LOVE, SPIES AND CYANIDE

GALYA'S STORY

By
R. K. Price

Based on True Events

Love, Spies and Cyanide
Galya's Story
Copyright © 2014 R.K. Price

This is a work of fiction. All of the characters, organizations and events portrayed in this novel are either products of the author's imagination or are used fictionally. Any resemblance to persons living or dead is unintentional.

The views expressed in this work are solely those of the author and do not reflect the views of the publisher, and the publisher hereby disclaims any responsibility for them.

Cover Design by Jennifer Welker
ISBN-13: 978-0-9898331-6-5

Published by Quiet Owl Books
P.O. Box 58
Montrose, PA 18001
www.quietowl.com

Printed in the United States of America

Quiet Owl Books are available for bulk purchases in the US at special discounts. For more information please contact the Special Markets Department at sales@quietowl.com.

Fond memories and special thanks to my editors George Luby and Chuck Campbell of the Pueblo Chieftain who were with me all the way when I broke the Galya Tannenbaum way back then; to Janet, my wife and Juliette, my friend, who helped shape the manuscript and correct my many spelling errors; to the glorious new mother Angela, my publisher, and to Sara, my baby girl, who is just now old enough to read what I write."

LOVE, SPIES AND CYANIDE

GALYA'S STORY

PART I

Chapter 1

When the call came in at 2:40 am on a Sunday morning Victor Bravo, captain of police detectives, had been awake for some time. His bedside phone often rang around that ungodly hour. And as expected, he heard the dreaded voice of on-duty night dispatcher Corporal Benjamin Smothers come on the line.

Recently Victor had been having trouble sleeping. He had no solid explanation for his insomnia but he had a darn good theory. Rosanna wanted another baby. They already had three children but she wanted four to round out the family. She was convinced that their two boys would overwhelm their one girl. Sibling gender balance was important in her opinion, which made the risk of trying for a second girl worth taking. Plus she was nearing the end of her time. A year or two from now would be more difficult, her doctor had said, maybe impossible. She was adamant. Victor wasn't so sure.

Victor agreed that an even number four would equalize the pairings but four would mean having all of them in seven short years and that was all the time he and Rosanna had been together. He made good money and they lived fairly well on a top cop's salary but it had its limits. Four kids would stretch them thin, maybe too thin. Besides he was just past forty. A little grey at the temples. A slower gait at times. Lighter weights during bench-press workouts and a belly slightly sagging over his belt buckle. Rosanna, the raven-haired former queen of the Cinco de Mayo parade, had just turned thirty-seven. Their house on Abriendo Street had four bedrooms on the upper level and two in the basement.

The mortgage payment ate up exactly twenty-three percent of his take-home pay.

So Victor was particularly on edge that night having denied Rosanna her pleasure for the very first time.

"Captain, are you there? I said, they found another stiff out at the loony bin."

"I heard you Corporal," Victor whispered angrily, "Stop with your stupid commentary and just give me the facts!"

Smothers, slow and methodical, laboring through each word with his South Carolinian drawl, took his time as always to respond with, "Female, forty years old, they think. Pretty bitch, they said. Red head, found in her cell by a male orderly stark-ass naked. Real pretty bitch I suspect. No tellin' why he was male. The guy who found her, that is. Thought only women worked the women's wards, but anyway, she's dead. No outward signs of injury; trauma, they called it. She's alive at midnight, layin' there on her cot in her cell readin, so says the male orderly, and the next thing he knows, she's dead. No rope; didn't hang herself, didn't stab herself, so no signs of foul play."

Victor listened impatiently, finally interrupting his unwanted caller with, "God damn it Corporal, why do they want me out there at this time of night? Is there something suspicious?"

"Don't rightly know, Captain," Benjamin responded, "They just said they wanted you out there to take a look around."

By this time Rosanna had sat up and switched on the night light next to her side of the bed. Victor glanced in her direction noticing that her pale blue silk gown had come askew to expose most of her left breast. Instantly his concentration was lost, replaced by the alluring sight and the quick decision to seek her forgiveness for his earlier rejection; what a fool, he told himself, he had been.

"Don't be so loud; you'll wake the kids," she quietly admonished.

"Coroner there?" Victor asked the dispatcher in a hushed tone.

"Guess so, don't rightly know, Captain. If he is, I suspect he's probably drunk," Benjamin observed.

"Can it corporal! Tell them I'll be there in thirty; no, make that forty-five minutes," Victor instructed, as he moved his free hand to coax his wife nearer. Victor hung up the phone, brought Rosanna to him and whispered, "I'm so sorry." A sweet smile cross her lips and the extra fifteen minutes they spent in astonishing passion were without worry or concern about the possibilities of baby number four.

Later, as black night still lingered and dawn evaded its beckoning, a certain foreboding swept over Captain Bravo as he drove through the crumbling red-brick archway suspended hauntingly over the ornate iron main gate of the Asylum; his city's pillar of progressive mental health care. Without fail, and tonight was no different, his drive-through reminded him of entering a graveyard on a cold, stormy Halloween night. Yet at this hour conditions were even worse than normal since a frigid Chinook wind wailed off the southern Rockies and wisps of snow danced about the headlights of his unmarked cruiser. Despite his repeated instructions otherwise the Asylum gate had been left open and unguarded. Passing through Victor swore at the blatant security breach. Barely beyond the portico with his obscenity still piercing the air a tree limb twice the girth and length of a baseball bat plummeted from the angry sky above and smashed squarely onto the hood of his car. Startled, Victor violently jerked the steering wheel and instinctively reached for his shoulder-strapped pistol at the gunshot-like sound. Thick bundles of broken branch pine needles obscured his vision as he braked and inched slowly into the nearby parking lot. His anger boiled after emerging from the car to remove the fallen branch. With intensifying obscenities he examined the perfect crease and cracked paint left splayed straight down the middle of the hood of his recently commissioned Dodge Corona.

Disgusted, he turned from the damage and began his labored walk through the nearly vacant lot toward Women's Ward Number 3. To shield against the howling breath of God he pulled the collar of his wool J.C. Penney's navy blue overcoat tightly around his neck and sprung into a rapid trot toward the light and the sign above the main entrance. Approaching the door he thought of suicide.

Recalling a recent internal Departmental report, since August of last year, there had been seventeen confirmed suicides at the Asylum, known to many but not him as Colorado's premier mental institution. Reaching for the door handle Victor reckoned if this death proved to be intentional, which it probably was, it would be number eighteen in eight short months.

On nights like these Victor Bravo, veteran police officer, decorated often in the line of duty and the epitome of professionalism can slip into a rather macabre mood. When he does, his frame of mind is generally prompted by scenes of self-inflicted deaths about which he had been required to investigate.

Victor abhors suicides. He hates investigating any death, accidental or willful, but suicides, Victor says, are the worst. That's because normally there aren't any witnesses. There's seldom anyone to talk to, to get the facts. The motives of suicide are never clear and his job requires that he always must treat them as suspicious until proven otherwise. Captain Bravo can never mourn the victim or pity them because they are the victim and the perpetrator. Victor is Catholic, and Catholics can't abide suicide and that may be part of Victor's problem. He's not sure. No one is. But it is particularly hard for him, and he usually ends up blaming the poor stiff and no one else. He despises what suicides represent. Despair. Despair beyond repair. Victor believes life is forever precious given not only to the person who's living it but also to those who have cared. And there is always someone who does care. And when someone cares, no matter whom they are or were, Victor thinks that life is worth preserving. To a point, that is. Victor doesn't mind, in fact celebrates when a cold blooded killer, rapist or child molester ends it by their own hand and saves the state piles of money housing, feeding and clothing the miscreants for the rest of their miserable lives. Someone might care about that dearly departed low-life but society is better off, so, Victor says, let them suffer.

Victor has a best friend named Johnny. They have a pact when they go fishing together. They do their best to avoid re-telling tales of their work. Their sanctum is Johnny's fishing boat rocking gently on tiny swells of deep blue crystal-clear reservoir water just a few miles outside of town. That's where they go to escape. To catch rainbow trout, drink beer and seek the calm. But no mater how hard they try there are occasional lapses in their pact. And Victor is usually the instigator. When that happens, Johnny forgives him because he realizes his friend has something to expel and cast into the air to be cleansed and cooled. Much of what Victor Bravo experiences boils up and spills down the sides of his brain to ignite a flash fire burning in his soul. If he can't douse the flames Victor would not survive. Johnny understands that about his friend.

One time when casting for trout Victor told Johnny about a skilled, yet horribly paranoid auto mechanic assigned to the Asylum's motor pool. One day for lunch the mechanic washed down his ham and cheese sandwich with a pint of fresh, slightly chilled battery acid. They found a sliced lemon in the bottom of the smoldering glass from which he drank.

Then there was the time, he said, when a sharpened bed spring, carefully removed from beneath the mattress of a failed schizophrenic medical school student was used for self impalement in the fashion of a cork screw opening a fine bottle of Bordeaux. The deranged dropout managed to remove his spleen, gall bladder and a small portion of his liver before he bled to death, never uttering a sound during the entire procedure.

But Victor's favorite and perhaps most baffling was when two spinster sisters who had pitch-forked their aging parents to death and fed them to their pigs somehow managed to simultaneously hang themselves with toilet paper rope. Kept in separate cells for their own protection, nevertheless the unhinged pair crafted their twines of death by weaving them in an intricately beautiful pattern to rival that of any master shipmate spinning cords on-board an 18th century whaling vessel. The loving dual had collected what may have been thousands of yards of the flushable kind, twisting, turning tying and weaving sheet after sheet until the desired length and strength of their lethal masterpieces were sufficient. Although housed apart, with great precision and timing they dropped and swung by their necks in tandem both from suspended ceiling fans, which spun their bodies like macabre high-wire circus acts. No one could understand why they didn't simply tie their bed sheets together.

Victor was greeted inside the entrance to Women's Ward Number 3 by a uniform officer who Victor immediately recognized as Corporal Harvey Kirk. Victor knew Harvey's personnel file well. Harvey was probably sixty but remained a patrolman second grade. His dossier made it clear he had trouble with Math, English and Demerol, the latter to quell his claim of thirty years of chronic back pain.

"Evenin', Captain," offered Harvey, "She's up on the second floor, cell 218, on your left. Awfully good lookin'. Down right shame. Damn back's killin' me again. Think I might end the shift early, Captain? Kind of need the rest."

Ignoring the request Victor grunted the corporal a greeting and began climbing the steps to the second floor. Over his shoulder he called back to Harvey, "Don't leave your post until a replacement comes. We're supposed to be in lock-down until the coroner arrives to release the body. Then, yes, go home and take it easy, Harvey."

"Thanks, Captain. Coroner's here already. Think its Dr. Korman. You know the one with the first name like me. Harvey Korman, Funny hum," Harvey mused.

Victor ceased his climb. Exasperated, but somewhat amused, he turned and smiled down at the patrolman. "Harvey, that's Harper Korman, Dr. Harper Korman, not Harvey. Harvey Korman is the comedian on television."

"Oh, yea, that's right" Harvey agreed, then looked perplexed.

"You sure about that Captain?"

"Yes, Harvey, I'm sure. Good night."

"Good night Captain. Thanks."

Victor turned to continue his ascent to the second floor. At the top of the stairwell he pushed open the heavy metal door. It creaked loudly. He stepped into the corridor and was stunned by the spectacle stretching into the expanse.

In a dim, shadowy overhead light, the grey walls ceiling and floor dulled his vision but slowly the bewildering scene became clearer. Crowded rows of sleeping cots lined each side of the hallway. A narrow path separated the beehive packed passageway. He could tell most were occupied by sheet-covered female forms lying prone. At first he thought he'd taken a wrong turn into the morgue. Hesitantly he stepped forward, searching for cell number 218. Finally he spotted it, far off into the distance. In the foreground one form moved, turning on its side. Then another. Then he heard a moan, and next to the sound came a sneeze. Then another exploded, expelling foul smelling gas. Not the morgue but a cesspool of misplaced humanity. Others stirred, sensing a presence. To get to Cell 218 he had no choice but to wind his way through the horrifying labyrinth. He would try his best not to disturb its inhabitants, but after just a few steps in near darkness he tripped on the leg of a cot and tumbled onto one of the occupants. A muted yelp ruptured the quiet. Just then from another cot next to where Victor had fallen a figure lunged at him, screaming, "COME FUCK ME, COME FUCK ME!" This obscene outburst rioted the others and soon screeching pierced the stale, now urine-tinged air.

Victor quickly rebounded to his feet and launched a hurried pace through the tangled maze. He dodged outstretched arms pleading to be touched. He sidestepped attempts to topple him with bare, extended legs and naked torsos thrust in his path. One, clad in nothing but a hospital gown secured Superman's cape-like by a bow at her neck, leaped from her roost and briefly came down on his back. She lost her grip on his shoulders when he spun in a gridiron maneuver similar to those he perfected as a teenage pass-catcher on the field of play.

The din was deafening. He looked up to see four attendants in white coats cheering him on like enthusiastic fans watching from the grandstands. He moved forward with haste, his eyes straight ahead. But on the last cot, positioned at the end of his journey through this tile-floored hell, he saw her lying there shivering, crying, terrified; her knees drawn up in fetal position. Her hands were tightly clasped around her shins for protection. Transcending down one forearm to the elbow and down one thigh to a knee were long red rows of evenly spaced ladder-stepping razor cuts. Her sheets and pillow were wrapped in a ball at her feet. Blood stained her otherwise bare mattress. Victor momentarily stopped to stare. She looked up and he caught her tear-filled eyes for just an instant, but long enough to think she didn't belong there.

He stooped to help her up but halted when she screamed in terror. He fell back and stepped away. He had to. He could do no good. Besides, he had finally finished the gauntlet of anguish. Seconds later he arrived at the doorway of Cell 218 and the awaiting orderlies, but he looked back once more to see her being pulled from her sacred space to be sent crashing onto the cold hard floor. Someone wanted what she had and she couldn't defend it. Her pillow.

"Aren't you going to do something to quiet them down?" Victor berated those in their white coats.

"Don't worry," one-stepped forward to reply, "Now that you're gone, they'll exhaust themselves pretty soon. The medication will take over. See, some of them are already lying back down."

Repulsed, Victor pushed past the foursome and stepped into Galya's death chamber.

Chapter 2

When Victor Bravo was growing up in the southern Colorado town of Pueblo, his mother would hug him gently after each razor strap thrashing administered by the wide sweeping arc of his father's beefy arm. Victoria Cardenas, daughter of Helena and Carlos, was sixteen when she married Salvatore Bravo, a truck driver who hauled lettuce from the flat fertile fields that stretched across the southeastern Colorado plains. On the nights following a day marked by one of Victor's whippings, Victoria would silently slide out of the bed she shared with Salvatore and trek gingerly down the hall to Victor's room. There her son would expectantly await her loving grasp accompanied by her soothing murmurs. Salvatore would lie awake for her return, never revealing his knowledge of the motive for her absence.

Victor likely deserved many a sting from that well-worn strap, but his mother would never acknowledge that. Not for a second. He could do no wrong in her eyes. He was a perfect but perpetually soiled angel. Divine but devious in every way. Perhaps that was because she swears to this day when, after twenty-seven hours of agonizing labor, a ripped open uterus and the loss of two pints of her blood splattering across the St. Mary Corwin Hospital delivery room floor, she sustained a jagged emergency Caesarean section to extract the nine-pound six-ounce hue-blue baby boy from his undersized vaginal entrapment, a heaven-sent shower of moon light beamed down upon mother and child the moment her Victor was placed in her arms. They both shared the same birthday. It was Victoria's seventeenth. She could produce no sibling for her son. The damage to her body was too great.

In later years, objectively thinking back, Victor would disagree with Victoria's assessment of him, accepting that some of his backside blisters may have been warranted.

Like the time he shattered seven out of eight neighborhood street lamps with precise single shots from his Daisy lever-action BB gun. He missed the eighth overhead beacon when his father's unexpected shout of reproach startled him the instant he was pulling the trigger.

Or the time he flung two overly ripened apples from his tree house perch, each splattering precisely in the center of the windshield of Sheriff's Deputy Jack Ames' sparkling new Plymouth patrol car. Few in the neighborhood cared much for Deputy Ames but that was no excuse.

Victor's true sidearm sling was maddening enough, but when with a third hurl he hit Jack's forehead with such velocity that it pitched him backward like a well-placed uppercut, sending his shiny black- brimmed cap somersaulting into the rain-filled gutter, the consequences were to be aptly applied. Deputy Jack was so angry he ran three blocks in the opposite direction of Salvatore, finally helping him trap the fleet footed lefty in an alleyway lined with fences too high to climb for a deft escape. Jack delighted in witnessing Victor's punishment that day, and that night while she held her son in the darkness of his room, Victoria snickered at the memory of the furious cop wiping rotten-apple smear from his face.

"I was a mischievous kid, for sure," Victor would admit. "My mother let me get away with everything, but my father, if he caught me, would dole out the penalties in big doses. On reflection, no doubt my father was mostly right and my mother generally wrong on that point."

And then he would add. "She should have been stricter with me and supported my father's discipline. Instead she babied me, which caused a great deal of confusion. Sometimes I think I acted out just to please her."

To even the score, Victor's father made him work off everything he damaged or destroyed. He spent one whole summer picking cantaloupes on the farms around Rocky Ford to pay back the city for the broken street lamps. He spent another summer mopping the floor, polishing desks and emptying ashtrays at the Sheriff's Department headquarters. Every day for a month before his reprieve Victor shined the brim of Jack Ames' cap at the end of each patrol shift.

Victor told those stories often when his upbringing was a topic of interest to others.

Which was often the case. Because in that part of the state, actually in that part of the country, Victor's professional status was quite unusual. And how he reached the height of his profession was an anomaly by all standards. Sons of first generation Mexican immigrants, especially farm laborers with teenage wives who both lacked formal educations, generally didn't make it much past their parent's position in life.

Not Victor. He was different. He would buck the trend. His parents demanded it. He demanded it of himself.

Through his adolescent years Victor grew tall, angular, straight-backed and agile. His skin was chestnut in color turning dark oak in summer under the blistering southern Colorado sun. He could palm a basketball at thirteen and could grab a one-handed pass while sprinting down the sidelines away from defenders. His jaw line jutted outward to prominently display a deep crevice in the center of his chin. His elevated cheek bones and cavernous deep-set brown eyes gave him the look of an Apache chieftain, evidencing that some of that ancestral Native American blood may have been flowing through his veins. His parents had no way of disputing the speculation. They had no reason to try, but the stubble of his beard sprouting early in his fourteenth year seemed to dampen the presence of dominant Chiricahua genes.

Naturally, his hair shined bright ebony. He grew it straight and long to his shoulders during his fifteenth summer and tied a red scarf around his crown. Mocking whoops and cries echoing from a feigned Indian war dance prompted Victor's single-handed assault against the offending trio of classmates resulting in a three-on-one baseball field brawl. The melee produced a broken nose for Victor that Dr. Stein absently left crooked and bent. His omission only added to Victor's physical mystique as he matured. After the fracas he cut his hair only because he hated the excess sweat his long locks produced while he worked the fields with his father to pay off another obligation incurred from one of his menacing childhood pranks.

Johnny, his fishing buddy, cherished Victor's friendship. Johnny was a Sicilian kid from the Bessemer neighborhood near the steel mill section of town who grew up poor like Victor yet proud and defiant. Their alliance was peculiar in itself. Mexican kids in that part of the country, especially in Pueblo, did not befriend Sicilians or Italians. They stuck to themselves, apart from others. They left the wops, as they called the Mediterranean breed, alone, while the wops left the Mexicans, or the spics as they called them, alone. Not Victor and Johnny however. Their union was born in the Central High School boy's locker room shower after football practice one day when members of the offensive line, made up mostly of Polish or Slovenian bruisers, whom everyone called bojons, thought it would be humorous to test the will of their new pint-sized freshman would-be halfback. Their strategy was to corner the unsuspecting try-out and administer a snapping towel initiation as he exited the shower stall.

Johnny stepped from the shower, realized his predicament and tried breaking through the ring of tormentors, but was pushed back into the center to receive a barrage of wet stings and hyena-like ridicule. That was until the split-end with the sticky fingers showed up to end their fun. Victor calmly stepped into the circle and in mid-flight snatched a rocketing towel whip aimed directly at Johnny's unprotected genitals preventing it from reaching its target and sending the victim into spasms of sheering pain. Not to mention the possibility of a childless future.

The protests from the first-string guards and tackles were loud and threatening, but Victor's angry insolence soon prevailed, ending the festivities with just a few red welts rising on Johnny's backside, shoulders and belly. No one on that offensive line challenged their star receiver since he was directly responsible for seven touchdowns in their first five games and the lead in the Southeastern Colorado class AAA football league standings.

From that point on Victor and Johnny were nearly inseparable. Among many other beneficial life lessons, Johnny taught Victor how to shoot eight-ball pool and snooker at Joe's acclaimed billiards emporium and Victor tried his best to teach his friend the art of dodging a tackler with a spin move in mid-stride. They laughed often, fished whenever possible, snuck beers from Joe's cooler when he wasn't looking, lied about the girls they loved, and formed a bond lasting their lifetimes.

After the war began and Johnny joined the Army and left for Europe, Victor waited a mere week before enlisting in the Navy to serve in the Pacific. When they returned home, neither of them would talk much about the horrors they saw. Those were about the only secrets they didn't share.

Victor's calling after the war was into law enforcement. Johnny's became the business of food, libations, and entertainment. Through years of struggle Johnny became a restaurant and nightclub owner of some renown while Victor methodically rose through the ranks of the local police department to eventually earn Captain's bars and the appointment to head the detective division. The paths they took crossed many times through the years, with one or the other stepping forward to ease the pain or spread the joy of life in the place they chose to call home.

And what a place it was. Pueblo was a pristine paradise for some, a garbage pit for others. Its steel mill smoke stacks rose high into the crisp, clear mountain air, emitting plumes of soot and ash, yet with each twelve-hour shift of thousands of overall clad men, millions of dollars poured into the coffers of the above and below ground economies. The money brought with it certain limited prosperity for the otherwise jobless, less skilled and under educated manual laborers, while others donning pin-striped suits, silk ties and gold cuff links, and not much education either, accumulated immense wealth from a deeply embedded criminal element with roots winding and twisting across the globe to the southern Mediterranean. In the days of Victor and Johnny's post World War II rise to some local prominence Pueblo reached its pinnacle as the western hub for the notorious Sicilian La Cosa Nostra.

Victor and Johnny soon found themselves in a decades-long battle with the Mafia's vicious, corrupt elements displaying what some people said was a strength and courage arising from the battlefields on which they fought in Europe and in the Pacific. Their friendship was further fortified when mob henchmen, spanning several years, burned their properties, stole, and tormented, kidnapped, raped and even brutally murdered members of their families. But finally in a series of running battles with those responsible, their terror ended with the mysterious deaths of a mob assassin and an equally disreputable police sergeant. Those brutal but some say justifiable deaths remain unsolved to this day.

Following the bloody demise of these two hoodlums and the welcomed death of the Mafia chieftain they called "Black Jim", came an agonizingly slow, methodical decline of mob influence in the region. And with it came a certain serenity that settled over the lives and families of these two unlikely kinsmen.

Victor and Johnny remain satisfied with their decisions to take different paths in their lives yet they never know if circumstances might force yet another collision piling wreckage at the intersection of their otherwise peaceful existence. In Cell 218 as Victor eyes the still warm corpse of Gloria Forest aka Galya Tannenbaum there's no way for him to know that her death would prove to be a runaway train careening head-on toward a fiery life-changing crash.

Chapter 3

Just seventeen miles from the mark on the water where Victor and Johnny usually catch their limit are the front gates, never locked and seldom guarded, of the Colorado Asylum for the Habitually Insane. The barren three- hundred acre, tumbleweed-infested moonscape swoops down below the horizon just enough to block line-of-sight vistas in all directions. The City's leaders prefer it that way. Conveniently tucked away for no casual observer to see. Victor knows the history of Asylum well. He is repulsed by it's past and present, and shudders in disgust when forced on site for an investigation.

Although shielded from view and never discussed in polite society, Victor and most local citizens are well aware and covertly reminded that the Asylum heaps truckloads of state money into the hands of contractors, vendors and a few caregivers who thrive on, yet seldom promote speedy recoveries of the endless stream of psychopathic killers, lobotomized manic depressives, or serial kleptomaniacs. These so-called medical specialists, who Victor describes as parasites, have sympathy for but overwhelmingly appreciate the high admission rates of the drugged up prostitutes, devil worshipers, and accused cannibals. And then there are the countless traumatized and terrorized women who escape the death penalty after x-rays introduced at trial show broken bones which never healed from the beatings administered prior to the fatal shots they fired into the heads of their sleeping husbands. Not guilty by reason of insanity. To others who purposefully block the ungodly place out of their consciousness to ignore its searing reality, it is as if the Asylum wasn't there at all. Some believe those in denial belong in the Asylum instead, but none will ever get within ten miles of the place.

Victor was an early supporter of Gilbert Esposito, who ran for mayor in November 1968. Gilbert asked during one campaign appearance, "Who wants a horde of criminally committed outcasts living and lurking within a short distance from our neighborhood elementary schools?"

And then the candidate had the audacity to add, "Especially when the grounds are encircled by porous chain-link fences and security guards who often sleep or drink through their eleven-to-seven a.m. shifts."

Esposito had been an accountant at the Asylum for five years before he ran for office. He was fired for insubordination after a board of inquiry found him guilty of unfounded, libelous accusations against his fellow employees. The Board especially didn't like the audit he produced on the superintendent's slush fund for personal travel.

Victor saw it coming but could not influence the outcome of the election.

Despite all the evidence his favorite candidate was defeated in his quest for office by a two-to-one margin after the Chamber of Commerce made sure Gilbert's campaign contributions dried up and his credit at the local bank was frozen forcing a foreclosure on his house.

Victor realized Gilbert Esposito would soon fade into his City's checkered past unlike many figures influencing Pueblo's history who are revered and become subjects of local lectures at Friends of the Library meetings. People like Kit Carson, who was said to have searched the wilderness nearby; steel baron John D. Rockefeller and his son Junior who owned the steel mill, First Lady Mamie Eisenhower who lived in the city as a child, and the obscure yet in local circles, widely acclaimed Dr. Hubert Work.

Victor was especially amused by the works of Dr. Work.

Dr. Work, noted for his study of mental diseases and alcoholism, served as the Asylum's superintendent for nine months. He resigned to become Secretary of the Interior under Presidents Warren G. Harding and Calvin Coolidge. Few people could understand how his credentials as a mental hygienist might qualify him to oversee the nation's lands and natural resources. But somehow they did, and he is footnoted in the history books.

However, one who is seldom if ever mentioned in the history classes, and certainly not in polite society, is George M. Chilcott, Colorado's first U.S. Senator. He was the scoundrel, as some like Victor call him, who donated the first forty acres of his land northwest of the city as the site on which the Asylum's first buildings were constructed. His benevolence is bemoaned even today by a large segment of Asylum critics; Victor among them.

Knowing the history of the Asylum as well as he does Victor lectures others who will listen in an ongoing attempt to improve the lives of those who inhabit the horrible hovel today. He often tells fellow critics that the year of the good Senator Chilcott's bequeath was 1879, but it took until 1883 to open the first of a cluster of cold, dark, dank and extremely terrifying wood, brick and plaster chambers soon to be encrusted in green mold and infested by scampering hordes of rats. These structures were to permanently house a growing population of mostly improperly diagnosed mental misfits.

Victor notes the first of their number to be incarcerated was eleven, and then there were twenty, then fifty. Soon more inhospitable dwellings were built to house a hundred, then two hundred. Three hundred soon came. As the state's population swelled, so did its discards, the unwanted, the unclean, the misunderstood or the downright dangerous, all mixed together.

"A mound of humanity about as homogeneous as hungry sharks among baby seals," Victor explains. "The treacherous preyed on the vulnerable and feeble, and cures were seldom found or even tried. It was better to lock them away, provide scanty clothing, bad food and worse treatment than to let them wander free to victimize or simply challenge the patience of the upper crust."

It was clear in Victor's research that Pueblo's Asylum quickly became the state's dumping ground for the bothersome who disrupted the desirable tranquil. It was such an attractive place, Victor points out, that officials from other states and even neighboring countries paid handsomely to deposit their outcasts allowing them too, to forget with clear consciences. The early census of inmates included malcontents as far away as Missouri, Montana and Mexico.

Preceding Dr. Work was the first long-tenured superintendent, a former Civil War Surgeon named Pembroke R. Thombs. Most people, including his patients with sufficient cognitive ability aptly called him "Tombs" in recognition of the environs in which his patients were housed. Thombs remained on the job for twenty years. During his term he became a stalwart community leader appreciated throughout the region for his medical and administrative skills. His stature gained him ever-increasing budget allocations from crony state lawmakers who gladly funded his ever-expanding catacombs to incarcerate a burgeoning patient population. Victor is particularly repulsed in describing Thombs as well known for his creative experimentation in the black hole science of mental illness. His theories about what made people violent, taciturn, prone to addiction; cunning, moronic or simply overly shy were mostly assembled on the battlefields between the Blue and Grey.

"Thombs liked to cut," Victor maintains. "He was a surgeon after all, adroit with the scalpel maneuvering about the scalp. He had no one to challenge his forward-thinking experimentation at altering patient behavior. His preferred technique was to remove those portions of the brain, which, in their absence, he argued, would restore a certain equilibrium to their poor miserable, unbalanced lives, or as equally beneficial to society, permanently place them in a vegetative state. Many never made it off Dr. Thombs' operating table."

Beyond Thombs' legacy as a renowned wielder of the knife, he also left behind the burrows. Measuring nearly four miles in distance he began the uncanny, inexplicable construction of a winding maze of subsurface passages, which ostensibly were to be used to connect the aboveground buildings with a more efficient route for transport of goods and equipment.

"Anyone with a single brain cell should have realized that the pitch black, sweltering, persistently rancid tunnels costing many tens of thousands of dollars to dig, mainly proved to be a convenient avenue of escape, or better yet, a hideaway to stalk and murder unsuspecting users, many of them female Asylum employees," Victor says.

"I've been down there. They still exist. They were catacombs of death."

"Several attempts to seal off the tunnels were unsuccessful as crafty inmates unceasingly found ways to reopen them for their often deadly exploits," he adds.

But this is only the beginning of Victor's treatise. He goes on to say that Thombs was succeeded in his job by a succession of Asylum directors including Dr. H.A. LaMoure a real medical doctor who assumed the post in 1913. "LaMoure did little to improve the plight of his wards but he did have the foresight to recognize the onslaught of feeble minded would eventually far exceed the capacity of the facility."

"He was right," Victor affirms.

"Dr. LaMoure launched a campaign to convince politicians in Denver to build a second, and even a third warehouse for his lunatics in proximity to the more heavily populated Capitol City. His request set off a firestorm of protest. Soon, led by the most gluttonous beneficiaries of the Asylum's largess, Dr. LaMoure's ideas were soon snuffed out. Pueblo had and would continue to monopolize the region's maniacs."

Meager structures begat more meager structures on the sprawling, windswept site, but, in Victor's words, "the scant building program could not keep up with the demand. Soon patient numbers overwhelmed the limited availability of private living quarters for the less impaired as well as locked-down cells for the truly violent. Patients, both on men and women's wards, lived on nothing more than cots aligned in endless rows along every building corridor.

"Side by side, inches apart, no matter if they howled with night terrors, wet the bed sheets or tried to smother their neighbor with a pillow, there was no place else to put them. These gauntlets of despair remain today," he says. I know from first hand experience."

Finally, instead of building adequate annexes, in a sweetheart deal with a local landowner and large contributor, legislators forced the purchase of a nearby run-down sanitarium. "Problem was the place was more dilapidated than the existing buildings, and worse, it was extremely close to the flood-prone Fountain River. Shortly after cramming nearly 300 mostly elderly transferees from the region's "poor-houses" to their new domicile the infrequent rains came, predictably flooding the area and sweeping away part of the complex along with a few inhabitants who were never found."

Dr. LaMoure finally relinquished his post to a man named Dr. Frank Zimmer, who held the job for thirty-three years. At that point the Asylum was still woefully overcrowded but, thanks to Dr. LaMoure, it did have a brand new morgue, chicken and dairy farms, a state-of-the-art hydrotherapy ward and several heavy sedation treatment centers. "A maximum security building was built for the uncontrollable but it was located so close to the non-violent patient barracks that guards and counselors were besieged with separating the two population segments. The problem was particularly acute at night when males cohabitated female cots for overnight, often times, consensual copulation."

A measurable upsurge in unexpected pregnancies kept the two-bed maternity ward full. That was until the sterilizations began.

It's generally at this point in Victor's history lesson that he has to stop, catch his breath, re-compose himself and search his core for calm. Otherwise he often fears he would break many laws in an attempt to close down "the rat hole," as he describes it.

Beginning again, Victor states with certain disgust that shortly after Dr. Zimmer's arrival and routinely under his watchful eye for more than three decades the fallopian tubes of countless women were tied within or removed and stacked high on the Asylum's operating room floor. "All Dr. Zimmer needed was a declaration from the Colorado Lunacy Commission to permanently obliterate his patient's wanton urge to reproduce oddballs. So he did so with relish."

Troubled teens, rebellious runaways, nervous orphans, adolescent alcoholics and even a few with eating disorders were spayed like dogs in heat, Victor asserts. However he hastens to add that the problem was Dr. Zimmer's neutering practice was profoundly illegal. Some states at that time allowed forced sterilization, but not Colorado. Nothing in the state law library permitted Dr. Zimmer's unfettered butchery, yet it went on without interference, ignored and hushed up. In the end, only a check mark by his patient's name and inmate number accounted for his acts. "Dr. Zimmer was never challenged. It was the right thing for him to do. He had every justification since those wayward women had no business reproducing. They were incapable of motherhood, slight birth defects or mental infirmities aside. They deserved what they got. Besides, their doctor had other issues to contend with, like a patient population now approaching six thousand. He needed to buy more sleeping cots," Victor states with dripping sarcasm.

Months later after immersing himself in the life and death of the corpse he was about to view there in Cell 218, Victor would insert in a written report that, "It was here at the Asylum for the Habitually Insane, which is now preferably called the State Hospital, some fifty years after Dr. Zimmer's reign but with few advancements in either treatment or accommodations, that the Denver, Colorado District Court committed Mrs. Gloria Galya Tannebaum, formerly known as Gloria Ann Forest, for forging her lover's name on a money order. Her indefinite sentence for indefinite mental evaluation and treatment ended with the discovery of her cold, naked body, a figure too beautiful to comprehend; ending a life too extraordinary to imagine."

PART II

Chapter 4

He saw her seated in the second row, paying little attention to his forthcoming incredibly sage observations. Her eyes were cast downward, apparently more interested in the papers in her lap. As was normally the case in situations like this, Dr. Thomas Riha had immediately become enraged by her willful insolence. From his lectern he glared at her bowed head and silently vowed to severely punish this rude and obnoxious individual who is refusing to sit in rapt anticipation of the wisdom I am about to bestow. But then, alas, after checking his enrollment sheet he discovered that she is not one of my students after all.

The interloper held her place in the history section of the University of Chicago's main library, which set adjacent to Dr. Riha's lecture hall, a cavernous two hundred-seat auditorium. The cramped anteroom was adorned with dark-stained twenty-foot high-coffered ceiling and paneled oak walls. Dr. Riha had rented the room for the evening to pitch his new book to a cadre of obliging students seeking his adoration and high marks. Now as he gazed at the stranger he hoped she too would make a purchase to allow his vast knowledge to somehow seep into the brain residing under that stunning mop of perfectly coiffed auburn hair.

I wonder what she looks like, Thomas pondered. Look up; let me see your face, he silently commanded.

Professor Thomas Riha, then entering only his third year as a yet-to-be tenured faculty member of the University's history department, had hurdled over many of his more seasoned and certainly more respected colleagues to publish what some critics were describing as one of the most "laudable chronicles of Russian history modern civilization has ever received." And this night, the night of the unveiling of the three volume set aptly entitled, "Readings in Russian Civilization" would finally put its author in the spotlight, at least in his own mind, where he belonged.

At a mere thirty-four years of age, carting a doctorate from Harvard and a string of notable academic achievements Dr. Thomas Riha had hit his stride. Yet just as he began reading from Volume II, "Imperial Russia, 1700-1917, to the second-row redhead and a modest assemblage of seventy-five or so, he stumbled over his first words and had to stop and re-group; his composure momentarily lost.

Her incredible shamrock green eyes had slowly risen to lock on his. His wish for her attention had finally been granted.

My God, he found himself inaudibly gasping. She is gorgeous. She smiled. He swooned.

Thomas stepped back from the lectern, willfully breaking her stare. And then he was angry with himself. It was her alluring look that had bored deeply into his skull shattering his concentration and rendering him weak-kneed, tangle tongued and red-faced with embarrassment. Get control of yourself.

"Excuse me ladies and gentlemen. I shall begin again," he declared, clearing his throat and nervously stepping back to the podium. He stood between book shelves stacked high filling every square inch with bound volumes of mankind's remembrances of events long past. In the annex of the University's main library the history section alone counted its collection of hardbound editions in excess of three hundred and fifty thousand. Thomas' podium was square in the middle of the twenty-seven rows of shelves on which these blessed books resided. Thomas was in his element.

The goddess in his presence dropped her gaze gracefully allowing Thomas to continue. If she hadn't the night might have ended before he found the resolve to begin it.

Jesus, Thomas thought, what the hell is she doing to me?

Despite this monumental distraction Professor Riha finally undertook his recitation.

From the section of his self-proclaimed classic Second Volume chapter, entitled "Catherine the Great's Instructions" he got underway by quoting from one of the queen's most profound declarations. "You must add to this," he said she proclaimed in 1767, "That two Hundred Years are now elapsed since a Disease..."

"She was supposedly talking about smallpox here," Thomas interrupted himself, and then continued with her quotation,

"A Disease Unknown to our Ancestors was imported from America, and hurried on the Destruction of the human Race. This disease spreads wide its mournful and destructive Effects in many of our Provinces. The utmost Care ought to be taken of the Health of the Citizens. It would be highly prudent, therefore, to stop the Progress of this Disease by the Laws."

Thomas paused. He lifted his eyes from the text to span the faces in the crowd. He found most of them, including his earlier second-row nemesis, now attentive to his reading. He smiled after a moment and posed a question.

"Now, for one minute do any of you believe the great Queen Catherine, whom I believe and have written extensively about as the only intellectual ever to sit on the Russian throne, was really talking about smallpox in this example of her numerous instructions to her subjects?"

He waited for a response; for one hand to go up. None did. So he proceeded.

"If my memory serves me correctly, this little country of ours hadn't yet been hatched when Catherine spoke. Further, how she found it prudent to blame America for two hundreds years of the scourge, putting us back to when red tribes men still freely roamed the forests of Manhattan, poses an intriguing question in my mind. How about yours?"

Again he searched his audience. Again all were silent and still.

"Well, okay, let me tell you. Catherine's true genius is illustrated profoundly here in this one passage. She's warning her countrymen about America; not the threat of smallpox. She sees clearly that America is the Disease. While George Washington was surveying the western provinces for wealthy land speculators, Catherine already had figured out that talk, even talk, of democratic principles, free elections and representative government would be her scourge. Left alone, not treated, not vaccinated against, would allow these diseased concepts to infect her world and bring it down. She had foresight. She was fearful and had every right to be. Catherine was an advocate of collectivism. She lived and breathed socialist ideology long before Karl Marx scratched his beard and picked up his pen. Even as a monarch she knew that power ultimately lies with the people in the fields. She had it right. Listen to another of her instructions to her people.

"Here she has to begin with outwardly staking her claim to her throne by saying, "The Sovereign is absolute; for there is no other Authority but that which centers in his single Person, that can act with a Vigour proportionate to the Extent of such a vast Dominion. The Extent of the Dominion requires an absolute Power to be vested in that Person who rules over it."

"But is she really talking about a single ruler? About herself?

"Of course not. "No other Authority but that which centers in his single Person"...The worker, the masses, not the resident of the castle. She strengthens her argument later by instructing that....

"The method of exacting their Revenues, newly invented by the Lords, diminishes both the Inhabitants, and the spirit of Agriculture in Russia. Almost all of the Villages are heavily taxed. The Lords, who seldom or never reside in their Villages, lay an Impost on every Head of one, two and even five Rubles, without the least regard to the Means by which their Peasants may be able to raise the Money.

"She doesn't stop there." And neither did Thomas.

"It is highly necessary" she declared, "That the Law should prescribe a Rule to the Lords, for a more judicious Method of raising their Revenues, and oblige them to levy such a Tax, as tends to least to separate the Peasant from his house and family. This would be the Means by which Agriculture would become more extensive and Population be more increased in the Empire."

With that, Thomas closed his text and stepped back from the lectern. He had his audience now. He could feel it. He looked out and saw heads bobbing in agreement. Expressions acknowledging his theory about Catherine; his interpretation, his insight, his wisdom. Every one of them would buy the book. He knew it.

"Thank you for attending. I will be at the librarian's main desk to answer any questions, and if you so desire, to sign copies."

She was the last one in line. She had waited for nearly two hours for others before her to collect his signature and quiz him endlessly on his literary license and theories. It seemed as if every one had a point to make while he scribbled personal notes and autographed inside book covers. While accommodating his admirers and jousting with a few brave adversaries who didn't need his class to graduate, he had looked for her in line but didn't see her until she appeared at his table and placed her copy before him.

"You were magnificent," she smiled.

"And you are likewise my dear," he responded, ignoring her request to personalize her purchase; rather holding her playful stare.

"Please make it out to Galya; no, I changed my mind. Gloria. Yes, Gloria. I prefer Gloria."

"As you wish. But who is Galya?" His eyes remained fixed as he waited for an explanation about her curiously altered request.

"Well, I am. I go by both names, you see."

"Very well. So, today you are Gloria. Tomorrow you will be Galya?"

"Please don't mock me. If you don't want to sign my book, I shall take it blank, as it is," she huffed angrily, and reached down to retrieve the book from the table.

A momentary panic rose in Thomas. He pulled the book back from her and held it. He could not let it, or her vanish from his view.

"No, please. I apologize. I am not mocking you. Both are beautiful names. I can tell. You are a person of such omnipresence as you easily fill the lives of two people. You deserve two names."

She withdrew her hand, and displayed a bashful grin.

"That sounded almost poetic. You are a poet as well?"

Thomas began to write as he spoke. "Only when it suits me. Only when poetry fits the occasion."

"I am writing passages for both of you. For Gloria and for Galya. I want my words to find you; whomever, wherever you are. To have meaning so you remember."

"My, now you are a romantic. A man of many talents. A man of letters. A historian. A scholar. A poet, and now a big fat flirt."

His eyes darted up from his writing at the last remark. He was delighted to find a broad smile. Her hand on her hip thrust sideways in a provocative stance.

"Yes, I admit it. Guilty on all counts. I am flirting with you unabashedly."

"I hope that is a gentlemanly remark. It does sound terribly forward to me. Decadent, perhaps. You are not so arrogant as to assume I will easily be beckoned by your call."

"No. Oh, no. Absolutely not. I am only wishing. Hoping; yes, praying you will accompany me for coffee and perhaps a snack at a delightful establishment nearby. I am done here. You can see you are the last in line."

"What? Are you too cheap to buy my dinner?"

Following a sumptuous Italian feast and two bottles of a fine Chianti Thomas failed to lure either Gloria, or Galya back to his apartment. Her rejection of his request was polite but firm. Later he felt she was tempted yet he contently completed the evening alone stroking the soft fur of his prized Persian cat while lounging on the white leather sectional couch placed before his living room's floor-to-ceiling glass windows. His panoramic view of center city Chicago was breathtaking.

Someday soon she will be here to enjoy all the pleasures I have to offer, he assured himself.

But he was not lulled into thinking the prize she held would be easy to capture.

Chapter 5

The day after Thomas met Gloria Galya Tannenbaum he became moderately perturbed to have received a handwritten note in perfect fountain-pen script from the chairman of the University of Chicago History Department. In polite yet pointed prose the chairman, Dr. Horace Finlayson, PhD in 19th and early 20th century German history, summoned Thomas to a private conference in his chambers promptly at 4 o'clock that very afternoon.

Thomas finished his 3 pm lecture to second year undergraduates at 3:45 pm in preparation for the meeting. His topic that day had been based on an excerpt from his prized work, Readings in Russian Civilization, Revised Edition, entitled The Falsehood of Democracy authored by the noted Russian philosopher Konstantin Pobedonostev.

"It is an absolutely brilliant treatise," Thomas had stated in his introductory remarks to his students.

Thomas departed the lecture hall promptly upon conclusion of the class and leisurely began his stroll to the chairman's coveted office, which was located on the third floor of Rosenwald Hall overlooking the main campus mall. His walk from the Social Science Research Building, the site of his lecture, to Dr. Finlayson's quarters would normally take five or seven minutes, at most, but this day Thomas purposefully decided to take his own sweet time. He would be late and old Horace would have to wait.

Thomas knew what was in store. He faced yet another stern dressing down by the chairman who Thomas firmly believed harbored secret fascist anti-socialist sympathies. All German professors are closet fascists. If it weren't for Horace's Irish heritage, Thomas could have easily classified the stale, senile old coot as a true Nazi. He found it odd that an overt Mick like Horace would embrace radical Kraut dogma, but he did, and ever so openly, Thomas was convinced.

As he ambled down the winding sidewalk that bisected the lush grassy lawn, he eyed clusters of coeds in their miniskirts and short shorts lounging in the sun, either with books in hand or chatting gaily among themselves. His lecherous gazing was interrupted when he thought back on the topical emphasis he had placed during his most recent lectures. Each study session had centered on Pobedonostev's profound pro-Communist works, and Thomas surmised those scandalous topics had likely prompted his summons to the chairman's lair.

Most particularly during his short but deliberate meandering Thomas convinced himself that the point of contention with Horace would be Tuesday's session during which he frequently quoted Pobedonostev, and took no means to rebut or contradict the esteemed author's hypothesis. Thomas let stand without challenge Pobedonostev's fundamental question being:

"What is this freedom (The New Democracy) by which so many minds are agitated, which inspires so many insensate actions, so many wild speeches which leads the people so often to misfortune?"

If that wasn't enough Thomas pressed on, quoting the text word for word.

"In the democratic sense of the word, freedom is the right of political power, or, to express it otherwise, the right to participate in the government of the State. This universal aspiration for a share in government has no constant limitations, and seeks no definite issue, but incessantly extends (and) for extending its base the New Democracy now aspires to universal suffrage---a fatal error."

The implied, if not blatant attack on universal suffrage leveled by Pobedonostev and seemingly endorsed by Thomas, the lecturer, had sparked faint protests from his quasi-attentive class members but that hadn't deterred him from offering even more biting rhetoric.

"In a Democracy, the real rulers are the dexterous manipulators of votes, with their placemen, the mechanics who so skillfully operate the hidden springs which move the puppets in the area of democratic elections. Men of this kind are ever ready with loud speeches lauding equality. In reality, they rule the people as any despot or military dictator might rule it."

Puppets...that got their attention, Thomas recalled. But even calling them that still didn't upset his students all that much.

That was Tuesday's theme. The Falsehood of Democracy. Thomas had slammed his message home, and he was sure Horace had heard about it. But he still wasn't finished. He played out his theme again on Wednesday. Pobedonostev's enlightenment once more took center stage.

"The extension of the right to participate in elections is regarded as progress, and as the conquest of freedom by democratic theorists who hold that the more numerous the participants in political rights, the greater is the probability that all will employ this right in the interests of the public welfare, and for the increase of the freedom of the people. Experience proves a very differing thing. The story of mankind bears witness that the most necessary and fruitful reforms---the most durable measures---emanated from the supreme will of statesmen, or from a minority enlightened by lofty ideas and deep knowledge, and that, on the contrary, the extension of the representative principle is accomplished by an abasement of political ideas and the vulgarization of opinions in the mass of electors."

So now voters are vulgar? Voting in mass is debasing? Demigods must rule because they are the only enlightened. God, that was brilliant stuff, Thomas thought as he entered Finlayson's outer office. I am sure he is really pissed off. And I love it!

Chapter 6

"Yes that's exactly what he said," Thomas exclaimed. "He came at me like a wild boar. Teeth bared, nostrils flaring. It was insane. He is insane."

"But why did you provoke him? Why are your lectures so deliberately provocative? Are you not satisfied with simply stirring debate? Why must you step so close to the edge?" Gloria Tannenbaum, who said to Thomas earlier that evening that she preferred to be called Galya, at least for the next few hours, questioned the man across from her at the linen-clothed, candle-lit, remote corner table.

Goddamn, she's wonderful. Not only is her beauty incomparable, her mind is expansive, deep and voluminous, Thomas thought, staring like a lustful yet forlorn schoolboy into the bashful eyes of his first-date ingénue. He didn't respond; only gawked to the point of shamefulness.

"Well, answer me," Galya demanded. "Don't just sit there. You look like a panting dog waiting for a bone."

At that Thomas' spell was broken. He lifted his glass of crimson Bordeaux to shield a shade of red-faced embarrassment. He took a sip and finally spoke.

"Old, miserable Horace Finlayson is beyond redemption. His myopic view of the world narrows by the day. His conventional political views are far outdated and smack of spoon-fed democratic pap that is stale and rancid. He is clueless and blind."

"Just because he challenges you on your endless stream of anti-American vitriol?" Galya was quick to challenge.

"Anti-American?" Thomas came back. "I'm not anti-American. I love this country. I just oppose its political system. It is oppressive, tyrannical, and unrelenting in condemning other points of view. And it offends me when people like that old bastard can use his position to intimidate others who have contrary positions."

"Are you afraid of him? Can he successfully suppress your ideas? Your ideals? Will you let him? Will you mute your voice in the face of his clinched fist?"

"I will never be silenced!" Thomas sneered a little too loudly; causing those at tables nearby to turn in their direction at the angry retort.

"Excuse me," Thomas suddenly announced, "I need to find the rest room." He rose and threw his starched, now wadded napkin on to his empty plate. Galya had grasped his hostile emotion some moments before and took a stab at levity to quell the tension with, "Beyond the ladies room. Thomas, please hurry back. I'm hungry. I will miss you and I can't wait to continue our cheerful banter."

He caught her mood-altering commentary and released a quick smile before turning toward the room at which she was pointing.

Following the bathroom break, their evening rebounded with satisfying rounds of lovely shrimp cocktail appetizers, tossed salad with a fine olive oil and lemon-based dressing, followed by a chateaubriand encased in a delectably butter crust, flaky and moist to the point that both agreed it was the best either had ever consumed. Their orange sherbet was crisp and refreshing, and the port and espresso brought each to a light-headed state of pleasant, giddy-like enchantment.

By the end of the evening they had examined the chandelier above their heads, speculating that the suspended crystal pendants amounted to more than one hundred. Their conversation had been interrupted twice by the pianist at the Steinway on a riser placed in the opposite corner of the room. He was accompanied by a strolling violinist playing seven minutes of Beethoven's Moonlight Sonata Movement 3 Opus 27 and they wondered aloud if the music should have remained pure without the strings. They chuckled mischievously at the rotund cue-ball bald tuxedo-clad gentleman when he unsuccessfully attempted to grope his young-enough-to-be-his-daughter date, but instead tipped the ice bucket and its recently opened champagne bottles, tumbling each to the floor to shower two tables of nearby patrons.

They had purposefully steered far away from further examinations of their respective political views. The topics of academic freedom and overbearing department heads were ignored, and in deference, they settled into what second or third-date adults more commonly debate. Was it time and did the chemistry exist for a lusty go at it in bed?

Thomas desperately hoped she would consent. Galya knew it was time to grant his wish. That was part of her job. He had no inkling that she was on the payroll.

Chapter 7

Thomas' stark vision of Gloria Tannenbaum reclining luxuriously on his white-leather sectional couch refused to fade from memory.

Her long lean neck had stretched back so her head had come to rest on the padded sofa arm. Her eyes had closed dreamily. A half-filled champagne glass tipped precariously in her hand. Her naked legs had arched and crossed at the knee, allowing the pale blue velvet robe to slide down provocatively to expose her rounded hips while the garment remained partially closed at midsection to modestly cover her breasts.

He dwelled on the sight constantly. He examined it with the same intensity as he probes 1914 Vladimir Lenin treatises for inspiration. Their first night together had seized his soul. He relives it just like he thought he would. Just like he planned it on the night of his book signing when she refused to accompany him home. He knew it would happen. Her position on the couch. The lights of the skyscraper city illuminating the background. Ella Fitzgerald serenading from stereo speakers. He, boney and bare-chested, clad only in his silk pajama bottoms desperately avoiding her ogle.

She became Gloria when she had agreed to accompany him home that first time and all times since. He didn't ask her why her name and persona must change, but quickly he knew, or at least surmised, as any self-respecting holder of a PhD would. She was Galya the thinker. Galya the inquisitor. Galya the pure intellect who could wring the truth out of him no matter how hard he tried to shield it away, but she became Gloria the seductress when the mood struck her and she acquiesced or promoted his advances.

Thomas was satisfied with both parts of her; ecstatic in fact. He found Galya as his lightning rod to ground him when the sparks flew from his high voltage brain inflaming controversy and consternation from an unenlightened faculty or student body. And now, glory be to God, he got Gloria as his mistress to exhaust him with her body slicing away at his outer core to expose an infantile nature in need of mothering and bottle-feeding. He had quickly become addicted as if by the most potent spoon-cooked heroin.

The only problem was that she would not move in. She had refused his repeated pleas to cohabitate. He could not understand why. She said she had her own place but he was never allowed to see it. She had her life away from Thomas and she would not share it. He complained about that but she was unrelenting. It had to be that way or she said she would disappear. She would entice him with long lustful weekends together, but she would depart on Sunday evenings, sometimes not even saying goodbye. He would often return to an empty room where she had just been, and his heart would break again.

They became a public couple; together attending Thomas' long list of obligatory University-related functions, but their status was awkward until Galya finally permitted Thomas to present her as his fiancé.

She had agreed to accept her public label only on the condition that Thomas find a real wife. He was dumbstruck by her demand. It came during a brisk, brusque silent single-file walk along the Navy Pier on a Saturday evening after dinner at Miller's Pub on Wabash Street. There they had fought viciously over Thomas' scoffs at the wall-mounted photographs of Chicago's famous patrons, ranging from Milton Berle to Mayor Richard J. Daley. Thomas had declared each among them as bourgeoisie elitists who could never relate to the working class on whose backs, Thomas asserted, they rose to prominence. Galya was furious at his narrow minded, even bigoted view of humankind outside the Communist sphere and threatened to break off their relationship if, "your tolerance for diversity of thought did not manifest itself pretty god-damn soon."

She stormed out of the esteemed Chicago eatery forcing Thomas, in pursuit, to throw a fifty-dollar bill at the waiter to cover the tab, resulting in an outrageous tip.

He had caught up with her two blocks away with shouts of apology and promises of open mindedness, but she kept on walking ahead at a faster pace refusing to permit him to stride by her side. Her hidden smile at her veiled anger was lost on a trailing Thomas but it prompted curious looks from passersby meandering on her left.

After their night of turmoil, Galya had remained Galya, denying him at every turn. During a ten-day hiatus of intimacy she accepted six dozen roses, but refused countless remorseful telephone calls. She even tore up a love poem written in the style of Boris Leonidovich Pasternak, who famously penned the acclaimed novel Dr. Zhivago, even though she had read the book and passionately loved the love story, as well as Thomas' poem. She finally gave in to his invitation to attend a black tie fund-raising affair for the Chicago Symphony featuring the music of Nikolai Rimsky-Korsakov for two reasons. The first because she had forever been awestruck by his masterpiece, The Flight of the Bumblebee, and secondly, because her bosses had told her "enough is enough."

After the concert that night, while she sat fully clothed on the white leather sectional, absent the shimmering light from the city due to a raging thunderstorm, she had told him why a spouse was essential at this stage in his life.

"You need such a person to advance your career. A dutiful wife is essential for an individual at your station to fully realize one's professional goals. I will never be that person, Thomas," Galya had said. "I cannot fill that role. I carry too many burdens, and adding you, and the dreadful thought of children to them, are more than I could possibly bear."

"I promise I will change," Thomas had pleaded. "I will become more tolerant. I will tone down my tirades in deference to your views. I will become a model companion; someone you will be proud of. I will expand my studies beyond the borders of the Russian motherland. I will even pledge a serious review of the merits of democracy. You'll see. I will be better. Just for you."

"Don't be ridiculous Thomas," she had lectured in response. "You are who you are. I would never attempt to change you. And this is not about you. It's about me. I'm the one who must resist a permanent relationship with you. My condition is this. I will remain your lover. Your passionate and willing lover. I will be your soul mate in body, and yes, in mind when you race headlong with your tongue wagging toward the cliff, but I will not, ever, marry you. You must find a willing wife who compliments your being; fixes your meals, irons your shirts, mends your socks and washes your dirty underwear. And yes, even bears your children if that must happen. There are many women out there who fit that description and will leap into your arms if given the chance."

He had sat in bewildered, stunned silence. Staring, not at her long luscious sheer-nylon-swaddled legs swinging before him; but rather at the ceiling; numb.

Chapter 8

Thomas struggled through the bitter Chicago winter as Galya continued to prod and push him toward accepting a spousal partner other than her. He grew more suspicious by the day that she was using her harebrained theory as a ploy to leave him, alone, searching and grasping for solace and satisfaction while she ventured off in search of new conquests. He felt abandoned and violated, having heaped his unrestrained devotion on her while she schemed to cast him off to fend for himself in the wilderness of dating and mating. He was furious one moment and begging her for reconsideration the next. She, however, stood firm. Finally, coaxing him like an exasperated father demanding his skittish son to leap into the deep end of the swimming pool, she said, "If you won't take the plunge, I'll do it for you."

"So, you are going to find me a wife? Is that what you said?" Thomas responded indignantly.

"Yes, that appears the only way we will find a solution to this problem," Gloria gasped as she rocked rhythmically on Thomas' erect status sending spasms of delight through both of their steaming bodies.

After a final thrust Galya rolled off onto the damp silk sheets, caught her breath and added, "I know exactly what kind of woman fits our definition. If left alone to the task, it will take you years if not decades of searching and still you may never find the perfect specimen. I will sort through the mobs of desperate women out there and capture an ideal partner for you. Wait and see. You will be pleased."

At that particular moment Thomas was too spent to argue further. His chest heaving; his mind still under control of her loins, he simply said, "If you insist."

Six weeks later Thomas met Helen.

Three weeks before that Galya met Helen.

She spotted her in the University library, sitting alone, intently scouring a book on Eastern European history. Galya's focus was on her furrowed brow; eyes squinting through an oddly misshapen pair of oversized reading glasses. Strands of mousey brown hair dangled over the frames obstructing her view. A tear rolled down the side of her nose and hung from its tip. She was clearly distraught, and Galya, unconsciously abandoning her mission objective, found herself suddenly equally curious and sympathetic. Their location was not at the University of Chicago library. No, hunting female quarry so close to Thomas' domain was too risky. Galya had chosen the Northwestern University campus for her pursuit that day.

Galya strolled in quiet circles around where she sat like a wolf stalking a lost fawn. On one passing at her back, Galya could see that her book was open to a section entitled, "The Trials and Tragedies of the Czechoslovak Nation." My God, she thought, this might be too good to be true. She had to get a closer look. A better scope. The hunt was on. With the fourth pass completed, Galya sat down across from her, not speaking, rather discreetly but intently observing. Her muted sobs had subsided, but her nose remained red and moist. She was childlike, not pretty but somehow delicately handsome behind the unsightly spectacles. Porcelain features, Galya could tell, fragile and glistening. A sculpture still in unmolded clay. Galya waited for a moment and silently rose from her chair, returning a few moments later with an identical text in hand. She opened it, unnoticed by her tablemate, and absently began leafing through the pages.

At last Galya decided the time was right to speak. She addressed her in a low whisper. "This is quite impossible material for a freshman level-one course, don't you think?"

The young woman was startled by the hushed interruption. Her glasses slipped down her nose as she raised her head to search for the source. Galya winced at her reaction and contritely offered, "I'm so sorry to disturb you. I saw you were studying the same book there and I just sort of blurted it out. My frustration, you know; this stuff is so hard to get through. I'm sorry, please forgive me."

The woman's riveted concentration on the section of the text was now clearly broken, but she did not display irritation, rather offering a warm smile in return.

She responded with, "I too find it exceptionally difficult, not the material itself, but the fact that this particular section reminds me of home and the plight of many people with whom I remain close." She flipped around the open text and slid the pages across the table for Galya to observe.

"Oh, I see. I found that chapter more boring that most of the others. Why, are you Czech?"

"Yes, at least my ancestors were."

"Interesting. That why you were crying?"

"Yes, I'm so embarrassed."

"Don't be. Excuse me, but I must get back to work," Galya declared abruptly, rather harshly ending the exchange.

The woman shrugged, pulled the book back in front of her and resumed reading; this time stoically, without outward emotion.

Confidently returning to her strategy Galya had chosen to temporarily ignore the woman's friendly overture. Inwardly she was ecstatic. A Czech. Just like Thomas. I must be dreaming! Not going to let this one get away. Following course, Galya pretended to bury her nose in the book and fell silent as if her target had never spoke. Thomas had spent too many long hours with her in private discourse about his native land, so Galya did, indeed, find the struggles in Czechoslovakia under Antonin Novotny's iron-fist rule tedious and monotonous. So instead of absorbing more of the book's contents her brain was working deviously to calculate her next move.

In the silence Galya often glanced up from her text to further size up her quarry. At the right moment she would reignite the conversation with renewed affability if her unsuspecting target began to stray.

When engaged, Galya was prepared to discuss specifics about the contents of the book in question. Her fundamental appreciation for and acute knowledge of world history was intense, and thankfully, this time, Thomas' incessant drumbeat on the subject, particularly related to the Eastern European bloc, by the grace of God, had prepared her exceedingly well for this fortuitous encounter.

Galya's high acumen played well in academic settings, but her real forte was falsehood, forgery and deceit. She had to make this young flower; this unblemished but blossoming infant, believe she too was an aggrieved, fledging student, older perhaps, but no wiser, whose purpose in learning paralleled her own.

That opportunity came when her prey unexpectedly pushed back her chair and quietly rose to her feet. Galya then looked up with feigned curiosity. Before moving away the woman leaned across the table and whispered, "I'm afraid I have disturbed you now, and for that I do apologize."

On cue, Galya pounced. "Oh, it's not you. I just found a particular passage somewhat interesting and got carried away. Don't be silly, you didn't bother me. Please sit down, and please, let's both avoid at all costs any discussion of the whole god damn topic of world history."

"I'm Galya by the way."

"I'm Helen," and she smiled and retook her seat with an inappropriate student library guffaw prompting long "shhhhhhs" from those around them. An hour later they were in the student cafeteria and their discussion had covered a number of wide ranging topics, most of which to that point had any academic application.

That afternoon Galya learned that Helen Dobrinski was a native of Chicago, born into modest wealth to a third generation Czech family who occupied a three-story Victorian off Lake Shore Drive. And she was not a first year, right out of high school, preppy as Galya had suspected from her first observation. On the contrary Helen was proud of her legal drinking age of twenty-three, and her two-and-one-half year stint in the Peace Corp in northern Africa before returning to the homeland and into the welcoming arms of a partial scholarship to the famed Northwestern University campus. Helen loved the social sciences but hated all of her other subjects including chemistry and physics and all they stood for. She was planning on dropping those courses unbeknownst to her father, a pediatric surgeon, who was thrilled at her sojourn home from the third world and the assumption that she was, at-last, destined to follow in his size-twelve footsteps into the wondrous galaxy of medicine. Helen, however, knew her calling was elsewhere and was simply terrified to tell her good old dad differently. Instead of doctoring the sick she told Galya she longed for a culinary career.

"I want to feed the people not cure them. Strange, huh?" she offered.

"No I don't find that strange at all," Galya responded. "But let me ask you why?"

Helen did not hesitate. "In Africa, the procurement of food is a life-long pursuit. Society is either shaped or shattered on whether people are well fed. History tells us so. Diets dictate prosperity or poverty. America and free countries eat the best food; the third world now including

Eastern Europe under the Communists, the worst. I know I can't change any of that so what's challenging to me is when you find any thing to eat, trying to make it taste good; no matter what you've gathered on any particular day. You might eat monkey and turnips one day, and boiled alligator eggs and nothing else the next. I find it most fascinating, and yes, intensely stimulating to take whatever comes your way and make a delightful meal out of it."

"Monkey. Is that right?" Galya quivered. "Taste like chicken?'

Helen emitted another loud burst of laughter. "No, it tastes like rotten tree squirrel unless it's boiled for half a day, then sautéed in a peanut oil-like substance and some mysterious herb I was too frightened to ask about, and then dipped in stale, crumpled bread crumbs and deep fried over an open flame in a black skillet filled with three inches of pure lard."

"Sounds enchanting, very healthy," Galya suggested.

"Mouth watering," Helen confirmed.

"The only use I have for basic chemistry is the knowledge gained to concoct good ingredients for fine cooking, much to the future chagrin of my father," she added.

Their conversation continued through the afternoon hours and into the evening reaching a point when the topic of well-prepared food overtook them and they caught a cab for a French bistro on Michigan Avenue.

To Helen, Galya revealed little, most of which was pure fabrication. Helen was led to believe her companion was twenty-five, recently divorced from a Chicago Board of Trade statistician who was fascinated and preoccupied with the parallels between rising oil prices and the falling money supply among the established nations of Europe. Galya said she had had enough of the monotony a year prior. Her divorce settlement, she lied, was sufficient to pay tuition costs, not at Northwestern but at U of C, and fund a fairly nice one-bedroom apartment six blocks east of the campus. She wasn't working just then, only studying, Galya said, but she had recently applied for a part time, paid secretarial position with a history professor at U of C, who was said to be quite witty and extremely good looking. She too despised chemistry and was axing the course the following Monday as soon as she could meet with her advisor. Her plan was to load up on creative writing classes.

"Then why were you at our library rather than yours?" Helen inquired.

"I just needed some new scenery. That place is so dry and full of itself. Northwestern seems vibrant, alive, much more interesting and fun. I come here a lot to meet new, refreshing people. Like you," Galya lied again.

Galya continued embellishing the last part of her personal history, which became even more horrendously false than the first. What she studiously avoided telling Helen was she was not a registered student, and she loved chemistry, a skill she often applied.

Their evening ended with a pledge to meet for brunch on Saturday at a restaurant near Garfield Park Conservatory, and Galya learning that Helen's atrocious glasses were only for reading. Nonetheless she vowed to promote the idea of contact lenses at the first opportunity.

Saturday came quickly.

Their meal and follow-on activities on that day also proved to help advance Galya's agenda. They visited an expensive hairdresser who, with Galya's prodding, promptly altered Helen's color from ugly, dull blonde to a vibrant chestnut brown. They shopped at Marshall Field's Department store for more than two hours in the afternoon purchasing a number of lovely outer and under garments, including, with Galya's strong encouragement, an evening dress for Helen for an upcoming event to which she was destined to attend.

"It is a dinner/dance at the Chicago Hilton sponsored by the local chapter of the AFL-CIO. This man I was talking about; you know, the professor I started working for this week, is a keynote speaker that night. I don't know much about him yet, but I do know he is quite a talker, and people have told me he is some sort of an activist for poor working people. It should be fun. He's invited me and said I could bring a friend. What do you think?" Galya queried.

Helen was hesitant at first. "I don't know. It will be kind of odd going without dates. And if my father knew I was going to an event supporting labor unions, he would have a fit."

"What do you mean?" Galya was genuinely curious.

"My father's a physician. He's quite conservative about politics. He thinks the unions in Chicago are all run by a bunch of gangsters; some of them as bad as Al Capone back in the Twenties. You should hear him rant and rave about the corruption, and how union bosses are all rich and steal from their own members who are out there working, digging ditches and collecting garbage. I don't think I believe him, but I really don't know that much about it," Helen explained.

"Well, neither do I," Galya lied again. "But they say it's going to be fancy with an orchestra in one ballroom for the older folks, and a rock and roll band in another ballroom for younger people. And I'll bet with all those young, handsome, big, strong, muscle-bound hard working ditch diggers there's got to be two of them who just might like a gentle touch from ladies like us. What do you say?"

Helen's resistance was broken by then. "Well when you put it that way. Why not?"

The dress Helen bought shimmered in lemon yellow silk, cut low in the front and slit too far up her right thigh. Her new hair color and style accented the look perfectly. Galya said she already had a dress, equally sexy, but in shamrock green. It hung in her closet, she said, having been worn only once to a Christmas party this past December. She lied about that as well, surreptitiously knowing that Thomas would be shelling out big dollars in a day or two to dress her equally as well for the upcoming event. Shoes to perfectly match came next.

Along with Helen, Galya also purchased an expensive pair realizing with great confidence that full reimbursement from Thomas was forthcoming when presented the receipt.

They were giddy with excitement by the end of the shopping spree; Helen, by then, having shed her initial forbearance; now rather looking forward to the night ahead with growing anticipation. Before they parted for the day Helen asked with a hint of shyness, "Do you think I will be able to meet him?"

"Who's he? Who are you talking about?" Galya, knowing full well to whom her friend was referring, asked in return.

"The professor, you silly. The tall, debonair, smooth talking, radical; that's who."

"Oh, him," Galya came back, "Well if you want to, I suppose that can be arranged. I'll see what I can do," she smiled. "And by the way, he's not so tall," Galya corrected, "but everything else you said about him is true."

Chapter 9

The main ballroom of the Chicago Hilton was garishly decorated in predominant greens and oranges of different mind-twisting shades. The hotel staff had been instructed by the public relations departments of competing shop stewards to match their emblematic colors, many of which were adopted from sister union locals in Ireland and Scotland. The result was a surrealistic kaleidoscope of visual nausea that covered everything from the tablecloths to the dyed carnation bouquets that served as centerpieces. Even the napkins were alternating oranges and greens. The hotel ran out of water glasses of those prime colors, so many were substituted in colors of blue and red.

"This room looks like Jackson Pollack on a weeklong drunk might have decorated it," Helen laughed as she and Galya entered the expanse at the assigned eight o'clock hour. Festivities had just begun by the time they arrived.

With an off-key big-band orchestra striking up a tune they thought they recognized from the 1940's as a musical backdrop, they were immediately struck by the appearance of many who wandered about the room. Clad in mostly ill-fitting tuxedos, some of which were accented by brown shoes or scuffed work boots, the gentlemen mostly displayed wide, over-the-belt waistlines.

And it was hard for Galya and Helen to avoid gawking at their lady companions decked-out in garish lavender and pink frilly bride's maids looking outfits that, "should have remained in their respective cedar chests for eternity," Galya opined at one point. This hideous exhibit of what not to wear was especially true, Helen remarked, when she saw one immensely oversized breast nearly burst from its binding when its possessor leaned over to retrieve another glass of cheap, rather warm champagne.

"Where are all the hunks of man flesh you promised me?" Helen teased her companion.

"Oh, don't you worry your pretty little head, dear Helen. They're lurking nearby. We just have to weed them out. Let's find the bar. One thing we know about events like this is these people know how to drink."

They shimmied through the crowd, turning heads of both sexes, prompted by either sheer lust or boundless envy. They found the bar and ordered dry, gin martinis, both with three olives. Helen had never tasted a martini, but admitting so to Galya was as likely as another size-four female scampering to her side. They clinked glasses and scanned the crowd for more amusement. Then came a light, gentle tap on Helen's bare shoulder.

She turned to seek out the source of the touch and stared into the face of Dr. Thomas Riha.

"Well, good evening, my ladies," Thomas proclaimed, "You both look absolutely astonishing."

With Helen's back to her and Helen's eyes locked on the professor's broad grin, Galya produced a pronounced wink of satisfaction to which Thomas caught a glimpse, responding with a nonchalant nod in return.

"I believe you are Helen," Thomas said, to which Galya stepped forward to interrupt with, "I'm so sorry, Professor Riha; how rude of me. Yes, this is Helen Dobrinski, my friend. We are so grateful to you for inviting us this evening. It is bound to be a wonderful event."

"Well, Miss Tannenbaum, it is, indeed, ordained to be a magnificent evening of fine dining if you adore cold chicken breasts, over-cooked brown rice, green beans sprinkled with stale almonds, topped off by a delicate Jell-O butterscotch pudding for dessert. My advice is to go heavy on the martinis to deaden the pain and quell the indigestion, while you wait out the frightful dinner hour until my speech."

Helen cocked her head curiously, sensing a slight arrogance in his remarks, until he laughed aloud and followed with, "You see I am the star of the show tonight, just a step above the jugglers, magicians and fortune tellers due any moment."

"You are joking, aren't you?" Helen queried quite seriously, turning to Galya in a momentary plea for assistance in finding an escape route.

"Oh, yes he is, dear friend. I've known him only a week, and I can assure you that he is quick with a joke but is quite humble," Galya responded. "No need to panic."

Thomas belly laughed at that plus Galya's additional remark of, "This afternoon while you were out professor, I snuck a peek at the text of your speech tonight, and I might agree that it is worth waiting for; plied, that is, with another martini."

"Coming right up, my ladies," Thomas said. "And by the way, I was fibbing about the jugglers."

As predicted the dinner feast was genuinely awful. Helen and Galya joined their dining companions at a big round center table by devouring their portions as the gin and vermouth had the opposite effect of stimulating rather than dampening their appetites. Even the pudding went down quickly. Thomas could not join them at their table. Instead he had a prominent seat on the dais, right between the exalted AFL-CIO leader George Meany and his equally venerated wife Eugenia. Meany's billowing cigar smoke hung as a thick blue-grey cloud over the head table, at times, blurring Helen's view of Thomas who was paying scant attention to the labor boss and spouse, choosing instead, to keep a watchful eye on the enticing Miss Dobrinski. She's Czech. Fantastic. Galya, I love you, Thomas muttered under this breath. Helen caught his pleasant gape and several times looked away in embarrassment.

She'll do quite well, Thomas thought as he ignored Mrs. Meany's chatter about her new post as head of a labor initiative to organize the nation's hospital nurses. She is attractive after all; fine figure I suppose under that slinky dress Galya convinced her to buy, so the sex should be acceptable, but I'm sure not as vibrant as with Galya; but no matter, she will perform as instructed and provide certain entertainment. Plus she will look good on my arm at functions like this and also should prove capable of carrying on a rather intelligent conversation, perhaps even in my native tongue, judging from our earlier discourse. All- in-all a fine choice, my darling Galya. Fine choice.

Thomas' daydreaming was interrupted when Brother George rose to introduce him. Meany's comments were short and direct.

"I give you a clear thinker. I give you a man who should live in your hearts, if he doesn't already. I give you a socialist working man's champion; a man who will help the world's laborers organize and suck every last dime of profit out of the corporate money changers who control our economy," Meany roared. The crowd cheered. Thomas Riha took the podium doubtful the applause was for him.

That night Thomas chose to talk about his favorite author, Russian journalist, Vissarion Belinsky. Thomas knew how dangerous it was to speak in lofty, high brow terms to this peculiar audience, so his challenge was to make his point clear and succinct without violating the fundamental theme of Belinsky's most famous and poignant work; his renowned Letter to Gogol.

"Nikolai Gogol lived from 1809 to 1852," Thomas began. "In his short life span he gained wide recognition and was considered by some in elite circles as the conscience of Russia; its headmaster, its mentor and defender."

"Yet Gogol died young and broken," Thomas continued, "On the receiving end of Belinsky's poison pen. His crime: Totally misreading the conscience of Russia with his perpetually condescending commentary. Gogol was like the Barry Goldwater of his day. And Barry, God-bless his evil soul, should have cracked his Russian history books and listened to the people."

Despite full bellies and many wobbly cocktail-laden heads, the mere mention of the demonized 1964 Republican presidential candidate brought the crowd to rapt attention in short order.

"Belinsky died young as did his adversary but, unlike his opponent, he died a satisfied man. During his short life, he took on the role of our Walter Cronkite. He strongly criticized the heretic Gogol with grand narrative rebukes, correctly describing the mindset of a downtrodden Russian society in the mid 19th century."

"Listen to Belinsky's words of a hundred and twenty years ago," Thomas patiently instructed his audience. "I will quote them directly, but with two exceptions. Where, in his indictment, Belinsky cites his beloved Russia, I will substitute with my beloved America, and I will let you draw the uncanny parallels to today's America; an America I suspect many of you out there are longing, and some would die, to change."

"Belinsky wrote as an angry man to a docile man, a man without scruples, he alleged; a man who ignored reality and rested his weight on the backs of the suppressed. Here's exactly what he said."

What America needs are not sermons; she has heard enough of them; or prayers, she has repeated them too often. What America needs is the awakening in the people of their human dignity lost for so many centuries amid the dirt and refuse. She needs rights and laws conforming not with the preaching of the church but with common sense and justice, and their strictest possible observance. Instead she presents the dire spectacle of a country where men traffic in men. A scattered applause caused Thomas to pause. He then plunged deeper.

A country like America where there are no guarantees for individuality, honor and property, and even no police order, and where there is nothing but vast corporations of official thieves and robbers. The most vital national problem in America today are the abolition of serfdom and corporal punishments and the strict observance of at least those laws which already exist.

With that said, Thomas broke off again; waiting for a response. It came louder and more universal this time. But they were on their feet with....

This travesty is realized by the government itself which is well aware of how the land owners treat their peasants and how many of the former are annually done away with by the latter, as is proven by its timid and abortive half-measures for the relief of the white Negroes and the comical substitution of the single-lash knout by a cat-of-three-tails. Such are the problems, which prey on the mind of America in her apathetic slumber!

And they remained standing, at least those who could, when Thomas railed on with....

You, as far as I can see, you do not properly understand America. Its character is determined by the condition of American society in which fresh forces are seething and struggling for expression.

Why if you Mr. Gobol, my Mr. Goldwater, had made an attempt on my life I could not have hated you more than I do for these disgraceful lines which you teach the barbarian land owner in the name of Christ and Church to make still greater profits out of the peasants and to abuse them still more.

Thomas stepped back from the podium as pandemonium ensued. The clamor finally died down after Meany, cigar flaming, began banging his fist on the table knocking over glasses and spilling food-crusted dinner plates on to the floor.

Thomas had at least fifteen more minutes of scheduled commentary, but scuttled the thought of continuing any longer. So, when the crowd obeyed their leader's command to quiet down, Thomas finished his remarks with, "No you are not Russian peasants. No you are not slaves, but yes, you and I are oppressed. You, you socialized workers of America, are its backbone. Belinsky's landowner is our General Motors.

Our Westinghouse; our Carnegie Pittsburgh Steel; our Standard Oil. His apathetic government is our apathetic government; his plight is our plight. But you, members of organized labor, you can tell Mr. Goldwater and his right-wing maniacs America will change or there will be no America!"

By the time Thomas re-took his seat Helen Dobrinski thought she might be in love.

Chapter 10

Their courtship was a brief one. In the early days of its four-month span it was mostly filled with laughter and gaiety, fine wines and food, operas and lectures and the occasional public protest attended by Thomas and a select delegation of radical friends. At times they attempted to converse in the Czechoslovak dialect, but abandoned that effort when both admitted to the difficulty of adequately expressing themselves in a language long ago forsaken. Helen longed to cling to Thomas' side from that first night, but soon her plans were frequently sidetracked by Galya who had suddenly become an all-too-frequent third wheel. Thomas brushed off Helen's complaints with shallow excuses that Galya added balance and perspective to their coupling. Besides, he said, "I rely heavily on her for my work. It's impossible for me to suddenly stop my thought process at five o'clock quitting time. My brain works constantly; my speeches come at all hours; my lesson plans evolve unexpectedly. I must have her near, if possible, as a sounding board; a backstop against which I fling my ideas."

As the weeks went by Helen's resistance to Galya's omnipresence slowly waned. Her protests about Galya gradually subsided, while other complaints involving Thomas professional activities intensified.

Since Thomas' resounding reception before Chicago's organized labor force, his star not so quietly rose to a zenith among the city's more vocal, radicalized left-leaning populace. His celebrity resulted in frequent invitations to repeat his message before ever-expanding, clearly sympathetic crowds. He was keynoter at union gatherings of miners and autoworkers. He addressed the garment workers, the taxi drivers, and municipal employee assemblies, and even the Socialist Workers Party convention. But when he was announced as a featured lecturer at the Communist Party of America's annual congregation, Helen threatened to walk out. She could not face her father if confronted by the assertion that her boyfriend, perhaps fiancé, as she put it, "was coaching Communists on how to overthrow the government."

Thomas and Galya were stunned by her vehemence, and surprised she would challenge Thomas in that way. They feared she wasn't bluffing. Thomas tried his best to placate her fears and diffuse the tension with a promise to, "Stick to recitations on the common man's grievances against oppressive regimes rather than presenting an instructional manual on how Lenin, Trotsky and their cronies sacked the Romanovs in 1917."

Helen was not persuaded. She held to her opposition by refusing to attend his lecture, and reluctantly accepted Galya's offer to accompany him in her place. Helen sat alone at home that night occupying Thomas' white leather couch, sulking and staring at the brilliant city lights while consuming a fine bottle of white burgundy.

Despite his assurances otherwise, Thomas' speech to the Red Party hierarchy was a stem-winder. Not unlike his address to the AFL-CIO confab he had the delegates on their feet several times with broadside attacks on the most fundamental of democratic, free market principles. He drew the loudest, longest applause with his full denunciation of fellow professor Milton Friedman, the messiah of free enterprise, and his rousing 1962 best seller Capitalism and Freedom. Thomas labeled the renowned work as worthy of nothing more than toilet paper.

He ranted that he was ashamed to be teaching at the same University that had paid Friedman for so long, allowing him to "continuously spray his venom over an ignorant populace."

On Communist Party President Gus Hall's personal instructions Thomas and Gloria, the guise she took on for the night, had been chauffeured to the convention hall in a stretch Cadillac limousine which, after his performance, they used as a not-so-comfortable, semi-secluded lovemaking boudoir during their twenty-minute ride back across town. Except for one late afternoon tryst in his office they hadn't copulated since Galya had Helen burst onto the scene, so they quickly but not so quietly made up for lost time.

Galya had taken full responsibility for their forced separation and she had remained steadfast on the advantages of Thomas and Helen remaining a rising couple in Chicago society.

All that came crashing down, when, on the day after Thomas maligned Milton, Professor Riha was fired.

His dismissal notice was delivered to his office by special courier. The messenger handed the sealed envelope to Galya who found it curious and decided to open it. After reading the terse sacking, penned personally by Dr. Finlayson, she cried out in anguish loud enough to attract the attention of a secretary seated across the hall. At the sound the woman came quickly to Galya's aid, but as a would-be Good Samaritan, was harshly waved off followed by a slammed door in her face. Inside Galya wept openly, terrified over how she would break the news to Thomas upon his return from his early morning class.

There would be no appeal. Thomas did not have tenure. His time on the teaching staff was short of securing that cushiony safety net. Understanding that, Galya immediately knew he was out on the street with a month's severance, and overnight, a social standing below a student dormitory janitor.

When Thomas arrived and read the pink slip he surprised Galya with his reaction. Actually, he said, he expected it, and without her knowledge, had prepared for it. On his own, typing his own letters, he revealed an ongoing correspondence with the head of the history and social studies department at the University of Colorado at Boulder. Thomas called Professor Edward Reznick the day after Dr. Finlayson's letter arrived, and the day after that, he had a job in Colorado teaching Russian and Eastern European history, beginning that next semester.

"But that means we have to move," Galya whined. "I love Chicago. How can you uproot me like this?"

Helen was astounded by Galya's outburst, which came as the three of them were having dinner at a lower-scale diner on a side street off Michigan Avenue. Thomas had insisted on the reduced- cost fare since his paycheck had vanished just days before.

Still astonished by the remark, Helen glared across the table at Galya somehow hoping she misunderstood what had just been said. But, instead, her anger reached its peak when Galya added, "Our arrangement here has been nothing less than perfect. We are advancing up the social ladder, gaining acclaim and prestige with every step. Could you not seek appointment at Northwestern?"

"Galya, don't you understand? I've been blackballed here in all academic circles. Finlayson and his allies have seen fit to guarantee my exile. I have been banished, overthrown, deported. I shall await my execution by firing squad. My only escape is a midnight ride through the castle gates on a trusted steed, head covered with black hood, my tempered steel sword my only defense against those longing for my demise," Thomas jokingly waxed poetic.

"Don't be ridiculous; this is serious. You make fun," Galya angrily retorted.

Helen fumed, caught her breath and finally said, "You two make me sick. What am I in this whole sordid mess? Thomas, I'm supposed to be your girlfriend. At one point in this relationship I thought, just maybe, I was your fiancé. I'm nothing more than your whore. That's right! I sit here listening to you and Galya moan and bitch about losing your social status as if she's in control of all that's important in your life. How can you not be sleeping with him Galya? And you Thomas, you don't even address me with this news. You speak to her. This should be a private matter between us. But no, she not only comes along, she's the center of your attention. Every move you make, every decision, it seems, revolves around her; her opinions, her point of view, her recommendations. Well, mister, I've had enough. You and Galya decide what to do. I'm out of here."

Helen's voice had risen above the surrounding ruckus, turning a dozen heads in the packed, noisy eatery in their direction.

But despite her best effort, tears had welled in Helen's eyes. Thomas reached for her hand. She jerked it away. Galya sat, stifling a smirk, yet she knew quick action was in order. Helen pushed back her chair and stood. She looked away and found the restaurant patrons gawking. Galya quickly glanced at Thomas motioning for him to act. Few others were eating their meals; instead watching the drama unfold. Helen turned to walk away. Galya silently mouthed the words, "Don't let her go." Thomas leaped to his feet. To his surprise, Helen spun around for a final word.

"By the way, in case you are interested, I love Colorado. I would have gone there with you in a minute."

Thomas caught up with Helen as she scurried toward the exit. He grabbed her elbow. She let him hold it. Gently, he turned her toward him and hugged her tightly. She buried her face in his shoulder to muffle her crying. A cheer rose up from the patrons inside. Wild applause at the scene. Thomas grinned and waved to those offering their accolades. He escorted her outside.

Galya withstood the silent scorn of the surrounding customers by saluting them all with a full glass of cheap Chablis. Alone, she finished her dinner and the bottle, less mindful of their piercing stares with each empty glass.

After a week of intense pressure from Galya and a promise from Thomas that Galya would remain behind, Helen agreed to his marriage proposal. The ceremony was brief and sterile. The Cook County Justice of the Peace hurried through his lines. He had nine other ceremonies to perform before his lunch break.

Following a leisurely drive West, Thomas and Helen arrived in Boulder a week later. Thomas' fall semester classes began September 10th, which gave them plenty time to find a home, receive their shipment of furniture, un-pack and settle. Thomas left the white leather sectional couch behind. The couple sub-leasing his apartment wanted it badly and paid handsomely for the privilege. He missed Galya terribly. His first lecture was a thorough examination of the wisdom and wit of Karl Marx.

PART III

Chapter 11

It was remarkably warm for late February in Colorado. So warm that the buds on the matching pair of cherry trees in the rear yard of Professor Thomas Riha's brick and dark wood-stained siding Tudor two-story near Pearl Street were prematurely beginning to flower.

This freakish weather phenomenon was simply Mother Nature's wanton act of cruelty, Thomas thought, as he sipped his morning coffee and gazed through his kitchen window at the infant white blossoms that sprinkled about the branches of his prized samplings. Having now lived in this bustling center of classic liberal arts academia for nearly forty-eight months, Dr. Riha had come to recognize the weird weather patterns that played havoc on the normal seasonal cycles of vegetation that flourished in the region. Chicago had prosaic climatic change, Thomas recalled. He liked that. He didn't like the prospect of a frigid spring storm sweeping across the Rockies to annihilate his blossoms and neuter his cherry crop for another year. The weather report said a blizzard was on its way with temperatures forecast to drop thirty degrees by mid-afternoon.

In Chicago, the weather was either hot as the Amazon or cold as Siberia, nothing in between, and always predictable during the same months of each year, Thomas silently asserted, while peering intently through the window glass. He shivered at the thought of another wintry blast.

Much in Thomas' life had changed since his arrival in Boulder four years earlier. To his delight the University had granted him full amnesty from his forced Chicago banishment and all but removed his academic shackles. He was free to espouse his theories in a freewheeling atmosphere of Vietnam War-induced, anti-American radicalism. He could not have found a better home. Now his principles would never be compromised. With this backdrop he self-imposed a higher standard for his message and his discipline hardened. Over the preceding months he had honed his precise, rule-book-thinking brain to work in straighter lines; start to finish; no diversion or contradiction. He was true to form. That's the way he was taught and how he now taught his students. His Russian history classes were not for the timid or faint of heart. Bigoted thinkers need not apply. His empathy with the Russian people and their strict obedience to autocratic rule made them exceptional, predictable; the envy of the world of astute intellectuals.

It didn't matter to Thomas Riha that the Russian populace suffered in poverty under a grim tyrannical regime. He ignored that common fact. What mattered to Professor Riha was that Russians were survivors and conquerors. They were rugged and rigid; withstanding all adversity and thriving in spite of it all. Just like Thomas himself. Being a Communist, a Stalinist, a Marxist, Jew, Muslim, Christian, or Orthodox were all meaningless to a true Russian. Thomas could be any one of those archetypes. Religion, philosophy, or political adherences were of no consequence to the People. Being Russian was the only worthwhile identity. There was purity to this transcending affinity that Thomas found intoxicating, and he applied its spiritual qualities in his writings and lectures with certain revitalized vigor. Undoubtedly Thomas was a true scholar on the country and the people he adored, and his depth of knowledge of the Soviet empire was bottomless. In Colorado he was flourishing in this liberated philosophical environment. His only shame was being born a Czech.

Although Dr. Riha was not without his critics, his status in the subject realm among peer academics was unchallengeable. How gratifying it was to him to be standing at this high water mark. And at such a young age. At forty he had yet to reach his prime. Tenure in the University of Colorado History Department system was only a matter of time. Short as it was. Today, if anyone asked, he was beyond reproach. With staunch conviction he could successfully argue all elements of Russian socialist doctrine with all who may query.

Thomas smiled at his self-induced gratification, then realized his coffee was growing cold and soon he would be late for class. Reluctantly he poured the remaining drops down the sink and turned from the window to retrieve his briefcase from the countertop nearby. In his musings he had forgotten to eat his breakfast, which he had prepared only moments before. He grasped a warm piece of dry toast on his way to the front foyer to find his heavy winter coat before venturing outside into the crisp, bright sunshine.

Galya was still asleep. She didn't like to cook, hence in the early mornings and often at dinnertime, he rummaged for himself. Unless he took her out. Which was often. It was easier that way. She may not rise until noon, but of no consequence. He remained obsessed with her, even more so today than in their years together in Chicago; before she joined them in Boulder to help him secure new opportunities and explore an expansive world of study and discovery.

On his way to his car he thought of Helen. There was no remorse. No regret. Their marriage had lasted a mere two and a half years. After Galya arrived one year into their residency in Boulder, Thomas knew his journey with Helen was doomed. Galya had said it was okay to end it whenever he saw fit. After surveying the ranks of those who mattered, she concluded that Helen was an expendable asset for Thomas, if not a languishing liability. No one knew them in Colorado. They had no real history here. They were an enigma. Thomas and Helen were seldom seen together in public. Thomas had hid himself and Helen from social gatherings, choosing instead to concentrate on refining his message for the lecture hall. Helen was locked inside her own world, frustrated and soon furious and remorseful of her pursuit of this inexcusable villain of a husband. Thank God she never got pregnant.

Their agonizing time together ended the night of a drunken living room brawl with Thomas stepping between the women and taking a blow intended for Galya's left cheek thrown from Helen's well-toned right arm. Prior to the altercation to compensate for his incessant criticism of her physical appearance and caustic rebukes over her failure to appreciate his superior intellect, a good deal of Helen's spare time had been spent in the University gymnasium where she had shaped her figure and bolstered her strength. Thomas had a very hard time restraining her from inflicting more serious damage to both him and Galya during the fracas.

By morning Helen's suitcase was checked for her flight back to Chicago. She filed divorce papers two weeks later and with a good lawyer took not only her possessions but also a good deal of Thomas' in the settlement. Financially she was sound but mentally her humiliation was pervasive.

Thomas never could determine whether it was Helen's plain looks and lack of sexuality that was disconcerting or his overwhelming fixation on the woman in his bed upstairs. Probably a little of both had created endless bouts of tangled discord. No matter. Helen was gone and he was glad. As he drove toward campus he dismissed his trivial thoughts and returned to the task at hand. His day ahead.

Dr. Riha was not particularly fond of his lesson for this Thursday's senior level class. It will be based on another of the countless Cold War encounters between the two superpowers. He despised the subject, no matter how big and splashy the day's headlines had been. But he was told he must teach the subject nonetheless. Despite his pleas to the Department chairman to avoid lecturing on events currently surrounding this mindless Soviet-American chess match, it was a topic, the Chairman had made clear, "not to be shirked before a classroom full of budding adolescents yearning for knowledge directly affecting their daily lives and well-being." Yet Thomas would make the best of it. He would avoid the common trap of allowing his students to pick sides in the conflict between democracy and socialism because, inevitably, regardless of their current disdain for their homeland, most would "crawl back to the nest" of American comfort if presented a balanced view surrounding the whole affair.

Thomas would have much preferred to lecture on the brilliance he exhibited in one of his most recent books. A fine example of subject matter of much more importance in his mind would be discourse on excerpts from Volume 1 of "Readings in Russian Civilization," Russia Before Peter the Great, 900-1700."

This may have been his finest work, he often espoused. Its publication date was only weeks before. Initially, sales of his masterpiece, which included a second volume, had been slow, but recently were picking up according to his publisher. Especially in the past few days when one-hundred-fifty copies had been ordered in a single block purchase. Thomas had been pleased to have been informed of the large procurement but was curious and cautious as to its origin. In his highly competitive world of examining such topics, large one-time purchases of a work usually meant some contingent of academic adversaries was searching for flaws. Or potentially investigating the subversive mindset of the author.

No one was more careful than I in my representations, Thomas muttered to himself as he backed from his driveway and steered north on Folsom Street toward the main campus.

As he drove away Thomas was oblivious to the two linesmen from Public Service Company who were carefully inspecting a hot high-voltage power cable from the cherry-picker bucket hoisted skyward from their truck parked opposite and one door down from his residence. The workmen had watched him intently as he exited his house, entered his car and drove off into the distance. One of the crew, his coveralls sparkling clean and his hardhat shining in the sunlight, spoke to the other. "Don't touch that wire; don't even get close to it. It'll fry you like a burnt pork chop."

"Don't you worry about that, I ain't goin' near it," said the other equally pristinely dressed workman.

Twenty minutes later Thomas hurried through the side-door entrance to his lecture hall strategically located in the heart of the Norlin Library Building. The oversize classroom was filled to capacity. A few students, some not even enrolled in the class, stood at the back waiting for him to shuffle his papers lying atop the lectern and begin. Dr. Riha's lectures had become renowned among the student body. His kindred spirit popularity was unmatched by other members of the young faculty intelligentsia. He was a ringing voice among the elite for his toxic anti-Nixon, anti-American rhetoric that had already begun to envelope many college campuses at that time. Nixon had hardly had time to find the White House men's room before Thomas and his counterparts began spewing their venom at yet clearly defined policies, especially about the war in Southeast Asia.

One never knew what Thomas Riha might say next. And that made him ecstatic.

This day, Thomas had decided, the war in Viet Nam will bear the brunt of his wrath. Dr. Riha credited himself in leading a select few who blamed Johnson initially and now Nixon for America's latest globetrotting imperialism in Southeast Asia. It is an obsession, he alleges, with destroying the Communist Eastern Bloc, and particularly the Soviet regime. Thomas' lecture notes emphasize his firm belief that Viet Nam was simply a by-product of hysterical anti-Soviet dogma. An unnecessary, wasteful and deadly extension of the Cold War. His theories may not be widely accepted, but that would be no deterrent to him today.

He was fit and primed. He would not disappoint, and he took the stage at full tilt. Soon he would have the rapt attention of them all. He stood erect, grasping the sides of the podium. He peered across the expanse. Remaining silent, he allowed the anticipation to build. He grinned. Play-acting shyness. His dark grey Brooks Brothers suit was perfectly tailored. His trademark yellow boutonnière was firmly secured in his left lapel. His long angular face, deep-set laugh lines and creviced wavy-lined forehead displayed a man, without knowing otherwise, to be somewhat past his forty years. Yet his long, black slicked-back hair, at times hanging in his eyes or flopping over his ears projected a more youthful appearance.

Thomas fought the disobedient pelt by constantly running his fingers through it like a primping model ready for the runway. Galya often nagged him about this un-kept look, coaxing more frequent haircuts, but he refused, silently believing the length preserved a deceiving childlike cast. With one last corrective sweep through his beloved locks he finally began.

"Nixon should be impeached!" he exclaimed. The crowd murmured its approval; the manner of classroom protocol prohibiting outright cheering.

"Nixon is a foreign policy neophyte. He never learned his lesson, and his incompetence is dragging us deeper by the day into the quagmire of Southeast Asia. He thinks because, just once, he offered a weak-kneed rebuttal to Khrushchev during the hyped-up "kitchen debates" a few years back, that he deserves center stage with Ho-Chi-Min, Leonid Brezhnev, or for that matter, any of the Premier's underlings in the Politburo.

"No, all of them already have Nixon on the ropes. The Communist insurgency in South Vietnam is a mystery to him. He can't effectively deal with the Arms Race, control of nuclear missiles, oil exports, grain sales; even currency exchange. This man can not understand the Russian state of mind, let alone that of the Vietnamese," he asserted. Thomas paused to let it sink in and then began again.

"Set forth by Vladimir Lenin in his Decree on Peace during the great revolution, Nixon cannot even comprehend the dual nature of Soviet foreign policy. It quite simply encompasses both proletarian internationalism and peaceful coexistence. Lenin had it right, Nixon has it wrong. He does not perceive how rational proletarian internationalism embraces the common cause of the working classes of all countries in their struggles to overthrow the bourgeoisie and to establish regimes intent on peaceful coexistence. Russians don't want war; they want open measures to ensure relatively peaceful government-to-government relations with capitalist states," the professor declared.

"As Nixon rattles his saber and slaughters Viet Cong, the Soviets and Vietnamese call for peace. Peaceful coexistence does not rule out but presupposes determined opposition to imperialist aggression and support for people defending their revolutionary gains or fighting foreign oppression.

"Why can't he just leave them all alone? Why can't our government step back off the threshold of nuclear conflagration and let the Russian and Vietnamese people pursue their own interests as Lenin so eloquently laid out for them some sixty years ago?" He asked rhetorically.

"Because Nixon is an idiot!" Thomas bellowed in answer to his own question.

This drew a smattering of applause at first; then it spread with many rising to their feet.

Soon a thundering clamor echoed down the aisles.

Dr. Riha, attempting without much enthusiasm to quiet the throng, failed to notice the demure garishly clad girl in the aisle seat in the third row to his right. She too was standing among those offering praise for his rousing remarks. Her face was mostly shielded by unruly strands of a bleached blonde mane that fell over her breasts and down to the middle of her back. She wore clothing perfectly in style for the times. A flowing flowered skirt hung off her waist to the floor. Open toed sandals encased her feet. A boy's pale pink linen shirt that was partially concealed by a tanned-hide fleece-lined vest hid her upper torso. Her wrists were encircled by leather strap bracelets measuring three inches in width. A turquoise squash blossom necklace dangled from her neck. She felt like a fool but admitted to herself that her disguise was perfect for the occasion and exceptionally comfortable. Except for the wig. It had to go.

The outfit had been foisted on her by a supervisor who had left it lying neatly across her hotel bed that morning. Other than this embarrassing get-up, all she had to wear to Dr. Riha's diatribe would have been her navy blue pantsuit uniform tailored just right to conceal the bulge of her 9-millimeter semi-automatic. Being out of place would have been an understatement if had she opted for the pantsuit. Practically speaking the shirt and vest nicely hid the pistol holstered to her shoulder. She suppressed a fleeting impulse to retrieve it and fire a bullet into the demented brain of this fanatic to whom she was paying false acclaim.

Instead CIA Field Operative Agent Catherine Benson along with her fellow classmates slowed their applause, and a minute later all had quietly returned to their seats.

She watched Dr. Riha take a sip of water. His smugness was nauseating. Fuming but following the lead of those around her Agent Benson pulled out her note pad and pencil to record his brilliant remarks for posterity.

The rest of Dr. Riha's lecture that morning was even more hysterical hyperbole and just as maddening, Agent Benson later reported. She listened intently as the professor launched into his comparison between the Brezhnev Doctrine and the Doctrines of Truman and Johnson, claiming the similarities are "irrefutable."

It particularly didn't sit well with her when Thomas claimed Brezhnev's Doctrine was announced to justify the Soviet invasion of Czechoslovakia the year before, and in the next breath, said the Johnson Doctrine promoting Communist containment retroactively justified the American invasion of North Vietnam.

"The Soviets invaded Hungary to put down the uprising in 1956. That action was a blend of Brezhnev and Khrushchev Doctrines, strikingly similar in nature to the Truman Doctrine that justified the invasion of North Korea."

"Soviet military interventions are meant to put an end to democratic liberalization efforts and uprisings that have the potential to compromise Soviet hegemony inside the Eastern bloc. The American interventions are meant to put an end to the spread of communist influence thus protecting the American flank in all four corners of the globe," he said, and added rhetorically, "Who's right in either case? Why should we impose our democratic principles on a socialist society when they are perfectly content with what they have? And vice versa. The problem is the Soviets promote peaceful co-existence while we can't wait to pick another fight."

With those remarks, Agent Benson, pressing hard with her pencil as she scribbled notes on her pad, shattered the lead in disgust. Her seatmate, a boy with hair as long as the annoying wig that was beginning to irritate her scalp, glanced over at her inquisitively, appearing to question her actions. Apparently satisfied, a moment later he solicited her agreement with the professor's latest proclamation by giving Catherine a thumbs-up to which she promptly returned with an identical gesture and an artificial smile.

Agent Benson regained her composure for a short time, but Dr. Riha's next assertion nearly brought her to a fitting homicidal rage.

"The Brezhnev Doctrine promotes a policy of limited independence of the satellite nations providing a buffer zone between the Motherland and NATO forces which are clearly intent on surrounding it and choking off its economic lifelines. The Soviet hierarchy is left with the responsibility of defining socialism and capitalism, implementing the powers and rules of the central government, such as free trade, common currencies and mutual defense.

"What does this system clearly emulate?" was his next rhetorical question, which he promptly answered with, "The United States....don't you get it?"

"The Soviets are quite simply copying us. We have a central government, which sets national policy. The American states, just like the Soviet satellites, have certain rights and freedoms, but they are restricted for the good of the nation as a whole. Don't you think that if a state were to secede like we all remember happened a hundred and eight years ago, that our FEDERAL military wouldn't be dispatched to suppress the uprising? Of course they would...in an instant. And by de-facto adherence to the U.S. Constitution the states have signed on to their participation in a democratic system exactly like the Soviet states have signed one treaty after another pledging their allegiance to the hammer and sickle.

"Again, who's right? I'm taking the side of peaceful co-existence," Thomas exclaimed. "I am tired of unchecked imperialism for the sake of proselytizing a philosophy half the world rejects on principle. Sure, it would be nice if we all had Republicans and Democrats swarming all over the earth competing in free and open elections every two and four years, but that's a childish pipe dream.

"Wake up from your nap, Mr. President and love thy neighbor as thyself."

Agent Benson cringed, and gritted her teeth. Suddenly she had to use the bathroom. She thought the urge had something to do with expelling the poisons that had soaked into her mind and body while she sat cross-legged for Dr. Riha's performance.

Then she heard him finally conclude....

"Your assignment for the day is to bring me two neatly-typed pages refuting, if you can, my theories expressed so eloquently for you in this morning's session. Your reasoning must be sound and strongly supported by facts; not with emotion, not grounded in party affiliation, and certainly not bound in flag-waving patriotism. Dig deeply my children and you will find satisfaction and solace, but I warn you, the mineshaft of truth about which I speak is bottomless. Good luck. Class dismissed."

Loud groans replaced the adulation of a short time before. Agent Benson's shaggy unkempt seatmate turned to her and said, "Impossible, fucking impossible. No one can dispute his arguments."

PART IV

Chapter 12

"You can cover her up now," Dr. Harper Korman instructed the rookie patrolman who stood at the foot of Galya Tannenbaum's bed, gawking at her face-up corpse. The young officer, barely in his twenties and at his first death scene since joining the force, stood frozen, his eyes transfixed on the remains, fantasizing how, at any moment, she would awake, seize him with hands now resting over her pubic region, to coax his mounting with passion and skill.

"Times up!" Captain Bravo sneered at the rookie, "Put your eyes back in your head and do as you're told. Then get the hell out of here and back on patrol."

Patrolman Youngblood was startled out of his stupor by the harsh order given. He stepped quickly to bring the blanket over the body in repose. He presented a starched salute, and "Yes, sir, sorry sir," before nearly sprinting out of the room.

"Everyone else out," Victor ordered, "Including you all." He pointed to the three attendants, all female, who remained in the doorway having reformed their circle after the dress-downed patrolman had hurriedly passed between. Their amiable chat had been rudely interrupted by Victor's command.

"You stay," Victor said, pointing to the fourth orderly who stood in the far corner of the room opposite the deathbed. "You're the one who found her. Correct?"

"Yes, sir," came the response from the sole male attendant, also youthful in appearance but his manner stoic, staring at the floor. "I found her," he acknowledged, glancing up briefly at Bravo and over to Dr. Korman who was seated at a tiny wooden desk which stood along the wall next to the entry door. The other three attendants scurried away.

Dr. Korman, a tall, lanky, rail-thin man with huge claw-like hands, sharp, protruding fingernails, and snowshoe-sized feet was writing in his report ledger. Victor once remarked that "with those talons of his, he might not need instruments to perform his autopsies." It was a good joke often repeated in the squad room. Victor regretted his stab at humor when he heard it mimicked so frequently.

That night, as always, Dr. Korman displayed his signature ear-to-ear stringy brown comb-over, black horn-rimmed glasses, red bow tie and brown tweed suit. His white shirt was stained with what resembled spicy marinara sauce probably from Johnny's restaurant where he ate frequently.

"She was a good person. Frightened, all the time. She told me someone was out to get her. She didn't belong here. Really intelligent. Elegant. Beautiful. Desperate to escape. They knew where she was. They put her here to watch her and wait for the right time. She needed to disappear; to vanish, so they couldn't find her. Now it's too late. She was an easy target," the attendant rambled on with increased intensity, absent any prompting from Victor or the coroner.

At the outburst Dr. Korman looked up from his writing with bewilderment and then glanced over at Victor who had a hard, curious look on his face. He shrugged and went back to his writing.

"Hey, calm down young man," Victor commanded with no hint of compassion.

"Before we get into what you just said, let me ask you why you were on duty here tonight? On the women's ward? It's my understanding that male attendants are banned from these wards."

"And another thing, why did the deceased have her own room when all the others are crammed together on cots out there in the hallway? What made her so special?" Victor continued.

The attendant stepped back, retreating from Victor's barrage until his back was pressed to the wall. He stammered, trying to speak. Victor let a moment lapse.

"What's your name young man?"

"Samuel, sir, Samuel Richards, soon to be Dr. Samuel Richards."

Dr. Korman remained passively at work on his report, seemingly oblivious to the drama unfolding around him.

Samuel stepped away from the wall, cautiously more confident.

Head up and chin out, he said, "I have no idea why she was one of the few to have a private room. She just did. No one told me why. And normally, we are, sir. Normally, that is, barred from working in here, but lately we have been short-handed of female nurses and aids, so those of us who can be trusted in here are assigned. Tonight was one of those nights for me."

Victor's disbelief did not subside. Accusingly he responded with, "So at night you are trusted with all these women; all by yourself, patrolling the wards, spying in their rooms, comforting the patients when they're lonely and depressed. Helping rid them of their misery. Satisfying them when they're horny?"

The aid bristled and stood erect with shoulders back to face his accuser. "No sir. Absolutely not! I take offense at that. I am a professional. I am in my fourth year of medical school and studying to be a psychiatrist. I take my work seriously. I use my skills to counsel patients, both men and women, not to abuse them, sir!"

Victor anticipated the response, and took another tact. "Maybe I was a little hasty there. I'm sorry, but you can understand. I suspect that most people, especially wary cops like me, would be more than a little suspicious of a young, good looking fellow like yourself being here all alone with all these vulnerable females many of whom are just a little if not a lot, say, touched? I just experienced quite a bit of that borderline lunacy getting in here tonight."

"These are desperate times, Captain, and these are desperate people. We are under staffed, under funded and over crowded. These folks need our help, not our ridicule. Yes, many are too sick to cure. On the other hand, many can be cured. And some are here because the state or some uncaring relative thinks they're odd, and can't figure out what to do with them, even though they are as sane as you and I. But there are none like Miss Tannenbaum. She was here because someone put her away until they could find an easy, unsuspecting way to kill her."

With that, Victor could not hide his surprise. Dr. Korman rose from his seat. Victor thought the latest comment might have stirred his attention.

"Why do you say that, Samuel?" Victor lurched.

The orderly silently shook his head appearing to regret the statement.

"There's no way of confirming the cause of death until the autopsy is complete," Dr. Korman unexpectedly broke in. "Let's reserve judgment here. At this point I have no reason to suspect foul play, however; she was a young woman, I believe thirty-eight; no forty, by her chart. Outwardly, by the look of her; vital, in fine physical condition. I do see some discoloration under her fingernails, however. But there are no signs of struggle, bruising, abrasions, or cuts. The skin shows a slight pink-like hue but that is probably due to nothing more than over exposure to the sun. Frankly she looks like she's in a deep, restful sleep. Even her hair is perfectly coiffed."

"In addition, of course, we have the letter which appears to be a suicide note."

Victor listened to Dr. Korman's summation as he caught Samuel's eyes and stared into them deeply, probing for a hint of disingenuous expression. He found none at the moment.

"I am releasing the body to be transported to the Asylum's morgue. There, I will perform the post mortem examination and report back to the authorities within twenty-four hours." The coroner was speaking as if addressing a congregation of the faithful or a press conference of inquisitive journalists.

"Doc," Victor said, "I'm right here. Remember?"

"Oh, yes, Captain. Yes, you are." Awakening from his apparent daze the doctor looked stunned. Victor only smiled at the creature. On this occasion he reminded Victor of a lean, hungry jackal.

"I believe my duties here have been completed for now, so I intend to depart. I will wait in the morgue for the arrival of the remains to begin the process." Dr. Korman, papers in hand, announced to no one in particular as he moved toward the door.

"I want a full toxicology work-up on her," Victor ordered as he stepped aside to allow the doctor to pass.

This remark finally caught his attention. "Oh. very well then," the doctor responded. "Do you have reason to believe a self-administered ingestion of a lethal substance may have occurred?"

"Yea, Doc, I do. Unless this woman died of a sudden heart attack or brain hemorrhage, or some other internal malfunction, she poisoned herself."

"Or more likely, someone poisoned her," Samuel Richards quietly offered.

"A toxicology screen will take more time to complete than what I've allotted for his case. And it will cost the city an additional fee," Dr. Korman proclaimed.

"I don't care, Dr. Korman. Just do it, please," Victor patiently reiterated.

"Very well. If you insist."

"I do," Victor smiled and watched the coroner slither out the door.

Abruptly he turned back to face the orderly.

"And was that someone, you, Samuel? Did you poison her?" Victor sneered.

But the onset of his probe was interrupted as two city fire department paramedics pushing a gurney emerged from a service elevator across the hall. They noisily wheeled the unit into the room and stepped toward the body.

Samuel glared at Victor with loathing. Neither spoke. Victor would be patient with his questioning.

Samuel wasn't going anywhere.

Victor noticed Dr. Korman was midway down the corridor moving in the opposite direction of the sleeping horde of cot-bound inmates. He shook his head in dismay, realizing there was not only a service elevator to this hellhole but a back entrance as well. If he had known that, Victor thought, he could have avoided his trek through the maze of unfortunate malcontents earlier that morning.

This was going to be a bitch of a day.

Victor and Samuel watched intently as the paramedics gently lifted the body onto the gurney and carefully tucked the sheets around to tightly wrap her head and frame. They were gone with her within a minute, finally leaving Victor and Samuel alone.

"I want you to wait outside for me," Victor instructed. "Shut the door behind you. This may take a while. Stay put. Don't go anywhere. If I have to, I will bring up an officer to watch over you until I'm done."

"That won't be necessary Captain. I have no place to go," Samuel replied, exiting and closing the door behind him.

Victor began his search. He was torn. Indecisive. What was he looking for? Was the kid right to be suspicious, or was this just a routine self-inflicted departure? He kept asking himself those questions as he examined the small collection of jars and bottles on the top of the three-drawer dresser next to Galya's bed.

He read the letter. Written in beautiful, flowing calligraphy. Words on paper like monk-script in a monastic biblical translation. But nonsensical. Something about her work for the government. She, being a rising star, then shamed and put away. Now being threatened. Fearing for her life. Afraid of being tortured. So death by her own hand may be preferable. Very strange, but this is a strange place full of strange people. He put the bizarre missive down. He'd read it again after his search for clues.

Why did the kid say that? He seems genuinely upset. What went on between them? Anything? Was he actually trying to help her? Victor questioned as his rummaging continued.

Something may not be right here. The words of the would-be psychiatrist kept coming back to him. Pounding in his ears. Could he dismiss the attendant's hysterical comments? It's only an irrational diagnosis by a kid who still needed years of training and experience with the mentally imbalanced.

No one in this God-forsaken place thinks they belong here. They're all wrongfully committed. They've all been treated unfairly. They're all being watched, and many are convinced someone's out to kill them. Paranoia is as common as a three-day cold, Victor silently rationalized.

He finished his examination of Galya's clothing and other personal belongings, meager as they were, and neatly placed them back on the shelves and into the drawers where they belonged. The nagging thoughts would not leave him, so he pressed on. With his pocket flashlight in hand, he shined the beam in every corner and along the ceiling and floor of the room. He took out his penknife and unscrewed the screws holding the ventilation air-duct screen in place. Nothing was hidden behind it. He turned over her mattress and upended the single bed, carefully searching for stowed-away contraband. Nothing. Not a sign of objects foreign or out of place. He then opened the door. Samuel was leaning against the wall outside.

"Not done yet," Victor said, "I need a broom."

"Over there in the closet next to the service elevator," Samuel replied.

Victor found what he was looking floor; returned to the room, closed the door and began sweeping. Carefully he formed a small pile of dust and debris in the middle of floor and went to his knees looking fixedly for powder residue or other abnormal material of any kind. At first, nothing; then he saw them. He thought it was a reflection of light off the dust particles, a tiny twinkle that disappeared when his eyes moved out of the light ever so slightly. He looked again. He changed the angle of his flashlight's ray. There they were. Three tiny shards of glass. All about half the size of a pencil eraser. He separated each one out of the dust pile. They were too small to confidently pick up with his fingers. He was afraid of dropping and losing them.

That's odd, he thought. But then again, someone probably broke a light bulb or maybe a drinking glass and didn't clean up all the pieces. They could easily be missed. They are so small. And thin. Too thin for a drinking glass. More like a vial or test tube.

He looked around the room for something to aid in capturing the pieces. He remembered the roll of Scotch Tape inside the top drawer of Galya's dresser. Moments later he laid the strip of tape face up on the desktop with each miniature shard safely stuck to it in a neat line. Then he also remembered the magnifying glass. It too was in the top drawer of the dresser. He went to retrieve it.

Odd that she had such a thing. And then he looked inside the drawer again. Three pairs of eyeglasses, each in their cases, scattered about in the drawer as well. He flipped open one case. He noticed how thick the lenses were. She must have had poor eyesight, he thought. But three pairs? Why so many? And why did she need the magnifying glass? To read with?

Victor brought the magnifying glass over to where he had placed the up-right tape and its secured bits of glass positioned all in a line. On the first piece he focused the image to several times its normal size. Nothing stood out in his view. Just sharp, jagged edges. The second piece in the line displayed the same characteristics. But the third appeared a little larger and dissimilar to the others. A tiny but distinct red line ran up one side.

I need this in a lab. But why am I bothering? It's just broken glass. Could have come from anything. This is crazy. I'm wasting my time. But a red stripe on one side? It looks like it's painted on there.

Victor folded the strip of tape in half and wrapped it in the handkerchief he pulled from the breast pocket of his suit coat. He tucked the wad of cloth and its contents in his pant pocket. Evidence? Evidence for what? What the hell am I doing?

Victor stood in the middle of the room, turning in a complete circle, eyes slowly scanning up and down, left to right, for one last look. He kneaded the cloth in his pocket. Then he knew. He'd seen enough of them crushed on the floors of the city's heroin dens.

He turned and opened the door; exited, closed it behind him and stepped before Samuel. "Do you have a key to the room?"

"Yes, a master key," Samuel answered.

"Good. Lock it up."

Samuel did as he was told.

"Is there a phone nearby?" Victor asked.

"Yes, just down the corridor. We keep it in a locked cabinet so the patients don't have access."

A few minutes later Victor spoke into the receiver.

"Superintendent Meredith; this is Captain Victor Bravo. I am sorry to wake you, but as you may have been informed, I am here at the hospital this morning regarding the apparent suicide sometime earlier last night of one patient, Miss Galya Tannenbaum, Women's Ward Three. Room 218.

"Yes, sir. Indeed, I fully assumed you had been informed. Yes, sir, I appreciate the fact that you are notified of all deaths at your facility; no matter the time of day or night," Victor said.

"Yes sir, I believe you are concerned about all of your patients, and deaths are always a tragedy, never to be taken lightly. And yes, yes sir, properly mourned by everyone. Yes sir, thank you sir.

"Well, sir, I have a request. I need you to do something for me. I need you to secure the room of the deceased for the time being. No one is to go in or out of that room without my explicit consent. Until further notice I need you to post a twenty-four hour guard. Yes, Superintendent; that's right. A twenty-four hour guard. No one in or out. Until I say so. Yes, I understand you need that room, oh, you call it a cell, okay a cell, to house waiting patients. But for the time being you have no choice in the matter, Superintendent. Do you understand? Thank you. Until I say otherwise. That room, ah cell, is off limits. Under my control, not yours.

It is a crime scene. Have a good evening, or morning, Superintendent. Again, sorry to wake you."

Victor replaced the receiver and turned to Samuel who was standing nearby in earshot of one side of the conversation. He had a wide grin on his face.

"What's so funny, Samuel," Victor asked as he approached him.

"Nothing, Captain. Just thinking about the Superintendent. He doesn't like to be told what to do."

"I gathered that," Victor replied.

"Now, Captain, how can I be of further assistance?" Samuel asked urgently, and added, "I desire to be dismissed. My shift has ended."

"Oh, yes you can Samuel, be of assistance, but you are not dismissed."

"No?"

"No, Samuel. I see outside that the sun is coming up. Time for that morning cup of coffee, wouldn't you say? Is the cafeteria serving this ward open yet? I see it's just six o'clock."

"Yes Captain; its open. But I'm off duty now."

"Now Samuel, I think you need that cup of coffee. You see, you're not going anywhere until I tell you you can. And if I'm not satisfied with the results of our little chat you're not going anywhere but to jail. Shall we make our way?"

The service elevator took them down to the first floor leading to a long empty hallway at the end of which was the cafeteria. The heavy metal accordion gates were being pulled back by an attendant at the moment they approached.

Victor and Samuel took a table in the corner by a window. Soon a few workers, mostly in clean white uniforms but a few in grey jumpsuits signifying their janitorial positions, arrived for first-shift duty. Mostly, they too ordered coffee. Some were alone. Others began talking quietly with co-workers. Victor, however, said nothing to his companion, instead he stared out the window glass at the blazing red ball rising over the Eastern plains.

"Beautiful, don't you think?" Victor declared, breaking a long, silent interlude.

"Captain, what do you want from me? I've already told you what I saw; how she was lying on her bed, fully clothed, reading, the last time I saw her."

"And what time was that Samuel?"

"Like I said, Captain, around ten o'clock."

"Ten o'clock you say. And when did you inject the poison?" Victor's gaze was hard and cold.

Samuel jerked back in his seat. His mouth went agape.

"What are you talking about? I have no idea what you mean. I, no, you're crazy. I didn't do anything. Poison. Me? This is insane." Samuel's voice rising to a shrill.

'You're the one who brought it up Samuel. Don't you remember? You said someone wanted to kill her. You said she didn't belong here. Someone put her here to watch and wait for the right time to do her in. A little earlier you thought poison might have been the murder weapon. Well, why wasn't it, and why wasn't that someone with the poison you?"

"I was giving you a summary of her condition. I was just trying to be helpful. I was counseling her since she became so consumed with fear over her confinement. Paranoia, at times, overwhelms a patient's behavior."

"But before, Samuel, you were so sure. You seemed to have taken her so seriously. Like her story was not a mental condition, but rather the truth." Victor was calm but unrelenting. He let it sink in before he leaped again.

"I'm telling you I think you're right. Miss Galya Tannenbaum was murdered tonight. Someone injected her with, or forced her to ingest, a legal toxin. I don't know what it was yet, or how, but the lab tests will tell me. I'm sure during the autopsy even our esteemed coroner will find one, possibly more pin pricks or needle marks cleverly concealed in the folds of her skin. Or maybe he'll find residue in her mouth. I don't know.

"And Samuel, after she was unconscious you removed her clothes and had your way with her. Necrophilia. Shame on you. How unbecoming of a would-be physician. But in your ecstasy somehow the syringe you used was knocked off the nightstand, onto the floor. Much to your dismay it shattered into tiny pieces. So after you blew your rocks, you got dressed, went to the broom closet, the one you pointed out for me---and I thank you for that---and you got a broom; swept up the glass and needle and left. But you missed just three ever-so-tiny pieces that bounced under the bed.

"Why Samuel, why didn't you have the decency of putting her clothes back on? Leaving her naked for all the world to see? Didn't you think someone, someone like me, would notice the white, creamy glob you left entangled in her pubic hair? I'm pretty sure it's your wayward deposit.

Stunned and recoiling, Samuel tried to speak.

Victor raised his hand to halt Samuel's attempt.

"Just a minute more, Samuel. If you please. I have a question and then you can talk, you can talk to me all you want."

"Did Miss Tannenbaum have poor eyesight? Was her reading or daily activities aided by eyeglasses?"

Samuel's mouth and throat were too dry to immediately respond. He gulped down the cold coffee remaining in his cup. A waitress came by offering refills. Victor waved her off.

Samuel took a deep breath in a desperate attempt to calm himself.

"Captain, yes, Galya had poor eyesight. I had noticed it was deteriorating rapidly. She was getting a new pair of glasses every month or so, each with stronger lenses. She was growing fearful of going blind. In the last few weeks she resorted to using a magnifying glass for reading. It was especially bad for her at night when she tried to read in that cell with such dreadful lighting. It was particularly troublesome for her.

"That was my thought as well. Thank you for that Samuel. I appreciate the insight." Victor said.

"Please go on Samuel, Take your time," he coaxed.

Samuel's hand went to his mouth. Tears welled in his eyes. His voice cracked.

"I loved her, Captain. She was a spectacular woman. I couldn't have killed her. I wouldn't have harmed her in any way. She loved me too. I was terrified for her, possibly going blind. We could not understand why. She was having other problems too, becoming fatigued, weak, even in the mornings after deep, restful sleep at night. She developed frequent headaches and was sometimes dizzy. Last night; oh God, last night she was short of breath when we....."

"When you were having sex," Victor offered.

Samuel began to weep. The waitress approaching their table a second time with coffee pot in hand, turned away when she saw him.

Victor waited.

Samuel brought his hands from his face, shaking his head, "Yes,

Captain, when we were making love."

"Samuel, you are under arrest for murder. The murder of one Miss Galya Tannenbaum. You have the right to remain silent. You have the right to counsel. If you cannot afford counsel one will be appointed for you. Any thing you say, can and will be used against you in a court of law. Do you understand?"

"Captain, I loved her. Yes, I admit we were lovers. I know that was wrong. I lied to you, but I'm not a killer. I know it was unethical behavior and I know I will probably never practice medicine. But I did not kill her. I swear."

"Son, besides going to jail for the rest of your life, you probably wouldn't have made it through medical school in the first place. Ever heard of cyanide? Can't you even recognize the telltale signs of cyanide poisoning?"

"Please stand up and turn around. Put your hands behind your back." Victor handcuffed Samuel and began to lead his prisoner toward the cafeteria's exit.

Mary Louise Henderson, night nurse, Women's Ward Three, overseer of cells 200 through 250 on the second floor, sat at a table next to the cafeteria's exit door watching Victor and Samuel approach. Samuel's eyes were closed. His head slumped to his chest. He shuffled along. Victor's hand grasped his arm to quicken his step. A momentary pang of sympathy arose in Mary Louise but was quickly suppressed by a baleful smile. Neither Victor nor Samuel noticed her expression. The plan had worked. It had worked, oh, so well. And I only stood-by.

She remained in her seat to allow a few moments to pass before departing herself. Her night shift was over. Her duties fulfilled. Rewards awaited. She looked around the room for her but instead several tables away caught sight of a young, somewhat attractive woman, dressed in a candy-striper nurse's aide uniform, crying uncontrollably. Between sobs the woman glanced back at Mary Louise as if she was the reason for her sorrow.

Curious, Mary Louise thought, but no matter. She's probably just been reprimanded. Few of them ever do things right. Silly little girls. I'm chewing one of them out all the time. Always bellowing like babies when I do. Usually it's the bedpans they spill.

Wonder where she went? No matter. My work is done.

Night Nurse Henderson pushed back her chair, rose to her feet and walked slowly toward the cafeteria exit. She paid no further attention to the mournful glare of the nurse's aide as she wiped her tears and wondered how long her real job would last after what had happened on her watch, hours before.

Chapter 13

Victor read the would-be suicide note again, admiring for the fifth or sixth time how artful hand-scribed words can be even if they formed a tragic message. He put Galya's epistle down, still unconvinced of its meaning. He reached for and pulled the coroner's report from the orange envelope resting on the desktop beside him. He adjusted his reading glasses and scanned the document. In the upper right hand corner of the first page he noticed the telltale ring left from the bottom of a leaking coffee cup. Dr. Korman was not known for good table manners.

Victor quickly flipped through that page and the two behind it. He was quite familiar with the forms Dr. Korman used to document a death, suspicious or otherwise. His interest at that moment was directed toward the attached toxicology report, which, he believed, would affirm his suspicions about the true cause of Miss Tannenbaum's death. It had taken the esteemed coroner two weeks to produce his findings. He claimed a backlog existed at the laboratory of the Colorado Bureau of Investigation. Dr. Korman also was not known for promptness. And his tardiness had caused Victor to erupt in rage when he was forced to release his prime suspect in the case, one Samuel Richards, student psychiatrist in training, who had found the body of the deceased and for sixty hours of combative interrogation remained steadfast in his denial of any wrongdoing.

Samuel's smooth-talking barrister, Michael Bluestein, had sprung his client after Victor failed to establish just cause for holding him another minute. Bluestein, a few years back, was a venerated prosecutor, who had won Victor's praise in helping establish the identity of a major organized crime figure. The suspect, however, was never brought to justice in the criminal courts; instead meeting a fiery death in the explosion of his big baby blue Lincoln in which he had sat parked under a willow tree on the property of a renowned Mob boss and rural cheese distributor. After that incident Bluestein launched a full-scale investigation into the cause of the blast and demanded a manhunt for the perpetrators. Much to his dismay evidence surrounding the fatal car bombing was scant and disjointed.

Bluestein grew even more frustrated when he had turned to Victor for help in the case only to be told that all witnesses had disappeared and the vehicle and the remains of the victim also had vanished. All Bluestein had to go on was a scorched piece of dry dirt fifty yards wide, a few fragments of a chrome bumper and shards of glass scattered over an eighth of a mile radius of the detonation. Victor's unwillingness to pursue leads, minimal as they were, led Bluestein to accuse the detective of a cover-up from which a deluge of protests from an outraged local citizenry washed over his office. After that, Bluestein reluctantly closed the file and two months later found his own pink slip in his in-box offering him six month's severance and medical insurance for a year thereafter. Bluestein didn't wait that long to turn defense counsel and swore from that point on to frustrate Captain Victor Bravo and his cases at every turn.

Gaining Samuel Richards' release without charges being filed was a major victory for Bluestein and he let Victor know that he was out to destroy any further prosecutorial pursuit of his client. There were no witnesses to the death, and there was very little evidence of foul play for Victor to cling to. Certainly Richards was a charlatan, likely preying on an innocent, mentally disturbed patient, and yes, he exploited her vulnerability to the extreme with regular sexual encounters, but he was no rapist, or murderer, Bluestein had maintained. Besides, Richards had lost his job over the matter and found he could only seek further training in Panama or Haiti if he chose to travel there for medical degrees of suspicious value and tenuous recognition in the U.S. That was punishment enough in Bluestein's view.

Victor knew Bluestein was right. His case against Samuel Richards was weak. Victor's sense was the toxicology report he was about to read would substantiate the cause of death but he had little hope that the document would unveil the killer.

He leaned back in the swivel desk chair, propped his feet on top of the desk and began to read. Soon, his suspicions were confirmed. Correct on both counts. The report confirmed death by cardiac arrest brought on by the ingestion of "measured quantities of cyanide" which, immediately or over time, according to the report Victor now read a second time just to make sure, "makes the cells of an organism unable to use oxygen, primarily through the inhibition of cytochrome c oxidase."

So, essentially the victim suffocates, Victor concluded.

His second and perhaps equally important theory also was borne out by the report, which stated that, "tiny prick marks were found in folds of tissue under the arms and behind the knees of the deceased indicating multiple injections of unknown substances over time."

The report further explained that, "ingestion of high concentrations of cyanide causes a coma with seizures, apnea, and cardiac arrest, with death following in a matter of minutes. However, Galya Tannenbaum may not have succumbed quickly. She may have been given or voluntarily took lower doses which caused "general weakness, giddiness, headaches, vertigo, confusion, and perceived difficulty in breathing."

At the final stages, the report theorized, "the deceased lost consciousness, likely with her breathing becoming erratic and rapid, although the state of the victim appears to have progressed towards a deep coma accompanied by pulmonary edema, and in this case, finally, cardiac arrest."

Prior to the fatal dose, the report corroborated that her skin color had become a bright pink directly attributable to concentrated cyanide-hemoglobin complexes. Victor continued reading, noting that a fatal dose for humans can be as low as 1.5 mg/kg body weight and was stunned when he arrived at the section of the report which stated that Galya's body contained 2.75 mg/kg body weight.

"Cyanide concentrations in her blood could have killed a person three times her size and weight," the report noted, and it was through her blood sample that the report concluded a crime had taken place by, "providing the means of assistance in the forensic investigation of a criminal poisoning."

Planting his feet back on the floor he removed his reading glasses and rubbed his weary eyes.

Jesus Christ, the poor woman endured prolonged suffering in pure ignorance by the hand of a vicious, heartless, yet patient killer. She couldn't have had any idea what was happening to her, Victor mumbled audibly.

Time passed. Victor sat in silence. His mind recalling the pink, pale tone to Galya's otherwise flawless skin, thinking how idiotic he had been to pass on the mindless coroner's notion that she was "probably working on a tan."

Over exposure to the sun! My ass. For Christ's sake, how stupid was that. Asylum inmates don't go out sunbathing. And in the nude! What a moron I am, Victor chastised himself in disgust.

Still shocked after absorbing that section of the report he was equally struck by the next paragraph, which read: "Cyanide toxicity can occur following ingestion of amygdalins found in almonds and apricot kernels."

Goddamn, Victor muttered under his breath; how did I miss that?

He picked up the telephone on his desk and called barrister Bluestein.

"Well, well Captain Bravo, what can I do for you this fine day," Bluestein sarcastically chirped. His secretary had told him who was on the line so he had time to rehearse a biting repartee before picking up the receiver.

"Cut the crap, Bluestein. I need to ask your client two more questions," Victor responded.

"Captain, lest I remind you that in the course of your botched investigation into the death of Miss Tannenbaum, before I became my client's counsel, you had nearly five straight uninterrupted days to harass and torture him with hundreds of questions all of which have been answered truthfully. With the innocence of my client now firmly established I also remind you that you have been forced to release him without charges. Why in God's name would I subject Mr. Richards to further harassment, because, after all this time, you conveniently forgot some inconsequential tidbit you think might be relevant to your trumped up case," Bluestein proudly pontificated.

"Bluestein, you can sit there and dish it out all you want. I don't care what you think or what you believe, but this is important, and yes, it is something I overlooked. I received the toxicology report today and it brought to mind the existence of certain evidence that needs to be pursued. Your client would do himself a big favor by simply answering my questions. You can either cooperate with me on his behalf or I will re-arrest him and you'll have to come down here to the station and spring him again after I'm done. And since you're such a busy man with all those important clients clamoring for your precious time, I'm sure you'll lose more money than I make in a year wasting another day fighting for his release. So be nice, stop your blabbering and act like the good lawyer I'm sure you are," Victor said with equal verve and satisfaction at his comeback.

And then he added, "I'll be at your office in thirty minutes. Have Mr. Richards there or I'll find him and this will get a lot more complicated."

"I'll have him here. Make it forty-five minutes," Bluestein said.

"Forty-five then; fine," Victor agreed.

"Yes, she was fond of almonds. She ate them all the time," Samuel Richards responded to Victor's first question. Samuel sat fidgeting in his chair, which sat across the desk from his attorney. His unease was apparent. Victor sat in the adjacent chair, calmly making the inquiry while shielding the anxiety he felt by the critical nature of his questioning.

"The bowl on her nightstand was nearly empty that night, but I noticed there were a few nuts remaining in the bottom," Victor offered somewhat off-the cuff.

"I really didn't pay much attention, Captain. Like I said, she munched on them constantly. The bowl was there, I think, all the time, either full, or partially so, every time I came into her room.

"So, would you say she had an obsession for almonds?"

"I don't know, Captain. Like I said she ate them constantly and seemed to have them in ample supply," Samuel reiterated.

"Ample supply. Okay. Did you make sure she had them in ample supply?"

"Wait a minute. This is much more than what we agreed to Captain," Bluestein interjected.

"It's okay Michael. I don't mind answering," Samuel said. "No, Captain, I didn't get her the almonds. They always seemed to be there, fresh in that bowl by her bedside, every time I came by."

"Did she buy them?"

"Maybe, but she never had any money that I knew of."

"Even for a bag of nuts?"

"Even for a bag of nuts."

"So, if you didn't supply them; who did?"

"I have no idea. Maybe one of the other attendants. "

"Humm, maybe so, but you didn't. You're sure?"

"I'm sure, Captain."

"Samuel, if I find out otherwise, there will be trouble," Victor warned.

"Can we proceed Captain? Please stop with the threats," Bluestein sneered.

"Okay. Now, one other question," Victor began; switching course.

"This better be the end of it," Bluestein tried to warn.

Victor ignored the latest intrusion. Samuel appeared to do the same.

"Were you ever with her when she had lunch or dinner?"

"Occasionally, yes."

"Did you ever notice her having apricots?"

Samuel pondered the last question for a time, but then answered with, "Yes, Captain, come to think of it, I did see apricots on her plate quite a bit. I don't like them myself, but she seemed to gobble them up, almost like she did the almonds."

"So she liked almonds and apricots. I wonder Samuel, have you ever had apricot kernels?"

"No, sir, I don't think I have."

"Did you know they look, and sometimes taste like almonds, and they are often mixed with almonds and served as a snack."

"I didn't know that, no."

"Did you know that almonds and apricot kernels contain high concentrations of amygdalin, a substance that can elevate levels of toxic cyanide in the bloodstream, and when ingested with other excessive doses of cyanide from other means, such as injections or by capsule, can lead to a particularly agonizing death? Did you know that, Samuel?"

"She really did die of cyanide poisoning. Is that what you're saying Captain?"

"That's what I'm saying, Samuel. Just like I said before. And it wasn't suicide. Just like you said before. You were right with your first impression. Someone very cleverly killed her, aided by her favorite snack. There were either injections or pills that caused her heart to stop at that inconvenient moment when you were copulating. What do you think of that Samuel?"

"Dear God in heaven, I can't believe it. You said that night; the night she died, that she presented symptoms of cyanide poisoning, but I never connected it all. How could I have been so stupid not to realize what was happening to her. Her skin color. Her deteriorating eyesight; her weakness; her lethargy toward the end. Yet she still had desires, till the end. God, how stupid I am. I could have protected her. How callous; how uncaring. I thought only of myself." Samuel began to cry. His head slumped into his cupped hands. Now choking on his words, he added, "She said it in the letter."

"You read the letter Samuel?" Victor asked.

"Yes, she showed it to me a few nights before. I didn't know what to believe. But I couldn't do anything about it. The suicide part I dismissed believing above all she was a survivor."

"Obviously she failed at that," Victor offered.

Samuel continued to cry.

Victor watched him closely, scrutinizing for any sign of emotional fakery. He found none. Victor decided to let him suffer a moment longer in his evident grief. In his own humiliation. Victor then knew he had the wrong man. Bluestein sat by silently, unsure of the detective's thinking, but with growing confidence that his client might be off the hook for good. After a lapse in time to allow Samuel to regain his composure, Bluestein's wish was granted when Victor said, "Okay Samuel, you're free to go."

Chapter 14

"We couldn't let that son-of-bitch Hoover get his hands on him," the Director of the Central Intelligence Agency, Richard Helms, said to the CIA's former head of science and technology, Albert (Bud) Wheelon. The two were seated in Helm's opulent office overlooking the lush, properly groomed and heavily fortified Virginia forest that surrounded the headquarters of the nation's spy apparatus.

Helms, a sleuthing maven whose clandestine resume spanned decades, was one of the few high-ranking holdovers from the Johnson to the Nixon Administration. His credentials in the undercover business were impeccable, dating back to his service in the Navy's Intelligence Branch in World War II and subsequent lofty affiliation with the Office of Special Operations, the forerunner to the CIA. At the ripe age of thirty-three he had landed the job as head of intelligence and counter-intelligence in Austria, Germany and Switzerland. His dandy dress and demeanor, plus his noted "intolerance for fools" mantra ingratiated him well with Nixon who kept him on after his election over the strong objections of many in his own Party who laid much of the blame on him for repeated intelligence failures in Viet Nam.

"Helms knows Eastern Europe and Russia, but he can't find Southeast Asia on the map," one of his
strongest critics liked to charge.

Until 1969 Bud Wheelon was Helms' top scientist. Holding a PhD in theoretical physics from MIT, Wheelon was the Agency's brain trust responsible for everything from guidance systems for long- range ballistic missiles and early space projects, to radio wave propagation and fluid flow. He became the storage house for technical data collection and analysis for U-2 over-flights of the Soviet Union, plus he was in charge of the early military and security satellite systems that were increasingly circling the globe. His job, at that time, one that didn't come close to testing his scientific prowess, was head of the 303 Committee.

"I can't believe you still had your eye on that leftist, pinko professor from Colorado," Wheelon said with a great deal of revulsion in the tone of his voice.

The Director turned from the window and his unobstructed view of the luscious grounds to stare across his antique leather desktop at his trusted friend and confidant to say, "We certainly did Bud. Riha was perfectly suited for the job. The 303 Committee's purpose precisely suited his skills. All we had to do was keep him away from Hoover, and make sure the bullshit that spewed from his mouth during his classroom lectures was all a clever cover for his true feelings about this country."

"Remember Bud, all the Committee and its field operatives needed to do was keep the airwaves open. The Soviets were spending hundreds of millions each year jamming our signals. Voice of America had been off the air for weeks. Nixon was furious when he learned about it after taking office. You know how he felt about bombarding those Commie sons-of-bitches with our message of freedom and democracy. The President insisted we allocate another twenty million dollars that year alone to support the program. Radio Free Europe was not enough. Their message was good but often lacked our strength and conviction. We needed unfiltered propaganda; damn good American propaganda. We could alter the frequencies, but the KGB was good at tracking the changes and adjusting their equipment to disrupt the broadcasts.

"We knew where their base of operations was. Near the center of Moscow, close to Red Square, and even though they were pouring piles of Rubles into jamming equipment the site was not closely guarded. The device our lab tech guys developed was ingenious. It simply plugged into an outlet in the body of the main power unit. It looked like it belonged there. Just another condenser, or conductor, or whatever. Anyway, once activated, clean and pure American truth would flow freely into the hearts and minds of our Russian brethren, all the while the KGB would still think the jamming was going on.

"Dick. I know what it looked like. Remember? We called it the virus. I know how it worked. It was my department. My invention. And yes, a ten-year-old child could plug it in and activate it. That wasn't the problem, Dick. The problem was we could never be sure about him. We were never sure Thomas Riha was the right man for the job," Wheelon reminded his old boss.

"I know we couldn't," Helms responded, "It was a gamble. Riha was so well steeped in the Russian language, its history, culture and Soviet politics that he stood apart from all the rest for that assignment. He infiltrated so easily, even into the upper echelons of Soviet society. That one time in Moscow he was seated on the third tier of the reviewing stand in Red Square for the May Day Parade, for God's sake. He didn't need any special technical skills to complete the work. We taught him how to do it. He had access and the ability to shake the tails of the KGB who used to follow him everywhere but virtually gave him free rein after growing accustomed to that goddamn pretty face of his."

"Dick, it wasn't your fault. No one could have predicted....." Wheelon started to say.

Helms interrupted his friend with, "Bullshit, Bud. I sit in that chair now, and still do until Frank Church and the rest of those miscreants in the Senate have their way with me."

Wheelon couldn't rebut Helms' last statement. The Church hearings, chaired by the senior Senator from Idaho and chairman of the Senate Intelligence Committee, which oversaw the CIA, were just two short months away. They had to prepare. Both were quiet for a while, reflecting on the events.

Wheelon spoke first, offering, "Dick, let's take a few minutes to review his case file. You snatched Riha up for a reason. You didn't just go with your gut."

"All right," Helms agreed, "I've been through it already but one more time won't hurt."

"Great. Recall, most of what we had on this character came from FBI files leaked to us right under Hoover's nose by a friendly agent in their surveillance branch in DC. Apparently they were also watching the Professor for several years."

Wheelon removed his reading glasses, cleaned them, adjusted their position on his ski-slope nose and began to read from the Top Secret file he held in his lap. "Riha was born in Bratislava, Czechoslovakia in 1929. Immigration had him entering the country in 1947 after somehow surviving the War. Nothing we had indicates he took sides either with Germany or the Soviets, yet he came to this country with a decent understanding of military protocol having learned it somewhere, from someone. In any event, he joined our Army after the outbreak in Korea and served over there in the intelligence branch. Army records have him only rising to the rank of corporal, mainly assigned to radio communications intercept and language translation. His linguistic skills apparently proved useful in assessing whether the Russians were trying to elbow the Chinese aside for influence in the conflict and the region overall.

"While in Korea, everyone connected to him said he played it pretty straight. There was no hint of Communist sympathy or collusion but more than one source found him strange and distant. Apparently he never seemed to get exited about the job, or anything for that matter. He never expressed anger toward our enemies and seemed to think the South Koreans were as bad as those in the North. His ledgers were clear and concise but lacked emotion or conviction even when the Commies were kicking our butts down the peninsula and Truman was firing McArthur for insubordination.

"So he's honorably discharged and comes back to the U.S. He enrolls at the University of California at Berkeley. There are symptoms of socialist leanings while he was a student; but hell, half or three quarters of the students and most of the faculty there are Communists themselves, or at least sympathizers. So that was no big deal. His academic record is superb. Nearly straight A's according to his transcripts. He likes girls, and that cute little smile of his, and his long, wavy black hair seemed to attract a lot of female companionship. Rumors of wild sex parties abound, but no hard evidence exists."

Bud paused and stifled a chuckle at the unintended implications of the last passage. Helms, however, broke out with a loud guffaw. "Nothing hard, huh?" Helms laughed. I missed that part." When both had caught their breaths, Wheelon continued.

"Okay. Where were we? He gets a Masters Degree in language arts in four years, not five, and enters Harvard to pursue his doctorate. That takes him a while because he's working part time at odd jobs to pay tuition and write his dissertation. Eventually he gets that done and takes his PhD. to Chicago for a teaching post at the University beginning in 1960. That school thankfully isn't quite as bad as Berkeley in terms of leftist politics but Riha does find a group of questionable characters among the faculty and student body who write and speak in unflattering terms about Cold War policy, the Arms Race, the Cuban Missile Crisis and other incidents making headlines and causing us grief.

"Some of his papers are here in the file but, again, nothing outlandish enough for us to worry about. He lives well in Chicago. Eventually, he gains a reputation as a real party boy, maybe having a harder time, this time." Wheelon smiled at his emphasis on the word. Acknowledging the joke Helms smiled and waved him on.

"Anyway, there's one woman who appears more regularly on his arm than all the others. Her name is Galya Tannenbaum. A.K.A., Gloria Forest. Striking woman. Rita Hayworth type. Long, sleek body; red hair. Fits into a low-cut cocktail dress better than a snake in its skin. Those are my words, not the FBI's."

"Poetic, Bud, poetic," Helms offered.

"Riha meets her in 1964 at a book signing, celebrating the publication of his terribly pro-Communist "Readings in Russian Civilization." Can't tell you why she went. Looking at her dossier, there's no knowledge of or even a hint of an interest in Russian history. He writes for a very limited audience of academics as do most on their way to University tenure, so it's a real mystery why she showed up that night. But she did. They had dinner but didn't spend the night together. She took a cab home. After that they were soon inseparable. She went everywhere with him. They were big on the school's social circuit and she spends many long nights at his apartment near the campus on East 58th Street. Yet there's no evidence that she ever moved in. She doesn't work, apparently, and he doesn't make a lot of money but they are still swimming in dough. Dressed to the nines, both of them. Driving around in a new Buick."

Wheelon paused from his recitation.

Helms looked up from the papers on his desk and said curiously, "That last part is new. It wasn't in the file before; at least when I read it last."

"What last part?"

"About the Buick. I thought it was an Oldsmobile," Helms said.

"Wait a minute!" Wheelon exclaimed with an unintended shrill to his tone.

"Dick, what's going on here? My records on Tannenbaum stop there. Are you telling me there's more?"

"Yes, we knew a whole lot more about her," Helms came back

rather sheepishly, but he stopped when his friend interjected with,

"Okay, now I'm gonna stop, and you're gonna talk," Wheelon said with less than subtle indignation.

Helms paused. Hesitating, he scratched his forehead, removed his glasses to clean them, adjusted his tie and moved the papers on his desk to the side. He was calm. Thinking how to put it. Wheelon waited patiently, having known his former boss long enough to realize the time had come when the Director would either reveal the depths of his knowledge or clam-up all together.

Finally Helms looked in the eye of his trusted ally and said, "Embezzlement and forgery convictions back in 1959 are what brought her to our attention. She was serving her time at the Federal facility at Marion, Illinois. She was convicted of forging names on stolen Social Security checks for a bunch of widows at a nursing home in Springfield. These old biddies had a scheme going. When one of their friends' husbands died they would con the Administration into believing he was still alive. The checks kept coming, and lovely Gloria or Galya, she used both names, kept signing the dead one's name and cashing them. She and grandma would split the money. And then, when one of the widows died, a friend of the dearly departed would pilfer the checks, now two of them, and Gloria would visit the bank teller twice.

"Her skills were remarkable. She could forge the original signature of John Hancock off the Declaration of Independence well enough to convince the best handwriting expert in the land that it was authentic. Swear to God. She was the best."

"How'd we catch her?" Wheelon asked, forgiving Helms' reticence to come clean at first. Now he was anxious for the Director to assemble the puzzle for him.

Helms paused again, stood from the chair behind his desk and began pacing the room. He spoke as he strolled around the spacious bug-proof office with his hands clasped behind his back.

"A bunko squad detective in Springfield had a grandmother at the nursing home whose bank account suddenly swelled to five-thousand dollars. The detective who happened to be her trust administrator got suspicious; cracked his grandmother, gave her a pass, and eventually found his way to the gorgeous redheaded forger. It took him three weeks of hard interrogation to gain a confession. She was tough and combative. During that time he became so impressed with her work, he alerted a local Fed who was smart enough to clue us in. The Fed, by the way, is a field officer for us in Vienna right now," Helms added, offhandedly.

"We made sure the local cop got his just reward. I think he's now a deputy chief." The Director paused once more, sipped water from his glass and continued.

"In your prior position with us you weren't normally exposed to these activities. You flew the satellites at two-hundred-fifty miles up, tuning the gadgets so we could spy on the bad guys at war games along the Caspian Sea coast or monitor Soviet warships congregating in the North Atlantic. Some of us still have less exotic duties. Some of us stay on the ground doing the grunt work like chasing our enemies down dark alleys. Well, the astounding Miss Tannenbaum, in exchange for a reduced sentence and an ongoing stipend to keep her in those cocktail dresses, became the best damn forger the United States Government could buy."

Wheelon's outward expression didn't change but inside, his mind churned with Helms' disclosure.

Helms was right, Wheelon thought to himself. I had no idea.

Wheelon had freely acknowledged to colleagues in the past that he seldom took part in the inner workings of his Agency's basic mission. His lab coat was clean when it came to "boots on the ground" covert action. Spies and counterspies, agents and double agents, undercover action crossing the legal boundaries were mostly out of his immediate domain, literally removed from his radar screen. He designed and perfected the instruments that allowed men and women to remain in cubicles behind new- fangled analog computer terminals, reading and interpreting surreptitiously obtained documents, photographs and all sorts of communiqués, which exposed the enemy's deeply held hatred for his country and their schemes to destroy it.

"I suppose forgery skills are good to have," Wheelon offered somewhat in jest as the Director made his second lap around the office.

"Sometimes just as valuable as a new lens on a high speed camera shooting pictures of missile sites from fifty-thousand feet," Helms replied.

"So that's why they were living high on the hog," Wheelon said. "We were supporting them."

"No comment," Helms said, avoiding a response to the assertion.

"Again it was a friendly former FBI agent who alerted us to her talent. She could copy handwriting with incredible accuracy and speed.

It's like her mind saw it and her hand reproduced it precisely, stroke for stroke, swirl for swirl for each letter, even to the point where her imprint depth on the paper measured the same as the authors'; down to the micro-inch. She could spot forgeries of others just as well and make them her own."

"Okay, that's great, but how did we use her?" Wheelon asked.

Helms stopped his pacing on his fourth lap and returned to the chair behind his desk.

"Passports for one. We didn't have one with her handiwork carried by any of our agents turned back or even closely inspected by border guards stretching from East Berlin, to Peking, and points in between. She was fantastic with bank deposit or withdrawal slips especially when we wanted to freeze or temporarily sidetrack funds freely moving between parties with unfriendly dispositions toward us. And she was great at helping transmit disinformation to ornery governments who only respond to handwritten notes inserted in diplomatic pouches from trusted allies.

"Plus, like I said, she was extraordinary at identifying forgeries and counterfeiting. Hardly anything got by her.

"Her original sentence was for ten years. We had to keep her there for three years just to make it look good. But she went to work for us right away, while still in custody. It didn't take much persuasion, I might add. Our deal was to spring her in thirty-six months and set her up with all the comforts. When we let her out, she chose to stay in Illinois and work out of Chicago," Helms continued.

"And I suppose her meeting Thomas Riha was no accident?" Wheelon probed.

"They made a fine couple," Helms observed. "She called him Tom Cat. He called her the Colonel."

"Big promotion, I would say," Wheelon chuckled, "thought he only made it to corporal."

Helms grinned. Wheelon pursed his lips and shook his head with amusement.

"Sounds like she deserved the rank," Wheelon managed in addition.

"Riha had been in our sights since he went to Moscow in 1958 and spent a year there roaming the streets and absorbing the ambiance of the Kremlin. He needed further Russian study like I need another snot-nosed Senate staffer sniffing in my underwear drawer."

"Go on, Dick."

"All right. During that one year Russian sabbatical, without prompting, or for that matter interference from us, Riha quickly found himself mingling with all the right people in all the right places. We suspected he was picking up more intelligence then that of ten of our field agents put together. His appeal to the Soviet elite was under the guise of soliciting research material for a series of ultra-flattering Russian history books mostly containing indictments against the succession of ruling monarchies. We assumed he was well received by Soviet civilian and military high-brow society with this approach, particularly coming from a well educated American; a Czech immigrant, U.S. Army veteran, respected professor, major university; all of that nonsense."

Helms paused and filled his glass from the silver water pitcher on the corner of his desk. He offered Wheelon some, but he declined. Helms drank and continued.

"So, as you know he comes home after a year and declares himself a mouthpiece for Soviet success and world domination. He writes reams of pure crap about every subject from Russian advancements in agriculture to their marvelous achievements in outer space, but he doesn't publish anything until 1968 with the release of that shitty paperback you mentioned earlier. His classroom lectures become vitriolic indictments against the U.S., and uninhibited praise of the Kremlin. He stirs the pot at every opportunity, gaining a real following among radical leftists and a gaggle of naïve do-gooders who think imperial America should be bridled by a ring of Soviet SS long-range missiles along our borders.

"Finally, after one particularly outrageous outburst the administration at the University in Chicago gets fed up and fires him.

"Am I right so far," Helms asked with a mischievous grin.

"Yes, sir, almost word-for-word in my report, right here."

"Okay Bud. Sure we planted her. We wanted her to cuddle up to him; encourage him to bust at the seams with his own bullshit. Make the Russians think he's truly one of them; a convert, unafraid to spread hateful Soviet doctrine right here in the heartland. All she had to do was screw him occasionally and look pretty at the cocktail parties and off he'd go on another tirade. She was fantastic at it for a while, but then the dumb bastard had to fall in love.

"Who fell in love?"

"He did. He wanted to marry her!" Helms nearly shouted. "She wanted no part of it. We wanted no part of it. He persisted. She resisted, but then she had an idea. It wasn't ours; it was hers. She'd find him a wife, or better yet, a waif to put him to the test. She convinced him that another woman was better suited right then to augment his career. Someone who was smart, an adequate companion, yet modest and reserved. But there was a catch. Galya had to stay in the picture until he was ready, or we were ready to snatch him up, as you say."

"Frankly Dick, this is really out of my league, but I do find it quite fascinating," Wheelon offered.

"You have to remember something here, Bud. This guy was captivated by this woman. Enchanted was not the word. Beguiled is better. He would do anything for her. She could cut off his balls and he would thank her. Obsession was nowhere near an adequate description for it. So it wasn't too tough for her to convince him to take a wife to help promote his cause as long as she remained available to him and pushed the right buttons for us."

"Perverse, I would say."

"Yes Bud, yes it was perverse yet it worked. She found him a perfect match. Fairly good looking. Smart, and be damned if she wasn't a second generation Czech. Could even speak a little of the language. Incredible. Galya found a needle in a haystack Czech for his lover. A match made in heaven. So, it didn't take her long, and soon they were a loving trio."

"In all ways? You know Dick, I wasn't born yesterday."

"Not that we know of. The two rival ladies soon developed a vile animosity toward one another, so it didn't appear that the three of them enjoyed a carnal relationship at any time. However, Dr. Riha certainly took advantage of both his wife and the girlfriend. Even after the marriage he remained in close contact with our little forger.

"Great; how convenient for him."

"About this time he gets the boot in Chicago, quickly finds another job in Colorado, at the University there in Boulder. He marries our stand-in, mail-order bride, shall we say. They move. He's lonely. Galya waits patiently in Chicago for our next move. Riha is welcomed to Colorado with open arms by an even more radical faculty and student body. He steps up his speechifying; gains an even bigger following, even gets some national press, and then we send Galya back in. She promptly destroys the marriage, sends the wife packing back to Chicago, and the blissful couple is destined to live happily ever after; at least in his mind. He passes the test with flying colors."

"But Dick, why torture that poor woman, whoever she was? Why put her through all that and then cast her aside? Damn heartless, if you ask me."

"Bud, we were sorry about that. She's apparently a fine woman and found a new life. Yet it was the only way to see if Galya really had him, and whether she could actually stage-manage his mind and his actions however fundamental they might be. If he would do anything for her, he'd do anything for us, whether he liked it or not. He was the perfect candidate for this mission. Christ Bud, we watched him for years. We protected him from zealot right-wingers who wanted to taste his blood; cops who yearned for five minutes alone with him in a holding cell, and nearly every true patriot who vomited at his antics and would have paid dearly to see him hang in the town square."

"So when did you give the order?"

"To grab him, you mean?"

"Yes, to snatch him up." "About ten minutes after Hoover gave his order."

Chapter 15

Catherine Benson never imagined she would ever become a field operative for the Central Intelligence Agency. At one time that was the farthest thing from her mind. Originally, she wanted to be a fashion designer. To work in New York for a while and then design costumes for motion picture actors in Hollywood. But here on this gorgeous, bright, sunny, fall afternoon in Boulder, Colorado, instead of pinning chiffon gowns on newly minted starlets, she was shadowing a seedy, blow-hard, left wing college professor whom her bosses back in Virginia believe will make a good spy for America in its ongoing cat-and-mouse game with the Soviet Union.

Talk about taking a different path, she thought as she strived to keep pace with this mop-haired Communist bastard while decked out in her full, faux hippy regalia, floppy sandals, flowing skirt and tie-dyed blouse absent a bra to accentuate the image and affect.

Never would have dressed even my worst enemy in this outfit.

To make matters worse, her 9-millimeter strapped to under her arm was beginning to chafe at her skin. Her breasts hurt from all the jiggling, and the highly annoying stringy blond wig was slipping down over her forehead, loosened by the sweat beads appearing at her temples.

Catherine's fate in becoming a favored domestically assigned spy, one of the few females, or for that matter, males at the time, had been sealed during her final year of graduate school at the University of North Carolina. Her U of NC counselor, who happened to be the CIA's ex-station chief assigned to the U.S. embassy in Warsaw, had marveled at her academic achievements, paying particular attention to her Master Degrees with honors in both accounting and economics.

Catherine took dual degrees in those subjects because her ultimate goal was to have her own design studio, and to assure success, she had to understand accounting principles and international economics as thoroughly as she could sculpt sleek, flowing lines from bolts of silk and lace. Her standout academic achievements, coupled with unrelenting pressure from her counselor, clearly contributed to her decision to switch careers. He was persuasive but it still took him six months to bring her to her senses and send her off for training at a base in southern New Mexico.

The CIA was not supposed to deploy field agents within America's borders. Catherine knew that. But it didn't matter to her or her superiors. Intelligence activities, or more accurately, spying inside the U.S., was allegedly the exclusive purview of the FBI. The CIA, by Congressional edict, was the nation's international clandestine force, charged with protecting the homeland borders from foreign intrusion by those intending Americans harm. However, everyone in the Agency that Catherine knew ignored that bureaucratic line of demarcation when the mission called for it and the politicians would look the other way.

Operating with impunity and, if necessary, immunity she could maneuver in that underworld as easily as she could thread a sewing machine needle or hit a moving handgun target at fifty yards. So, Catherine Benson, former fashion maven, now sporting blistered toes and a raw underarm, was a sanctioned rogue spy known only to a few. If confronted for her activities, imprudent as they might become, she was to remain quiet, speaking to no one, particularly local law enforcement. She was to make one phone call which, in a matter of minutes, would result in her release and her return in from the cold.

With the sun in her eyes and the wind of her nation at her back Catherine remained in hot pursuit, keeping stride-for-stride yet some thirty yards behind Thomas Riha, her renegade prey, as he hurriedly wound his way through campus heading west.

Thomas soon reached the crosswalk at Folsom Street and stopped. The traffic was heavy at the moment so he couldn't proceed across. "Thank God," Catherine murmured under her breath, quickly stepping behind a tree to rest against it and remove her right sandal to gingerly massage her foot. She had a good forty-five second respite before Riha was on the move again. Catherine grunted and pushed off from behind the tree at the sight of his quick step, noticing for the first time that he favored his left foot. She made a mental note to determine the cause and hustled to re-form her trailing march.

This probably wouldn't be the night Thomas Riha would be escorted to a secure location to begin his re-education; that would likely occur tomorrow or the next evening, or the next. Catherine was not sure. Her job was to monitor his movements, understand his routines, and determine where and exactly when to grab him. She liked that part of her assignment. Especially given the thought that this scoundrel, this demented Soviet apologist; this evil enemy of her country, would finally be given a solid slap with America's backhand.

Riha kept hiking west, crossing Folsom now laboring at his pace toward 13th Street. Catherine snickered, realizing his direction was toward The Hill. Catherine knew The Hill was not really a hill, but a maze of intersecting streets, including College Avenue, that form an ill-defined neighborhood filled with clusters of bars, dead-beat nightclubs and falsely advertised gourmet restaurants. It stretches for several blocks onto which thousands of students flock each night to quench their under-aged thirsts and look for love.

Riha soon reached his destination. The Sink. The place to be if you're a college senior with a perpetual hard-on, seeking to score with an unsuspecting freshman three months out of high school. But for Riha. He was definitely out of place. Catherine watched him squeeze through the throng of Coors long-neck-bottle drinkers and enter. She stood two doors down in front of the Buff Room, named for the school's beloved bison mascot. Through the window Catherine could see the professor meandering through the crowd until he found a seat at the bar. She moved toward the milling mass of hard bodies who still blocked the entrance, but she was given a clear path to the inside accompanied by a few annoying "hey babies and nice tits." If they only knew that with one blazing jab she could relocate a larynx through the far side of a spine, but instead, she only smiled and gave a little shake, prompting even more whistles and cheers. She noticed that Riha was looking in her direction when hearing the commotion. Just as she had hoped. She wandered inside just long enough so it wouldn't look obvious before taking the bar stool next to where Thomas sat.

Only a few moments passed before Riha struck up a conversation. Just as she had hoped. In his opening overture he feigned concern over her rude treatment at the door, apologizing for the behavior of the "riff-raff", and then quickly offered to buy her a drink.

Which she gladly accepted.

Their conversation ensued with one-sided vigor, but was interrupted several times by shattering glass, stumbling sophomores and a girl-fight over a misplaced tube of lipstick. In spite of it all Catherine and Thomas quickly became, as he put it, dear friends, while she silently plotted the where and when of his capture.

What Catherine also noticed during their two-hour beer and bar-nut feast were the two less- than-qualified utility linesmen who sat three stools away sipping iced tea and thoroughly pissing off the bartender who figured his tip would be less than fifty cents.

Chapter 16

Gordon Peterson and Rico Hernandez were not iced tea drinkers. Gordon liked scotch and Rico liked tequila and they were unhappy with their forced abstinence while conducting on-duty surveillance of another one of the FBI Director's targeted Commie sympathizers.

"If this puny, stick-up-his-ass, big mouth pinko could ever really be a threat to the security of the United States of America, I'll kiss your balls in the middle of Pennsylvania Avenue on Inaugural Day," Rico whispered to Gordon as he rose from his bar stool for another trip to the men's room.

Rico was seeking relief from the enormous liquid intake he'd consumed over the past two hours. At Rico's astute observation, Gordon shook his head in affirmative disgust and turned again to cautiously observe the professor and his oddly attractive, stringy, blonde-haired hippy companion. But there was something about her that Gordon couldn't quite reconcile. She, too, seemed misplaced among the sweaty, belching, screaming throng of juveniles who Gordon suspected at any moment would break out in riot, forcing him to produce his weapon and fire warning shots into the ceiling to regain order.

She doesn't quite fit in that costume.

And certainly not with him. It's not her style. She doesn't belong in here at all.

I'm not one who goes in for that body language crap, but she's uncomfortable here, hanging with this guy for so long. It's a put-on. She ain't what she's displayin'.

Gordon's speculative but fairly well trained examination of the scene was interrupted by Rico's return. He re-took his seat with his back to the couple, not realizing they were finally getting up to leave. Gordon lifted his chin slightly and shifted his eyes in their direction. That was Rico's cue to carefully turn to observe their departure for himself. He was damn glad he had peed now that they were probably on the move.

Catherine Benson had had Gordon and Rico in her sights the moment she entered the uproarious beer joint. To her, they were hiding in plain sight. They might as well have displayed their FBI badges on their front shirt pockets. It's that obvious. What she didn't know for sure was their motive, but she had a good idea.

Dr. Riha's freedom would be coming to an end earlier than she once thought.

Chapter 17

"Yes, Superintendent, you heard me correctly. Not only do I want Miss Tannenbaum's complete file, I want a complete roster and the personnel files of all employees who had either direct or indirect contact with her from the moment she entered the institution. And yes, that means their work hours, their employment records, their home addresses and their telephone numbers.

"No Superintendent; that will not be an impossible task for you. It will either be accomplished resulting from this friendly request or you will receive a subpoena delivered by an on-duty sheriff's deputy this afternoon. And for good measure you might expect to greet a newspaper reporter or two seeking an explanation for the subpoena. Which will it be, Superintendent?

A pause.

"Very well, I will send a deputy to your office at 2 pm to pick up the files. I appreciate your cooperation. No Superintendent; no reporters." He hung up the telephone shaking his head in disgust.

"The man's a genuine asshole," Victor said aloud to no one but himself.

Captain Victor Bravo was in no mood for stonewalling or tolerating even the slightest resistance to his request for material to aid in his investigation. Especially from the obstinate head of his city's esteemed mental health institution. He knew his demand for Asylum personnel records would result in a mountain-high stack of paper from which he would examine every possible clue, which might link one, or more of them to what has become, in his view, a vicious, contemptible, perhaps strung-out over time, homicide. To cull the list, he faced countless hours of interviews with an eternal succession of persons of interest. But no matter. In the end someone in that horde had to have known about, or done something themselves, to help end the short tortured life of the lovely redhead.

Victor absently stared at the plastic envelope containing three tiny shards of broken glass. The encasement was affixed with staples to the manila file folder lying open in the middle of his desk. The lab report confirming that the splinters had indeed once formed a vial to which normally a needle had been attached, was partially hidden by the packet. Victor didn't need to read the report again. Three times were enough, and each time his frustration grew when reading the section that described inconclusive chemical tests as to what substance had been inside the shattered syringe. But was that gap in the evidence chain all that important?

There was conclusive, beyond a doubt, substantiation that Galya had died of a sustained intake of cyanide aided by a lethal diet of snacks containing amygdalin. So, the lack of scientific proof of the vial's contents may not be all that detrimental to his case. And then again, it could be a problem if some shyster defense lawyer like Bluestein could exploit the evidentiary breach. But Victor was getting ahead of himself. He had a long way to go. All of the other pieces of the Tannenbaum puzzle had been assembled save only one...a suspect.

Victor was hungry. He craved a bowl of spaghetti and meatballs. He closed the file, retrieved his coat from the hook on his door and exited his office for the short walk to Angelina's Fine Italian Restaurant. He knew Johnny was working the luncheon crowd. Seeing his friend always brought Victor out of the doldrums, which were generally prompted by a baffling case or an argument with Rosanna.

A Silly spat; pure nonsense, Victor thought. This one was over the choice of purchasing either a gas or an electric stove. Victor wanted gas. Rosanna preferred cooking with electric. In the end electric had won out and both wondered why they bothered debating the point in the first place. Get over that and go on to the next problem, like this case, which he sensed was bound to take a heavy toll.

As Victor ambled across the street toward the savory Italian specialty that awaited him he reflected on the two eighteen-hour workdays, which had preceded his current hankering. During that time Victor's list of targeted Asylum personnel with direct or indirect contact with Galya Tannenbaum had been narrowed to thirteen. Their titles ranged from the line cook in the cafeteria, to the head nurse on the woman's ward. Nurse's aids, janitors, security guards, and Galya's own therapist also made Victor's list. He had been shocked to read the profiles on a few of those he now favored. A PhD from Harvard; two high school drop outs; the former now polishing floors on the night shift while the latter two were somehow counseling bipolar teenagers. Some, including the man carrying his doctorate degree, had been patients who had found gainful employment following their confinement and perceived recoveries. Victor was dismayed that anyone, irrespective of their past condition, could spend one more second in that dismal, dysfunctional compound once given the choice to leave.

An hour later Victor emerged from Angelina's, renewed, refreshed, with belly full and clear determination at hand. His interrogations would begin in thirty minutes and he was ready. His drive to the compound would take less than fifteen minutes. His unlucky list of thirteen awaited him outside the superintendent's conference room.

He began with the line cook. His questioning spanned the obvious to the ambiguous. Was she tainting the deceased's food by spiking portions with chemical compounds that make up amygdalin? Did she even know what amygdalin is, or what cyanide is? Did anyone ask her to prepare any special meals? Did she ever see anyone tampering with the meal trays? Who delivered the trays? And then the nurses' aides. Who had access to medical supplies? To syringes in particular? Who knew how to use them? Who was trained to give injections? Who had knowledge of chemistry? Who could gain entry into a locked cell at night? Janitors? Orderlies? Who ate a lot of almonds? Who bought a lot of almonds? Who befriended her overtly, beyond a professional relationship; besides, of course, Samuel Richards? For that matter what did they think of Samuel? Did he act peculiar? Particularly around Miss Tannenbaum? Did others find him attractive? Did he make passes at anyone else? Any strangers try to visit her, and most importantly perhaps, and this one, coming two exhausting days later, was saved for last. What was her psychiatric diagnosis? Was she paranoid? Was there any basis for her feeling threatened or endangered? Did she show the suicide letter to anyone else? Was she justified in thinking someone was out to kill her? What was discussed in her counseling sessions?

"Yes, captain, she did suffer from hysterical paranoia. She had delusions of naked vulnerability; a feeling of hostility constantly aimed at her. She sought comfort, shelter, security, protection; claiming her past acts had put her in danger. Fear of her imminent death haunted her. She could trust no one, confide in no one," explained Dr. Sylvia Gladstone, Galya's shrink who Victor quickly considered bad at her job at best; a quack at worst.

"Except, of course, Samuel Richards; correct Dr. Gladstone?" Victor queried.

"Samuel Richards. The same Samuel Richards who was on our staff? I'm unaware of his association with Miss Tannenbaum. He was not treating her. I was her doctor," she replied with a hint of indignation, but showing signs of concern.

"You mean as her therapist; the one treating her for all those serious conditions. The one person assigned to aid in her recovery and you knew nothing of her lover? The individual who offered her much more than a shoulder to cry on. Why do you think he resigned so quickly? You realize I arrested him; held him as a suspect for nearly a week? And you knew nothing?"

"I don't read the newspapers, Captain. I am devoted to my work. We do not practice our professions in a public forum. We do not thrive on rumors. Medical students come and go. He was of no concern to me," Dr. Gladstone responded flatly.

"I believe Miss Tannenbaum took her own life. She was psychotic. Impossible to counsel. At one time, I believe, she was highly intelligent. She had exceptional skills. Her handwriting, for instance, was exquisite. Calligraphy was her forte. It was the one thing she was most proud of," she added without prompting.

"I would say. She was committed for forgery. Did you know that?" Victor responded.

"I believe I read that excerpt from her file."

"So, you think she killed herself, somehow smuggling high doses of cyanide into the hospital, injecting or ingesting them over a period of months, slowly causing her own blindness, making her weaker and sicker by the day. And while all of this is going on, she is banging the brains out of a horny medical student, whom she believes can protect her, maybe help her escape from this shit hole and save her life? You never got that far doctor? With her so-called therapy?" Victor could hide his anger no longer.

"Please don't be crude or attempt to ridicule me Captain. You have my professional opinion on this case. The death was self-inflicted. You have the suicide note. I will always have much more insight into the victim's mental state than you. I am the one who is qualified to judge the outcome of a patient's treatment. Not you! Sometimes it is successful. Sometimes not. In this unfortunate circumstance, the patient was determined to end her life in the way she found most fitting. If you have no other questions of me, Captain, I have patients to see."

"Oh, just a few doctor," Victor said, motioning for the psychiatrist to re-take her seat.

"Earlier in passing, doctor, you mentioned that Miss Tannenbaum's past acts made her feel threatened. Which past acts was she talking about?"

"I'm afraid I can't answer that question captain. Patient confidentiality, you know."

"Doctor, lest I remind you, your patient is dead, perhaps, due in part, to your incompetence. You have a choice here. You can either answer my questions, truthfully and completely, or I just might find some way to charge you as an accessory, before or after the fact. I'll have to think about which one is easier. If that doesn't stick I will personally see to it that you're brought up before the Medical Society's review board and the state licensing authority for malpractice.

Dr. Gladstone's arrogant expression faded instantaneously. Her jaw dropped. She couldn't help it. Her eyes widened. She stiffened in her chair.

My bluff may be working.

It took Dr. Gladstone all of forty-five minutes to re-tell Galya's tale. She began with Galya's time in prison for crimes she claimed she never committed. She told of her passion for beautiful handwriting.

"For calligraphy. She was a scribe in the truest sense. A master of the curves and the swirls of the written form. She made letters and words jump off the page. And sing. Becoming art. A painting, not a scribble. A fluid, confident hand motion, she would say, is like floating on a quiet lake in late summer." As she spoke Dr. Gladstone fell into a monotone chant of sorts as if reciting the events relieved her of a heavy emotional burden.

Her recitation continued but nearly at an inaudible volume. Victor moved his chair closer to catch every word. He did not interrupt until she posed a question.

"You are aware Captain she was imprisoned before."

"Yes, I am aware of that," Victor responded.

"Well, Galya's craft became her way out. Her means of escape. To freedom. Her chance came unexpectedly. From a stranger. She called him her guardian, a man who presented a plan with conditions for an early release. She accepted without hesitation. Her sentence was cut short, but it still lasted three years. A long time, but it passed quickly for her. Her work kept her busy. She was moved to a better place, while still in jail, but to a better place, nonetheless, for her to meet her obligations. She was better fed; had better clothes. They liked her work. Copying the signatures was her favorite part. Copying so no one could tell of even the slightest variation. Also falsifying letters. Making up things that were untrue to cause trouble. That was the most challenging of her tasks, and she was good at it; the best, her guardian would tell her."

"I need a glass of water," Dr. Gladstone suddenly declared in a stronger voice. Her pronouncement startled Victor. His riveted concentration on the psychiatrist's monologue had unexpectedly been broken. He rose to fetch the drink for her but soon realized he had no idea where to find one. By then Dr. Gladstone was on her way to the bathroom adjoining the superintendent's office. She returned quickly with a full glass but offered him nothing. She sat and sipped, again commencing to deliver her words in subdued resonance.

"Then at last, she was free. They gave her money; lots of it. She had an apartment. They paid the rent. She was liberated and happy but she knew they were always lurking around. She kept working; doing her best for them; copying the works of others, making everything perfect so they could use it to cause their enemies trouble.

"And then came her next assignment. Different this time. She was to meet and befriend a man. Not any man, but a man who the stranger said would cause more trouble for the stranger's enemies.

She paused to drink again. Victor silently urged her on. He was enthralled .

Finally, she continued. "He turned out to be a fine looking man. She was pleased about that. She had to avoid other men; all except this one, or the stranger would quit paying her. She was told she didn't have to become his lover; but he implied his friends preferred she did. She first met the man after listening to a speech he made and signing a book he had written for some people in his audience. At first she didn't particularly understand his speech or the importance of his book, but that didn't matter much. As instructed, she bought a copy of the book and waited in the back of the line for the others to have theirs signed. She wanted to talk with him alone. As instructed. The stranger said it was best that way. Right off, she knew he was interested in her. She said she looked particularly attractive that evening and he took notice. He immediately began flirting with her and asked her to dinner. She accepted, but declined to accompany him to his apartment after they ate. Early on, she decided to sleep with the man in an effort to be more productive for the stranger, and possibly earn more money. To make the man want it that much more, she decided to wait a while before giving in."

Victor's mouth and throat were suddenly parched. He held up his hand for the doctor to halt and quickly moved to help himself to water from the adjacent bathroom faucet. He repulsively noticed the only glass available was smudged with a pale pink half-moon of lipstick. A special guest of the superintendent, he mused. His sudden thirst overcame his revulsion at the smear forcing him to drink from the other side. He cringed and swallowed. The water was warm and an awful chemical taste lingered on his tongue.

She didn't wait for Victor to re-take his seat before beginning again.

"As the weeks went by she learned much more about the fine looking man. He was a professor at the University of Chicago. He taught Russian history, and was somewhat famous in his field. She didn't care much for the subject; his job, or what he had to say about it, but over time she established a fairly well grounded understanding. Since he was an expert on the country and its satellites, she concluded their manufactured relationship might have something to do with all the papers she was working on for the stranger. She was never absolutely sure of this, but many of those papers were written in Russian."

"The man's name was Thomas Riha."

Startled once again, Victor interrupted her with, "Wait a minute. Stop. You said Thomas Riha. Thomas Riha was her lover?"

"That's precisely what I said, detective. Are you familiar with him?"

Victor hesitated.

"Thought I recognized the name from somewhere," Victor finally replied, attempting to shield his initial reaction. "Somewhat unusual name. Probably not; no, don't think I am familiar with him," Victor lied.

"Sorry. Go on."

Victor's mind raced back to a stack of mail on his desk at the station among which he had noticed the latest FBI's missing person's bulletin seeking the whereabouts of one Dr. Thomas Riha, prominent University of Colorado history professor. Victor had only glanced at the sheet when he arrived for work that morning. Despite routinely screening dozens of these Bureau dispatches each week, the image of the man's broad grin, weathered face and wind-swept coal-black hair had struck his consciousness, and now came back to him into sharp focus.

Before he could reorient his thoughts the good doctor was already pressing on.

"He had a doctorate degree in Russian history. At times he would speak to her in Russian. This annoyed her a great deal especially when he spoke to her that way when they were making love. She didn't understand a word he would say, and he was loud and spewed spittle, of all things, when he shouted in that dialect during the climatic moment of sex."

At that Victor had a hard time suppressing a chuckle at the imagined sight and sound.

Undaunted, Dr. Gladstone rushed ahead.

"Evidently they became quite a notable couple. She accompanied him to various events, usually at the University or at some library or bookstore where he was trying to sell more of his books. He made many speeches. Sometimes people cheered at what he said. Other times they booed him. When they booed, he got upset and would later label his critics as imbeciles, or worse. That was one of his favorite words. Loosely translated in Russian it means abnormal. Despite his abnormalities, she tolerated being with him; in fact, grew to appreciate her position when he began buying her clothes and some fairly expensive jewelry. Wherever they went she always looked her best. Even with his offensive behavior, she gradually grew fond of Thomas and began to call him "Tom Cat." That was her favorite name for him. He taught her how to say it in Russian....Volume Llat.

"Her guardian told her to make a big splash with Riha. Whenever possible go everywhere with him, he instructed. To help make him more famous. After he told her that, the stranger wanted to know everything that was going on between them. Everything Thomas Riha said; everything about the people they met; the people he worked with, even his students if they were around him more than usual. She told this mystery man everything. The money kept coming in. She was happy.

"After a while Thomas became serious about her. In fact, he told her he wanted to marry her. He became obsessed with the idea. He talked about it all the time. He wanted children by her. To live happily ever after, he said. She wanted no part in it. She had no intention of marrying him. The stranger agreed, but told her to keep him thinking that she might.

"So, she came up with an idea. At first her guardian didn't like it. But over time she convinced him it was the best thing to do. She would find Thomas a wife; someone other than she. It had to be a person who was easily influenced, even controllable. Someone who was lonely and vulnerable who would be attracted to Thomas for what he was and what he stood for. She would convince Thomas that he needed a different woman to help boost his career, but it had to be someone who was intelligent enough to succeed in the social and academic circles in which he was often the center. She took the idea to Thomas. He was hurt and angry in the beginning, but when she carefully reasoned with him that another women who both of them could control would better serve his purpose, he relented. A big part of their agreement was that she would remain loyal to him, celibate except with him. She would continue to serve his needs in every way. Exclusively. She would work closely with him and remain at his side forever."

Victor shook his head in disbelief. This was nothing more than a twisted fairy tale, not suited for the young or the morally well grounded. She ignored his groan and went on.

"Galya found that person after a short but intense search. When she met her, Galya knew quickly that she was the right person for the role. Her name was Helen. She was pretty but plain. She could never match Galya's beauty. That made it easier to make her choice. And she was of Czech decent which made her even more suitable since Thomas was born in Czechoslovakia and could speak the language. A perfect match. It didn't take long before Galya got them together. The three of them became inseparable. The arrangement was truly bizarre even in this modern age. At first Helen accepted the situation, strange as it seemed, but soon grew frustrated and even bitter, once threatening to end the relationship. When that would happen Galya would fade away for a time to allow Thomas to lure her back. Once he did, Galya would reappear and the cycle would begin again.

"In the middle of this convoluted romance Thomas went overboard. His writing and his words became spuriously radical. He started offending more people than he pleased. He soon became isolated, even shunned by his superiors and peers. He became insufferable both at home and at work, even at times with Galya. And when he refused to tone down his offensive remarks, the University fired him. He was devastated. Galya was too. She saw her plan unraveling. On the other hand, Helen surprisingly stood up for him, promising Thomas her unending support, even love. Thomas was touched by her sincerity. Galya was concerned. The stranger told her to make amends. Don't lose him, he advised. She heeded the warning. All it took was one long night in bed and she had him back.

"Like Tom Cats do, Thomas abruptly landed on his feet. He was out of work for only a short time. A teaching post in Colorado came his way through an old friend. He had no choice but to leave Chicago to take the position. Galya said she wouldn't go with him, but her refusal was half-hearted. Helen said she would go, gladly, but only if he would marry her. Thomas was unsure about the proposal and sought Galya's advice. She said it was okay, but made him promise to remain loyal in his heart only to her. So Thomas and Helen married and left for Colorado, leaving Galya behind.

"But not for long."

"You mean to tell me he married her knowing full well that Galya would be following them here. Why did he bother?" Victor asked, truly baffled.

"Detective, I'm a psychiatrist. I have treated many patients in relationships with conditions much more peculiar than these. I admit this one was uncanny in many respects but I assure you these individuals are not without peer. My hypothesis, hearing from only one member of this strange trio, that being Galya, is that Helen believed she could win him over with gentleness, kindness, sympathy and, yes, love, but she was sadly mistaken. The intensity of feeling, or raw passion Thomas had for Galya was irrepressible. He would do anything for her, perhaps even murder," Dr. Gladstone said.

"Doctor, you're not going down that path with this, are you? At the beginning you said you believed she committed suicide. Are you suggesting otherwise? Did his fixation on her take a wrong turn?" Victor probed.

Her eyes rose from the notes in her lap from which she had been referring and froze unblinking on Victor's intense expression.

"No, detective, I am not altering my view in this case. Thomas Riha had nothing to do with her death, because, I believe, as did Galya, that he was already dead when she died."

"Is that a fact? So how did Thomas Riha die, may I ask?" Victor's smirk was apparent.

"He was murdered."

"Okay, now you're telling me Galya Tannenbaum committed suicide after her lover was murdered. A lover she cared little about?"

"Yes I am detective. That's what I'm telling you."

"I see. Now, since you have all the answers, tell me who killed Thomas Riha."

"The United States government," she responded adamantly.

"Ha! Doctor, you are truly amazing, and amusing" Victor exclaimed. "I suppose some might find your humor entertaining, but doctor, I am quite tired of your bullshit. Get off it or I swear the licensing board will...."

Cutting him off, she calmly said, "Detective, if you would please let me finish describing the events which led up to Miss Tannenbaum's confinement perhaps you will see how I..."

Victor cut her off by saying, "Nothing you offer doctor will ever convince me that our government would murder one of its own citizens, and secondly, your conclusion regarding the cause of Miss Tannenbaum's death, in my view, is confirming my suspicions of malpractice. But as you wish, doctor, please proceed."

Seemingly unfazed by Victor's charge Dr. Gladstone stared down at her notes, shuffled a few pages and began again.

"Galya's plan to reunite in Colorado took form. They spoke frequently by telephone. Phone sex was a regular occurrence. After these torrid sessions they would discuss the right time for Galya to join them. And, above all, the stranger liked the arrangement, Galya maintained."

"What, the phone sex?" Victor broke in with dripping sarcasm. "He got off on hearing about their long distance mutual masturbation?"

"Detective, I have no idea, but Galya thought it was important to present that fact in her sessions with me, so I presume the stranger encouraged the activity to keep them close and intimate."

"Lovely, just lovely. Intimate with their own digits and palms. This can't get any weirder. Sorry doctor, I just can't help myself."

Again ignoring Victor's interruption she continued.

"Once during more friendly times, Helen confessed to Galya that she didn't believe in the things Thomas preached. She didn't believe America was evil and Russia was utopia. She said she was often ashamed at how Thomas always criticized the United States and democracy, while praising how the Russians lived and supposedly thrived under their Communist form of government. She said she was trying to overcome her concerns about Thomas' beliefs because she loved him. But her doubts persisted. Confiding in Galya proved to be a terrible blunder.

"Galya used Helen's admission to convince the stranger that Helen had become a liability sooner than expected. Pressing her point she maintained that Helen could indeed jeopardize the entire plan. She argued that they could not risk having someone dampen Thomas' meteoric rise in notoriety. What was needed to effectively carry out the plan was a strong, like-minded supporter; not someone, especially his wife, who didn't share his convictions. In Chicago Thomas needed a demure, non-assuming wallflower on his arm who kept her mouth shut, but in Colorado it was different. The more flamboyant the better. In Colorado, Thomas found a new, more sympathetic audience eager to soak up his vitriol, and Galya was much better equipped to help polish his radical public image.

"However, it must be understood that Galya's beliefs were not rooted in his politics or anyone's politics for that matter. She cared less who said what to whom about most topics. She believed only in herself, and selfishly cared solely about making more money. Lots of it.

"The stranger accepted Galya's premise and endorsed her early move, but it came with a warning. He told her things would be different in Colorado and to accept the idea that Thomas would soon be gone for long periods of time. And when she arrived she was to aid Thomas in preparing for his assignment. She didn't question her new role. She was fine with it as long as the money was there.

"As expected Helen was very unhappy when Galya unexpectedly appeared on the scene. Thomas apparently tried to convince his wife that he could not succeed without her. He needed Galya, he supposedly asserted, as his assistant, so he told Helen he had hired her to work with him at the University. All part of a well-rehearsed plan. If he were ever to meet his full potential, he claimed, Galya had to be with him, advising and coaxing him to greatness.

"With Galya's arrival Helen's relationship with Thomas deteriorated rapidly. Their arguments intensified and became more frequent. After a while, as things got worse, Helen forbid Galya from visiting them, but Thomas insisted on her presence at every opportunity. Finally, one night the situation exploded with shouting and crying and items hurled about their house. Helen accosted Galya during the melee requiring Thomas to intervene. The next day Helen was gone, later filing for divorce and seeking a handsome property settlement. Apparently she returned to Chicago. Neither Thomas nor Galya much cared where she went. Neither did Galya's handler. The couple was finally openly reunited having learned from their mistake, and that nothing or no one would ever come between them again. At least that was Thomas' fervent belief.

"The stranger also agreed that it was a better arrangement but he continued to caution Galya that Thomas would soon be traveling for extended periods of time. Galya was ambivalent. Truthfully, she admitted that she looked forward to the times when he would be away.

"Their lives together settled into a docile routine. They made frequent appearances on the local social circuit and were often included as guests at rarified cocktail and dinner parties reserved for only a few in the affluent inner circle at the University. Thomas was popular in these settings, frequently sparking lively debate with controversial remarks, "better suited for a vodka-slinging drink fest in the Kremlin."

As if to emphasize the point, Dr. Gladstone looked up from her notes and said, "Galya actually used those words. I wrote them down and later asked if that was her view of Thomas' behavior. I remember she shrugged and said, no; she'd overheard some belligerent tweed-suited fat man say it at one of the parties where Thomas was being particularly obnoxious."

"Got it, doc. Go on."

"Galya told me she delighted in igniting her own furor during these gatherings. She took every opportunity to engage flirtatious male attendees in close quarter encounters. Her glamorous looks and rapturous smile cast a hypnotic spell causing jealous wives to storm about with threats slightly short of castration."

"That's rather creative prose, doctor. Did she actually say that?"

"No, detective. I must admit I crafted that statement, embellishing in my words her more, let's say, crude description of the events."

Victor suppressed a chuckle. He found himself warming somewhat to the good doctor, deciding it best to encourage her candor and revelations of detail. It was rare for a shrink to be this forthcoming on a case, and he sensed she was so taken by Galya and her story, that it had evolved far beyond a customary psychological examination. She needed to tell someone, and sharing it with him was safe for her professionally and intellectually. Going forward Victor changed his tactic. No more threats. Just good cop; no bad cop.

"If I may?" she asked.

"Yes, by all means continue. But if you please, I have a question." Victor politely requested.

"During this period when these social butterflies were flitting around town, was Galya in touch with this guardian of hers? Did she continue her work for him as a master forger? What occupied her time during the days and nights between dinner parties and satisfying her lover?"

Dr. Gladstone's face seemed to light up with the question.

Her response was animated. "No, detective she stated that weeks would go by without contact from the stranger, and despite asking for work, she was told she was no longer needed. This frustrated her tremendously as you can imagine. She became anxious and tense, fearing her value to him and those he represented had diminished. She was terrified that the money would dry up and she would become dependent on Thomas.

"By this time she had stashed away nearly thirty thousand dollars in a bank account unknown to Thomas or anyone. But she knew if she left him, that amount would be insufficient to maintain her lifestyle for very long. Plus, on her own, her most rewarding means of livelihood had landed her in jail before, and without the protection of her guardian, she panicked at the thought of getting caught again if she was forced to venture down that treacherous path. But eventually to her great relief the stranger resumed contact. When he did he reassured her all was well, and that her only job at that point was to prepare Thomas for his upcoming trips.

"How was she supposed to do that? I mean, was she given instructions on buying luggage and making travel arrangements?" Victor asked lightheartedly.

"She never said. All she was told to do was help him raise his profile at the University. They went to parties and lectures, and of course, she attended his on and off campus speeches where often there was media coverage. Certainly his views were controversial, and he was frequently quoted by local and national press, especially when the U.S. would step up its criticism of the Soviets. Thomas became an apologist or defender of the Communists which made him a reliable quotable source for ambitious journalists."

"Okay, so he's riding high on this crazy anti-American soapbox. When did it all come crashing down?"

"A few days after he disappeared."

"Really!" Victor could not hide his astonishment.

"Yes, detective, shortly thereafter she was arrested."

"Damn, it happened all at once."

"Yes detective, all at once.

Both fell silent for a time. Dr. Gladstone calmly reshuffled her notes. Victor stroked his chin and aimlessly gazed about the room, avoiding eye contact. All the while his mind churned through the incredible tale he had just heard.

Breaking the uneasy interlude, Victor said, "No other questions, doctor. Thank you. I really appreciate your help. I mean, I apologize for being rude there at first. You know. I'm stalled on this case. What was first a routine, run-of-the-mill suicide has possibly turned into some kind of secret government scheme involving star-struck lovers, loony Communist college professors, sex triangles, secret agents, another mysterious death and God knows what else. I don't have the time or resources to investigate this thing. It's too big for me, I think. And if the government's involved, who can I turn it over to and expect a fair handling? Somebody killed that woman. Its murder, and its in my backyard. I'm responsible and now I've got to figure out if Galya Tannenbaum was linked somehow to the disappearance of Thomas Riha or if he was out there in the shadows orchestrating her death.

"Christ, he might have done it himself for all we know. Maybe he pushed those needles into her butt or made her swallow those pills. Or how about this? Maybe she killed him and then she was killed in retaliation. Man, this is really fucked up.

"Excuse me doctor. That was rude."

She hastened only momentarily before saying, "Don't worry about it detective. Listen, I may be wrong myself. Less than an hour ago I was convinced beyond a doubt that Galya killed herself, but now I'm not so sure. You've helped me question my own theories as a clinician. I'm trained to draw sound conclusions on cases like these. Now, I have to rethink my position, and I thank you for helping me discover things I may have inadvertently ignored before."

"Well, what I've done, Sylvia, is confuse the situation that much more. Sorry, may I call you Sylvia?"

"That you have, detective; yes you have confused things greatly. And, yes, you may call me Sylvia."

"Thanks. It's Victor."

"Victor, are we done now?" she asked.

"Yes, Doctor, I guess so," Victor responded, then hesitated as he pushed back his chair and rose to leave. As an afterthought he added, "To your knowledge did Galya ever leave the compound for any period of time. Was she ever granted a pass? Is that what you call it here? A pass?"

"Yes, we call it a pass or leave, either supervised or un-supervised. One time during her confinement Galya was granted a temporary release. I believe she was gone but a day or two. She was not a danger to society, detective, and we were told she was being supervised. She returned to the hospital as scheduled without incident."

"Supervised by whom?"

"I assumed the authorities."

"Her guardian, perhaps?"

"I don't know. That's an interesting question."

"Okay, just curious. Thank you Doctor, ah, Sylvia. I truly appreciate your help. I will be in touch."

"I hope you will detective. Victor, please understand now sensitive my situation is here. I have violated every canonized ethical standard there is for my profession, but I, like you, am bound and determined to find the true cause of this woman's tragic death. If there is anything I can do to assist in your investigation, please call on me."

"You've been a great help already. I will do just that if the need arises."

That night Victor sat at Johnny's bar sipping his second rum and coke. Johnny leaned across the bar into his friend's face and quietly said, "No Victor, you don't have a choice. You've got to dig through this one. No one else will. If you don't, they'll sweep it under the rug and it'll rot there and stink and you'll smell it in your sleep."

"Shut up and give me another one."

"Nope. Go home to your wife and kids. I have a feelin' they may not be seein' much of you for a while."

Chapter 18

"No, I'll walk. I just live over there in Libby Hall," Agent Catherine Benson lied. Her feet hurt so badly from sprinting around the campus after this prick she could scream, but instead, she walked steadily, expecting any minute for blood to spurt through the ends of the obscene-looking sandals, which bound her ten toes.

"Okay, if you're sure. I don't mind. I can drive you. You were great company. I enjoy mingling with my students on their home turf, you know. It gives me a unique perspective on your views and beliefs. Part of my research. My laboratory. You can tell so much about a segment of society by just listening to their barroom banter. True insight. Thank you Monique."

Dr. Riha held out his hand for Agent Benson to shake. She nearly gagged at the thought of accepting the offer, but grasped it firmly in response. A gentle shake followed. He released her quickly and stepped back.

Catherine was surprised that he did what he did. She would have bet half her pension twenty years from now that he would have made a move on her. Hey, a rather young professor. Ladies man reputation. I'm not that bad looking. Even in this ungodly outfit. He's glib and cocky. I should be ripe for the taking. But no, he's gonna go away, and leave me standing here.

The look on her face caught Thomas' parting glance. Having only half turned from her, he pivoted slightly and grinned. "No dear, I know what you're thinking. I'm not going to have sex with you even though I suspect you truly desire it. I have someone waiting at home who puts you to shame."

With that, he turned and strolled toward the faculty parking lot.

Catherine needed a moment to steady herself before shouting under her breath, "you pompous motherfucker."

"Good-bye professor. Have a nice evening," she called out so he could hear.

Then she too grinned in the same sinister manner as he, and said to the giant maple tree beside her, "If he only knew what's about to happen to him."

Gordon and Rico, two of J. Edgar Hoover's best, were positioned about a hundred yards away each peering from behind a similar ancient maple, one of hundreds which dot the campus landscape. Gordon had a small but high-powered pair of binoculars leveled to his eyes.

"He's walkin' away. We were both wrong. He didn't hustle her after all," Gordon announced.

"Maybe they're planning on meeting up later," Rico speculated.

"Don't think so. Don't get the sense. Kind of a cold handshake at the end. He's not looking back. And she's sittin' on the grass rubbing her feet; not looking after him neither. No. Ain't gonna happen. Let's move. He's heading for his car."

"No come-on body language, you sayin'?" Rico asked.

Don't believe in that bullshit," said Gordon.

"Sure doesn't sound like it."

Agent Benson watched the two overall-clad utility men as they jogged toward a parking lot restricted to campus security vehicles.

How blatantly obvious they are, she thought. They even got free parking.

She gingerly rose to stand on her throbbing feet. Her sandals in her hands. She couldn't wait to throw them away. The cool grass felt good. She moved as quickly as she could to a nearby telephone stand; one of those placed along main walkways for emergency calls, but mostly used for drunks trying to reach wayward girlfriends stuck in their dorm rooms. The hood over the receiver looked like a seashell, an odd amenity, Catherine thought, for a sweeping lawn at the base of the Rocky Mountains.

Catherine would use her restricted code number to connect directly with the deputy director at Langley. Luckily the phone she found worked. The seashell blocked the sun's glaring light. She gave her code to the operator who answered.

"Operator, now get off the line. This call is a matter of national security," Catherine hissed into the mouthpiece. The connecting line clicked and seconds later she heard a familiar but unexpected voice say, "Yes, Agent Benson. You have my attention."

Catherine audibly caught her breath. "Director, Director Helms I, I...."

"Catherine, this is an extremely important matter for all of us, as you know. You have my personal attention. What is your recommendation?"

Catherine said in a forceful tone, "Sir, we must take him tonight."

"Very well, Agent Benson. Recommendation approved, we take him tonight."

Chapter 19

Moments after Thomas Riha's self-satisfying discernment that his denial of sexual favors would have a profound effect on his afternoon drinking companion, Galya Tannenbaum answered the telephone at their home on the third ring. Without introduction she immediately recognized her handler's voice. His instructions were welcomed and perfectly clear.

"Pack an overnight bag and leave the house immediately. Drive into Denver. Check into the downtown Marriott. The reservation for your room is under your real name, Gloria Forest. In the room there will be work for you to do. Your specialty. Payment for the work will be made in cash, and delivered in an envelope slipped under your door while you sleep. Leave your finished work in the room sealed in the envelope in which it came. It will be retrieved while you are out. While not working, make yourself visible. Take attractive clothes. Spend time in the bar. Eat dinner in the restaurant if you choose. Attract attention. Make sure people see you. But do not bring anyone back to your room. Remain alone there at all times. I will let you know when you can return home. You have fifteen minutes. Please hurry."

The line went dead.

Galya placed the receiver back in its wall cradle. She knew she had to obey and act quickly.

Great, she thought. Some time away. By myself. Work to do. Nice hotel. Some money. It's about time. If I run out of clothes I'll buy some. I'll be out of here in ten minutes.

And she was. By the time Thomas pulled into the driveway at their home, Galya was three miles away, heading south toward Colorado 36 which would take her east toward Denver and a delightful retreat which she hoped would last a few days, not just one.

Thomas was unhappy and undeniably aggravated when he parked in the driveway and switched off the car's engine. His self-congratulatory reproach of the cute but unappealing student had left his thoughts long before. Sitting in traffic along Broadway while those idiots pushed their pickup truck out of the intersection caused him precious time away from his woman and his scotch. And now. Where was she? Her car is gone. She knows I'm always home around this time when I'm not speaking to some adoring assembly. Well, she'll be back soon. We'll drink, have a nice dinner and fuck all night.

Rico and Gordon had also been stuck in the same traffic jam sitting, idling in their fake decaled utility truck, three cars behind Thomas' vehicle waiting for the intersection to clear. The chorus of blaring horns still rang in their ears. None of the clamor seemed to have prompted the occupants of the disabled vehicle to move it any faster. It seemed like they were deliberately causing the delay.

"Christ, I'm getting hungry," Rico said as Gordon pulled the truck to curbside a block away from Riha's residence. "And I need to piss again."

"You'll have to wait. We need to make sure he's in for the night. It looks like his lady friend might be gone. Her car's not there. See?" Gordon said, pointing in that direction.

"Well don't blame me if I have to whip it out and drain it in this Coke bottle," Rico warned.

Thomas ambled through the eerily quiet and clearly empty house already feeling alone and un-appreciated. The place was stifling without her. Despite surroundings of what Thomas boasted as his exquisite décor of mainly eastern European black walnut living room tables, side chairs, dining table, sideboards and even picture frames, his somber feelings that late afternoon were even darker and more pervasive.

The tick-tock of the black forest grandfather clock in his foyer seemed to clang in his ears. The thick-piled brown mosaic wool carpets spread throughout the main floor rooms irritated his bare feet rather than soothing his walk. Thomas always shed his shoes and socks upon entry. He found bare feet erotic. To please him Galya had adopted his practice in spite of an annoying chill, which always ran through her lower limbs, especially when barefoot.

He sorted through the mail stacked on the kitchen countertop.

She was here just a while ago. The mail isn't normally delivered until three o'clock.

Thomas left the kitchen and climbed the stairs to his second floor bedroom to change his clothes. He sat on the mattress of the heavily-carved teak four-poster bed and sighed, failing to notice a drawer in Galya's high-boy dresser standing partially open exposing the strap of one of her white lacy bras hanging over the side. He shed his clothes, carelessly tossing each piece onto the shamrock green upholstered chaise positioned in the bedroom's far corner. He stood and walked naked into the bathroom to retrieve his robe. He would remain clad only with that article until she returned and then he would punish her for her absence by requiring oral sex while seated in his favorite chair in his library.

She doesn't like doing it in there, but tonight she'll do what I say to quell my anguish over her unexpected absence.

From his nightstand he grasped his vintage leather-bound second-edition copy of Fyodor Dostoevsky's "Brothers Karamazov" which he was reading for the second time.

The English translation he held while descending the staircase to make his way to the main-floor liquor cabinet was second rate in his mind. He long sought the first edition, published in 1880 in Dostoevsky's native tongue, but he was consistently outbid at auctions where one occasionally was offered by a New York collector who had a ready after-market among the Orthodox Jews in Brooklyn. On his bookshelf, however, Thomas proudly displayed first edition copies of "Possessed" and "Crime & Punishment".

He filled his cut-glass crystal tumbler full of his favorite brand. It rested on a side table beside him under an antique hand-painted glass shade Handel lamp, glistening in the multi-colored light. He reached over and gulped down two-thirds of his drink and settled into the soft brown button-tucked high-back leather chair, trying to relax. He opened his robe and inspected his genitals imagining the pleasure she would soon bring. His book lay unopened, sharing the table top with the newly opened bottle of Macallan 18. He couldn't get comfortable. His book didn't interest him. He drained his glass and poured another.

God damn it, where the hell is she?

"Okay, my guess is he's not going anywhere at least for a while. I see the light on in his library. I think it's safe to grab some food and for you to drain your pecker as long as you're back here in twenty minutes. I'll get out and act like I'm reading meters or something," Gordon said.

"Yea, like that won't attract attention. In case you haven't noticed, it's damn near dark outside. You go into somebody's yard now, you're liable to be shot," Rico chuckled.

"Get me a pastrami on rye, mustard only, chips, a pickle and ginger ale," Gordon ordered as he exited the vehicle.

"What am I a catering service?" Rico retorted, slamming the truck in gear and speeding off. Gordon stealthily moved behind a tree, heeding Rico's advice not to trespass.

About that time Galya stood at the reservation desk awaiting her room keys. She was stunning in a mid-thigh, blue-sheath mini dress, matching blue heels; her long slender legs exposed without stockings. Hair down, falling over her shoulders. Her black mink jacket, the one Thomas bought her on the anniversary of Helen's departure, was draped over her shoulders. Out of habit she smiled flirtatiously at two well-dressed three-piece business suit types who walked by on their way to the lounge.

The suits had looked like they might be good for free drinks and dinner since she had offered coquettish hints but she reminded herself that she really didn't care since she could pay her own way now that the clerk had presented the envelope at check-in. Shielded in her purse, she opened it to find three one-hundred-dollar bills she presumed were her guardian's good faith deposit toward her forthcoming assignments. Keys in hand, she declined bell service and strolled to the elevator. Her Louis Vuitton overnight wasn't that heavy so she carried the bag and purse over each shoulder, her mink removed and now safely draped between the leather straps. Life is good. Good to be back to work. Good to be alone. Arriving on eleventh floor she walked to her room. To the right of the elevator and straight away to the end of the hall. A suite, no doubt. The lock clicked. She entered and switched on the light.

She was right. A room larger than Thomas' parlor and dining room combined. A pile of tan manila legal-size envelopes rested on the writing table of a very old but beautiful tiger maple secretary placed by the window. She pulled back the curtains. The lights of downtown flickered on. The fading remnants of a blazing sunset over Longs Peak. She shed her dress, catching it with a toe as it fell, and flinging it expertly onto the king size canopy bed decorating space across the room. She stood at the window in matching blue lingerie with bare feet sinking luxuriously into the beige carpet. This time in this place there was no chill moving up her calves. A bottle of fine Dom Pérignon was nestled in an ice-filled silver bucket on a stand adjacent the secretary. She decided she would bathe with a tall glass and candles burning before dressing in her white full-length spaghetti-strap gown, slit to just below the panty line.

Thomas finished his third glass and fumed. He checked his genitals again. They seemed to have shrunk.

Rico and Gordon sat cramped in the truck cab. It was getting cold outside. They had put on their jackets also displaying phony pasted-on utility company decals. The windows were fogging over. The inside reeked of Gordon's dinner. Discarded leftovers gathered at their feet. The light in the Riha library still shone. Occasionally a shadow passed by a window seemingly circling the room.

"We'll wait until the light goes out and we see one go on in his bedroom. Then we're off duty," Gordon declared wearily.

"No argument there," Rico responded.

Agent Catherine Benson was flanked by two men she'd met only an hour before in the K-Mart parking lot off Highway 36 near the Broomfield interchange. They were clad entirely in black, even the hoods over their heads and their crepe-soled shoes. Catherine felt much more comfortable in this outfit than the one she had worn that afternoon. But her feet still hurt despite the salve she had spread over her blisters.

It was near midnight. She and her companions moved in a slinking bandit-crouch through Thomas' rear yard toward his back door. Their vehicle was parked in the wide alleyway directly behind them. It was to be a simple snatch, Catherine had told her accomplices. The house is isolated. High hedges border the sides and rear of the yard. An unlocked gate will provide convenient access, she had said. The door entering the house is at ground level at the rear. No security system; just a single push-button lock. No dead bolt.

Catherine's only concern was the size and capability of the two men on either side of her. They weren't much bigger than she. Could they carry him away without struggle or resistance? They were at the door. Catherine's shiny thin-bladed pin knife slipped easily into the keyhole. She turned it one way, then another. The button on the other side of the knob popped back with a click. She pushed the door open. No sound. She knew there wasn't a dog.

Thomas, Gordon and Rico were all sound asleep as Catherine and company crept through the house toward the light. They didn't know where their target was, but all other lights in the house were off, so they suspected he was either in that lighted room or in a darkened bedroom upstairs. Silently they stepped closer. In her right hand Catherine held the syringe she'd retrieved from her belly pouch. The cap covering the needle was between her teeth. From her earlier encounters Catherine knew Thomas was a little guy, so the sedative dosage would be minimal. Catherine reached the wall separating the hall from the library and peeked around the corner to peer inside the well-appointed space. She heard loud snoring and stopped her movement. She smiled.

This can't be this easy.

But it was. Within twelve minutes, Thomas Riha, still snoring, lay comfortably on a fine mattress in the rear of the windowless panel truck. His nude body had been wrapped in his silk robe and was covered with a down comforter for extra warmth. His head rested on a foam pillow. A set of clean set of clothes was stacked neatly at his bare feet. Shoes, socks, belt, pants, shirt and jacket all color coordinated. His underwear didn't match, however. All she could find was pink. The suitcase nearby was full of selections from his extensive wardrobe. He would sleep, sedated for the next eight hours allowing his captors plenty of time to reach a remote airstrip near the Kansas border.

In a jump seat next to him Catherine stared down at her hostage, thinking of the days ahead beginning with their flight to Virginia where she would spend days, if not weeks, training Thomas Riha for his new mission in life. The extent to which the time and effort spent on his instruction would depend entirely on him. The longer he resisted, the more difficult it would become; not for her, but for him.

In the waning moonlight Rico awoke to the sound of a passing car and shouts from its occupants, one of whom hung precariously out the window of the rear door vomiting. He nudged Gordon who apparently had heard nothing of the commotion. Gordon sat up and looked toward the house. The library was dark as were all the rooms. "Shit, fell asleep. Oh well, he never moved," Gordon said.

"He's in bed for sure. Damn, apparently she's not home yet. See, her car's still not there, and its, Christ, its five o'clock," Rico exclaimed.

"I won't tell if you won't tell," Gordon offered.

"Off duty now for sure. Probably shouldn't put in for overtime,"

Rico said.

"Yea, probably shouldn't. Its Saturday so what you say we take the day off," Gordon proposed. "Can't imagine Headquarters is gonna want us to grab him today."

"Can't imagine that neither. Okay with me then; day off," Rico agreed. He started the engine and slowly drove past the house, and said. "Bet he's got a broken heart. She's steppin' out on him for sure."

Catherine rested beside Riha's repose. Her back against the truck's side panel. Her legs stretched out across Thomas' covered, padded torso rising and falling in rhythm with his heavy breathing. She sipped strong black coffee. Her un-named counterparts had promised to drive the whole way to Kansas allowing her to sleep if she chose to do so. They were good guys. Professional. She would never know their names. She wouldn't ask. No need. What she knew was while she had gathered Thomas' clothing they had carefully lifted him from his leather throne, and with ease and undetected, hauled him to his resting place. Catherine's injection into his jugular had assured a prolonged rag-doll state.

"You pretentious bastard. You have no idea what comes next in your fucked up life," Catherine whispered to her supine foot stool, his breathing unconsciously halting at the noise, but his face still shining serenely from the glow of dashboard lights.

Chapter 20

They had found her irresistible, but after about fifteen minutes of inane conversation with the two imbeciles attending an insurance company retreat, Galya determined neither was worth her time, even though both had offered spectacular dinners and gaiety to follow. She excused herself for a ladies' room visit, and when returning, had found a seat at the opposite end of the bar. When one rose to occupy the empty seat beside her she had sternly waved him off. He got the not-so-subtle message and soon departed with his buddy for more fertile hunting grounds elsewhere.

Soon without her objection an older bookish-looking fellow sporting a bow tie and silk-suit-pocket kerchief, round glasses and manicured nails took the seat beside her. Their conversation turned out to be amiable and fairly interesting, but had lasted only an hour before the gentleman excused himself to escort a lady to their table upon noticing her arrival at the hostess desk.

Uncaring Galya paid her tab and returned to her room to order room service. She dined alone on fairly decent king crab, for a Colorado import, a petite medium-rare filet mignon, house wine from Napa and a splurged-on chocolate sundae.

She had opened the first envelope from the top of the deck about the same time her unconscious lover was being placed inside the panel truck. Thomas hadn't crossed her mind for a second since she began examining instructions to alter an intercepted letter from the prime minister of Cambodia to the Laotian ambassador demanding cessation of support for Communist insurgents crossing their border. No doubt a properly forged document would cause chaotic confusion and antagonism between the two nations since both provided safe harbor for

Viet Cong forces fighting U.S. ground troops in Viet Nam.

Galya was certainly up to the task but remained unaware and totally unconcerned about the international implications of this or any of her other forgeries. All she cared about was perfection in her craft, no matter the content, and continuation of stellar wages. She worked until four a.m. falsifying these and other documents; copying and changing key parts of important diplomatic correspondence, and even signing counterfeit bank notes for an unsuspecting North Korean treasury official who would most assuredly be accused of embezzlement and probably executed without trial.

Still sheathed in her gown she finally moved to her fabulous bed for fabulous sleep.

They would let her rest and work a few days before her arrest.

Chapter 21

"Mary Louise Henderson, night nurse, Women's Ward Three, overseer of cells 200 through 250 on the third floor. Is that right Miss Henderson?" Captain Victor Bravo asked, his eyes rising from the personnel file laid open on the superintendent's conference table before him.

"No sir. That is not correct," Mary Louise responded.

"What is not correct Nurse Henderson? You are Mary Louise Henderson, are you not?"

"Yes sir, I am Mary Louise Henderson."

"And you are a registered nurse employed at the Colorado State Asylum for the Habitually Insane. Is that not correct?"

"Correct."

"And you are typically assigned to Women's Ward Three. Mostly the night shift?"

"Correct."

"Then what is not correct about my statement, Nurse Henderson?"

"Second floor. Women's Ward Three is on the second floor, not the third."

Victor struggled mightily to control his temper. Condescending bitch, he thought. What did I do to deserve her?

The beginning of his interview with Mary Louise Henderson, second floor pain-in-the ass, had marked Victor's seventh straight hour of interviews with Asylum personnel, other than Dr. Sylvia Gladstone, who had been on duty the night of Galya Tannenbaum's murder.

Victor couldn't describe his meetings with this long list of hospital staff members as interrogations. And he had no reason to label anyone who had been seated before him since seven that morning as a witness, or for that matter, a suspect. As he labored through the meetings it became increasingly apparent that they all just might be innocent bystanders doing the hard work of caring for the state-declared mental cases in their stead. Seventeen people had punched their time cards in that night, all of whom could have had access to Galya on the night she died, or the many nights before when the deadly doses were being callously administered.

But why would any one of them want to kill her? He kept asking himself during each session.

So far, nothing; no one, including Night Nurse Henderson fit the profile.

Victor's only suspect, short-lived as he had been with that status, was not on Victor's list of appointments this day. He had exhausted all reasonable efforts to link Samuel Richards, would-be shrink whose libido had ruined a promising career, to the crime. So Victor had to move on. Somebody in this nut house, patients and employees similarly categorized for residency therein, knew something, and the Captain of Detectives would not rest until someone cracked. To this point all their shells had been made of lead, eight-inches thick.

"So sorry, Nurse Henderson. Second floor, my mistake," Victor sneered.

"Thank you, sir. I just want to keep everything very clear and precise," she further lectured.

"As do I, Mary Louise. May I call you Mary Louise?"

"I would prefer Nurse Henderson, sir."

"Very well, Nurse Henderson. Then let us begin. Nurse Henderson, why did you kill Gloria Galya Tennenbaum? Were you paid to do so or did you dislike her so much that you couldn't stand to let her live?"

Mary Louise gasped. Her hand went to her mouth. Her eyes wide in shock. "How dare you!" she exclaimed. "I will not sit here and be accused of causing her death or anything for that matter. I'm leaving." She leaped from her chair.

"You will leave when I ask you to leave Nurse Henderson. Please re-take your seat." Victor's tone was as stern as his expression.

Mary Louise slowly sat back down.

"I'm so sorry, Nurse Henderson. That was probably discourteous of me. You see I'm very tired. And you really pissed me off with your attitude a moment ago, so I just thought we'd cut to the core here. You see, you are number seventeen on my list of appointments today. That is, I've talked to sixteen of your fellow professionals who were on duty with you that night. And, you see Mary Louise, every one of them, right down to the poor guy who cleans the toilets, tells me you were the only one who had access to the pharmacy on the night in question. And it also seems that every night you work, you keep the magic key to the drug vault all to yourself."

"Is that correct, Mary Louise?"

Her previous reaction to Victor's shot-from-the-hip accusation had vanished. She came back at him with harsh directness.

"When I work I am the head nurse on duty. I am senior to the other nurses. I am there to seal off those premises from the patients, and yes, sir, occasionally from the employees. I am responsible for monitoring medications and maintaining the pharmacy records.

"Your implications, sir, are extremely offensive. Libelous in fact. Neither I nor anyone at the hospital had anything to do with her death. She committed suicide. It is well known. The coroner's ruling confirmed that. And from what that lawyer for Samuel Richards said in the newspaper, you agreed, so why are you wasting my time and yours? And please, before I have my lawyer intervene to stop your nonsense, I ask you, politely, never to accuse me of such a thing again."

It was Victor's turn to repel but he didn't outwardly show it. He kept a straight, unaffected expression. Damn, she's good, he thought while closely examining the rigidity she restored to her look and the calmness exhibited in her voice.

I've never seen anyone recover so quickly from a gut-shot like that. She's one tough cookie by nature or she's well trained to be that way. I like the term she used...seal off. Sounds kind of military to me. Or cop-like. Wonder if she was.....

"Do you have any further questions of me, Detective?" She asked, interrupting Victor's thoughts.

"Oh, yes, Mary Louise. We've hardly begun. So please be patient."

Victor hesitated then added, "For the moment, I'll ignore your comment about needing a lawyer. When someone says that to me, I can't help but think they have something to hide."

Before she could react again, he quickly continued.

"So, Mary Louise, how well did you know Miss Tannebaum? Had you reviewed her case file? Were you aware of the reasons, or should I say, excuses for her confinement? Did you ever observe her behavior? That is, in the manner of detecting any suicidal tendencies to justify your conclusion?"

Victor could tell she was still fuming over his last remark and sensed she was groping to cover an exposed vulnerability.

She coughed. It seemed like a nervous impulse. Then with an indignant tone, she said,

"I am responsible for dozens of patients while on my shift. I do not have time to familiarize myself with their individual case files. No sir, I did not come to know the lady at all; nor did I inspect her file or become familiar with her particular affliction."

"I see. Yet you conclude like most people that she committed suicide. Am I to assume that because of your heavy workload and the fact you have no idea about the condition of many of your patients that when one of them kills themselves, you seldom question why? It's just a matter of, well, inevitability, you might say. You don't even wonder?"

She sat erect, placing her elbows on the tabletop, which separated them, and stared straight into Victor's eyes.

"I care about my patients. I care what happens to them but I don't crawl inside their skulls. We have a fifteen-percent suicide rate at the Asylum. Maybe that's too high. I'm not here to judge. I do my job. Some die. Some get better and are released. Some stay inside forever. If I allowed myself to get attached to these people I'd go crazy myself."

She has a point.

"But Nurse Henderson, what you don't realize is Miss Tannenbaum couldn't have killed herself. She died of cyanide poisoning. She succumbed after a long, agonizing time-span of torture. Not from a large single dosage. Rather from small doses which, over a prolonged period, attacked her brain, her central nervous system, and eventually shut down her vital organs after gradually causing an onset of blindness. Did you know that Nurse Henderson?"

She didn't flinch. No reaction at all. Her expression did not change.

Not news to her, Victor thought.

Yet she came back with, "No sir, I did not know that. Cyanide you say? Interesting. Strange way to do it. If she didn't do it all at once, it must have taken a lot of discipline. No detective, there's no cyanide in my medicine cabinet if that's what you think. Somehow she must have smuggled it in from the outside, like some of them bring in guns or knives. It's quicker that other way you know."

Then she smiled. Not quite diabolical, but almost. Victor's slightly convulsed reaction did not go unnoticed.

Damn! Jekyll and Hyde.

She jumped in with, "You had your suspect Detective. The best one you will ever

have. Either you let him get away, or you couldn't pin anything on him because no crime was committed. Now you're groping for another suspect. Get real Mr. Copper, it ain't me. It ain't nobody."

Mary Louise Henderson leaned back in her chair and offered Victor a look of total self- satisfaction; an arrogant air of accomplishment.

Well trained. That didn't come naturally, Victor thought.

Victor let her bask in her brief moment of glory. He broke her gaze and looked down, acting as if further studying his files. A few awkward moments of silence passed between them before he said, "Well, Mary Louise, let's see what we do next. How about you give me your keys to the pharmacy. How about right now. And I give them back to you when I'm done going through every prescription bottle in the place. If I don't like what I see or if anything appears to be out of place or maybe not quite properly labeled for what's inside, I'll have it tested. What do you think of that plan, Head Second Floor Night Nurse Henderson?"

She flinched this time. Victor saw it clearly. She swallowed hard.

Mouth went dry with that one.

Finally, trying to suppress a rasp in her voice, she said, "I can't do that. I am responsible for the security of the pharmacy and all of its contents. I do not allow those keys to fall into anyone else's hands."

"Oh yes you will Mary Louise." Victor's smile was purposefully menacing.

"You see Nurse Henderson, I have a very good friend who is a damn fine pharmacist; actually trained as a chemist. I'm sure he won't mind helping me go through the inventory. He's so smart. You see, he knows drugs so well he can spot bad ones, outdated ones, liquid or solid, counterfeits, sugar pills when they're not supposed to be there, phony substitutes, and yes, probably poison in whatever form it might take. He's the best. I'll probably get started with him tonight, so I'm going to take your keys and have your private personal narcotics stash sealed off, just like you do it yourself.

"Please hand me the keys."

The blood drained from her face. She couldn't help it. She had nothing to say.

Mary Louise pulled the ring of keys from the pocket of her frock and laid them on the desktop.

She remained seated. "Are you done with me Detective?"

"Do you have anything to tell me Mary Louise?"

"No sir. Nothing at all."

"Very well. Then you may go, but please, as a courtesy, and for your own sake, do not leave the area."

She pushed back her chair, gathered her purse and unsteadily walked to the door.

"Are you sure you have nothing to say?" Victor called after her without turning to view her exit.

"I might be able to help you. I don't think you did this alone."

There was no response. A hesitation and then the door opened and shut without Victor hearing another word.

The body of Head Second Floor Night Nurse Mary Louise Henderson was found two nights later. It lay at the bottom of a ravine, which angled two hundred feet sharply down from the two-lane roadbed leading west to the mountain town of Gunnison.

The wreckage of her demolished late-model station wagon was spotted by a terribly inebriated teenager who had stopped to relieve himself over the steep ledge before returning home from a late-night beer-keg party at a friend's house ten miles away.

Through the blackness, he had seen slowly blinking headlights eerily signaling the crash site far below. At the sight his hefty stream had gone awry to wet his sneakers, yet he waited until arriving home and finding his parents asleep before calling the Sheriff's Office, which notified the Highway Patrol.

Investigators later concluded that Mary Louise Henderson had been thrown from the vehicle as it careened down the near vertical decline and tumbled into the deep and dangerous God-made crevice. Her skid marks indicated she left the poorly paved surface at high speed through a gap in the guardrail. She was wearing her night nurse's duty frock when she died. She displayed ghastly injuries including a crushed skull. Victor requested, and the patrolman on duty agreed, to close the road and cordon off the fatal scene. The patrolman diverted traffic for three hours

LOVE, SPIES AND CYANIDE

while Victor and five sheriff's deputies combed the area for clues. They found her purse under a bush some twenty-five yards away from the body. It contained thirty neatly wrapped one-hundred-dollar bills.

After his heated interrogation of Night Nurse Henderson, Victor had ordered all city cops to keep an eye out for her vehicle and to alert the Highway Patrol if they spotted her leaving town. Patrol officers had a description of the station wagon and were asked to inform him of her movements, and if possible, follow her to her destination. They had no reason to stop and detain her. Victor only wanted to be aware of her activities, he had said, since she was a person of interest in an ongoing criminal investigation. The patrolman first-to-arrive on the death scene recognized the smashed-up automobile as the one Detective Bravo was interested in, and called to make him aware of the crash.

When Victor arrived at the spot where Mary Louise lay he was hard-hit by a fleeting notion of personal responsibility for her death. Somewhat at least. Despite his promise to thoroughly search the pharmacy he had had no intention of doing so. Truth be known, Victor was clueless how to detect pharmaceutical contraband. The only pharmacist he knew was the one who occasionally filled his prescriptions for high blood pressure. His condition often fluctuated when the stress got too great; which was one of those times, so he would probably need a refill soon. The only chemist he knew was his high school teacher whom he suspected of routinely sniffing some of the concoctions they had mixed up in class.

Victor stared down at her mangled body and reflected on his recent actions. His ankle hurt. He had twisted it scaling down the sheer cliff to find her.

Victor's ruse with Mary Louise had a greater impact than he'd anticipated. He didn't expect her to react so strongly, or move so quickly. I saw it in her eyes. The terror. The guilt. The need to run. Was I correct? My tactic with her proved fatal this time, and damn it, I didn't mean it to be. I needed more time with her. To crack her lead shell.

Victor later learned the best chance he had had to again confront Mary Louise was lost when she slipped out the back door of the Black Cat Bar & Grill while first-year detective Ronnie Sapp munched on a beef and cheese burrito seated in his unmarked patrol car a block away from the tavern's front entrance. When she didn't come out of the joint at closing time rookie Sapp went in to investigate. He was shocked to learn that two hours earlier she had told the bartender she was being followed and harassed by an old boyfriend, and asked him to aid in her escape.

The tavern attendee had agreed, and stood watch over Sapp, identified as the one being spurned, as he dozed in the driver's seat on a full stomach moving not a muscle to further stalk his lovelorn prey. She was gone long before Sapp knew it and was never seen alive again. What the bartender and Sapp had failed to notice was the car parked catty-corner from the cruiser, which, with headlights doused, moved in behind Mary Louise the moment she sped away.

Victor desperately wanted, but now will never have another opportunity to pierce Mary Louise's protective shield. Let alone ask about the money. In his frustration he planned to deal Sapp a stern reprimand and likely demotion to beat cop when the case finally closed.

If that ever happens.

Was she on the run? Probably. Where was she going? She still had her nurse's frock on. Purse loaded with cash. Did she intend to return to work? Was she being followed? Did someone force her off the road? That goddamn rookie. Was this just an accident?

Besides the purse the deputies eventually found nothing but crumpled car parts strewn far and wide.

No one would ever blame his investigators for missing the pinholes punctured at strategic points in the brake line by the tip of a super-sharp ice pick, or the scraped bumper from the speeding car, which tapped it as she attempted to slow and maneuver through the abrupt highway curve.

Victor watched the paramedics place her remains in the body bag. They tied it down on a toboggan-type sled, attached a rope, and pulled it up the steep slope to the awaiting ambulance.

Dr. Korman's post mortem would reveal nothing more than the plainly visible signs of massive internal and external injuries.

Victor arrived home as the sun peaked over the eastern horizon.

Christ, all these night shifts are killing me.

Rosanna stirred and pretended to sleep. She would be up in an hour to get the kids off to school.

Another night. Another wasted night away from us, she thought. Still feigning slumber she signed heavily. I can't let this go on. I've got to say something. Do something. He's not the same man. It must be this case. Not like the others. This one has torn him apart and maybe us.

Victor sensed her consciousness. He moved in beside her. Quietly. Hoping to quell the concern he knew she had. "I'm sorry," he whispered. "I'll try to cut back. Limit my time on it."

"No you won't," she responded without turning to face him. She suppressed a sob. Her voice cracked. "It's what you live for. Cases like this. It's all about the mystery. The obsession you have to solve it at all cost. Alone. No one good enough to help, or that's what you think." She pushed him away and rose quickly, turning to glare down at him just as a sunray burst through a sliver in the open bedroom curtains. "It's a high price you're paying for being away. Victor, someday you'll have to make a choice."

"Don't say that. Come back here please."

"Sorry. Some other time. The kids need their mother and their father."

Retrieving her robe from the bathroom door hook, she was gone in a blink, closing the door with a muted click.

Exhausted, his head splitting, eyes afire with fatigue, Victor could not plead again. His head found the softness of the pillow and his naked body the coolness of the sheets.

I'll deal with that another time, he thought, and before he dove deep into restfulness his mind raced not after her but back to the hours before.

Now I have no choice but to search the pharmacy.

Looking for what?

Night Nurse Henderson wouldn't have been that stupid to leave telltale signs of a killing potion, her murder weapon, right there for someone to find. She would have destroyed any remaining traces.

But why did she panic when I took the key from her? Must be hiding something.

I'm going to sleep till noon.

He didn't awake until three that afternoon. The kids were home from school by then. He had a snack with them and was gone before Rosanna returned from the grocery store.

Chapter 22

You here in Chicago?"

"Doesn't matter. You okay?"

"Yea, I'm fine. Couldn't be better."

"She with you?"

"No. She took an earlier flight. We don't travel together. We'll meet up there. She's still pretty upset. She thinks she's responsible, but I'll explain things."

"You're sure about that?"

"Yea. I'm sure."

"Accidents happen for the right reasons. You said it yourself. The nurse's time had come. She did her job well. We may have been able to use her again. Perhaps Galya too. But that became impossible. Bad luck that Mexican cop had to stumble on to her. We will deal with him later. Right now you're telling me there's nothing left in that dung- heap town for us to worry about. Right? Two dead women. Both served their country well. Clean exit, right?"

"That's right. Clean exit."

"Good. So, they've put you on leave for six months. Right? Good. Report to me after that. Either one of us. Same way as before. We know where you're going. Back to your old post. Vienna, right? Have a good time."

"Wait. Before you hang up. You promise me this action had approval all the way to the top. Correct?"

"You bet. Not to worry."

The airport pay phone went dead. Three seconds before, he heard the encryption "click" on the line. The sound comforted him confirming the secrecy of his call and his work overall. Satisfying. Rewarding. Justified for the good of the People.

I have to trust them. They're my superiors.

Galya's former handler walked toward Gate 31, B Concourse, O'Hare International Airport, Chicago, Illinois. His flight to Austria would leave in an hour and stop in Madrid. The extra six hours to return to his foreign post was of little concern. Six months off was a long time, but he needed the rest. How long had he been with her? Five years? No seven, or more since I first discovered her. Could never understand why she preferred the name Galya over Gloria? If anything it should have been Galya, or Christ, Gloria is so much sexier. G-l-o-r-i-a, you know, like the song. Good song. Man, she was the best ever. No one, by far, could forge handwriting like she could. Personal signatures copied with the greatest skill, undetected by every expert we have.

I knew it. I told them so.

Went through money like shit through a goose. No one seemed to care. And then hooking her up with that jerk-off professor. What a waste. Why couldn't it have been me to enjoy those perks?

But who am I to question?

He found his seat in the waiting area. He would be among the first called to board. He would always fly first class from this point on. Not in government coach. He had the money now.

And then you'd think by putting her away in that hell hole on that trumped up charge would be good enough. But no. After they decided to kidnap the professor she had to go too.

Disposable, is that what they said about her? Like those new baby diapers for my nieces. To top it off, my Agency turns the case back over to the FBI; assigning my old buddies. And putting a woman in charge, no less. Never thought that would happen. Don't really know why. Politics, I guess.

Maybe Gloria knew too much. The nurse sure did.

It was great seeing Gloria that one day they let her out. She was thrilled to be free, but already feeling bad. I could tell. She wanted to get back to work. Itchy fingers, I guess. She would have done anything for me, anything at all, if I could have sprung her for good.

But why use that flaky broad for the dirty work. I told them she wasn't qualified. She lacked the skills, or maybe just the guts. She was not cut out for the job. Can't imagine why someone besides me didn't realize that.

So, again, I had to clean up the mess. But I'm good at it. Didn't have to do much. Ice picks leave such tiny holes, and just a nudge at the right time and away she went.

The gate agent called for his flight. The giant Pan-Am 707 First Class section was still spacious and luxurious. He would sleep only part of the way, dining first on a fine meal and drinking all the wine they would serve. He settled into the soft leather window seat and ordered a vodka tonic.

That cop was smart.

He might have realized something was haywire about that nurse. A soft spot maybe. She let her guard down with him. That guy might be trouble. The only thing I wonder about is what she did with that last vial I gave her. The last big dose. A syringe or a capsule? Both are equally effective. I wonder if she got rid of the leftovers.

No matter, it was in a cough syrup bottle. No one will ever find it.

He sipped his drink and asked for a pillow for his neck. Lobster and a rib eye were on the menu. Ten, maybe twelve hours and then shacking up for six months. I like it when she wears that red striped nurse's uniform for me. The one she took from the nuthouse. Candy stripers, they call them. Sweet candy in my book.

With nothing on underneath and so much to taste.

Life is good.

And who's to say, if that spic cop gets too close maybe they'll let me take him out when I get back.

PART V

Chapter 23

The wheels of the Gulfstream luxury modified military jet hit the runway hard. A steady rain and cross wind forced the CIA-trained pilot to accelerate his approach and brake quickly after touchdown.

His designated landing strip, located at a remote section of Andrews Air Force Base, was the shortest among the maze of hardened reinforced concrete that checker boarded the huge airfield. The jolt brought Thomas Riha out of his fitful fourteen-hour drug-induced sleep. He opened his eyes but saw nothing but the dim overhead lights illuminating the fuselage. He lay supine. As the pilot corrected a sideways skid caused by another strong gust, the sensation of movement, at first, felt like he was careening in a runaway truck. Then Thomas Riha realized he was in an airplane; a jet. He could hear the reverse thrusts of the engines. The tires of the sleek aircraft caught traction and the plane began to slow.

Thomas' senses sharpened. He closed his eyes to activate other sensations. He was warm. Wrapped tightly in something. He tried to move his arms; then his legs, but couldn't. He was restrained. Then he realized the sharp, jackhammer-pounding headache. A hangover like none before. He couldn't have drunk that much.

This is probably just a bad dream.

He was still in his library chair, slamming back another shot, growing angrier by the minute over Galya's absence.

But no. This is too real. And that smell. Is she here with me? Another appealing thing about her. That exotic scent of Chanel reminding him of his Christmas gift.

He opened his eyes to search for its source. Maybe she's finally home.

"Hello, professor. How do you feel?"

He looked to his left into the face of the sorrowful schoolgirl he had jilted just a few short hours before. She smiled. She looked different and even less appealing. The black turtleneck sweater she wore hid the cleavage he once momentarily admired that previous afternoon. Her hair was drawn back tightly in a ponytail. A black baseball cap covered her skull.

"Where am I you fucking bitch?"

Catherine Benson kept her grin intact.

"Now, now professor. You're all right. No one hurt you and no one's going to hurt you if you cooperate. We'll have plenty of time to explain your situation. It has changed, you know. Your classes will be cancelled for some time. All those impressionable youngsters you were mind twisting will go on without your nasty anti-American drivel for quite a while. Let's just say you've been drafted into the service of your country."

Thomas thrust his arms and legs against his bindings in a futile attempt to free himself and attack her. He opened his mouth, intending another profanity.

She gently placed her hand over his gape to quell the impending outburst. He shook his head, pointlessly trying to dislodge it.

"Professor, I will let you speak but you will address me politely. If you don't I will tape your despicable mouth shut."

He relaxed and nodded his head in agreement. "Okay," he managed.

Catherine removed her hand. He glared at her but did not utter another sound.

By that time the plane had completed its taxi and was entering a cavernous hangar. The lights inside lit up the jet's interior like it was noontime in July. Thomas blinked at the sudden glare.

"Who are you?" His speech hesitant, halting, indicating a hint of fear. "Have I been kidnapped?"

"In a manner of sorts," Catherine responded. "You are no longer in Colorado. In time you will know where you are and what your new responsibilities will be. As I said you are not in danger..."

A voice over the intercom crackled with, "Miss, as you can tell we have arrived. When do you wish to disembark?"

"Excuse me, Professor. I will be right back." Catherine rose from her seat next to the bunk-type ledge affixed to the side of the plane's interior fuselage upon which Thomas lay. Thomas tried to follow her movement but his view was blocked by a seatback in front of him. He calmed himself further. He sensed perhaps his life was not in immediate danger. *Why would they strap me down like this and fly me around to wherever the hell I'm at? If they were going to kill me, why go to the trouble? I don't have much money for ransom. Maybe Galya could come up with some.*

That is, if she ever comes home.

The last thought about his vanished lover renewed his misery, prompting him to momentarily set aside his current predicament.

God Almighty, where is she?

Catherine's return brought him back to his present state.

"As I started to say Professor, you are not in danger physically. We will treat you well. You will be comfortable for the most part. You are in the hands of the U.S. Government. My superiors are interested in utilizing your skills to support a special mission."

Thomas' bewildered gaze intensified.

Catherine continued, "We have arrived at our destination as you can tell. I told the pilot to give us a few minutes to prepare to deplane. I am going to loosen the straps around your hands and feet. I advise you not to struggle. If for some unlikely reason you were to get past me, be aware there are at least ten, possibly twelve, heavily armed Special Forces troops waiting at the bottom of the stairs. They will be escorting us to your new home where we will begin our discussions."

Catherine leaned down to address the first band securing Thomas' wrist.

"Don't worry," Thomas whispered quietly in Catherine's ear, his voice turning mellow and syrupy sweet, "I won't give you any trouble. You have captured my curiosity young lady. I am suddenly quite interested in what you plan to say."

Catherine freed Thomas' left hand and started on the right when he added, "And by the way I love the perfume. Where did you get it? Did you rummage through my lover's things after drugging me?"

Catherine jerked back at the snide accusation. Her response was frigid ire. "No sir. The only thing missing from your house is you and maybe your girlfriend. We locked the back door when we left. You should get a security system. Or at least a dog. If you must know, the perfume is mine. A weakness for a little vanity I must say. It was certainly not intended for you."

"Oh dear, please don't take me wrong. I love the scent. If you had worn it during our afternoon tête-à-tête I might have decided to take you up on your rather promiscuous offer."

Catherine reversed her motion and jerked the strap painfully tight around his right wrist. "Don't flatter yourself you little prick." Thomas yelped. She waited for his next move. His free arm hanging off the makeshift cot. He left it dangling. She would have broken it if he had moved.

"My apologies," he finally meekly offered.

"Good. Now be a nice little boy and in a little while we'll get you fed, and showered and tucked away for the night."

"Do you have an aspirin? I have a powerful headache?"

"I'll bet you do. Aspirin coming up."

Within two hours and with his headache nearly gone Thomas rode in a caravan of three black unmarked tinted-glass Ford police interceptor sedans as they sped past the "No Trespassing" sign and onto a gravel, properly groomed circuitous driveway which lead to what appeared from the main road to be a stone façade English castle. The edifice sat just off Route 522 on fifteen easily secured acres ten miles east of Culpeper, Virginia.

Catherine took the journey to the often-used safe house, a place the Agency called Longlea, in the back seat of one of the speeding sedans seated next to Thomas. Despite his loud protests she had handcuffed his tender wrists but unshackled his feet for the trip.

Agent Benson was particularly fond of Longlea. Not only was the main house architecturally magnificent, its outlying buildings accented the property with fine Colonial brickwork, slate roofing, dormer peaks and portico entrances. Being there was on par with vacationing at the best Southern plantation retreats. Agents on special assignment at Longlea were envied by their peers for the comforts of their private quarters, the fine meals served, and the abundant liquor supply.

Certain "guests" at Longlea were not so lucky.

The locals knew little of Longlea. They were told it was owned by an eccentric, very private ex-pat Brit named Baron Fisher who, rumor had it, hosted wealthy tycoons, European monarchs, Hollywood celebrities and high government officials for many spectacular weekend rendezvous. No one ever saw any of these notables come and go. His Excellency Sir Baron was occasionally spotted in town with ascot and cane, tipping his bowler hat to the ladies and sipping afternoon tea at the refurbished railroad station pub. He was polite to those who offered greetings but didn't mix with the populace.

One night local butcher Bill Barton's refrigerated delivery van broke down on Route 522. He managed to push the disabled vehicle off the main road and into a shallow ditch to avoid oncoming traffic, sparse as it was. Bill was tired and a little drunk so he decided to rest in the van's cab before hoofing it into town.

The prospects of a friendly neighbor coming by for a hitchhiker were slim. Just as he settled in for his short nap, much to Bill's surprise, he saw headlight beams off into the distance. He reacted quickly, climbing back up on to the shoulder, planning to present an outstretched thumb for the oncoming driver to consider. As he moved into place he did a double take. There were not one, but five bumper-to-bumper vehicles approaching at a high rate of speed. Overhead Bill distinctly heard the whirling thunder of a helicopter, and looked up to see its bright beacon sweeping side-to-side to cover a wide expanse on either side of the road.

Bill stood in awe as the motorcade sped by. The third vehicle in line, a Cadillac the length of Bill's house, it seemed, displayed fluttering flags on the front fenders and a gold seal on the driver's side door. Bill couldn't quite make out the lettering on the seal but clearly saw the symbolic eagle. Needless to say, no one stopped to pick him up.

In town Bill would tell his story over and over, but most of his customers were skeptical since Bill had a reputation for exaggerating certain instances in his life. He often claimed to have sat next to Elizabeth Taylor at the Plaza Hotel bar in New York City while on vacation. Few believed that story either.

If Catherine had heard Bill tell about the curious convoy on Route 522 that night she wouldn't have doubted him for a second. In certain need-to-know government circles, occasionally made public to ward off inquisitive reporters, the compound was vaguely described as either the National Security Caucus Foundation pavilion, or the headquarters of

American Security Council, or in some instances, the Congressional
Conference Center. Take your pick. Whatever name it went by, Longlea
housed a high-level national security and foreign policy think tank. It was
frequented by the foremost intellectuals in free-world foreign affairs and
strategic defense. It was America's laboratory for debate on how best to
foster U.S. interests worldwide and protect the country and its allies from
destruction either from within or outside its borders.

It was common knowledge among her peers that Lyndon Johnson
favored Longlea over other hideaways including Camp David. His
successor, Richard Nixon, also had a soft spot for the ambiance afforded
by the oak paneled walls, Persian silk carpets, mahogany sideboards,
heavy tapestries, crystal goblets and Tiffany sconces. Nixon also came
here as Vice President to attempt fly-fishing with President Eisenhower
on the shimmering Hazel River, which meandered through the property.
Rumor had it Nixon often became enraged when he consistently
entangled his line in the overhanging tree branches which lined the
shoreline. He clearly lacked the skill of his boss at the fine art.
Eisenhower seldom failed to catch his limit and delighted in chastising his
clumsy vice president.

If the good citizens of Culpeper only knew. But they didn't and
wouldn't until many years later when the Agency sold the property to the
American Chapter of Opus Dei, the much maligned conservative branch
of the Holy Roman Catholic Church demonized by Dan Brown's
depiction in The Da Vinci Code.

On the night Bill Barton gawked bewildered at the Cadillac's
whizzing by on Route 522, President Nixon was reading briefing papers
in the back seat of that flag-fluttering third vehicle, and the last thing on
his mind was a frustrating day casting for trout. He was traveling there for
a summit with his top military and national security advisors over the
planned carpet-bombing campaign in Cambodia designed to bring the
Viet Cong to its knees. Also on the agenda that weekend was an
assessment of Soviet submarine deployment in the Tonkin Gulf some
suspected was designed to discourage American aggression in the region.
National Security Advisor Henry Kissinger was already at Longlea
preparing for a heated weekend-long debate.

Baron Fisher's Longlea was the perfect front to house one of the
CIA's re-educational conclaves. There was no better place to host
clandestine courses in attitude adjustment. Fort Knox was not better

secured. On the opulent upper floors, heads of state, cabinet officers, military brass, pseudo-intellectuals, and just plain political pragmatists laid the groundwork for the next Cold War chess match, while down below the heavily-fortified, soundproof lower floors of Longlea contained the interrogation rooms for many of America's most ardent opponents.

That's where Agent Benson and her colleagues did their best work.

When she and Thomas Riha arrived at Longlea the top floors of the mansion were empty and silent. Not that they would have cared or would the presence of a full entourage of diplomats and saber rattlers really mattered since the bunker beneath was completely isolated and impenetrable. A few like the President and Director Helms knew what went on in the basement at Longlea. And they were generally happy with the results.

At the moment Catherine escorted her captive to his temporary quarters, Helms, for one, was ensconced in his Langley headquarters suite. His orders for Riha's treatment were strict and would be obeyed. By non-violent means if possible he wanted the professor convinced to fully cooperate, accept and execute his mission with an impassioned commitment. The Director would tolerate nothing less from the radical leftist, making it clear that Riha's confinement would become much more difficult to endure if he resisted fully embracing his mandatory task. If all else failed, he would be told his next stop would be FBI headquarters, there to be placed in Hoover's hands directly, with his last stop being a Federal penitentiary awaiting execution for treason.

The process of convincing the arrogant son-of-a-bitch to side with his captors would begin that next morning.

Chapter 24

Galya, meanwhile, couldn't have been happier. She'd been away from Thomas for nearly a week. She was not the least bit lonely. Besides, she was doing superb work having just finished a fine forgery of a scrawling, illegible signature of a Soviet Army major general affixed to an expertly doctored KGB intelligence report which under-estimated America's nuclear ICBM stockpile by five hundred launch-ready missiles. She was unconcerned about the contents of the document she had just endorsed. Her unmatched skill meant no one in the Kremlin could possibly question its authenticity.

She put down her Mont Blanc fountain pen filled with the best blue Russian ink, rotated her stiff neck and stretched her back. She was clad in a sheer rose-colored nightgown. The deep pile carpet messaged her bare feet. The light rap at her hotel room door was unexpected. She had not ordered room service deciding, instead, to sample Italian cuisine at Ronrico's in Larimer Square, an urban hot spot just a few short blocks away. She stood from her chair, slipped on the cashmere-lined robe lying across her bed and walked to the door.

"Yes, who is it," she inquired with some suspicion.

"Room service."

"I didn't order room service. You must have the wrong room."

"I am delivering a bottle of champagne. Compliments of the hotel, madam."

Galya opened the peephole in the door and looked through at a uniformed waiter holding a silver bucket containing a longneck green bottle. It certainly looked to her like chilling champagne. Moisture ran down the sides of the bucket. A starched white towel was draped over the waiter's arm. He tipped his head politely and smiled, knowing she was watching.

"Very well," she said, "That will be delightful."

Galya unhooked the safety latch and swung open the door.

Instead of the waiter marching through with his delivery, a man and a woman, both in dark, closely matching business suits, pushed past him through the doorway. Startled, Galya gasped and backpedaled away instinctively wrapping the robe tightly around her body. "What is this? Who are you? Get out of her. Waiter, call security," she screeched.

"Miss Gloria, Galya Tannenbaum, you are under arrest for felony forgery, theft, impersonating a government official, check kiting, and soliciting for prostitution. You have the right to remain silent. An attorney will be appointed for you if you cannot afford one, and anything you say may be used against you in a court of law. I have a warrant instructing me to take you into custody. Do you understand?" The woman standing to Galya's right extended her hand to present the folded judicial order. The man standing to her left remained a few steps behind to block the door. The phony champagne bearer retreated down the hallway.

Recovering remarkably quickly from the shock Galya responded with, "How dare you. Forgery. Prostitution! You have to be joking. I'm no hooker you bitch. Bring back that champagne!"

And then it struck her. Who would she call? She didn't even know his name. The stranger. Her benefactor. She had no way of contacting him, or anyone else to come to her aid. To vouch for her. The crimes, and they were many, could stick if no one other than she would say otherwise. Thomas couldn't. He knew nothing. And God knows where he is. I think they took him somewhere.

I'm alone. I've been set up. What a damn fool.

She sat on the edge of the four-poster bed. Dejected. Resigned. Her gown falling open. She scanned the paper in her hands. The two intruders, she presumed were police officers, stared at her intently.

Finally, the woman with some kindness in her voice said, "Miss, please put on some clothing. We need to take you in now. Your belongings will be gathered up for you and held securely until your release. You may take your purse after I check it."

Galya looked up from her reading and calmly said, "Oh, yes, excuse me." She laid the paper aside, rose and walked to the closet to pick out her outfit.

That's a real warrant. I can tell. I've been served before and I've forged many of them.

From the moment of her arrest, deep in her gut Galya knew she might never regain her freedom. Her worst fears proved prophetic. After sixty days in the woman's section of the Denver County Jail, unable to post bail because her accounts had mysteriously been frozen, and following an expedited sanity hearing, the District Court judge declared her incompetent to stand trial. She was remanded by the court to the state mental institution for treatment after two clinical psychiatrists maintained her manic depression, paranoia, fits of fantastical delusions and self-destructive aggression were all immediately incurable. The five separate criminal indictments against her would remain outstanding until she was deemed capable of supporting her own defense.

Galya's single court appearance, during which she was represented by a first-year public defender with a caseload that day of twenty, lasted only ten minutes. Galya stood before the court in stoic silence, refusing to defend her actions, or counter the clinicians' assertions about her mental condition. She was resigned in knowing no one would believe a single word about her vocation and the prolific products she produced, so she waited impatiently for the judge to pronounce his indeterminate sentence. At one point during the scant proceedings, in the faint hope her benefactor might be lurking nearby and sweep in to rescue her, she scanned the room for his familiar face. Her hopeless smile was one of resignation not joy at discovering his absence and finding no one to come forward in her defense, including even her harried barrister.

The prostitution charge was the only count the court dismissed. When given the single opportunity to speak, Galya was very lucid and convincing on that one allegation, and the judge believed her.

"Never have I sold my body," she roared when asked by the judge.

Well, maybe just once, she thought as she was led away.

Chapter 25

Captain Victor Bravo closed the file and grimaced is disgust. The last entry was dated July, 1969, close to the date when Galya's confinement began. Victor could tell it hadn't been touched since. He sat in a conference room adjacent to a gaggle of desks, chairs, file cabinets, debris and loud barking cops who occupied the main squad room of the Denver Police Department.

He'd been given access to Galya's file from an accommodating robbery detective who had inherited the cold case file with instructions to be prepared for trial if and when the defendant was deemed ready for the proceedings. She never was and now never will be ready for anything but her grave. Victor was further astonished to learn the obliging cop had no idea Galya Tannenbaum was dead. When Victor shared the news the Denver dick exposed a toothy grin as he pulled his rubber stamp from the desk drawer to mark the case file Closed. Victor stopped him with, "Not so fast detective. We're not sure down south there in what you guys call Podunk Pueblo that she actually killed herself."

"You're shitting me. Here. Take it." He meant the file. "There ain't nothin' in there worth nothin'."

Having finished his reading he convinced the detective to copy the file's contents for him. On his way out Victor asked, "By the way how did you end up with the case? Were you one of the arresting officers?"

"Nope, just got the short straw," he responded.

"So where are they? The cops who brought her in, I mean."

"Don't know. Both resigned some time back. Heard one went back East, maybe with the Feds, Secret Service, I heard, and the other, South, with some cushy job with the Border Patrol."

With the file under his arm, Victor made his way through the maze of cluttered desks, past stacks of coffee-stained papers, and overflowing ashtrays, dodging feet plopped on desks many with prominent shoe sole holes, all without one friendly greeting. Soon he was out the door and down the steps to the headquarters' main lobby. He found a drinking fountain next to the men's room. The water was lukewarm. He stood outside, leaning with his back to the wall for support. Near to where he rested, the faint smell of urine permeated through a pungent, piercing odor of antiseptic cleaning fluid splattered across the floor at the bathroom entrance. The privy door swung open giving the exiting janitor and his swabbing mop wide-sweeping access to the puddle at Victor's feet, forcing him to jump aside to avoid the splash.

Galya's file had noted the Boulder address where she had resided with Thomas Riha. Victor would go there next. He stepped around the nauseating yellow pond and moved quickly toward the heavy brass revolving front doors. They creaked and moaned as Victor pushed his way through. He found his car where he had parked it, as instructed, in a space on the street in front reserved for police vehicles only. As he approached he swore. A bright pink parking ticket, safely secured under the windshield wiper blade, beckoned his attention. Victor snatched the citation up angrily and tore it in half. He walked to a nearby trash bin and watched as the shreds floated down inside to mix with the other trash.

Chapter 26

"Okay Dick, so now we have him. We got him before Hoover could arrest and try him for sedition, or some such thing. Then what happened? Where did we take him for his so-called re-education?" Bud Wheelon asked Richard Helms who was now pouring them both a short glass of fine Kentucky bourbon. Neither wanted ice. Both preferred neat.

"You ever hear of Longlea?"

"Can't say that I have. What is it?"

"It's not an it; it's a place. If you left now you could drive there in little over an hour," Helms added.

Wheelon took a sip. The liquor burned his throat going down but he savored the flavor. It was going to be a long night. Helms had ordered dinner to be served at six o'clock in his adjoining private dining room. Wheelon waited for Helms to continue.

"Longlea is a safe house in the beautiful rolling hills of Virginia just west of here, near the town of Culpeper. Fantastic spot. Love going there."

"A safe house. You love going to a safe house?" Wheelon responded with surprise.

"Again not my bailiwick but what I used to hear was our safe houses were on par with the Tower of London in medieval times."

"Not this one Bud."

"Wait a minute," Wheelon broke in, "I remember hearing about some place out around Culpeper that was used as a sort of fancy retreat; a mansion, English country manor type, for top brass; senior Administration types, military, State Department, more for diplomatic think-tank activities. An alternative to Camp David; not as rustic..."

"You got it. It was Johnson's favorite hangout. Now Nixon claims it as his own. He can get away with just the boys. He likes to play poker there. Kissinger hates the place; says the rooms are too small and complains about the cold floors and drafty windows. Doesn't like the food either. Still a picky bastard if you ask me."

"And you're saying, Dick, this Longlea is an Agency safe house too?"

"That's what I'm saying, Bud. I've been there many times. Upstairs we deal with theory, examining and hypothesizing on every subject from Marine troop strength to the number of shoes in Imelda Marcos' closet. Downstairs, in the well-appointed basement, far from the maddening crowd overhead, we put those theories into practice."

"All right. So Riha's taken to this place called Longlea. I assume we treated him well even though we kidnapped him, probably drugged him, tied him up and hauled him all the way across the country; definitely against his will. That is a Federal crime, you know," Wheelon offered the obvious.

"Yes to all the above. We had little time by our standards to act. We needed Riha to come over to our side, train him, and put him in the field all in less than a year. We found out that he had been invited by the Politburo to a series of events celebrating Lenin's one-hundredth birthday that next April. So we had to move quickly. We put one of our best teams on him. We knew he was going to be a tough nut to crack. The man was so incredibly vehement in his beliefs, or so it seemed. First we had to break him down, dissuade him of his twisted philosophy and then build him back up as one of our own. One on whom we could depend."

"So all of this takes place while our President sits upstairs, shuffling the cards of a poker deck while shuffling fighter jets on the decks of our aircraft carriers," Wheelon proffered metaphorically.

"Good one, Bud, in a manner of speaking, that's precisely what went on."

"Like I said, Nixon was breathing fire down my neck on this one, so I had to go to him privately and explain the situation. I had to buy time. I spilled my guts to the President about Thomas Riha and why I was convinced we could convert him. He had the perfect cover. The Red menace loved him. He even had limited access to Brezhnev. I put my reputation on the line. Eventually, between hands of five-card stud, Nixon came around on my word. He said I had a year to bring Voice of America back louder and stronger than ever, to reach millions of Soviet citizens, not hundreds. It was to be a re-election triumph for him. Carrying the message of freedom to the oppressed while the oppressors remained oblivious."

"Looked good on paper, I bet," Wheelon injected.

"Yea, but I blew it."

From the crystal decanter placed on the corner of his desk Helms poured himself another glass. He offered the silver-spout whiskey-filled container to Wheelon who declined.

Bud allowed his friend a breather before asking, "Do I know the team you assigned to Riha?"

"Probably not," Helms responded after taking a large satisfying gulp. "It was headed by a woman."

"A woman? You have to be kidding," Wheelon came back truly astonished.

"That's right Bud, a woman and a damn good one. One of the best agents I had in the field at the time."

Chapter 27

"How was your breakfast Professor Riha?" Agent Catherine Benson inquired from the doorway of Thomas' single room suite.

"Excellent, my dear," Riha responded. The eggs Benedict were superb, although when the dish is next served, I would prefer quite succulent and tender Maryland crab cakes as opposed to the Canadian bacon if you please."

"I will see what I can do."

"Oh yes, and have the serving come with fresh asparagus. I am not partial to stewed tomatoes."

"I will see what I can do."

Thomas, seated alone at a fine two-person black walnut hotel-style dining table, movable on casters and adorned with a pale yellow muslin tablecloth, wiped his mouth with the matching pale yellow cloth napkin. He set his gaze on Agent Benson's face and said, "You are so lovely. Standing there in my doorway. Extending a most pleasant greeting. I do wish you would tell me your name; your real name, that is. It will be so much easier for my legal team to hunt you and your cronies down for your impending trials."

Catherine Benson could only smile.

"Perhaps in good time, Professor, I may feel you have earned that privilege. But you have such a long, uphill climb, and so many challenges to overcome before such a distinction comes your way."

"Once more, as I have said to you for the past three days, I have no intention of cooperating with you in any respect. I again demand access to a telephone in a private setting to notify my attorney of my whereabouts and criminal confinement. You are guilty of kidnapping, young lady, and I will see you punished to the fullest extent."

"Professor, yes, you continue to be quite eloquent in expressing your views and leveling your threats. All of your countless protests have been fully documented in your file, let me assure you. However today Professor we shall begin a new phase in the evolution of our relationship. One, which you may find less than desirable, I fear. I certainly hope that is not the case, but neither you nor I have a choice in the matter. We will make progress in defining our respective roles and responsibilities irrespective of your resistance."

"Are you threatening me with physical harm?" The tone of Riha's voice had changed. A slight hint of concern crept in for the first time.

Catherine did not respond. She turned to step into the hallway, which separated three other rooms, all of which were of equal size to Riha's and furnished as equally elegant.

"Where are you going you little bitch!" Thomas yelled, his face suddenly flushed. He leapt from his seat, spilling what remained of his espresso onto the right leg of his white linen trousers. "God damn it," he swore, "Come back here. I demand an explanation."

Catherine hesitated and turned back to face him.

"Thomas, it looks like you need to change your pants. You have several pairs, which we brought along from your oversized closet there in Boulder. I shall return in fifteen minutes. Please be ready and make yourself presentable. We have plenty of work to do today."

When Catherine returned to Riha's suite she was accompanied by two large and imposing male colleagues, both of whom were dressed all in white, resembling mental institution orderlies at a place similar to the one where he would soon be told his lover presently resided.

Catherine knocked at his door but did not wait for a response. All three entered the studio suite without invitation to find Riha, now in beige woolen slacks, seated at a red and gold chintz-covered love seat set along the wall opposite the off-white sectional couch that reminded him of the one on which Galya loved to lounge in Chicago. A stunning early 19th century Turkish carpet covered the wide plank, highly polished hardwood floors. His exquisite dining table had been wheeled out by an attendant dressed similarly to Catherine's companions only a few minutes before.

"Professor, please tell me we don't have to handcuff you," Catherine said.

Riha rose from his seat. "No you do not. Where are you taking me?"

"Not far at all. Actually just down the hall. To what we call our community room. Very comfortable. You will find the accommodations quite satisfying. We will begin our work there."

Catherine stepped forward and took Thomas' arm. She led him out the door, turning left for not a short but rather long walk down a narrow, winding hallway. They passed what seemed like dozens of unevenly spaced entryways blocked by closed doors on either side. Her fellow agents trekked two steps behind just in case.

Their day was set to begin at 8 am. Catherine couldn't predict when it would end.

Catherine's assurance of well-appointed, comfortable accommodations for their session proved to be an outlandish lie. When she and Thomas finished their long winding walk and entered the room he was struck by the stark austerity of his surroundings. Grey concrete block walls enveloped him. A cement floor. A square steel table, its legs bolted down, stood in the center of the room. A single-bulb lamp suspended by a long cloth- wrapped cord hung overhead providing the only light. Two steel folding chairs were placed on opposite sides of the table. Wooden, straight-back benches appearing as sterile and uninviting as pews in a colonial church lined the walls on two sides.

Off in the corner was placed an uncovered card table supporting a large commercial grade coffee maker. Paper cups were stacked high on each side. Restaurant packets of powered cream and sugar were strewn about the tabletop. Plastic spoons were jammed haphazardly into one of the cups. The room reeked of burnt coffee. In the shadows Thomas could detect the silhouettes of at least six people seated erectly on the benches. They were silent, unmoving; mannequin-like. He could not tell how they were dressed. The darkness veiled their appearances. Catherine led Thomas to his seat. The temperature in the room was oppressively warm.

"Now I get it. This is where my torture begins. You have captured a scene right out of a grade B Philip Marlowe movie script. Who was your set decorator? Alfred Hitchcock? This room is classic. Couldn't you have been more original?" Thomas sneered.

"Shut up, Doctor Riha, please. You are beginning to annoy me," Catherine said calmly without making eye contact. While seating herself across from his position she turned to face him and added, "You must decide, Professor. All of what comes next is up to you."

She paused, fixed her gaze and began.

"Doctor Riha, you are responsible for making this as pleasant or as unpleasant as you see fit. We are not here to coddle you any longer. We are here to work on your, let's say, outlook on life. We will conduct our business in this room with all of its glamour and charm, and when we are done, however long that might take, you will be returned to your room, and in a few short hours, depending on our progress, the process shall begin once again."

Thomas held her glare.

"Once more, whatever your name is, I say to you and the others hovering around, that I demand to be released immediately and be given access to my attorney who will pursue criminal charges against each and every one of you." Thomas' voice quivered with anxiety and rage.

Beads of sweat had already begun to collect on his forehead.

Catherine removed her suit jacket and from a pocket produced two clean, white cotton handkerchiefs. She handed one to Thomas and kept the other. With hers she dabbed moisture from her upper lip and spoke.

"Professor Thomas Riha, PhD, Russian History, University of Chicago, former U.S. Army corporal with service in Korea. Honorably discharged. You, Doctor Riha, are being charged with treason against the United States of America. If found guilty you will be executed. Probably hung. Evidence at my disposal is clearly sufficient to bring you to trial. Your actions, countermanding the safety and security of fellow soldiers in Korea, were egregious. You cavorted with, aided and abetted the enemy while on active duty. You engaged in overt espionage, revealing secrets to the North Koreans who were conduit lackeys to their Communist benefactors, the Soviet Union, and Red China."

"Preposterous!" Thomas screamed. "How dare you make such accusations. You have no evidence. This is a travesty. I am not a spy. I have never betrayed my country. I was a lowly corporal in the Army. In the communications section. I never had access to sensitive information, and if I had, I would never have provided such things to the Korean military. I demand my right to counsel. What is it? Miranda. Yes, that's it. You have abridged my Miranda rights. I'm no spy, goddamn it. I demand......"

Catherine permitted the Professor his rant for a few moments longer before cutting him off with, "Furthermore, Dr. Riha we have solid information that upon your discharge, and while a student at the University of California at Berkeley, later on the faculty in Chicago and most recently in Colorado, you continued your treasonous acts by funneling state secrets to Soviet agents at the embassy in Washington. You have been rewarded by the Kremlin for your invaluable service with open access to the highest Politburo members; paid cash, perhaps in the hundreds of thousands of dollars; given luxurious accommodations at Moscow hotels and rural dachas; provided willing prostitutes, and finally secretly awarded the equivalent of our Boy Scout Merit Badge for achievements above and beyond the call of duty." Catherine took a breath, then with pinched sarcasm added,

"Come on Professor, you can do better than that. Don't you realize your coveted Soviet medal is about as significant as that which our Boy Scouts earn when they're twelve years old?"

"It was for literary achievement. My books on Russian History," Riha responded defensively; his voice shallow and weak.

Catherine swallowed a wide grin and continued; cutting Riha off again with...

"And about those books and your lectures and public speeches. One of those Boy Scouts we're so fond of in this country could read them and easily conclude the subversive nature of their contents. Your vitriol against America is exceptional, over the top; outrageous."

Thomas came back, emboldened this time. He sat straight up in his backbreaking chair and growled, "Free speech you bitch. I can say anything; write anything, make as much money as I can from gullible liberals, socialists, Communists, whomever, and all you can do is wring your hands in disgust. Envious of my success. That's your problem."

"The First Amendment doesn't count when your outbursts contain coded messages to enemy intelligence officers."

"This is fucking ridiculous. You are out of your mind lady."

Of course everything Agent Catherine Benson, high on the list of favorites of Director Helms' covert CIA operatives, had just said to Professor Thomas Riha was totally false; a bald-face fabrication spontaneously contrived as she had gathered her thoughts after entering the stifling hot room.

She was sweating as hard as her adversary at the moment, but she was giddy with excitement. She loved the challenge presented by the scoundrel seated before her.

The sequestered audience perched on the parson's benches to the backs of the center-court combatants had not made a sound throughout the entire exchange. Catherine knew each audience member intimately. They were close professional colleagues. They were there to witness the proceedings and serve as friendly critics at the end of each session to help Catherine hone her interrogation skills. All had studied Riha's dossier in great depth. They realized his strength and had calculated his weaknesses; the most pronounced being Galya. But before Catherine would play that card she planned to deal several more hands.

"Now Professor. We've soundly established that you are an enemy of the United States. Why is that? Why have you sought to destroy our way of life? To shred democratic principles, to be replaced by a terribly flawed, oppressive system of collectivism where individual liberties and ambition and achievement are trampled by a military dictatorship and bloated, uncaring bureaucracy? You are an intelligent man Dr. Riha. Yes, you came to this country with certain ideals. But let me remind you, you survived the war only by the good graces of a liberated, free society, which rewards inner strength and personal initiative. What happened to you Professor?"

Thomas' gaze was blank. His eyes riveted on her, but his expression was hollow as if he had not heard a word.

"Are you paying attention, Professor?" Catherine asked with concern. She thought for a moment that she'd lost him.

He blinked, appearing to tune back in. "Young lady, you are truly ignorant; more than I first suspected. You have no idea what you just said. Yes, I heard every single, horribly misguided utterance. If you care for my response I will be happy to enlighten you," he offered.

"By all means, holy one. Enlighten me."

"As you wish. Perhaps you are right. Perhaps I am an enemy of the United States. And yes, you are correct, I despise its fundamental principles. They have served only to obliterate the common good of the common man. I cannot put it more succinctly. Free elections, open debate, capitalism running amuck have corrupted this society, leaving a class structure pitting rich against poor; workers against massive corporations; religious zealots against secular adherents.

"My poor, dear lost soul. May I give you a quick lesson quoting the master? One whose words, besides mine, will inspire all in this room?"

"Indeed, we are all ears."

"By the way missy," Thomas interjected, "If you think you can intimidate me by turning up the heat, literally, and confining me to this god-awful chair, you are so sadly mistaken. You have no idea whom you're up against. Frankly I'm beginning to enjoy this little charade of yours."

"Proceed Professor. I can't wait for your next line of bullshit."

"This will be fun. Now listen carefully. Of course my source, my rock, my foundation is Karl Marx."

"I figured as much. Get on with it, please."

"With pleasure. Karl Marx advanced a theory that would become the most useful tool ever effecting a revolutionary upheaval of the capitalist system in favor of socialism."

"As such, the crux of his arguments was that humans are best guided by reason. Religion, Marx maintained, is a significant hindrance to reason, inherently masking the truth and misguiding its followers. Marx viewed social alienation as the heart of social inequality. The antithesis to this alienation is freedom. Thus, to propagate freedom means to present individuals with the truth and give them a choice to accept or deny it. In this, Marx never suggested that religion ought to be prohibited.

"Now, you're going to preach me a sermon?" Catherine rudely interrupted.

"Yes, little girl, a sermon you would cherish if you possessed the least bit of intellect."

"I wait with baited breath you sanctimonious son-of-a-bitch."

"Marx believed Christianity teaches that those who gather up riches and power in this life will almost certainly be punished in the next. He often quoted the phase that it is harder for a rich man to enter the Kingdom of Heaven than it is for a camel to pass through the eye of a needle. I adore that one beyond all others, save what follows."

"Oh, please don't keep me in suspense," she chirped.

Ignoring her sarcasm, he pushed on. "While those who suffer oppression and poverty in this life, while cultivating their spiritual wealth, will be rewarded in the Kingdom of God. From that foundation comes Marx's famous line, Religion is the opium of the people. It soothes them and dulls their senses to the pain of oppression. Thus stands as his mantra to this day.

"Gee, I'm impressed."

"Central to Marx's other theories were the oppressive economic situation in which he dwelt in his day and we, in this society, remain burdened with today. With the rise of European industrialism, Marx, two generations ago, responded to what he called "surplus value." Marx's view of capitalism saw rich capitalists getting richer and their workers getting poorer. The gap, the exploitation, was how he measured the "surplus value". Not only were workers being exploited, but in the process, they were being further detached from the products they helped create. By simply selling their work for wages Marx knew workers were simultaneously losing connection with the object of labor and becoming objects themselves. Workers are devalued to the level of a commodity – a thing. From this objectification comes alienation. The common worker is told he or she is a replaceable tool, alienated to the point of extreme discontent. Here, in Marx's eyes, religion enters. Capitalism utilizes our tendency towards religion as a tool or ideological state apparatus to justify this alienation."

And so it went. Day after day. A week turning into two, then three, then four. Catherine enduring trivial ramblings, lasting hours, with Riha espousing over exasperatingly minute economic and social distinctions between the two super powers.

She grew increasingly impatient but bided her time. She learned to tune him out. Pretending to listen but drifting away at will, Catherine occasionally reentered the noise with snide snippets, which would temporarily distract him. Soon, however, Riha would regain his verbal footing and begin again, relishing in his own unending pontifications, oblivious of those in earshot, caring only to test his charged intellect and to wear down his listeners. On the third day of the fourth week came an admission.

"Yes, my dear, I am alienated from your society as are the workers of this country. Does that make me an enemy? In your eyes, apparently so." Thomas slumped back in his chair, shifting his backside in search of comfort, thinking his performance, once again, had been superb.

Despite the highly annoying self-satisfying gratification Riha took on this day, as he had in days past, Catherine saw her opening. She couldn't wait to heave it back at him.

"Yes, you are my enemy. Your talk is the most hypocritical, foul, gush of nonsense I've ever heard. It's particularly offensive today. Do you, for once, ever listen to yourself?

"Look at you. In your Brooks Brothers wool slacks, matching those you spit up on that morning weeks ago. No, I guess that was your espresso. Those two pairs of pants probably cost more than an average mine worker, or auto plant assemblyman makes in a week. You scum. How can you sit there all prim and proper and proclaim your allegiance to a false revolutionary deity. At least Karl Marx lived the part. He walked the walk, but you, you phony bastard, you get paid to spew your venom and you're chauffeured around in stretch limousines by big-shot union bosses whose drunken, big-breasted women spawn ten carat diamonds out their asses." By then Catherine was out of breath. The room was getting too damn hot again today.

She thought she heard a muffled giggle from the shadows behind her. The first sound in weeks.

But Riha was still sharp.

"You should be kinder to your sex, dearest. It is unbecoming," Thomas scolded. "Besides, looking at you, I can imagine some envy of those more well endowed."

Catherine resisted the urge to cross her arms; instead placed her elbows on the table. She stared deeply into Riha's eyes. She sensed that her latest outburst may have struck a nerve.

He's sensitive to that bit about hypocrisy, she thought.

She decided to pound away on that point.

"Don't you wish you could get your grubby little manicured fingers on them Professor."

Before he could react she pressed on. "Well, let's see. Let's talk about all of those other capitalistic-spirited possessions you cherish. For example, that quite lovely brick Tudor there in Boulder. In the most expensive part of town. Doesn't the president of the University live a block away, and two or three members of the Board of Regents around the corner? And what about those fine furnishings. All those beautiful ceramics. And that art collection. Wasn't that a Faberge egg I saw in the glass china cabinet all lit up nice and pretty? Must have been from one of those Russian plutocrats you hang out with. You see, I took a leisurely stroll around your house while you were slumped down in that genuine calves-leather armchair of yours drooling like a teething one-year-old.

And we could talk about all those vacation trips to Hawaii; Bermuda, and even Rio. Not where you'd typically find the toiling masses lounging on the beach."

Thomas visibly bristled.

She dug at him even deeper.

"And that wardrobe for you lady friend. Or is she your wife? We could never figure that out. Wife, mistress; it doesn't matter. The one you're fucking.

Thomas lunged at Agent Benson, reaching for her throat. It was an easy counter maneuver for her. She slammed his forehead against the hard, unyielding steel tabletop and pinned both wrists flat to the surface. Thomas groaned. The air leaving his lungs. A round of more pronounced snickers could be heard from the cast of observers stationed about the room. And they all remained in their seats. No reason for anyone to come to her aid. She held him down rather effortlessly sensing little resistance.

"Are you okay professor? I hope I didn't hurt you," she said, absent sympathy or sincerity.

"You leave her out of this you rotten slut," he mumbled, unable to speak clearly. Against the table's plane she held down his face as if in a painful vice. His lips puckered under the hammerlock pressure. His tongue unable to function freely. He tried to utter something again but abandoned the effort. A welt began to form above his left brow.

"If you act like a gentleman, and re-take your seat, I'll let you up Professor," Catherine prompted gently.

Riha nodded weakly. She eased up, permitting him to lift his head off the table. A tiny spot of blood had appeared on his forehead. Catherine dabbed the swelling bruise with a tissue, which she retrieved from her pocket.

"I'm sorry, Doctor Riha. It was not my intention to hurt you."

Thomas grimaced and slid back across the table to re-take his seat. He scowled at her and looked away sighing heavily with embarrassment and exhaustion.

She let several minutes pass.

"I think we've had enough for today Thomas. May I call you Thomas? Anyway, I think we made good progress here. Let me escort you back to your room."

When one of the two white-coated escorts swung open the door to

Thomas' heretofore suite he thought they had made a wrong turn down the wrong hallway. His luxurious accommodations now resembled the inferno-like interrogation room he had just left. Steel table. Steel chairs, and a steel-framed twin bed with a tattered lumpy mattress a little less than three inches thick. A single feather pillow, sporting a huge water stain and missing its case, lay at one end. Thomas' knees buckled. Catherine tightened her grip, which kept him from collapsing. She walked him over to the surplus prison bed without resistance or protest. Arriving, he shook loose of her grasp. She stepped back allowing him to gingerly climb up upon his foul-smelling resting place. He brought his legs up into fetal position. Still in his expensive garb he was asleep before she left the room.

She looked at her watch. It was shortly after three a.m.

Less than eighteen hours. Good day, she thought, marvelous, in fact. Moved along much better than I expected. We'll see how it goes tomorrow.

Chapter 28

Victor Bravo, still furious over the parking ticket, found a metered space on the street in front of the Boulder Police Department Headquarters. He parked, exited the vehicle, grabbed his briefcase from the front seat beside him, and to be sure, filled the time on the meter with nickels and dimes from his pocket. After a short distance he mounted the steps to the building. Awaiting him were search warrants for the private residence and the University faculty office of Dr. Thomas Riha. Entering through the heavy-glass front door he approached the desk sergeant who handed Victor the documents upon his request.

"Need anyone to accompany you Detective?" the sergeant asked, who to Victor's surprise, appeared friendly and helpful.

"Don't think so sergeant. I appreciate your help. I'll call if I run into trouble or find one of your citizens unwilling to cooperate, but for now, I won't bother your people."

"What do you think happened to him?" came a question from a uniform patrolman who was standing nearby and had heard Victor's exchange with the sergeant.

"Damned if I know. Maybe you could tell me," Victor responded.

"We turned over every rock in this town looking for that son-of-a-bitch. So did the force in Denver. Nothing. He vanished, man. We had two shifts out combing the foothills, even the Flatirons, looking for him. Nice overtime, but poof, he's gone. You know there was no sign of a struggle in his house. Everything was neat and tidy. Even the dishes were washed. We think some of his clothes were missing from his closet, but a full set of luggage, apparently his, was in the attic untouched. We didn't find his wallet or passport so we assumed he took them with him. I don't think he was kidnapped or anything. I think he went out there somewhere to cry in his beer over his girlfriend leaving him," speculated the young cop who had moved up to stand near Victor.

"Well, now he's really got something to cry about," Victor said.

"Yea, I guess so. Everybody around here is wondering why you're looking into her death. What we heard it was an open and shut suicide."

"Corporal. Is it Black?" Victor looked down at his nametag.

"Yes, Corporal Black," acknowledged Corporal Black.

"Corporal Black, don't you think it's just a little strange that he disappears; then she disappears. She's arrested in a swanky Denver hotel room. He's still missing. She says she doesn't know where he is and doesn't seem to care. Then she's put away in the state mental hospital following an awfully quick sanity hearing, and then some months later manages to smuggle in enough cyanide to kill a herd of horses and uses the whole batch on herself." Victor paused, hesitated, and then added.

"That nut house down in my home town is a lot of things, most of them bad, but one thing it does pretty well is control toxic shit. Hers is the first death from a man-made toxic substance in forty years. People do themselves in down there three or four times a week, mostly by hanging, a few by prescription overdose, more by stabbing themselves or bashing their heads against the wall, but poison, in such as massive dose. No. Hell no, Corporal Black."

Victor kept going. It was the first time that anyone, particularly in his profession, appeared the least bit interested in Galya's death. By that time three other officers had gathered around to hear more.

"You all knew this Riha character better than anyone. Do you really think he walked off from a high paying job; a popular tenured professor and all, with social standing here and some notoriety as a spokesman for ultra left-wing causes, to mourn over an unfaithful mistress?"

"Man I saw pictures of her. She was worth a week's drunk, if you ask me," said one of the officers in the group, which had then swelled to nearly a dozen. A chuckle at the comment came from here and there. The shift was changing. More cops were milling around. Several others stood nearby, curious about the gathering cluster and the stranger speaking to it.

Scanning the faces around him Victor continued, "Didn't you guys have some trouble with him? Or better put, because of him. Were there not threats over some of the things he said? His lectures? Some of his speeches? From what I hear he could stir up a crowd real easy. Didn't you guys think someone might have wanted to teach him a lesson?"

No one spoke. A few in blue began to drift away. Then one in the back whose face Victor could not see, said, "Better back off, detective; like we were told to do. For your own good."

With that, the entire assembly quickly dispersed. Victor looked down at the desk sergeant who was suddenly too busy with his paperwork to acknowledge him any further. Victor, now standing alone, snatched the envelope containing the warrants and made it toward the exit. He found no ticket on his car this time but his anger had returned, mixed with an uneasy feeling in his gut.

It took him nearly thirty minutes to find Riha's address. He had to buy a map at a gas station since he had failed to ask anyone for directions from his fleeing audience of curious cops.

He parked on the street in front. A child rode by on a bicycle. A man next door was mowing his lawn. Typical all-American suburban neighborhood. But not a typical all-American household, Victor thought. He sat in his vehicle taking in the scene. The house and lawn looked well kept.

Maybe the neighbor is mowing Riha's grass as well, not wanting it to go to seed. Also green; someone's keeping it watered. Driveway swept. Scrubs trimmed. Someone's paying attention. It's been several months since the place was vacated. Probably not by choice.

Victor caught the eye of the neighbor watching him from next door. He nodded a greeting. Victor got out of his car and walked across the lawn toward him. The neighbor had shut off the mower.

"Hi," Victor said with a friendly smile. "I'm Detective Victor Bravo. I'm from the Police Department down south in Pueblo. I'm here to inspect the house next door. I'm particularly interested in the woman who used to live here, and of course, Dr. Riha the owner. Do you mind telling me what you knew about them?"

"Which one?" asked the neighbor.

"Which one what?"

"Which woman? You know there were two, both at the same time; one time."

"Oh," Victor said, "The last one. I'm interested in the last woman who lived here with Dr. Riha."

"Mister," began the neighbor, "Pretty soon I'm gonna charge

admission. Or at least something for my time answering questions. You must be the twentieth or maybe the fiftieth guy carrying a badge asking me about them two freaks. The FBI's been here; Denver cops, Boulder cops, the Sheriff, even the IRS. Pretty soon the damn Coast Guard's gonna show up wondering if Riha stole a submarine or somethin'."

"Well, I'm sorry to bother you. I didn't know so many people had been around."

"It's okay. I'm just glad to get rid of them. All three of them. He was an embarrassment to the community with all his clamorin' about the government and such, and she, the last one, pretty as a picture, yet crazy as a loon. The other one, not so bad neither, but she didn't last long. Anyway, loud music. Late nights drinkin'; runnin' around. One time the red head stood damn near naked at her bedroom window. My grandkids, stayin' with us at the time. Got a real education that night, let me tell you."

"Did you know she was dead?"

"What? Really, how'd that happen?"

"That's why I'm here. She died a few weeks back at the state mental hospital in Pueblo. I am investigating her death."

"I heard she got sent there. In the papers, I think. Wow. That's too bad. She was nuts, you know, but still too young. I think if she coulda gotten away from him like the other one did, that being his ex-wife you know, she'd a been okay."

"Well, we're not sure about the cause of her death, so I'm looking into it just to make sure nothing strange went on."

He paused. The neighbor rubbed his chin and looked down as if inspecting his yard work.

"You taking care of the place?" Victor asked, sweeping his arm to indicate the adjacent landscape.

"Na. Someone comes once a week. A lawn service, I think. Not very friendly bunch. Just comes and goes; don't talk to nobody."

"Did you ever see anyone inside the house? I mean, after both of them disappeared."

"No. Can't say I have. Not here all the time, you know, but not too long ago my wife said she thought she saw a woman in there late at night. Flicked on a light for a second; then walked around with a flashlight after that. Thought she looked familiar. She didn't tell me anything about it 'till the next morning, so I can't say who it might have been."

"Well, thank you sir. What was your name, if I may ask?"

"Egbert, Gustav, they call me Gus."

"Nice to meet you Gus. If I have any further questions do you mind if I call you or stop by?"

"Guess not," said Gus. "Haven't had anyone come by for a while. Really, have to admit, it was kinda fun havin' all those people around. A mystery you know, like spooky stuff. Some say he's a secret agent or somethin', like that James Bond character, and she's like one of his concubines. She was a looker; that's for sure. Can't say I didn't take notice of that," Gus smiled and winked.

"Where'd you hear that; about the secret agent stuff?"

"Overheard one of the cops who was here jabberin' on about Riha bein' in cahoots with spies or something. Just talk. They were laughin' about it the whole time. Probably just a joke."

"Yea. Probably just a joke. Thanks for your time."

Victor turned and walked toward Professor Riha's front door.

The envelope he carried containing the warrants also contained the key. Victor pulled out the key and unlocked the door. He stepped inside. Startled, he caught his breath. The house interior was in total ramshackle. Walking through the main floor he found furniture overturned. Books strewed about. Drawers opened and contents scattered. Sugar and flour spread across the kitchen floor. Mouse tracks visible. Moldy lard covering the bottom of the sink. Toilets were clogged with tissue paper. Upstairs, bed linen was piled on the floors and crumpled on the beds. Clothes were ripped from their hangers and tossed about. Sleeves and pant legs severed. Scissors were lying on a bedroom chair nearby. Empty toothpaste and lipstick tubes lay beside the sink; their contents smeared on the bathroom mirror.

From one room to the next Victor discovered most were in worse condition than the one he had left before.

Returning to the main floor Victor stood in the front foyer and again viewed the room in amazement. Damn, the cops said the last time they were in here everything was spotless. Even the dishes had been washed. No reports of any break-ins. Someone was surely on a mission. Searching for something? Burglars or just vandals?

He re-traced his steps from before, thinking, No, it doesn't look like a burglary. This was malicious; hateful fury. Personal. Vandalism doesn't even begin to describe it. Or was it someone trying to cover up a search, to make it look that way?

Victor's mind raced in doubt and contradiction as he reviewed the massive disarray.

He cautiously stepped back into what appeared to be a reading room or library. The shelves were nearly empty with books strewn about. He pulled on a pair of gloves he had stuffed his jacket pocket. Can't touch anything. His eyes scanned the room. Then it struck him. He realized that nothing was broken. Just turned over. Pushed around. Apparently somewhat carefully. Yes, it was a sheer mess, but a neat mess. Like the intruder was protecting the valuables. Except for the clothes upstairs. Paintings were taken down off the walls but leaned against the baseboards.

Why didn't they break something? Slice up the paintings? There's plenty of fine stuff here to destroy, but every nice thing seems to have survived. Even that brass lamp with its lead glass shade is on the floor standing upright.

And that china cabinet. Looks antique. The door is open. Gorgeous thing. Looks like a silver stand there for hard boiled eggs. Awfully fancy for displaying breakfast.

He sat down in a comfortable wingback chair in the middle of the room to observe and think.

Even at that moment Victor was still questioning his decision to be there among the well-executed bedlam. What did he hope to gain by invading Riha's sanctuary? Galya died far away from here. This is not the crime scene. What evidence could he hope to find?

He walked back upstairs to inspect the medicine cabinets.

Nothing but aspirin, shaving cream, laxatives, sanitary napkins. cough syrup and more toothpaste. That would have been too obvious. As if I would find a bottle full of cyanide. Victor chuckled at his childish speculation.

Victor descended the stairway and returned to the library. He spent nearly an hour shuffling through papers on the floor and those remaining in the desk.

He found nothing of consequence. Only unpaid bills, travel brochures mostly about site- seeing in Eastern Europe and the USSR of all places, and checkbooks and bank receipts.

When he finished empty handed and frustrated he reached for the telephone on the stand next to the reading chair fully expecting the line to be dead. It wasn't.

Someone's still paying the utilities.

He called the desk sergeant who was not too happy to hear from him and reported the scene he had discovered. Soon a squad car arrived. Victor led the two patrolmen through the house. They casually walked about, taking a few pictures, said little, and were done in about twenty minutes. Victor asked whether detectives had been called. Neither knew, saying they were told to inspect the damage and report back to the commander on duty.

"Are you going to secure the premises? Victor asked.

"Weren't told to," one replied.

Victor looked away, shaking his head. He watched the two officers leisurely stroll back to their patrol car, get inside and drive off. Victor stepped outside and locked the front door. Gus was in his yard again, pruning a bush. Victor waved. Gus waved back. Victor would now try to find Riha's office. He had a map. It was leading him nowhere.

Chapter 29

Agent Benson had decided to skip a day. To let it rest. Just for a day. The day before she had thought it best to permit Professor Thomas Riha, soon to become a major figure in America's Cold War intelligence apparatus, to think about her closing arguments before she went at him again. Let him ponder his fate. Besides she needed a break herself. She wasn't sure why, but she needed time away from him. He hadn't worn her down. It was something else.

What is it? Recently, why did she find being with him a tiny bit titillating? Exciting. Possibly erotic? No that can't be. Fuck no! I detest the man.

Catherine had the covers pulled up to her chin. Her head resting on a fluffed up feather pillow. She was wide awake. Lying on her back. Her warm bed now not so comfortable. Sleep had left her long ago. She was focused. Rigid as she should be; yet this was really bothering her.

How could she feel anything but total disgust for this fundamental jerk? This self- absorbed narcissistic bastard who openly proclaimed his hatred for her country. He was her prey. Sitting in her sights. Especially now. A target for her taking. Someone she was about to turn. No doubt Thomas Riha was a man who presented an intellectual Mount Everest to conquer. He'd proven that. A rousing jousting match of words and emotions. Nothing else. This was her job. She had to hate him. She had no choice.

Wait a minute. Why am I questioning myself? I had him by the balls the day before yesterday. Should I have squeezed harder when I had the chance? Made him scream. I was in total control but then I let him go. I gave him time to regroup. Why did I allow a whole day to go by without seizing that part of his manhood again?

Catherine's day the day before was spent in debriefing sessions with her back-bench observers. She had announced early that she needed their critiques regarding the action which had taken place the previous day and to plan a strategy for the upcoming round. Catherine was ambivalent from the start. She neither needed their commentary nor wanted it. She knew that. What she wanted was an excuse to separate from him for a time, but it took her a while to come to that conclusion. Now she hated herself, admitting this flaw; a deep, wide gash in her otherwise steel-plated armor. She was the Director's favorite, by God, and what was going on between her legs or somewhere else in her fucked up anatomy had to be dealt with. Now!

Catherine turned on her side, slamming her fist into a pillow bunched beside her. She winced at the thought. She was attracted to him. No! He couldn't have that effect on her. Christ, this is awful. Was it his comment about her breasts? That spiteful remark about her wishing they were bigger. Suppressing the urge to show him he was wrong. How ridiculous. Or was it his obnoxious assumption she wanted to sleep with him that day in Boulder. Did she?

Catherine ripped off the blanket and jumped to her feet. She stood by the bed; Marine erect. Her standard nightwear tee shirt and gym shorts emitting a locker room odor. She craved a long, hot shower. She would not permit another crazy thought to muddle her brain. Catherine quickly stripped and stood naked in front of the mirror hanging above the dresser. She looked okay. Better than okay. Yea. Small tits. Perky. But great ass. Flat stomach. Biceps and forearms sculpted yet feminine. Let it grow, they like it bushy; down there. Shapely legs. She could run ten kilometers in under forty minutes. She hadn't had anyone for a while. That was the problem. Little time and too little effort. She decided to address her immediate problem.

The steaming water cascaded around her. She found her pleasure with little effort. Satisfaction without the complications. Only she could hear the moaning.

Despite the shallowness of her gratifying exercise Thomas Riha should anticipate a horribly trying day ahead of him.

What Agent Benson didn't know while in the shower preparing for the day was that the Professor had grown weaker, not stronger, in expectation of another grueling round of inquisition. The day off had done him more harm than good. In fact, his respite had worn him down even more than her intimidating words and the star-chamber setting of the day before. His twenty-four-hour confinement in the stark dungeon-like surroundings had contributed to his gloom, but his conditions, and her infantile attempts to coerce, were trifling in comparison to what he could normally withstand.

While lying on his metal cot staring blankly at the ceiling he had been reminded of his first few visits to the USSR and his treatment at the hands of a suspicious ruling oligarchy. His current accommodations were paradise in comparison to the Moscow holding pens in which foreign interlopers were placed until the KGB could verify that individual's true intent for their uninvited visit.

Thomas had convinced himself that the skill of his Russian captors far surpassed the temperate grilling of the temptress currently posing as his foremost foe. The Russians were the best, and back then he was at his best. Because he was on a mission. A mission to prove a point. He was then and now dedicated. Defeat in his quest to become a true friend of the Soviet Empire was out of the question. After three trips into the den of the Russian bear, countless nights freezing in ill-heated cells, plenty of rancid food and an even greater number of monstrous interrogators, Thomas Riha had emerged with a clean bill of Communist health. His perseverance in offering a consistent line of Marxist-Leninist logic, the Red duo's answer to every social ill, gradually earned him monumental respect as a rare American Soviet sympathizer. His reputation had grown quickly, beginning with the lowest of the night shift Gulag guards with whom he could converse freely, through the KGB intelligence bureaucracy, and in to the upper echelons of Red Square society. That journey was hard. The risks were greater with each step. It took guts. He had suffered but it was worth it.

Here, where he is now, is child's play. Given the time the day before to think clearly, Thomas saw the old pedantic pattern of brainwashing. His clear mind sorted through the course of events.

His first weeks in captivity were unremarkable. Frankly more bothersome than mind- altering. Accommodations were acceptable. Now, with this childish change in tactic, came a temporary headache, indigestion and a sore back from an old mattress. A nuisance was all. They didn't like his politics to the point where someone high up decided to make him an example. An example of what? Lively oppositional debate? And an example to whom? The college crowd?

I already have most of them. This country has lost its youth to my message. I've been on my soapbox for ten years. Why come after me now? They must have some sort of plan. They're not going to kill me. They would have done that already, so they hope to use me in some way. Twist and turn me into one of them.

Ha! Thomas laughed out loud. I got it. It's obvious.....A counterspy. Hilarious!

Here in this hellhole his only mission remains resistance. Stiff and unrelenting.

Thomas sat up. The bedsprings creaked. A broken wire poked through the cushion to scrape his fleshy backside. He barely noticed. Unconsciously, he rubbed the annoying scratch as he stood and began to pace his stark surroundings.

That's the silly game we're playing. Like the cruel trick the Japanese foisted on American prisoners during World War II. Or what the Viet Cong did to American fighter pilots a few years back. First you treat them well. Give them good food, new clothes, a nice bed, and then you beat them to a pulp and slam them into the worst God-forsaken conditions ever known to mankind. Then comes the promise to return them to comfort if they'll only betray their country and denounce its world-dominating intentions. Pretty basic stuff, Thomas concluded.

Elementary, you mousy cunt. For a moment I gave you more credit.

I still think you'd fuck me if I could get you alone.

That bitch's shallow motive is to bully me. Knock me off course with treasonous allegations she knows could never be proven. The Russians tested my loyalty. And I met that test. But these scoundrels aren't doing that. Their plot is different. The KGB never asked me to spy for them. The reason was obvious. I was too high profile. I was better fodder for Communist propaganda than if I was shuttling microchips stuffed up my ass.

With that Thomas' musing ceased. He abruptly halted his stride. It hit him like a blow to a kneecap. He sat, unable to take another step. Up to that point he had cleverly pushed aside the haunting notion. She had said it. She threw it out there for him to grasp, taste and smell. Like a rotting half-eaten carp washing up on a lakeshore.

What the Russians had, but never used, was Galya. But these people might. Galya changes the rules. Her presence, or even an allusion of her involvement, could be his downfall. Mentioning her name, while only in passing, was enough for Thomas to turn from stone to putty. Shielding her took precedence over his current predicament, and tore away his resistance to accept whatever these criminals have in mind.

She knew I would repel at the utterance of her name; then attack in her defense. Galya's too precious to me.

Keep her out of this. She has no role.

Wherever she is. I have to find her.

Chapter 30

Victor Bravo stood at the backdoor to Dr. Thomas Riha's Boulder, Colorado residence watching the beginning of a spectacular sunset.

They're always like this; this time of year, Victor thought. Love the sunsets.

His eyes momentarily dropped to span across the expansive lawn to the fence and the wide alley beyond. The gate connecting two lengths of the fence stood open. He didn't place any significance on what he saw.

Victor was tired, having risen at 4:30 that morning to complete some routine paperwork before driving the one-hundred-and-thirty-odd miles north to downtown Denver, and then the next thirty-five miles or so, west to Boulder. He was tired of the rude, condescending attitude of his fellow law enforcement officers; their way of letting him know how little they appreciated his presence and how much they were put off by this questioning. This should not be unfriendly territory, but in his experience, when cases took him north into the Capitol City and its suburbs, he was often treated with near disdain as a hayseed Barney Fife-like-character chasing a stray hound dog down a dusty Mayberry street. Cops from Pueblo were second-class citizens among cops from the Big City. Always have been, always will be.

No matter, Victor shrugged, turning from his westward view over Boulder's foothills to view Thomas Riha's cyclone-hit kitchen one more time. He was content with his status as a professional, knowing his acumen matched or exceeded his counterparts, regardless of the jurisdiction, which had handed them a badge. He'd go at this one alone, like he did most. In fact he preferred it that way.

He had spent just an hour at Riha's office. When he arrived it had looked like a maid service had been in there a full day. Nothing was out of place. It was spotless. Even the professor's black granite penholder, with a Soviet Hammer and Sickle Medallion embedded deeply into its two-inch thick base, was perfectly centered in the middle of his superbly carved mahogany desk. Not another object was close to his apparent prized possession except for a small, elegantly decorated glass shade reading lamp located in the desk's right hand corner. Victor had noticed there was no electrical cord feeding into its base. He carefully picked up the lamp to discover the wiring snaked down through a hole in the desk top, measuring the exact same diameter, to plug into an outlet in the floor. No clutter whatsoever. Not a speck of dirt to be found.

"He always kept it that way," said the security guard who had escorted Victor through the labyrinth of faculty offices to the space once occupied by the vanished professor.

"He was a neat freak; that's for sure. One night, I guess he was working late, I heard him yell and scream at the janitor for putting his waste basket back on the left side of his desk instead of the right side. I thought he was going to punch the poor guy. I came running when I heard the commotion. He backed off when he saw me, and the janitor ran in the other direction," recited the watchman.

"Thanks, Victor said, "It sure is clean and tidy. Now, if you'll excuse me, I need to concentrate while I'm here."

"Surely," was the reply as the guard shut the door, leaving Victor to his work.

Which had been halfhearted. Victor's instincts told him scouring Riha's office was a futile waste of time. Hundreds of volumes of books, many with Russian language lettering on the spines, lined his floor-to-ceiling shelves. Fine dark oak file cabinets with hanging folders precisely separated by class and lecture topic, semester by semester, all nearly the same thickness, hung systematically in each drawer Victor had pulled open. Soon he grew weary of looking at it all. Why would he hide anything here?

Riha was open about his radicalism. He was a self-proclaimed celebrity in his field. It wasn't as if he cared what others thought. He went about his business each day with an ego as big as the football stadium one could see outside his office window, and he tempted anyone to tread into his inner sanctum. When they managed, they had to be invited and certainly picked up after themselves.

After a few perfunctory inspections of desk drawers and an armoire, which contained a decent supply of liquor and an expensive black cashmere overcoat suspended by a padded silk encased hanger, Victor, inexplicably hesitant to disturb anything for fear of ghostly reprimand, returned to Riha's home for a second look. It was 6:45 pm when he arrived back at the house. Gus was apparently inside. His lawn looked like a putting green.

Like a gardener sowing precious seed, Victor tip-toed through the kitchen, stepping gingerly over a rows of flour and sugar crisscrossing the floor, to ascend the stairs to the master bedroom for the fourth or fifth time. He had lost count. Something up there didn't belong. Like Galya's multiple reading glasses and the almonds and apricot kernels in the bowl on her nightstand. This time he had brought along his 35mm Nikon camera with flash to record the scenes inside.

It was getting dark. He was glad he had remembered the flash. An orange glow cast by the descending sunrays was fading behind the jagged mountain range to the west. Victor turned on the wall-mounted light switch. Sconces above a corner-positioned tiger maple vanity provided sufficient brightness. Then he saw it. Small and much less pretentious by measure than the grace and style of other accouterments about. A hand-embroidered lace cover, reminding Victor of one accenting his grandmother's dining table, was draped over the vanity. Exactly in its center and capturing the light from above was a sparkling gold-linked necklace delicately displaying a tiny diamond or perhaps zirconium substitute; Victor wasn't sure. Victor bent over to inspect it closer. The necklace formed the shape of a Valentine heart with the stone at its bottom point. He couldn't tell if it was fake or real. He didn't touch it, whatever it was. Curious though, he thought.

Just lying there on exhibit for everyone to see. Certainly not an object to admire that much. Could be Galya's. Did she wear things like that? Probably not. Too cheap. Could be for a friend you didn't care much about or for whom you couldn't afford more. Could be for a child for that matter. Not a voracious lover.

Victor decided to leave the necklace where it was. He took four pictures of it from various angles, and then discovered he had only twenty frames to his film roll, so he would have to conserve the rest to adequately record the condition of the house interior. After two more tours through the ramshackle mess, using up his film but finding nothing of additional interest, he called it a day. He again locked the front door on his way out. He would keep the key in case he needed to return.

Victor kept himself alert on his long drive home, listening to the rumble and strife in the Big City on the Denver Police radio frequency, and thinking through what he had learned and wondering what he had missed.

Why the reluctance to release the files?

Why all the ambivalence about this case, or were they simply overwhelmed with too little manpower to care?

By the time Victor switched off his scanner to catch a baseball game on the big AM station that covered a four-state region, he had heard three DOA's broadcast from the City's General Hospital; two from gunshots, one from a pipe bomb. Minor league baseball, but baseball just the same. Better than homicide reports, he easily concluded.

Most of all, why the warning to back off from that unseen cop in the back of the crowd? Was that truly a threat, or just telling me I have no business playing in their backyard?

Why the mess in Riha's house? Who would do that? Why with such deviant precision?

And what about the necklace? The heart shape it was in just didn't happen.

Victor arrived home at 12:20 am. Nearly a twenty-hour day. Like several before. He fell into bed, alone again. Rosanna and his children were with her mother now going on three full weeks. I'll deal with that later, was once more his fleeting thought, and during that restful night, he was able to shut off the nagging questions that clouded his consciousness and had robbed him from hearing the final score of the game.

Chapter 31

"Sleep well Professor?" Agent Benson inquired from her position planted in the doorway of Thomas Riha's newly redecorated solitary confinement-like cell. As before she hadn't bothered to knock, although when she turned the key the loud crank of the unbolting lock alerted Thomas to her dreaded but anticipated arrival.

He resembled a condemned prisoner. Long gone were the pleated slacks and Egyptian cotton shirts, replaced by a jailhouse jumpsuit, grey in color, zipping up the front for easy removal. Also fleeting was the memory of his alluring, well-groomed, clean-shaven, yet purposefully unruly appearance.

Catherine silently chastised herself again. How could I be so stupid? There's nothing to this chump.

"You look a mess, Dr. Riha," Catherine offered with a visible smirk. "Your accommodations unsuitable? Perhaps I can do something about that." She stepped inside revealing the presence of the two dressed-like-psychiatric-ward enforcers who blocked the doorway double deep.

Thomas refused to acknowledge her, instead choosing to inspect his grimy fingernails as if he had just emerged from a summer spa with a manly manicure. He sat with knees crossed. The rubber sandal of his right foot flapping against his heel in drumbeat fashion. Catherine crossed the room and took the empty seat opposite him. She waited expressionless. After a moment, apparently satisfied with his cuticle review, Thomas dropped his hands to the table, which displayed the same grey metal motif as the one in the formal interrogation room. He smiled suggestively, and cooed, "If you tell your boys to leave us, I'll give you the ride of your life. I'll bring bliss to that pliable pulsating pussy of yours, in such a way you'll genuflect on my hard cock like a wildcatters oil rig drilling in the Texas panhandle."

Catherine didn't flinch. She held his hysterical gaze. He grinned. His breath stunned her like taking a whiff from an open sewer. His teeth yellow stained.

"Very poetic," Dr. Riha. "I didn't realize you were so adroit at pornographic lyrics. It must have taken you hours to come up with that."

Riha burst into uproarious laughter.

Minutes passed. She was silent. Remaining stoic. He abruptly stopped his outburst. Leaning closer he pointed his filthy finger close to her face.

"You have crossed the line." His voice quivered. His finger shook. He withdrew it and clinched a fist matching his other one resting on the table.

"Dr. Riha. Are we ready to begin sensible, adult discussions about why you are here and what my people have in mind for you?" Her tone was subdued, even gentle.

He was resigned. Talk of Galya had broken his resolve.

After a deep sigh he said with equal sincerity, "You must promise me that she won't be harmed. She will be protected at all costs. She must not in any way be implicated if my impending acts might threaten her freedom. I demand that she have financial support sufficient to maintain her lifestyle, and that I be given ample opportunity to communicate with her frequently including prearranged, private conjugal visits." Riha paused.

Catherine grimaced, then smirked and nodded in acknowledgement. The bastard is still thinking with his dick. Even at a time like this. He sure has his priorities.

She resisted a broad smile waiting for more. Instead of further demands, he was pleading, "Where is she? Do you have any idea? I am desperate for confirmation of her whereabouts and safety."

It was Catherine's turn to lean closer, but not threatening, she said, "We have her in our care. She has been taken into protective custody until such time as our arrangements with you can be finalized. She will not be harmed or intimidated. She has no idea what our discussions have been or will involve. Nor will she in any way be involved in your future activities, assuming you continue to cooperate. At a point in time she will be returned to your outstretched arms, and both of you will be free to go with the blessings of the United States Government, along with a sizable stipend for your time and inconvenience."

Almost all of Catherine's forgoing pledge had been totally fabricated. She was not partial to Galya's handling, nor was she privy to what the Agency had in store for her. She did know that Riha's lover was cordoned off somewhere where she could be closely monitored and influenced if need be. Catherine could only assume Galya was unharmed and safe, but she was clueless whether the length of her confinement was tied to Riha's potential service, or whether she would be compensated either with money, or sex, or freedom, or all three.

Catherine's words seemed to soothe her target. He fell back in his hard metal chair and sighed again. His eyes were closed. She thought she detected him mouthing the words, "Thank God," but corrected her impression with the notion that Communists don't believe in God, so why should Riha, this avowed atheist, go there?

She gave him time to collect his thoughts.

Coming out of what she surmised was a love-lost trance he said, "Okay. Tell me what you want me to do."

Thus began Thomas Riha's indoctrination as a secret agent for the country he despised.

PART VI

Chapter 32

"So Dick," Bud Wheelon began, "There's this super female agent of yours whom you entrusted with a career-saving assignment, and at some point I think I just heard you say you blew it. May I ask what you meant by that? Apparently you're still on the job, so something must have happened to; let's say it politely, save your ass."

Helms couldn't suppress a grin at his friend's poignant observation.

"Well for now anyway, until Church's Senate Committee has their way with me," Helms reminded both himself and his friend.

The Director hurried on.

"Bud, you have to understand. We fully expected this little prick to put up a solid wall of resistance to our request for his help. We planned, and at first my agent tried all the standard ploys from patriotic appeals, which he literally scoffed at, to accusations of treason, to damn near extracting his tongue with a pair of pliers. But he shrugged her off, clamoring for his lawyer and leveling counter-threats to bring kidnapping charges."

"For which you were certain to have been found guilty," Wheelon interjected.

Helms ignored his friend this time.

Wheelon probed further. "You still haven't answered my question. How did you blow it? Sounds to me something had to have happened to bring his guy around rather quickly. Records show Voice of America continues to broadcast free of Soviet signal jamming. This fellow did something right, motivated by some force, and I doubt he's missing a tongue."

Helms hesitated. Despite his absolute trust in Bud Wheelon there were still need-to- know matters that only the Director could determine were subjects to share. Wheelon sensed he had sailed into those unchartered waters with his old boss. He would go no further. Ask nothing more. Awaiting a response.

Helms eyed the remaining liquor in his glass. He was tempted but resisted refilling it.

"We anticipated a long protracted cat and mouse game with Riha before we could break him down. Part of that plan was to take out his girlfriend," Helms said while staring at his distorted reflection in the empty crystal tumbler he held in his hand.

As if ducking for cover Wheelon lurched backwards in his chair, unintentionally slinging the remaining nearly melted ice cubes out of his glass onto Helms' lovely Persian rug. If he hadn't been in a wingback he may have landed face up on the floor.

Before Wheelon could come back with the logical query as to what the Director meant by "take her out," Helms hastened to add, "No Bud, not literally. She was a pawn in our chess match with this fellow. We had to take her out of circulation. Control her whereabouts. We had to make sure it was impossible for her to contact Riha or vice versa, and in so doing, expose the mission. It was part of the plan. After seizing Riha we had to prohibit them from reconnecting, because if they did, we knew he would gain enough strength from her to resist us indefinitely. He depended on her immensely. It was strange how a man of such misguided intelligence relied so heavily on that woman for his strength and courage.

"So, we had no choice but to turn on her. Remember she was an incredibly valuable asset. We sacrificed someone whose skills surpassed those of our most nimble counterfeiters. Her sweeping stroke with that untrained pen of hers produced results far beyond the detection capabilities of any human or machine. She was the very best. At the pinnacle, you might say. To no longer have access to her talents set the Agency, in this particularly unseemly arena, back many years.

"Once Riha knew we had her, he cracked. Weeks went by attempting to turn him. With her now part of the equation, it only took three days. We were amazed how quickly he gave up. Her effect on him was astonishing."

"Where is she?" Bud cautiously queried.

Helms appeared not to have heard, but Bud knew he did. He knew he was again close to the edge with the Director, but by the way Helms carried on about Galya Tannenbaum, something beyond the mere loss of a master forger with a special flair had truly affected him emotionally. Wheelon plunged ahead even though for the moment Helms had remained silent, looking past him, refusing to respond.

"She's dead isn't she?"

"But we didn't kill her!" Helms exploded in a rage and slammed his fist to the desktop.

"Jesus Christ Dick," Wheelon said calmly in an attempt to quell his friend's fury, "I know the Agency wouldn't go that far, not for something like this. Tell me how she died."

Helms looked spent. Wheelon waited for him to regain control. Helms rose from his chair to resume his pacing.

"We had her arrested on trumped-up felony forgery charges. The Denver cops were duped into believing she was guilty of a number of offenses. She spent a few weeks in jail. Second offender, you know, flight risk, so bail was refused, and then we expedited a District Court hearing on her case convincing her attorney to, in turn, convince her to plead to temporary insanity. She was told if she didn't she would head straight to the penitentiary; this time for a minimum twenty-year sentence, all in maximum security. She took the bait after being assured her time at the state mental institution would be limited, conditions much better, and the chance for early release much greater when her mental state improved."

Helms was exhausted. He found one of a matching pair of button-tucked black leather couches positioned in the exact center of his office suite too enticing to resist. He lay down heavily, closing his eyes to shut out the world including specifically Bud Wheelon whom he knew would continue peppering him with questions.

Wheelon allowed a measured time lapse to occur. Moments into the interlude he was grateful when a gentle knock on the door announced delivery of their dinner. Served on a portable fold-top two-person dining table, the waiters were quick to present the meals, pour the water and sensible portions of wine, and scurry out the door without a word for fear of disturbing the boss from an apparent deep slumber.

Helms was not asleep; rather revived but still supine, he said, "Bud, let's continue with these unpleastantries over dinner."

As they ate Helms became more explicit.

"All along we had a trusted field operative assigned to Galya. From the moment he discovered her talents while in prison the first time, to when she died, this individual saw to her every need. He handled her assignments for us. He guided her movements from the first staged encounter with Riha at the book signing, through their love affair in Chicago. Then her search for the surrogate wife; their move to Colorado, the divorce, and finally his cohabitation with Galya in Boulder. Through our agent we paid her handsomely. At the right time Galya was told that Riha would be leaving for extended periods of time. We were surprised she showed little emotion to that announcement. Frankly, she appeared to embrace the prospect of his prolonged absences. We were fearful that their relationship was deteriorating. This prompted our move against her and our actions with him. Plus the fact the Big Anniversary celebration in Red Square was fast approaching."

Wheelon sat listening intently, yet by the moment growing anxious for an explanation about the death.

"When she was incarcerated, or better put, institutionalized we planted a female on the inside of the hospital to watch over her. Wouldn't have been smart to have our agent, her handler, showing up at regular visiting hours. Turns out this woman was inexplicably poorly trained. I was not aware of her inexperience in operations such as these, relying on the recommendation of our field agent who recruited her for the assignment. Later we learned they had had a prior relationship, possibly intimate, which most assuredly distorted his judgment," Helms said, and quickly added, "That's how I blew it initially."

Wheelon could not hold his tongue with that last remark, saying, "Come on Dick. How can you blame yourself for that? We all have to rely on certain decisions made by our agents in the field. You can't take responsibility for actions at that level when you're sitting here in Langley running the whole goddamn Agency."

Helms ignored his friend's effort to console. "She was completely worthless. Galya Tannenbaum was murdered right under her nose." Helms rasped with scorn at his own words.

In shock Wheelon spat out. "You didn't say she was murdered!"

Helms broke the glare leveled at him by his friend. Looking away, he said calmly, "Yes, unfortunately it appears that way."

"How?" Wheelon exclaimed, "How was she murdered?"

"Poisoned. Cyanide. Heavy dose, either all at once or administered ruthlessly over time until her system broke down completely. Essentially she was tortured. Nearly blinded before death. Truly a heartless act."

"Do we have any idea who did it?" Wheelon probed.

"No. Drawing a blank so far. But another death has occurred which makes us wonder. A nurse on duty the night of her death."

As if to expel it all at once, Helms blurted out, "And now she's dead, and the bitch assigned to protect Galya has run off with our trusted agent."

Startled, Wheelon gasped and nearly choked on a piece of the succulent tenderloin.

Shaking his head in disbelief or perhaps denial Wheelon was surprised when Helms provided even more.

"The nurse died in an automobile accident a few days after Galya's death. We believe it was an accident. No indication of foul play, however there is evidence that she was emotionally distraught at the time, driving too fast in route to a relative's house, losing control of the automobile, which plunged into a ravine. Killed instantly, according to local authorities."

Helms gulped down the last of his wine. Wheelon did the same.

When he finished the delicate cabernet Wheelon spoke first. "Where's our field agent, Galya's hander? What does he have to say about things in general?"

Helms responded with little hesitation. "Nothing. He's clammed up. Assigned back to Vienna, where he's going to stay; frankly in a desk job, until we can get rid of him. Early retirement, not to worry."

Bud struggled to shed his astonishment and managed a smile in saying. "Wasn't suggesting otherwise."

"And the girlfriend?"

"We fired her on the spot once we found her with him in Vienna. Can't do anything to her. At least she's off the payroll."

Helms continued. "Looking back, trusting those characters was my second big mistake. After Galya's death our agent started making noise about orchestrating a cover up of some sort. He wanted to get in the way of local police investigating her death. One fairly prominent detective in particular. This guy, a Captain, we're told, is extremely bright, meticulous and thorough in his investigations; especially homicides."

"His name is Victor Bravo. Appears to be a fine man. A great cop. We've gained access to his reports; that is, once we sent our rogue packing off to Austria, we worked through proper channels to silently peer over Bravo's shoulder. At first he suspected an intern psychiatric physician, whom to our utter dismay, was screwing Galya regularly..."

"This can't get more bizarre," Wheelon brashly interrupted.

Helms again ignored the comment and continued, "Be that as it may, Captain Bravo pounds his guy into the ground with intense interrogation, expertly conducted from what we can tell, until he's convinced the sorry bastard is innocent. In fact, he determined this would-be shrink was madly in love with her and had planned to help her gain an early release, perhaps attempting to falsify her treatment records."

Without invitation Wheelon once more offered sarcastically, "I suppose she could have found a way to forge them quite effortlessly."

"I suppose she could," Helms acknowledged.

"So Bravo cuts him loose but makes sure he's stripped of his temporary license to practice and he high tails it out of town. Right now he's in Vermont studying to be a chiropractor."

"Still alive?" Wheelon edged in cautiously.

"Still alive," Helms confirmed.

"This local cop also interrogates the nurse. He's suspicious of her, it seems, and has her followed. The Keystone cops on duty lose her, and the next thing he knows she's cold on the ground at the bottom of a ravine. So far, things haven't gone well for him or us in this nasty little affair," Helms offered the obvious.

"That's an understatement," Wheelon confirmed.

Helms became abrupt. "Remember, Bud, we wanted Galya back. She was there in that nuthouse only temporarily. She was a priority asset, damn near irreplaceable. So her death dealt us a severe blow, but after learning about this local cop's innate capabilities I decided to leave him be; let him do his job. I think he will eventually find her killer. Sure we will help in our own way if possible, but I would not allow him to be interfered with.

"In the meantime we turned our attention back to Thomas Riha, who at the time, only knew his lover was in our custody. He did not know where or for how long, only that we had her and she was safe......."

His voice trailed off. He looked for more wine but the bottle he shared with his friend was empty.

Chapter 33

Agent Benson had felt it was necessary to relocate Thomas Riha before his new vocational training began in earnest. Although the Longlea setting was ideal for coercing selective captives into service for the U.S. Government, she determined, and her superiors agreed, that the newest and perhaps most unlikely secret agent should receive his schooling at a facility far better equipped for such purposes. Not to mention escape proof, with elite heavily armed military guards in compounds encircled with razor wire.

Agent Benson's student had been happy to accommodate her relocation plan. He had grown quite weary of the loathsome conditions in which he dwelled, although after his pledge of cooperation and hearing an expertly dubbed and carefully edited tape recording of Galya Tannenbaum's voice on which she swore she was perfectly fine and anxious for his speedy return, the thickness on his mattress grew to a full six inches. Furthermore, his food and beverage improved, and he was given ample reading material, albeit mostly written by such authors as Adam Smith and Milton Friedman espousing the virtues of free economies, entrepreneurship and democracy, as opposed to oppressive Communist collectivism.

The books he received remained unopened but evidence showed Riha was sleeping better and had regained some of the weight he had lost since the onset of his ordeal. Plus he was paying more attention to Catherine's message. She had moved beyond the threats to a more conciliatory dialogue in an effort, she claimed, to understand Riha's point of view. In truth, she could care less about why the professor came to believe and uninhibitedly advocate his positions, rather she was angling to gain a modicum of his trust that her promises, particularly about Galya, were genuine and that she could deliver on those promises upon completion of his yet-to-be-described mission.

Also, in truth, neither Catherine nor anyone with whom she was associated had any intention of rewarding Thomas Riha for his service. On the contrary her agency fully expected to turn over his dossier to the FBI in hopes that its Director, Mr. Hoover, would reignite his original plan to arrest and prosecute the bastard for crimes against America.

On a bright, sunny Sunday morning, a day Catherine usually took off to remain in her Longlea suite watching her beloved Baltimore Orioles play baseball on television, or if they weren't playing, tour the quaint knickknack shops in nearby Culpeper and lunch at the rail yard station restaurant, instead, she appeared at Riha's door with an announcement.

"We're moving you this evening. We have another place that will better facilitate your forthcoming training. Also you will find your quarters much more comfortable. Perhaps not as elegant as those when you first arrived, but certainly much more to your liking, we believe."

"My training?" Riha asked, looking puzzled.

"Yes, professor, your training. You will receive instructions on what we expect you to do in the weeks and months ahead. It won't be too difficult, I assure you, for a man with your enormous talent. You clearly have the capacity to absorb all we have to teach, and to gain some proficiency in executing the tasks we have in mind," Catherine explained.

Riha sat listening, smiling, bemused at her casual self-assuring observations.

"Do you find that amusing," she barked.

"Somewhat," Riha responded. "Since I acquiesced to your plots and schemes against me, certainly not of my free will, you've now assumed that I will further accept some sort of directive to better equip me in carrying out these illegal acts. Indeed I find that amusing, even hilarious."

"Professor, Catherine said calmly, "I withdraw my earlier compliment. You are not only naïve, but rather stupid to think that we have gone to all this trouble to send you out into the cruel world on an assignment without pounding some basic skills into that thick head of yours. Not only will you be drilled on the technical aspects of your assignment, we will make sure you are physically prepared just in case you might have to run for your life"

"You can't be serious," he responded with certain trepidation, not finding her latest revelation the least bit humorous.

"Quite serious," Catherine said. "Your upcoming course of study will perfect your dexterity with certain scientific instruments as well as hone that masculine frame you vaingloriously hold so dearly into a well-oiled physical specimen capable of long, sustained exertion if it becomes necessary." She paused to allow that statement to sink in.

"This is incredible. Do you think I will allow myself to be subjected to..."

"We will leave as soon as it gets dark," Catherine interrupted. "You will be blindfolded and bound for your own safety. We will be traveling by helicopter. Our trip will take roughly forty-five minutes to an hour. Please relax; I advise you not to resist when my associates come to get you. I will be accompanying you to make sure you are well treated and to see you to your new quarters. You will be given a day to acclimate. Your new life begins the following day. See you in a few hours."

"Miss, Riha said almost in a whisper, "Go fuck yourself."

Catherine grinned and profoundly curtsied before turning and waltzing toward the door, closing it softly on her way out.

Hours later an accomplished Marine pilot was at the controls of the Sikorsky VH-3A. The advanced aircraft had been recently decommissioned from the Presidential Marine One helicopter fleet, and refurbished and reassigned for special use at the sole discretion of CIA Director Richard Helms. The spectacular flying bird thundered its way two- thousand feet above the fast-running Potomac River bisecting Georgetown from Arlington, Virginia. Recent rains had swollen the normally docile waterway, creating far too dangerous conditions for crew exercises and weekend boating.

Whitecaps from muddy river rapids glistened in the moonlight, clearly visible to Catherine as she sat peering out the side window of the aircraft, perhaps, she mused, the same seat from which Nixon himself may have recently gazed about. A wonderful airborne Presidential perch, Catherine smiled at the thought. As they approached the downtown Washington, DC skyline, she tapped the pilot on his shoulder and pointed her thumb downward in a gesture indicating her appeal to fly lower.

In the distance, the famed monuments were beacons in the night. The pilot bobbed his head affirmatively to acknowledge her request.

Seconds later, when the pilot eased forward on the cyclic stick positioned between his legs, Catherine felt the chopper start its descent. His motion tilted the massive rotor blades to take them down. After correcting for lift and power with the collective stick on his left, he then pressed the foot pedals controlling the tail rotor, which eased the big whirling bird toward Lincoln, under his gleaming dome, sitting forever placid on his magnificent roost. It was a delicate maneuver, but the pilot's skillful touch to the controls avoided a dramatic drop, lift or turn of the airframe.

As the Marine in control completed the slight change in course with the utmost ease, in a fleeting instant, Catherine was drawn to remove Thomas Riha's blindfold to provide him a glimpse of the spectacular vista. He sat unmoving beside her. Wrists and ankles shackled. The panorama, breathtaking as it was, would be enough, in Catherine's view, for any American left standing with a heartbeat to rise up with patriotic fervor. All except the shackled man to her right. The same man Catherine despised because he deplored all which was symbolized in Catherine's full visual span now only five hundred feet below. She left the blindfold in place and selfishly stared in awe at the stunning display beneath her.

The pilot had obtained special permission from National Airport air traffic control to fly at the lowest altitude possible. Catherine had never seen the City from the sky at night. Let alone like a bird in flight. She gasped at its splendor. The pilot, speaking to her through headphones which silenced the din inside the belly of the helicopter, said apologetically, I can only hold this position for a few moments."

"I understand, sir," Catherine acknowledged.

"No need to call me sir," he responded, quickly turning toward her to exhibit a wide grin. His helmet partially obscured a handsome face, Catherine realized, her view aided by dim light from the instrument panel yet sufficient for the confirmation. Her attention had been momentarily drawn away from the Jefferson Memorial and shimmering Tidal Basin, which were so close now she thought she could touch them. She giggled with delight. Soon, without further warning, the pilot pulled back on his cyclic stick and pressed his foot pedals to lift the aircraft aloft, nose tilting skyward to resume normal cruising altitude and speed. He swung the chopper to the right over Old Town Alexandria, and soon, flying along the Potomac shoreline, they were above the historic mansion at Mount Vernon en-route to his home base at Quantico, Virginia. The time and distance were short. They would land in less than twenty minutes.

Catherine had hung back several paces from her burly associates who were escorting Riha toward the hangar and the awaiting side-load panel truck that would take them to a remote facility within the compound for the commencement of his training. She was waiting for the pilot to complete his post-flight checks and disembark, planning to thank him for the aerial excursion and to get a better look. Soon he emerged from the passenger door and descended the stairway to join Catherine who had positioned herself at the bottom much like the Marines who greet the Commander-in-Chief each time he steps to the ground. She saluted him in jest. He saluted back and extended his hand.

"Nice to meet you Captain," Catherine said.

"Likewise," Captain James Hardaway responded. A nametag on his Marine flight jacket and the double bars on his shoulders revealed his rank and identity.

"Thank you for the grand tour. It was beyond magnificent." And so are you, Catherine thought. Her next glance was down to his left hand, which was carrying a clipboard, attached to which was a blank sheet of paper. No ring. No report. This flight never occurred. Neither did this meeting.

He fills out that flight suit quite nicely. And that Warren Beatty face ain't so bad either.

They walked slowly. Catherine looked toward the hangar. Her colleagues were standing on either side of the truck's wide-open double doors patiently awaiting her arrival. She presumed Riha was not-too-comfortably seated inside.

"I will be here for a while," Catherine suddenly announced.

"Good," said Captain Hardaway, "So will I. I'm stationed here for the next six weeks. On special assignment, but don't know what it is. Just told to stand by and have her ready on a moment's notice." He motioned toward the big machine behind them. The smell of jet fuel from the giant turbo-powered rotor blades still fouled the air. A maintenance crew had swarmed around the chopper to perform their inspections.

"Should be enough time," Catherine said. She pulled off her Orioles baseball cap. Her hair falling to her shoulders. She shook it loose. She noticed he noticed. She unzipped her leather jacket. It was warm outside.

"I hope so; that is, I hope it's enough time," Captain Hardaway said.

"I'm sure it will be. I will let you know where I will be quartered," Catherine said.

"I hope so," Captain Hardaway repeated. Catherine removed the glove covering her left hand. She lifted it for the Marine to see. Also absent a ring. He smiled.

It was then that Catherine reaffirmed that this entire mission, including its special benefits, never occurred.

Chapter 34

"So, now we have him at Quantico," Bud Wheelon said in an additional attempt to further prompt Director Helms to explain.

Helms had remained transfixed on his thoughts of Galya's stupefying death. He hesitated for an uncomfortable period before slowly mumbling a response. "Yea Bud, he was moved to Quantico."

Then, appearing to snap out of his languid state, Helms added, "Shortly after we placed him there I went to see him. No, I didn't speak with him. I just observed a portion of one day's instructions. He wasn't happy to say the least. In fact on that particular day he was incredibly obstinate, rude and vulgar. A genuine asshole."

"What did you expect," Bud asked rhetorically.

"You're right but we pressed on. Two months became four months, then five. My chosen team leader supervised the proceedings. Out of all of them she was the one who kept him fairly balanced. One minute the bully. The next, his buddy, and the next, acting like a drill sergeant. She charmed and chastised him as the situation dictated. She played to his ego, and cut him to pieces when his head swelled.

As if attempting to defend his decision about his special agent, Helms added parenthetically, "I've promoted her since then, by the way. She's the highest-ranking female agent we have at the Agency at the moment. Someday she or someone like her might take my job if politics don't get in the way."

"That would be a first," Wheelon said, rather stunned at the thought.

"Don't be surprised, but probably won't happen in my life time," his boss predicted.

Helms swung his high-back swiveling office chair away from his companion to face the blackness, which had consumed his wrap-around bulletproof window. All that could be seen were the occasional infrared beams flashing sporadically in their ultrasonic span across the night forest to warn of unwary or purposeful invaders.

Facing his back, Wheelon again spurred Helms on by asking, "How did he take to the device?"

Helms was momentarily silent, suddenly he began to spin in his chair like a schoolboy on a merry-go-round. Wheelon had never witnessed such whimsy before. He had to chuckle. Helms came to a stop, smiled, appearing to dismiss the tension, and said, "Not very well at first. He treated it like a dog turd, especially when my agent informed him what it was for.

"But I have to tell you, before telling him the truth, she said it was a nuclear trigger, for Christ sake, and I think he actually believed her!" Helms was belly laughing at that point. Wheelon couldn't resist joining in. "And then she warned him if he tried to destroy it, it could create Armageddon."

"What a gullible bastard. She had him tied in knots at times, wearing him down to near collapse and then propping him back up to the head of the class. Quite an extraordinary performance," Helms reflected.

Wheelon filled in another momentary gap in the conversation with, "It couldn't have taken him long to understand how the devise worked. My God, all he had to do was plug it in. We had diagrams of the Soviet's jamming equipment. I recall there were at least four outlets feeding frequency current directly into the Russian-made mainframe. All it took was to block one feeder system and the rest would also shut down, rendering their apparatus impotent, yet, when inspected, all systems would appear to be functioning normally."

"Yes," Helms agreed, "Once she leveled with him, he was quick to grasp the basic functionality of the device. It was electrical. All he needed to do was put it in the right hole. He had four to choose from. That's about it." Helms did not need to remind his colleague, but went on to say, "However, we had to be extremely careful not to reveal too much. Even though we had his sweetheart tethered and safely locked away, breathlessly awaiting his return, we could never trust him. He could turn on us at any moment. Jekyll and Hyde, you know."

Helms stayed on point adding, "Frankly we never told him the real purpose of his assignment. All he was told to do was travel to Moscow for the anniversary, attend all the functions, and one night, fake an illness, begging everyone's pardon for an early return to his room. The trick was shedding his KGB guides. He still had two thugs positioned with him throughout his stay. The Kremlin loved him, but they would never let him drive the pretty babysitter home alone, so to speak."

Wheelon forged ahead by asking, "I'm assuming the night in question he was able to distance himself from his guards and somehow make his way to the broadcast center. How did he get inside to plant our little virus?"

Helms smiled mischievously. "He got them drunk. Pretty smart for a Commie. When they got to his room, instead of saying goodnight, he invited his comrades in for some high quality Polish vodka he'd smuggled into country in his luggage along with the virus.

"By then we understood that Riha had sufficiently charmed his companions to such an extent that his invitation was too appealing to pass up. So they accepted, conveniently forgetting why they had left the party in the first place. Riha also promised those boys a visit from a call girl or two, but in little time, they also forgot about illicit dalliances becoming sloppily intoxicated to the point that both passed out. That's when Riha made his move."

"Pretty amazing. Sounds like Amateur Hour," Wheelon observed.

"No doubt, but it worked."

Helms continued without prompting. "Riha promptly left the room, the device in his suit pocket, and exited undisturbed from the hotel. He strolled two blocks to the broadcast center and walked right in. In perfect Russian, he convincingly told the security guard he was there to check reports of lax protection of the site by the watchman's Army unit, and cited the poor jerk on duty with the example of his own easy entry. Riha insisted on access to the entire facility to inspect for other lapses. The guard acquiesced, allowing Riha to walk freely about until he found the unit, inserted our magic plug and angrily stormed out, telling the poor bastard to expect severe punishment when his report was filed within the week.

"The guard never said a word. The KGB types woke up the next morning with brutal hangovers. They too remained silent. Embarrassed and concerned for their own skins, they beseeched the professor not to speak of their dereliction, after being assured by their ward that he had slept soundly through the night in the adjoining bedroom. Riha spent the next two days partying with the bigwigs. During that time we extracted the information I've just shared with you.

"How did that happen?" Wheelon asked.

"He was debriefed by a double agent of ours who casually met him at a coffee shop."

"Undetected?"

"Yep, undetected."

"Riha left Moscow with a first class ticket on an Aeroflot jet, changing planes in Brussels and landing at Kennedy where we planned to pick him up for further de-briefing before turning him over to the Feds. In truth, when you think about it, he acted like a pro. Improvising his own strategy, adapting to conditions, avoiding adversity and executing with fairly high-level precision. We couldn't have been more satisfied, quite frankly."

"Lucky, I would say."

"Can't deny that, Bud, but our luck was soon to run out."

"Yea, you've made that clear," Bud said.

"In the meantime things were better. It took us about a week to confirm that our broadcasts were getting through, once again unrestrained, sending a clear channel American message to the hearts and minds of the Russian people.

"I personally called Nixon to inform him of our accomplishment. He immediately ordered a special meeting of both the National Security Council and the 303 Committee. In their subsequent reports the mission was labeled an outstanding success. It couldn't have come at a better time."

"Why was that?" Bud asked.

"Senator Frank Church's Foreign Relations Committee was holding hearings on our new budget request to increase funding for the Committee's activities. Church himself presented the private Memorandum and recommended full funding for all freedom broadcast operations. He even quoted the White House statement. Listen to this," Helms said, pulling a Top Secret file from the middle drawer of his desk. He opened the file, retrieving a single sheet of paper to read:

"While these projects differ in their approach to the Soviet target, they share common objectives which provide the justification for

202

continued support of their activities. The primary objective is to stimulate and sustain pressures for liberalization and change from within the Soviet Union. The neuralgic points of this disaffection—desire for personal and intellectual freedom, desire for improvement in the quality of life, and the persistence of nationalism in Eastern Europe and among the nationality groups of the Soviet Union---are the main issues exploited by these projects. The secondary objective is to enlighten important third-country elites, especially political leaders and the public-opinion shaping professions, about the repressive nature of the Soviet system and its imperialistic and self-aggrandizing foreign politic."

He looked up at Bud and sighed. "Great irony here, don't you think? Everything Thomas Riha abhorred. Every damn thing that man opposed was spoken to with eloquence right there. Nixon's thoughts. Church's grand delivery. Riha's revulsion.

Helms put down the paper and paused for a breath. His recent pique was somehow gone. Melancholy returned to the room. Wheelon could feel it overtake him as well.

"We were riding high. Nixon had his campaign theme. A triumph. Church too. He was seeking re-election in Idaho. We had the budget we wanted, and most importantly our message of freedom was flooding millions of living rooms in that closed Soviet society like water gushing through a giant culvert."

"And then for fuck sake Riha really disappears," Helms said, closing his eyes as if to shield himself, and shaking his head in defeat.

"What did you just say, Dick?" Wheelon asked, stunned.

Helms stared at his friend, his eyes seeking compassion, understanding, and sympathy. "Yes, it's true. Riha returned to the United States all right. But he slipped past us. Right through the airport. He's vanished. We haven't told anyone, Church or the White House, but we think he might be dead too, just like his girlfriend. Just like the nurse. Somebody got to him Bud and we don't know who."

"Incredible; fucking incredible," Wheelon exclaimed; then mumbled sheepishly, "Please excuse my language. It's not like me. I got carried away."

Chapter 35

"Waiter, this coffee's cold. Damn it man, what does it take to get good service around here?" Captain Victor Bravo quizzed his best friend lacking his normal good-natured manner. He had occupied his seat at the restaurant bar for well over an hour grumbling to Johnny about everything from his job, his problems at home, to the miserable weather. And now the coffee.

"Too damn cold outside for early fall. Bet there'll be hell to pay this winter," Victor predicted.

"Hate to go to work today. Same old crap. Getting nowhere. Dead end, that's all I can say," Victor volunteered without prompting.

"Can it. Heard enough of your bellyaching. Drink your coffee and let me do my work in peace," Johnny scolded.

"You're no help," Victor replied, failing to mask an obvious whine.

Two months had passed since Victor's visit to Boulder and his wholly unsuccessful attempt to advance the murder investigation into the death of Miss Galya Tannenbaum. He was angry and frustrated at the unwelcomed hiatus.

Without reservation he displayed his aggravation nearly everywhere he went.

In the days following his inspection of Professor Thomas Riha's house, Victor had realized he could rely on no one but himself if any progress in the probe were to be made. It was clear that Colorado's two largest and supposedly most esteemed Metropolitan Police Departments had no intention of helping. In fact, neither had expressed further interest in the case despite Victor's repeated requests for assistance. For their convenience the case was closed. Captain Bravo had no choice but to venture forward on his own. It was akin to a walk at midnight in a sunken cave. Not even a flickering candle to guide him.

Victor Bravo was his City's chief of detectives. He was the man in charge. He had other cases demanding his attention but none like this one. He ran a small division and he trusted only a handful of his subordinates. Few in his command were comparatively competent. Most lacked the skill or ambition to perform, and no one had the gut-level instincts, or drive, to keep pace with their boss. Cases solved were Bravo cases. Make no mistake, both his advocates and detractors agreed. Either he spearheaded a team or he went solo. If that didn't happen, chances were clues went cold quickly; the guilty wandered off while their victims hid, too afraid to demand justice. Spread too thin was Victor's yoke and it was weighing him down. Despite the burdens he bore, not a day in the past sixty had passed without Captain Bravo searching desperately for that terribly illusive sign which might lead him to Galya's killer.

He had memorized the coroner's report nearly word for word. All the lab tests from Galya's autopsy had eventually read like grade school text; the scientific terms were now easily understood. Countless times he had reviewed the transcripts of interviews he'd conducted with all of those who were even remotely connected to the case. Even poor old second-grade patrolman Harvey Kirk, who had reluctantly held his post that night outside the entrance to Women's Ward 3 and complained mightily about his ailing back, was brought in for interrogation since he was the first to arrive at the scene and enjoyed a quick voyeurs' glimpse at the naked female corpse before scampering outside to call for backup. All Victor got out of that interview was a request to support Harvey's petition for early retirement with full pension benefits, and a complaint that he was being denied overtime for the off-duty chat. Regardless, Victor had re-read the transcription of that irritating conversation with dulled interest.

Johnny gazed at his friend after re-filling Victor's cup. The coffee pot in his hand was empty. Johnny realized Victor will have drunk it all when he finishes the mug in his grasp. Johnny wasn't annoyed at him, just worried. Thinking back, Johnny hadn't seen the Captain of Detectives like this since those ugly days and trying times not so long ago. It was then when his friend had met the Devil. An honest cop, saving a kidnapped child, watching as fancy cars exploded with gangsters inside, while others ran to hide. He had made the most powerful cower and crumble. The Mafia in their town had finally been splintered and shattered. In the aftermath trusted fellow police officers were fired or jailed for corruption, while the most crooked among them took a bullet to his brain. With Johnny's help Victor had survived those hard times because they depended on and supported each other. Finally, as time passed and memories faded, their lives had returned to resemble the just slightest illusion of normalcy. The Devil finally departing.

But is he back? Johnny pondered with fear.

Their long, lasting friendship had afforded Johnny the insight, perhaps more than anyone, about Victor's mental state and the cases, like the Devil, that tilted his balance one way or the other. This latest one, however, involving the horrific death by poison no less of a gorgeous maven entangled in the disappearance of her treasonous boyfriend whom she may not have cared that much about, because she was screwing her shrink while locked up for crimes she apparently didn't commit, because her other shrink thinks she's a spy and Communists were out to kill her while the coroner still thinks she committed suicide...

Whew, Johnny thought, Hell, that would drive anyone totally bat-shit.

"What are you staring at?" Victor unintentionally barked at his friend.

"Hey buddy," Johnny retorted sharply, "Don't jump down my throat. I didn't create this mess for you. I should have cut you off at two cups. Now you've had five and you're wound tighter than a nun's...."

"Don't say it," Victor warned half-heartedly. "I'm sorry. No excuse. But goddamn it, this one has me by the..."

"Don't say it," Johnny interrupted. "Who do you think you are anyway? Fucking Houdini, Sherlock Holmes, Agatha Christie, and James Bond put together couldn't figure this one out. Why do you think you can? You have no help. In fact, those fine boys in blue up north shit square in your mess kit when you asked for help. The coroner's been drunk for six straight years and your victim's last lover, who probably did it in the first place, got away with his shyster lawyer covering his tracks with a backhoe."

"With all of that square in your face, you haven't seen your wife and kids for, what three months, now? You're a mess. Sacrificing a wonderful family for what? The satisfaction of finding some crazy old hag's killer? What the hell to you care?"

Victor sat still, saying nothing, defeated by his friend's pure summary logic.

Johnny turned away, snatching the blackened coffee pot off the counter. He stepped to the sink, emptied the residue and began scouring it clean. Victor looked up and stared blankly at his reflection in the bar's mirror. Seconds later, over the running water, he heard Johnny ask, "Did you check the time clocks that night?"

Baffled by the question, Victor queried. "What time clocks? At the station? What are you talking about?"

Hand drying the sparkling pot, Johnny pivoted to face his friend. "At the nut house, you nut. Did everyone who was supposed to be on duty that night show up? Did the timecards match the number of employees walking the floors, probably wishing they could smother half of their patients?"

Not waiting for a response, Johnny stepped from behind the bar and into the kitchen. The coffee pot back in its place under the counter.

"Hold on. Where are you going?" Victor called after him.

Silence. The kitchen door swung inward and then immediately outward as Johnny emerged with a full plate of scrambled eggs, finely chopped Italian sausage, mixed with green peppers, onions, and thinly sliced plum tomatoes, plus two slices of heavily buttered toast piled high with orange marmalade. He slid the heaping platter down the bar to land right in front of his favorite friend.

Startled, Victor asked, a smile forming on his face, "Where'd that come from?"

"Man you are out of it. Carlo's been back there fixin' it up for you for the last half hour. Didn't you smell it cookin'?"

Now distracted by the food, Victor ignored Johnny's earlier question and gobbled up the deliciously unexpected meal.

"Did you hear me? I'll repeat myself, but just this once. For you. Nobody else. Did the time cards match up with the employees?"

Between bites Victor hesitated, thinking. He put down his fork, grabbed his napkin, extracted a droplet of luscious sausage grease from his chin, cocked his head in retrospection, and said, "Come to think of it, the timecards didn't match up with the sign-in sheets. There was one extra signature; it was damn near illegible as I recall."

"An uninvited guest, perhaps," Johnny suggested.

Victor was finished eating by then. He belched. "More coffee."

"Nope," Johnny replied. "Milk. A tall glass of mother's sweet creamy nectar is all you can have."

That afternoon Victor Bravo, Chief of Detectives, examined that extra signature on the sign-in sheet. As he remembered correctly, the name in the column was an indecipherable scribble. He'd never realized it before, but that out-of-balance roster resting in his hand just happened to be for employees assigned to Women's Ward 3 on the very night of Galya Tannenbaum's death.

"Damn, how could I have missed it," Victor cursed in earnest self-reproach.

Chapter 36

"The son-of-a-bitch is married," Agent Benson bellowed in anguish at her sister Karen.

There was silence. Catherine pulled the receiver away from her ear and eyed it, thinking the line went dead and immediately blamed AT&T for a bad connection.

"Hello, are you there?" She anxiously quizzed her older sibling.

"I'm here," Karen responded dejectedly. "I'm so sorry sweetie. I know how much you cared for him."

"Cared for him!" Catherine exclaimed. "I was in love with him. For two years. No, more than that. Three years nearly gone from my life chasing that bastard around the world, arranging complex work and travel schedules so we could be together. Prague, Istanbul, Rome, Melbourne; Christ, even Saigon. Somehow we managed to meet when one or the other of us would be on assignment there. I'd pull strings. He'd pull strings.

"Once I even begged the Director, Richard Helms himself, to let me take a stupid low- level drug smuggling case in east bum fuck Egypt, near Alexandria, so I could meet up with him in Cairo for the weekend. Come to find out the agent we suspected of being in cahoots with the Egyptian army which was shipping heroin into the country from Afghanistan was undercover in Bulgaria at the time, and our tipster mistook him for the mule driver coordinating shipment teams at border crossings...and..."

"Catherine, please. Come back to me. I'm here. I'm your sister. I love you. I'm here to listen. I don't need to hear about your work," Karen said with soothing compassion in an effort to calm her down.

"I know you are. I'm sorry. But I wanted you to know how difficult it was for me and apparently for him to carry on like we did. There was so much passion. So much joy, frankly, and he hid his secrets so well." Catherine choked on her last words.

Regaining composure she said, "I'm highly trained in this stuff, you know. I'm supposed to be skilled in getting the truth out of people, using whatever means I can to get them to spill their guts. With him I was ignorant. With him, from the first moment, sitting in that fancy god damn helicopter flying over DC like a wide-eyed tourist, and then seeing him in that flight suit; that swagger, that boyish, cute, self-effacing confidence. He had me. Blind as a bat. Pussy on a rope."

"Stop it. Come on, you can't apply your professional skills to situations like this. They're different. Emotions cloud everything," her sister advised.

"Yea, emotions and unleashed libido," Catherine responded sarcastically.

"A little of that goes a long way too. I admit. Results are like wandering in a sandstorm. You can't see a thing. You just feel," Karen said.

"Yes and it stings," Catherine replied.

"That's what I meant," Karen affirmed.

"Where is he now?" she gently inquired.

"Don't really know. After I found out by checking something I should have done in the first place...like his military record...how stupid of me...he went through the whole routine. I'll get a divorce. She means nothing to me. I can get joint custody of the kids. We'll make a go of it. Which was nothing but nauseating drivel I couldn't stand to hear, and then he said he would find me after returning from another sortie in Viet Nam, and I said, don't bother, and he said he'd still look for me and I said, fuck off, and he said, I love you and I said what about your career?

"That stopped him dead in his tracks." Catherine took a breath.

"His career. Obviously," Karen repeated with resigned acknowledgement.

"That's all it took. He's a full colonel now. Colonel Hardaway took two giant steps during our illicit courtship. From major to lieutenant, to full bird colonel in two years. Come to think of it, perhaps it was following me around, like he did, to all the places I went and all the assignments he took, some dangerous I suppose, so we could be close, and that got someone's attention at the Pentagon. Maybe that's the case. And now, since I've read his record, I know he's on track to brigadier in probably two or three more years. He's not about to ruin that possibility by fucking a low-life bureaucrat like me and having to fess up to his superiors."

"Don't ever describe yourself like that to me again dear sister.! I will hang up on you and we won't speak again until you purge yourself of those ridiculous, damaging thoughts," Karen furiously admonished.

Catherine had no response. She had sunk deep into self-pity and needed big sister's help with this one; the first time in a long time she couldn't stand straight up on her own.

As she pondered what to say next, she saw the tiny red light blinking on the secured-line portable telephone, which sat atop the scratched, and wobbly coffee table positioned across the room from the awfully uncomfortable motel bed on which she laid.

Seeing that flashing light and knowing what it meant suddenly snatched her off her weeklong lovesick, sometimes drunk roller coaster ride. She leaped off the bed and planted her feet firmly back on the ground.

"Karen, I love you. You've been a big help. I've got to go." Catherine said excitedly, her voice unexpectedly strong, willful, direct, and commanding. Her sister had heard that voice before. She knew she would be all right. Again.

"Love you too," Karen said, and hung up before Catherine had to.

Catherine scampered toward the receiver unit. The headphone slipped easily over her matted hair, which was still wet from the shower taken before her call to her sister. She recognized the voice immediately.

"Agent Benson. Director Helms."

"Yes sir, I'm here."

"In Des Moines?"

"Yes sir."

"I'm re-assigning you. Agent Kilbride will arrive at your hotel room in thirty minutes for your briefing. Your present detail has been downgraded to warrant the attention of someone with fewer years, let's say. I am indeed concerned about the rising tide of animosity against our country coming from certain Islamic groups in the Middle East, and yes, we should be following militant sects like the one represented by Mr. Khalani there in Iowa. I, too, am suspicious of that proposal to construct a Mosque right there in our heartland, but I must bring you back into this one." Helms' voice trailed off. Catherine waited. He did not continue just then. She spoke first.

"Yes sir. I understand. What is it? How can I be of service?"

"Thomas Riha has been missing, truly missing for nearly two years. We don't know where he is. He's vanished. He's been gone since the Moscow foray and a failed attempt on our part to debrief him after his arrival in New York. I purposefully didn't tell you this before. You were done with him. You prepared him well. He carried out the mission better than expected. He did what we wanted. We were through with him. We planned to turn him over to the FBI, and if they didn't do anything with him, we thought he'd just resume screaming obscenities about America until someone clobbered him for good. But he didn't. He just disappeared, and now, God help us, Galya Tannenbaum is dead."

Catherine reeled from her boss's revelation. She gasped. He could hear her reaction through the encrypted line.

Helms continued. "After he slipped away, we decided to keep her locked up in that shit- hole mental institution in Colorado, afraid that he would find her if she were free and they would embark on some retaliatory campaign against us. Reveal the kidnapping. Implicate you somehow. Me definitely. And blow the whole scheme about us blocking the Soviets from jamming our freedom broadcasts. The Reds still don't know why our signals are getting through unmolested.

"And now Galya's dead. Poisoned. The whole thing is playing out like some trashy spy novel."

Catherine took a deep breath. "Sir, do we have a suspect?"

"No. No one."

"Is her death tied to his disappearance?"

"We don't have a clue. That's why I want you home to head our investigation. No more overseas assignments until we get this one figured out. You're in charge. A team has been assembled and will be at your disposal."

"There's only one thing."

"And what is that Sir?"

"Well, not a thing. A person. A cop. Local. A good one, we think. Smart. Has been on the Tannenbaum case since the beginning. You'll have to deal with him."

"No problem Sir."

"I wouldn't be so sure, Agent Benson, I wouldn't be so sure."

Chapter 37

Despite her lofty position in the organization Agent Catherine Benson's new headquarters office was buried deep, four levels down below the surface of the manicured, fortified Northern Virginia countryside.

Her workplace was a twelve-by-twelve cubicle off a side-angling corridor, past the weapons lab and down the hall from the newly created International Investigative Division on Child Trafficking, Pornography and Exploitation. She loved the men and women who staffed the Agency's latest branch which is solely devoted to capturing, and she hoped, occasionally killing the despicable perverts who prey with pure evil on innocent unsuspecting adolescents whose lives are uprooted from homes stretching from Cambodia to Columbus.

A year before she had had the pleasure of helping raid the headquarters of a ring of traffickers in southern Albania who were kidnapping prepubescent East German girls and selling them as sex slaves to wealthy Filipinos. In a rare incident of détente, Russian KGB operatives cooperated with CIA-trained Special Forces to invade a remote farmhouse, freeing twenty terrified teenagers and arresting seven of the most revolting human beings Catherine Benson had ever encountered.

The KGB didn't know a woman was part of their squad since on the night of the raid. Catherine was dressed in combat fatigues, stocking hat and helmet carrying an M-16, .45 automatic and a surgical knife on her belt. Only three of their captives made it back to the detention center alive. Four tried to escape from the transport truck even though their hands and feet were bound tightly with nylon twine and their mouths

214

stuffed with used Kotex napkins found in the filthy vermin-overrun outhouse positioned fifty yards away from the barracks where the girls had been kept. Catherine helped bury the culprits and marveled how neatly a certain caliber bullet could pierce the human skull without much collateral damage to the interior of the truck in which they were riding.

Catherine sat behind her government issued, sterile, grey-metal desk cluttered with papers stacked high at all four corners. Files were strewn about, some dating back seventeen years or more. The CIA dossier on Thomas Riha filled two four-drawer file cabinets. Catherine had been through six of the eight drawers and was beginning on the seventh, remaining fascinated with much of the contents, which were graphically exposing the weird, wild and wonderfully exotic world of Galya Tannenbaum. A large portion of what Catherine had been reading was written in Galya's own hand, or by her mysterious handler, the man with no name who had been permanently exiled to Eastern Europe on the direct orders of Director Helms. It hadn't taken Agent Benson long to understand why.

No doubt Galya's CIA shadow for all those years had eventually lost it, Catherine concluded after finishing the handler's latest entry.

Toward the end of his assignment the tenor of his reports went from strange to utterly bizarre. It was clear to Catherine that he had begun to see himself as Galya's Svengali-like savior. One minute, in his eyes, she was a national treasure; the next, a blood-sucking parasite, living off government handouts. He found her work incomparably brilliant on Tuesday and worthless on Wednesday. In one rambling, convoluted report he had written that she never should have been incarcerated, while later he advocated a life sentence for her despicable acts.

Reading between the not-so-blurry lines of his dissertations, Catherine had become convinced he was in love with her but knew he couldn't have her. And when Galya died he had fallen into an emotional abyss. But what Catherine found most disturbing was an entry alluding to certain outside forces suddenly put in command of his activities, and as a result, he openly declared he was no longer bound to the Agency, rather to old friends who had been put in charge of his life in general, and the destiny of Galya Tannenbaum in particular.

As he continued, he referenced unnamed persons on the inside, presumably inside the Asylum where Galya was housed, who had been placed there to protect his prime ward but had failed to do so---since she's now obviously dead---so he would be the one to set things straight. Right the wrong. Bring things back into balance, was the way he put it.

Catherine reread that section again, and again. Unnamed persons on the inside. Certain outside forces suddenly in command. No longer bound to the Agency. Old friends now put in charge.

Old friends, wonder if he means the FBI?

She stood from her chair, arched her aching back and began to circle the room; those strange, disturbing passages running through her head as she paced.

No one else was put in charge. The Agency has had control of the case throughout, Catherine affirmed with each step. At least I think so. There's no reference to any collaborative effort involving any other Agency; the FBI included. This was a solo mission. At least I thought so.

Seeking a change in scenery and some fresh air she exited the stuffy office and walked down the hallway. Her child porn crime-busting associates had long since vacated their space for the night. Their cubicles dark. She searched for a drinking fountain, found none close by, but saw a distant sign marking the entrance to an employee cafeteria. There she purchased a soda from a vending machine and began her sullen stroll back to her office with the eerie case now dominating her every thought.

This guy had no authority. He was a lackey field agent just like me, but with a plum assignment literally of his own creation. He discovered Galya. He was smart enough to recognize her incredible gift and leveraged that into a ticket out of a dead-end FBI gig into the heady world of international espionage. So why jeopardize his career? Did he blame himself for her death? Did she reject him and he killed her in revenge? And why put all this down in writing? Normally Helms would have fired him on the spot. Instead he's exiled to Europe with an Embassy post and given no real responsibility. Doesn't make sense. Driving me crazy.

Is Helms keeping him away from the Feds? Is that why he's in Austria?

Now at her desk and sipping on the lukewarm Coke, Catherine began plowing through the final file of reports, becoming more confused and frustrated with each turn of the page. Nearly gagging she dumped what remained of the awful-tasting beverage in the trashcan.

Seems as if every man who knew Galya Tannenbaum, in more than passing fancy, fell deeply, inescapably in love, or lust; probably both, she thought.

In that case, as she read further, Catherine realized that Galya had not one, but other possible perpetrators accountable for her death, and if connected, also responsible for the disappearance and possible murder of Thomas Riha. If not a blank slate of suspects, perhaps she had dozens of other would-be culprits.

If the rogue agent didn't take her life, then who did?

Many men could have killed her and yet so few, if any, had reason, or motive, other than jealousy?

Unlikely.

Opportunity? Very limited.

She was locked up for Christ sake.

If the killer thought he couldn't have her for himself, why didn't he just stab her, or strangle her? Why expose himself by having to work on the inside of that chamber-of-horrors and go to the trouble of administering a slow, torturous death from cyanide poisoning?

Catherine's mind spun in circles.

Wait a minute. Could the murderer be a woman? Why not? Females are equally capable of wanton acts of violence, and most assuredly through Galya's adult life, she'd pissed off countless maidens whose partners were tempted or perhaps even succumbed to the counterfeiter's charms.

Did the Agency do her in? Were Catherine's own counterparts responsible? Is that what her handler meant by saying someone else was put in charge?

Was the threat of exposure of Riha's super-secret excursion behind the Iron Curtain enough to knock off both Galya and Thomas, or just her, while keeping Riha alive for future assignments?

His first venture into espionage had been a smashing success largely due to yours truly, so who's to say that he wasn't recruited again for more daring escapades? Just hide him away until the coach pulls him off the bench. Above all, the Agency apparently adored Galya Tannenbaum for her stealthy talents. The last thing any right-thinking spy wanted to see was their master forger dead.

A ten-thousand-piece jigsaw puzzle.

Through it all Catherine knew the Director would tell her only so much. And she knew by putting her in charge of the investigation that he trusted her judgment, and discretion. She would protect his interests along the way toward finding Riha and solving a heinous crime. Yet if completing one or the other might expose her benefactor to untoward consequences, she would be expected to exercise that discretion without hesitation.

How far can I go to protect him?

Catherine was the first to admit she wasn't a detective, let alone one steeped in homicide. And when, after two more hours of reading, she got to the sections of Riha's file where she became the primary author of its contents, she knew she needed one.

Whoever that might be must be pretty special. He has to be the kind of cop who can see the big picture in all of this sordid mess. Eye on the ball. Good of the country and all of that. Look the other way when it involves domestic spying, entrapment, kidnapping, judicial intimidation and possible bribery, obstruction of justice, evidence tampering; the list goes on but is meaningless when compared to the cause of spreading democracy.

Right? I guess so.

All of that seemed to work fine in Catherine's mind. What didn't work was murder.

No way could she justify a ruthless cold-blooded killing.

What she could justify was meeting Captain Victor Bravo. And soon.

Captain Bravo's name had first appeared in one of the last reports submitted by Galya's dearly deported handler. He wrote of his fear that this "hick-of-a-Keystone Cop" was snooping around her death, asking too many questions of too many people and getting dangerously close to exposing the Agency's connection to her.

The handler had speculated that if not thwarted by aggressive intervention the detective might link the confinement of Miss Tannenbaum to Riha's disappearance since there was some evidence that Bravo had gained access to her confidential medical and psychiatric files. Contained therein, the agent wrote, could be inflammatory accusations of overt domestic action by the Agency in contradiction of U.S. policy, if not in direct violation of the laws of the land. He wrote he was particularly concerned that Galya might reveal her historical means of financial support, courtesy of Uncle Sam, and how, if anyone closely examined the case, the Agency had "procured" her sexual services to advance its mission, hence the prolonged bedding of one Dr. Thomas Riha.

Pimping was definitely frowned upon by a suspicious, overbearing Congress.

Catherine was fascinated by the disgraced agent's summary of the facts as he saw them at the time. She sensed wisdom in his remarks and insight into the "what if's" that all decent CIA functionaries are trained to examine. But when she got to the part where he suggested that Captain Bravo be "eliminated", and that he was the perfect candidate for that task, she hastily put aside the file and called the document room staff operator to request "anything we might have" on Captain Victor Bravo, Chief of Detectives of the Pueblo, Colorado Police Department.

Two hours and forty-five minutes later the research analyst on duty called back to describe a two-page synopsis on the man which had mainly been taken from old local newspaper clippings. The articles, he said, described the range of cases on which Bravo worked, and some of which he was personally credited with solving.

At Catherine's insistence, the documents were whisked over to her office by special courier. She put aside the remaining Riha files to concentrate on Bravo's abbreviated profile. She found there was a decent digest on his advancement through the department ranks, along with an editorial, which fussily congratulated the "progressive nature" of the police force in recognizing the talents of the new Hispanic captain despite all the inherent shackles that traditionally bound that segment of the population. The editor's opinion was an extremely poor excuse for an "up-by-the-bootstraps" chronicle, which Catherine viewed as profoundly condescending.

When finished she called the analyst a second time and ordered a full "physical" on the guy and she wanted it in forty-eight hours.

Often when Agent Benson took on an assignment such as this she preferred to sleep through the day and work through the night. She was convinced that her brain functioned better that way. Her father had been a night-shift factory worker making heavy equipment for Caterpillar, and he swore that the darkness brought out the best in people while on the job. And that sage philosophical advice had stuck with his daughter ever since.

Catherine's nocturnal work habits had been a persistent irritant during her former conjugal visits with the esteemed soon-to-be general officer, who had thought bright-light day-time sex bordered on exhibitionism, preferring, instead, conventional under-the-cover groping during the black of night. Catherine often won out on this issue when she forestalled his advances until her reports were filed, which generally did not occur until well after sun up.

Those pervasive, still heart-breaking memories of her stolen days and nights with Colonel Hardaway came back hauntingly as she commenced work two nights later at 9 pm and opened the now thick, marked CLASSIFIED, envelope on Captain Victor Bravo.

If I was with the Colonel now, he would have to wait until noon. Before I'm done tonight, I'm going to know Captain Bravo better than his mother, Catherine whispered to herself while extracting the papers.

Catherine marveled at the intimate personal portrayal splayed before her. All gathered in just two days. For instance, she was sure Victor Bravo's mother had no idea that her son was accused of fathering a child with a sixteen-year-old high school junior before joining the Navy at the outset of the war. The CIA did.

That would have sent any fine Mexican mama over the edge.

However, when Catherine read further she was pleased to learn that he had been exonerated when the real father accepted responsibility in a letter to authorities before being gunned down while storming the beaches at Anzio. Victor's mother also would be highly distraught if she had known that at a young age Victor's father was alleged to have killed a bar patron in a knife fight while in a tequila-induced stupor.

He too was later cleared, the report said.

There are no secrets.

Catherine was now fully aware of Victor's height, weight, shoe size, pant and shirt size; his preferred color, his allergy to bee stings, his wife's proclivity to chocolates; that she lost their first child in her first trimester, and that her father was a regular at the local greyhound race track, losing more often than winning. Catherine didn't care to know that Victor preferred Fords over Chevrolets and that he was obsessed with football, claiming to be a human statistical textbook on the game. His favorite player was Johnny Unitas of the Baltimore Colts. Well that's a good thing since I love the Orioles. Moving on, Catherine was highly intrigued with an anonymous memorandum, somehow extracted from deeply buried police department files, which speculatively linked him to the gangland-style execution of a notorious fellow police officer during a sweeping probe of corruption a few years back involving the local Sicilian mafia. Nothing ever surfaced from the nameless author's theory, although rumors had persisted for months. Many leads, but no suspects.

Wonder if he did it?

Catherine now knew a lot about Victor's friend Johnny, the restaurant owner, and their close relationship which was further cemented during the Mafia-plagued days, and she was highly impressed with Bravo's professional track record, particularly his dogged determination to solve even the pettiest of crimes. His success rate on major cases like homicides was sterling.

All except two. A cop killing no less, and now this one.

In any case she had to meet him. She would arrange it soon.

And now that she had finished she knew him better than anyone.

Some things mothers should never know.

Chapter 38

Victor Bravo heard the dispatcher's summons over his police scanner as he walked back to his unmarked cruiser parked at the curb on the street bisecting a quiet, serene residential neighborhood in the southwestern section of the city. Victor had just emerged from the quaint split-level ranch home after receiving the wrath of a not-so-quiet and-serene crime victim. The distraught citizen had accused the Captain's forces of failing to thwart brazen burglars from entering his dwelling through an unlocked back door and pilfering the interior of all his wife's fine china and silver. Also missing was his grandma's jewelry left to him in her will, a coin collection containing a rare New Orleans-minted half dollar and a good percentage of his wife's silk underwear, not to mention several boxes of exquisite Cuban cigars.

Attempting to placate the hysterical homeowner Victor took full responsibility for the break-in, readily admitting that he and his officers should have been more diligent on their patrols of the neighborhood. The disgruntled dupe couldn't agree more but stopped short of his threat to sue when Bravo reminded him that possession of illegal imports from Castro's Communist Caribbean isle constituted a class-two felony, and that his remaining untouched stockpile of twenty boxes or so, indicated he might be a part-time smuggler subject to federal prosecution. The two antagonists had parted friends in the end with Victor's promise to search mightily for the thieves and a shirt pocket full of flavorful Cubana's.

"There's a woman in your office who's been waiting for you for over an hour now," Corporal Smothers informed the Captain when Bravo responded to the radio call. The dispatch came in on channel three, the scrambled frequency reserved for lieutenants and grades above who are out in the field and were in need to hear private, unmonitored messages

222

from headquarters, or more often than not, stern reminders from wives or girlfriends to pick up the dry cleaning on their way home.

Failing to mention he had finished dealing with the irate resident and had literally taken stock of the situation before acknowledging the message, Bravo snarled indignantly, "So, Corporal, "You think just because some woman wants to see me that that it is important enough to pull me off a crime scene to answer your call?"

"No sir. I mean yes sir. In this situation, sir, I think, or I thought it, ah, her, or this was something you should know about right away, sir. No doubt, sir, she's here. Right here. No, not right here, I mean in your office, sir. What can I tell her?" Corporal Smothers was truly having a bad day.

"Corporal, who is this woman? She has you talking like a babbling idiot." Being less annoyed; rather somewhat amused and becoming somewhat intrigued, Bravo's tone was slightly softer.

"Sir, she won't say exactly. She showed me some kind of strange-looking badge, or shield or something, and said she was here on official government business and that it had to do with national security and that it was imperative that I find you and that she was getting impatient....that was about twenty minutes ago." His delivery hurried and shrill. Smothers' shift ended at 3 pm. He couldn't wait to rush out the door.

National security. Now that's a new one, Bravo thought. "Tell her I will be there at three o'clock. I want you to remain at your desk, even though I know your shift is over at that time. I want you to brief me before I go in to see her. And if she is some kook who's bamboozled you into thinking she's important, I might insist that you return to the police academy for further basic training."

Over the airwaves Bravo clearly heard a pronounced gulp as Smothers swallowed hard. Bravo smiled at the audible response, thinking how easy it was to haze the disheveled dispatcher who constantly took the brunt of non-stop ribbing over his resemblance to Tommy Smothers, the bumbling brother of Dick of late-night television fame.

Actually he's a pretty good cop.

"Ah, gee, acknowledge that, sir. Roger, 10-4. Copy that sir," Corporal Smothers stuttered, obviously crestfallen with the order to remain at his post.

Upon his arrival at the station some fifteen minutes later, all Victor got out of his interrogation of Corporal Smothers was a physical description of his awaiting guest, kind of cute, and the fact that she had placed her heavy .45 caliber automatic in the temporary storage locker when the desk sergeant on duty saw it lodged on her hip and partially covered by the business suit jacket she was wearing. She had cooperated willingly, according to Smothers, and handed over her firearm without protest.

With that Victor had dismissed his informant with a half-hearted warning about the Corporal's potential re-training. As he walked past the sergeant's desk Bravo unconsciously placed his hand over his shirt pocket to hide the Cuban delights, and while closing the distance to his office, he began to speculate that his forthcoming meeting just might have something to do with Thomas Riha and Galya Tannenbaum.

He was so right.

Catherine Benson had caught Victor Bravo's silent greeting nod to the short, stocky square-jawed man when they entered the restaurant. His nonchalant gesture seemed to set everything in motion. Not unlike the shielded, casual signals between agents passing by at night in the foreign field, Agent Benson had thought.

Interesting.

Turned out the guy at the door was the owner, Johnny was his name, and that was all she got, although from her reading she knew a lot more. Without further prompting or formal introductions of the mysterious lady with the Captain of Detectives Johnny had immediately taken charge of their accommodations.

The proprietor had a twinkle in his eye but the hardened look of long years of street-wise experience. Catherine studied the unspoken, yet clear understanding between the Captain and their host over the seriousness of their presence.

Not a social event. Strictly business. No questions. He knows the routine. Ask no questions. Serve the food and keep others away. He's handled situations like these before. I like that.

Johnny had seated them at the most isolated table that the expansive dining area had to offer. Sound muted by a half-encircling partition so voices would not carry.

Didn't matter much at first. Since meeting in the Captain's office and suspicion immediately arising over her appearance, they had had little to say so far, other than Catherine telling Victor she was starved and before they could continue she would have to eat.

It had been a grueling day. Up at 4 a.m., she had been forced to travel from Langley on a commercial jet through Denver. For some peculiar, totally unforgivable reason, all Agency aircraft had been pre-commissioned resulting in her inability to catch a convenient military hop. Instead she found herself on a much-delayed non-stop flight from newly completed Dulles International Airport. And then a two-hour drive in a rented Volkswagen bus without an adequate heater and an engine that sounded like a broken washing machine. She was tired and hungry and was in no mood for that god-damn desk sergeant taking my gun, or that lascivious dispatcher eyeing my ass, and now this detective who's proven to be nothing but a pompous prick.

Catherine Benson nursed her half-empty glass of Chianti and wished it was full again. She'd never tasted better. Nor had she ever consumed a more scrumptious lobster linguini. The garlic bread also was mouthwatering. The salad, crisp and tangy. She wondered how the lobster tasted so fresh. She could have easily been somewhere along the coast of Maine, not sitting in the southern half of far-flung Colorado, right in the middle of nowhere, at a place called Angelina's Fine Italian Restaurant.

On a full stomach and her mood much improved she decided to look past her initial dislike for Bravo and try a different tactic. He had proven to be quite difficult to reason with, much more so than she had hoped. Yes, pompous was the best description. Prick; let's see. Maybe I was hasty.

"Captain," Catherine quietly and calmly began again after dabbing her lips Victorian ladylike, which was a curious thing for her to do. Paper napkins to wipe her greasy chin and blow her nose while seated in mess halls among rowdy military recruits more closely resembled her practice and experience.

"I flew all the way out here today to ask for your cooperation in this matter. No Captain, not your cooperation. I asked for your assistance. I need your support and frankly your expertise. I have been tasked with finding Dr. Thomas Riha. I told you that. No matter the cost in time or money. Or the number of bodies I have to step over, and feelings I have to hurt, or jurisdictions I have to invade, I will find him dead or alive. My government, your government, Captain, needs to locate this man immediately and I believe your investigation into the death of his former companion, lover, wife, concubine, whatever she was, could be of great help. Why don't you understand that?"

Victor eased back in his chair keeping his eyes affixed on this highly annoying, totally obnoxious and completely fascinating individual with whom he had shared a scrumptious meal, albeit one horribly short on pleasant discourse. The food and the service had been superb as expected. Their seating was remote but inconsequential because few words had passed between them except for her recent recitation over ground they had already covered, perhaps three times before. Victor was not about to bend until his companion grew more forthcoming. He had an idea who employed Catherine Benson. He wasn't even sure of her name but suspected military intelligence, State Department, or maybe even the White House. The CIA crossed his mind but they weren't supposed to be mingling in domestic affairs.

However, one never knows in this cockeyed environment.

"Miss Benson. May I call you Catherine?" Victor didn't wait for an answer.

"Catherine, we are bound to be here all night, perhaps many days and nights to follow, and you'd better be prepared to climb over a heap of bodies including mine. I have absolutely no obligation to, as you say, support your search for this man. I am deeply involved in a vastly complicated murder investigation. That's my number-one priority. Yes, I believe there is a link in my investigation to your subject, but I know he didn't kill my victim so I am only mildly interested in him.

"You come here wanting me to turn over my files on the case with the hope the evidence I've collected will lead you in the right direction. And you ask me to turn my attention away from finding her killer to helping you track down some petty, two-bit, wanna-be teacher who should have been deported decades ago for treasonous acts too numerous to count. It repulses me, quite frankly Catherine, that my government is paying your salary to find this jerk in the first place. I hope he's in some Siberian gulag reading Russian poetry to a toothless three-hundred-pound male transvestite. I think the Soviets call them putahs."

Catherine couldn't hold back a loud guffaw. Loud enough for other patrons some distance away to inquisitively glance their way. Victor impulsively chucked in response.

"A putah!" She was still laughing. "Where did you get that? That's hilarious. I'm sorry Captain. I just had this image of Thomas Riha, the prim and proper bow-tied professor, a real ladies man in his own mind, cuddling with a lovely putah to keep warm in a filthy hut reading Marxist limericks by candlelight in January."

Their laughter died down, replaced for the first time by acquiescing smiles.

"Okay, Captain, I'm not supposed to do this but you're right; I need to level with you. Despite our rather rocky start today, I believe I can trust you. I'm told you're one of the best cops in this state, maybe in this part of the country. I should have respected your integrity and tried not to bully you or throw my weight around demanding your files and cooperation. That's really not me, and it's not the way my people expect me to act. Can we turn back the clock? Begin again?"

"Yes, we can Catherine by you telling me who you work for," Victor responded.

It was Catherine's turn to lean back, skeptically eyeing her companion, contemplating her reply.

"I should send you through weeks of background checks but we don't have the time, so I am granting you high-level security clearances, and therefore, access to top secret information," Catherine began, only to be interrupted.

"I'm not sure I want that. Don't do me any favors," Victor warned with a serious tone.

"Captain, please let me finish. I wouldn't be here about to share this information if my superiors and I did not recognize your patriotism, trust your veracity and expect your discretion. So, I am going to plow ahead like it or not."

Johnny moved from behind the bar to lock the front door to Angelina's Fine Italian Restaurant. It was ten past two. The third to-the-last patron had ambled out an hour before. Although Johnny had played host to Victor and many of his myriad dinner companions over the years this one was an exception. First she was a she. Victor had never been in there with a woman before. All the others had been male cops, petty informants, lawyers, judges, parole officers, jail wardens and even a few well-heeled hoodlums begging for leniency, but never a female and certainly never an attractive one.

Real special case, Johnny thought, wiping down the bar one last time. It already shined brightly enough for him to see his reflection. When he finished he strolled over to their table.

"Victor, I can lock up and leave you the keys," Johnny said.

"Why don't you do that my friend? We'll be here a while longer if you don't mind."

Two hours later Catherine finished her long dissertation on the Thomas Riha case and its broad foreign policy implications. She was beyond exhaustion and yawned uncontrollably. Her eyes occasionally unfocused from lack of sleep. Victor had been unrelenting. Not only had he come to know Catherine's employer, he knew all there was to know about deteriorating American-Soviet relations, his President's penchant for unabridged American-style propaganda, radio signal jamming devices, called viruses, crafty kidnapping techniques, an over-zealous field agent who'd volunteered to kill him, and how the CIA broke resilient targets, transforming them into cooperative pawns for their dirty work in the never-ending Cold War.

Catherine admitted she felt like Riha must have felt when she got done with him, or better put, when the transvestite was done.

Victor drove Catherine to her hotel. It was close to five a.m. They would meet early that next afternoon. His case files on Galya Tannenbaum would become her case files. A trusting partnership had been formed. His full cooperation promised. They'd find Thomas Riha and they'd find Galya's killer.

At least they'd try. Together.

Victor had lost count of the nights he had slept alone. This one would be no different.

Chapter 39

The slightly built man placed his red cashmere stocking cap on his head to cover his long, wavy silver-gray hair and stretched the warmth down over his ears. He wrapped his matching scarf tightly around his neck and zipped his quilted black down-filled ski jacket to the top. The temperature outside Montreal's famed Hotel Bonaparte was unseasonably frigid for this time of year. It was beginning to snow again. The man was accustomed to the cold winter. He actually thrived in it and was anxious to begin his walk. He wore expensive hand-tooled hiking boots and nylon fabric ski pants with straps at the leg bottoms securing a smooth comfortable fit and sleek appearance. His gloves were fleece-lined red and black leather accenting his other same-color apparel. He would have fit right in, perhaps even stood out, at the height of season in St. Moritz, Aspen, or Turin in the Dolomites of Italy.

The man welcomed the snowflakes with an upturned face and was charmed when they settled to melt in his full gray beard, which perfectly matched the color of his hair. He insisted on the harmonized look before recently allowing the effeminate male hairdresser to begin the dying process. In the end he had paid the salon owner handsomely and politely declined his offer to meet for drinks and dinner later.

The man had decided to take a long, snappish walk through the historic urban neighborhood surrounding the famed five-story, thirty-room boutique hotel before his planned attendance at the evening performance of Anton Chekhov's Three Sisters. The play was debuting at the Centaur Theatre just three doors away near the intersection of Rue Notre Dame. After inspecting his image in the huge gilt-framed mirror that adorned the south wall of the hotel lobby he emerged with satisfaction through the main passageway and stood under the oval green awnings to breathe in the icy air for delightful refreshment.

The man loved the Hotel Bonaparte for its rich heritage, its ideal location in the center of Montreal's most prized main business district and the fact that from its front door he had convenient access to Notre Dame Cathedral. Not that he ever ventured inside to pray; that was strictly against his nature, rather he relished the spectacular building for its architectural grandeur. After strolling past the church's ascending stairway, he had decided he would make his way through the public park to the Promenade du Vieux to walk the shore of the St. Lawrence for a least a mile, if not two. He knew his journey would encompass the better part of two hours allowing him plenty of time to return, shower and find his seat for the first act set to begin at 7:30. He would dine after the performance at the Auberge, the hotel's eatery renowned for its lemon-baked sea bass, baby carrots and mushroom and crab risotto.

He couldn't be more pleased and felt his destiny was further secured after discovering that morning that the Centaur, housed in the elegant stone façade Greek column edifice which was once the home to the Montreal Stock Exchange, would be opening their holiday series with his favorite play by his favorite playwright.

What could be more perfect for a man with my tastes, desires and passions than a day like this, Thomas Riha thought as he stepped onto the narrow sidewalk and turned right toward the intersecting street to the north of the city's most famous house of worship.

Feels like Moscow in January, and later Chekhov's fanciful tale to top it all off. Who could ask for more? Simply marvelous.

As he walked with a purposefully rapid gait Thomas remained alert. He had to. He was a man on the run. He fought with himself every waking moment in this lulling environment to be acutely aware of his surroundings and of the people nearby who could do him harm.

He had been in Canada since slipping past the pair of Kennedy airport greeters assigned from Langley to gather him up for debriefing upon his return from the Soviet capital. It had been easier to avoid their capture than giving a passing grade to a mini-skirted coed.

The rather homely, bad-toothed, stringy-haired Russian diplomat traveling to America to take her post at the consulate in New York had been the ideal shield he needed. He spent most of the eighteen-hour flight, two of which was on the ground in Oslo, convincing the poor, gullible flat-chested spinster in perfect Russian that he too was being assigned to the consulate, and they would soon be inseparable comrades surviving together in that debased American society filled with nothing but criminal capitalists. Their conversation was interrupted twice; the first time over the Swedish mainland when they squeezed into the on-board privy for a contorted tryst during which Thomas had to cover her mouth to suppress the loud groans that threatened to alert the Aeroflot stewardesses. The second time they gathered together was somewhere high above the North Sea but this event was planned differently and ingeniously executed.

It hadn't taken Thomas long to erotically engross his repulsive conquest with the declaration that he loved to dress in women's clothing and to fuck them when they were dressed in men's clothing. After much arousing deliberation on the topic, each participant retrieved the requisite garments from their suitcases stored in overhead bins, and an hour after their departure from the Norwegian capital on the last leg of their flight, retired to the same water closet, undressed, re-dressed, fucked again, and decided to remain cross-dressed for the duration of their trip.

Thomas thought she looked rather dapper in his blue suit, white shirt and red tie. His shoes even fit her enormous feet. However, Thomas would not turn heads in her dumpy black skirt, grey blouse, low block-heeled square-toed shoes and nylons with crooked seams running up his itching thighs. When they left the plane to snickers and finger pointing from the flight crew, who took note of the switch but did nothing to intervene, he had covered his head with one of her headscarves. It smelled of putrid perfume, cigarette smoke and was stained with bright red lipstick. She/he breezed through customs with genuine diplomatic credentials. He/she was stopped at the passport checkpoint, but after showing the officer CIA-issued papers and whispering about being incognito, Thomas was waved on without further questioning.

With each step Thomas scanned the crowd waiting for arriving passengers. Approaching an exit point, he quickly spotted two men who stood out most assuredly, watching intently for only him but not her.

He strutted right past his welcoming party and did not merit a second glance. His ludicrous looking escort took his arm like any proper male companion would do, and they strolled toward the egress and awaiting taxis. At the last minute, Thomas said he needed to use the ladies room. She chuckled at the thought and pointed out a nearby sign over the bathroom entrance.

Thomas entered the first stall and quickly removed her clothing and dressed in his own. He had a second suit and accessories in the suitcase he carried. For fear of arrest he knew she would not dare disturb him by entering in the outfit she now wore. He waited for the room to empty and went to the door. Fortunately she was looking the other way when he melted into a crowd of camera-snapping Japanese tourists scampering toward a tour bus parked at curbside.

Thomas broke off from the unruly swarm and found an escalator carrying him back up to the ticket counter. Unmolested, an hour later he was on the next Air Canada flight to Toronto.

There Thomas spent a number of weeks in less than desirable surroundings. His instincts had told him to find shelter in obscure hideaways deep in the city's center core where, dressed properly, notably unshaven, frequently un-bathed and generally slovenly in appearance, he would blend in nicely with local inhabitants. He moved from low-rent pay-by-the hour hotels, to youth hostels, even to occasional homeless shelters and the local YMCA to avoid continuity in his habits and locale. He ate in soup kitchens and took handouts, all the while carrying a key to a storage locker, which contained his suitcase-full of newly, purchased business and evening dress, and two hundred and thirty-thousand American dollars courtesy of the CIA's special project travel and expense fund. He had barely touched his original stipend. He was expected to hand over what was left upon his return.

It's mine. I earned it, he rationalized. So I'm keeping it.

Convinced in his seventh week on the lam that his clever shiftiness had thrown his adversaries, especially that shit-bag bitch Secret Agent, completely off his trail, he returned to the storage locker conveniently located next door to a Hertz Rental Car outlet. At the customer counter he used a new set of identification papers including a false driver's license and passport to rent a new Chevrolet Camero. The phony documents had cost him two-hundred-fifty Canadian dollars, about one-hundred-seventy-five American, secured through a chance meeting with a sleazy YMCA swimming pool towel clerk. He roared out of town in the Super Sport model that same afternoon and sped toward Montreal.

This particular early-winter day, to be spent on his walk, followed by the highly anticipated evening's theatrical event, was a rare pleasure for Thomas. Since his arrival, by all outward appearances, he was living well on the U.S. Government's dole. Opulent room, wonderful food, leisurely afternoons spent at the Russian section of the metropolitan library where his research for a new biography on Leon Trotsky was already in outline form, were ideal aggrandizements for a man of his stature. To add to his self- indulgence he had already enjoyed two delightful afternoon roundhouse romps in his chambers with bored wives of businessmen in town for mind-numbing conventions.

All of this had still failed to bring a sincere smile to Thomas' face. He missed Galya tremendously. He ached desperately for her touch, even the sound of her voice. He was frightened, terrified, in fact, of being caught and extradited to the U.S. to face fabricated charges, or worse, being murdered and his beautiful body unceremoniously thrown into an unmarked grave or the nearby icy St. Lawrence River.

As a backstop to those potentially gratuitous acts he had befriended a night clerk at the Bonaparte to whom he related a fantastically woeful tale about his long bout with terminal lung cancer. With occasional coughs and tears thrown in for good measure, Thomas told her of his heart-wrenching epic and asked the clerk to stow a letter for him. The letter was stamped and addressed to the editor of the New York Times. Thomas lied in saying it contained his personally authored obituary. He got the credulous teenager to agree to mail the letter if Thomas ever turned up missing or dead. If his corpse was ever found at or around the hotel, Thomas said, he would have likely peacefully passed on of his devastating illness, so, he instructed, act accordingly.

Explaining the missing but maybe not yet dead part, had been a little more complicated. It took a while but Thomas eventually convinced the clerk that if he ever disappeared it was because he had decided to die at a hospital instead of in his room or nearby. That fatal decision, he said, would have been made to shield hotel guests and staff of witnessing an ugly scene of rescue workers hauling his diseased body off to the morgue. With this haunting epistle the young woman broke down herself and swore to abide by his wishes in either case. Thomas paid her one hundred American dollars in advance for her future troubles.

The subject letter actually contained twenty-seven single-spaced typed pages describing in explicit detail Thomas' ordeal at the hands of the Central Intelligence Agency. Few parts were left out, mainly those dealing with Galya, otherwise it was a blockbuster front-page story, which, if printed, might lead to his freedom and exoneration if captured and convicted. Such an article was his only hope of being miraculously spared from demonic government assassins. Thomas tortured himself over it being a poor strategy, but it was the only option he concluded he had. He'd run out of all others short of defecting to Moscow. But that idea lacked substance since he knew he was more use to the Soviets espousing their sage propaganda in the free world than obtaining asylum and likely being reduced in prominence to teaching English to brainwashed Russian schoolboys.

Thomas Riha knew that his legacy might rest in the fingernails bitten-to-the-quick hands of a nineteen-year-old high school drop-out who still treated her acne, took the bus to work every day, and was primarily known beyond the hotel lobby for her ability to guzzle Canadian beer by the gallon.

What else can I do? Thomas often asked himself.

The snowfall had picked up and the temperature had dropped a few more degrees as Thomas neared the St. Lawrence shoreline. On this perfect Sunday, for the first time since his trek through Central Montreal had begun two hours before, he felt a chill. When a wintery gust off the river smacked him face-on, instinctively he wrapped his swinging arms around his torso to ward off the cold. He unexpectedly grew tired and looked for a place to rest. To his left he spotted an isolated park bench and made his way, abandoning the sidewalk to wade through the swelling snowpack that crunched under his feet. He sat and shivered, bewildered by his lack of tolerance for and endurance in the frigid outdoor conditions. By that time he could see only a few feet in any direction. An oncoming blizzard for sure.

I should keep moving, Thomas told himself, but I feel the need to sit.

Soon his decision to remain in place was rewarded by the arrival of a park-bench companion. She too was soundly encased; head-to-foot, in winter outerwear, yet her clothing did not hide a shapely figure beneath and a well-sculptured profile. Thomas soaked up the view when she strolled past him and was delighted when she returned to take a seat at the opposite end of the bench. She did not speak or even acknowledge his presence. Soliciting a response, Thomas held a longer-than-polite stare in her direction. He got none in return. Finally looking away through the swirling flakes, he squinted at a man peddling a bicycle against the howling wind. To his right he spotted a woman pushing a baby carriage and heard the cries of a distraught child from inside. He wondered why its mother was subjecting the infant to such rapidly deteriorating weather. Snow was swiftly accumulating around his feet. Thomas stamped his boots to clear them, and fearing his attempts at flirtation had been futile, rose to stand. Unexpectedly, she spoke.

"Please stay. Perhaps we can talk."

Thomas gasped. He knew the voice. How could he not? She turned to face him, confirming his suspicion. She smiled but her expression was cold, menacing and wicked in intent. His knees buckled. He felt weak, forcing his body to plop back down heavily.

"How did you find me?" Thomas' breath was labored.

Why am I afraid?

"It was not difficult. I lost you for a while when you went overseas, but my friends told me when you were returning. That was quite a trick you pulled at the airport. Scooting right past your escorts. Watched it all unfold. Nice outfit by the way. I knew you'd head for Canada. You always liked Canada, especially its big cities. Too bad you had to play hobo there in Toronto for so long, and I'm glad you finally decided to move on to Montreal. You always had good taste. The Bonaparte is such as fine hotel."

Stunned, Thomas' eyes went wide in wonder, then bewilderment, then unblinking in fright. He choked on his next words. The snow shook off his beard as his lips quivered. He didn't notice.

She did and it pleased her.

"What do you want?" He stammered.

"Satisfaction." She said calmly.

"Satisfaction? What do you mean?"

"For you to satisfy me for once." Her tone was more frigid than the atmosphere that
 engulfed them.

Striving to regain the dominance he once held over her, but still in a faltering delivery, he said, "Now then; come on, why don't we find a comfortable place to talk? Someplace warm and dry. You look lovely. What have you done with yourself?"

"Surprised Thomas?" She said. "Surprised to see me like this? Not what you remember. Right?"

"Most assuredly, my dear," He responded, regaining a steady cadence to his voice. "Oh no, I mean you were always lovely to me."

"Is that so? Gee, Thomas, you flatter me. Such kind, gentle words. But never sincere. Never satisfying. Always shallow. But soon, Thomas, you will satisfy me."

"Oh dear, I would be happy to do so," He chirped. "Let's go back to my room. Temperate and cozy there."

He started to stand and held out his hand.

In hers was a pistol.

He repelled violently. Instinctively. Terrified, legs giving out once again. He sat. The cold, wet bench shocking, soaking his backside.

"That's it. Sit down darling. We're going nowhere." Eyes fixed on the gun barrel pointing at his midsection, stammering, he managed, "Now, hold on a minute. What are you doing? You can't be serious. You probably have every reason to hate me, but this; you're going too far. Don't you dare threaten me. Put that away and we'll settle this. You'll never get away with it. You want more money? You want my house? You can have it. I'll tell her to leave."

"She's already gone."

"What do you mean?"

"She's gone. Literally. Dead, exactly like you're going to be."

Dumbstruck, Thomas choked. Air leaving his lungs. He fell back against the bench's armrest. He stared into her blank, death-mask expression.

She waited. Savoring the moment. Ready to strike if threatened.

Instead, his gaze on her remained. Frozen like the air. Then finally.

"You killed her. You did; didn't you? He whined. Tears welling. Thick mucus dripping from his nose, catching and coagulating in the bushy grey growth above his lip.

"Yes, my darling. It was slow and painful just like you treated me."

"How?" He cried. "When?"

"Poison. Just like I took from you. All the time we were together. The rest doesn't matter."

Suddenly emboldened, he snarled, "You don't have the guts. You were such a weak, sniveling little girl, always complaining, but never willing to stand up for yourself. You made me sick. Couldn't stand the sight of you. Plus you were lousy in bed. Fucked like a stone-cold corpse. Go ahead; let's see what you're made of. If you really killed her I have nothing to live for!" You might as well shoot me you ugly, mousy bitch! He exclaimed.

"Gladly."

The first bullet struck Professor Riha in the forearm, shattering the bone on its way through, to enter his abdomen and lodge in his liver. The impact from the powerful Berretta automatic slung his body sideways. Singed goose down from the hole in his jacket drifted into the air. His stunned expression instantly became one of anguish. He tried to speak. To cry for help. She stood, and before he could utter another sound, she slipped her pistol into his open mouth and fired, the projectile piercing his spinal cord to silence him for good.

No longer will disgusting words flow off your foul tongue, she thought.

Chapter 40

Following their initial rounds of rancorous meetings, Detective Victor Bravo and Agent Catherine Benson had reached a tenuous agreement on how best to conduct their investigation and themselves going forward.

An informal professional pact was formed calling for cooperation in and mutual support for their probes into the death and disappearance of their respective victims. In doing so each had granted the other access to all privileged documented evidence gathered thus far. However, when it came to next-step strategies, stark differences were soon commonplace. They argued about nearly everything.

First among their spats was that Catherine insisted on running the investigation from her office in Langley. Bravo couldn't appreciate a shred of logic in that plan. He refused to work that far from home. Doing so would force him to be away from his family for unacceptably long periods of time. At least that's what he told her since within the past six months only two weekends had been spent with his children. Rosanna reluctantly allowing them to be crammed into his studio apartment for two dreadful days and sleepless nights while their father caught up on paperwork. Nevertheless, countering Catherine's demand he felt they were best advised to remain in Colorado and set up shop in Denver. This came after he had convinced the regional FBI field director to provide office space and some logistical assistance.

Catherine finally gave in on that issue but then a greater problem loomed. Who was the boss? She had federal ranking. He could care less. He had more experience. She wanted to exhume Galya's body. "What the hell for?" He howled. The autopsy and toxicology reports were sufficient. Then she demanded they re-interview all the witnesses.

"Ridiculous. Listen to the tapes." His voice was hoarse by then. Later she said she wanted to re-inspect Thomas Riha's residence. He thought that would be a perfect waste of time. She insisted her priorities trumped his, claiming threats to national security. He shunned that notion outright, in favor of first finding a diabolical killer still on the loose. Back and forth it went until one day Victor received an early-morning telephone call.

The shrill of the ring shattered his dream. In the fog of slumber Rosanna had stood in the middle of a darkened street. Her back to him, neck twisted as she stared blankly with hollow face turned in his direction. A street lamp illuminating her shadow. Moments passed in silence. As if finally resigned her look softened. She shrugged in bewildered sadness and stepped out of the light. He called to her but his sound was muted. Behind him a siren screeched. His cruiser, driverless, lights flashing, inched forward. Bumper drawing closer. Like a phantom dog begging the attention of its master. Leash in its mouth. He could feel the heat of the engine. Denying the intrusion he looked for her but she was gone. Another ear-splitting blast. He was alone. No one beside him to stir at the sound. Cold sheets occupied her space. Nothing more. It was the goddamn telephone.

He reached for it to quell the noise. To end his loss of her. His senses returned. The voice on the line all too familiar.

"She said her name was Woods, Miss Rosemary Woods, and she would not take no for an answer. She was calling from Washington DC and it was imperative that I bring Captain of Detectives Victor Bravo to the telephone immediately," Dispatcher Smothers said in hushed tenor.

Then quickly he added more boldly, "She's a real snotty bitch, Captain. I told her it was four-god-damn-thirty in the morning out here in Colorado, and I didn't care who was calling, I'll be switched if I was gonna wake up my captain at this time of day." He paused, waiting for a grateful accolade that never came.

"Captain, are you there?" Smothers quietly probed, suddenly feeling sick. Another blunder? His throat went dry.

"Yes, corporal I'm here, Victor said calmly. "Where in Washington DC did this Miss Woods say she was calling from?" Looking at the nightstand clock, it shined a bright five-fifteen. The fog in his brain now clearing. He realized he was expected in Denver by eight that morning for a meeting with Agent Benson, two of her associates who had been temporarily dispatched as analysts, and a recent recruit fresh out of the FBI academy assigned by the Field Office Director to his first case, albeit part time.

"Captain, you won't believe it. I didn't. That's why I put her off. Told her to call back during normal business hours," Smothers courageously declared. His confidence temporarily restored.

"Well Corporal, you didn't wait too long. Where in hell did she say she was calling from?" Victor repeated, slowly losing his patience and soon his temper.

"The White House," Smothers uncontrollably blurted out a little too loudly. "Bitch said she was calling from the White House in Washington, DC."

"That's where it's located, corporal. Right there in Washington, DC. Corporal, did she leave a number?"

"Yes, sir. Its right here....somewhere." His voice now quivering.

Twenty minutes later Victor's heart thumped hard in his chest when he dialed the number Corporal Smothers had recited. He nearly dropped the phone when the familiar voice came on the line.

"Detective Bravo. Good morning. I hope I didn't wake you. I expect you know who I am."

"Yes, sir. I know who you are." Victor said haltingly.

He heard a distinct chuckle and then, "I hope you voted for me."

"As a matter of fact, sir, I did, sir," Victor lied.

"Very good."

"Now, I hear you're a fine man. A fine police officer. You know, I love coming to Colorado. You know, I've been out there plenty of times campaigning. Visited the Air Force Academy back in 1969. June, I think it was. Gave the commencement address. Fine speech, everyone said. Don't think I've ever been in your town. What is it called again there young man?"

"Pueblo, sir, Pueblo, Colorado sir." Sounding like his dispatcher, now it was Victor trying to speak with a parched throat.

"Right, certainly a fine city I'm sure. Now listen here Detective. I need to ask you a favor. I'm told you're a veteran cop, and I see here a Navy man. Damn fine thing. So I know you'll understand chain of command. Even though I'm not really your commander-in-chief, I'm gonna assume here that you'll see it my way. Do you think you might see it my way there, Detective Bravo?"

"Yes, sir, Mr. President. I suspect I will...see it your way."

"Fine; damn fine thing there detective. You see I need you to get behind us in helping address this little problem of ours. You know about this fellow we sent over there to Moscow to screw up their machines that were keeping us from broadcasting the truth about America to those poor ignorant Russians, and why those stupid Soviet bastards don't have a clue about what's good for their own people. And why those people need to oppose their own leaders from aiming missiles at us and building up their military when they can't even grow enough grain to feed themselves. You know all of that, don't you Detective?"

"Yes, sir, I know all of that."

"Well now this messenger of ours, well, I hear he's turned up missing. Vanished in thin air. And I hear this girlfriend of his is dead and there might be some connection. Sounds like a juicy dime novel murder mystery to me. Ha! But no, this is serious stuff. So I also hear that you're the man whose gonna solve the murder. That right Detective?"

"Yes, sir, I hope so, sir. We've got some leads."

"Well, that's fine. A damn fine thing. But the thing is, we need to find this messenger of ours first. You see. He's important to us. We can't let him run around out there shooting off his mouth telling some of his Commie buddies and the press, you know, what he's been up to. That's no good. We have to keep a lid on all of this.

"Right detective?"

"Right, Mr. President."

"Good. And I hear you could help us do that, but right now I'm concerned. You see Detective, I understand there isn't a display of good teamwork out there in Colorado, in the Land of Enchantment, you know. Ah. Maybe that's New Mexico. Anyway, I know you're damn smart. I know that about you. My people out there are also smart and they know what we need to do, and what's important to me. What's important to the country. So can I count on you to think like I'm thinking here, just for a while, until we find this guy and make sure he keeps his mouth shut? Can I count on you Detective?"

"Yes, sir, Mr. President. You can count on me."

"Good. Fine thing we have going on here. God bless you young man, and God bless America. Gotta go to work now."

Click.

The dial tone buzzed painfully in Victor's ear like a screaming train whistle. The coffee he was making had boiled black. He'd left the heat on high. He reckoned he'd probably be putty in Catherine Benson's hands from now on. Empty coffee cup in hand he sat down at his tiny, stained kitchen table, a broad grin crossing his face. He silently wished he had recorded the conversation with the President for his grandchildren to hear one day. Or maybe just his wife and kids, if he ever saw them again.

No one will ever believe me.

Victor's trip to Denver that morning took less time than normal. He covered the one- hundred-odd miles between the cities in a less than ninety minutes, door to door. He couldn't wait to see how Catherine Benson would act now that the Boss of Bosses had intervened. As he drove he struggled to reconcile many things. His dream for one. His temporary abandonment of his family for another. At least he hoped it was temporary.

But why? For what? There's no glory in this despite having just participated in a one-sided conversation with the Man himself. But I can't help it. It's an addiction. My addiction.

He gripped the wheel and swerved to the right to avoid an impeding motorist in the passing lane. "Get your ass out of the way," he yelled to no one but himself. Maybe that's what I should do. Get out of my own way. To prove something? That I'm better? A Mexican cop who made good in a lily-white world? Why not?

Two semi trailer trucks blocked both lanes ahead. Victor hit the brakes hard. This time his emergency lights flashed and siren squealed prompting a quick move to the right by the Wonder Bread truck and a clear path for Victor ahead. He thought of his dream, but remorse was not there, at least for now.

I'm not a drug addict; not a drunk, but seized nonetheless by this uncontrollable compulsion. So go with it. Slide in the needle. Puncture the vein. Swallow another shot. Make that commitment to the President. Come under his influence. And all the others. Take the glory. Bask in it. The family will wait.

As the mile markers sped by, no doubt he would throw his weight behind the Riha search rather than insisting his focus remain on finding Galya's killer. His myopic perspective on the case would change. Slowing to turn up the off-ramp all thoughts returned to the case. The dope of his addiction again filling his veins.

Frankly, Mr. President, I don't have one real solid lead, would have been the truthful answer Victor thought. And sir, Agent Benson could be correct in thinking that finding Riha may be the best and quickest way to capture his lover's slayer after all.

Not to fear, Mr. President, I'm your man.

As she awaited Victor's arrival that morning Catherine had been wrestling with events herself. Director Helms had briefed her earlier. She was amazed at the level to which the interest in her case had risen. To the highest level. With that, however, she realized that the pressure to find the bastard alive or dead, would mount each second. On the other hand, the challenge was intoxicating. She was tempted to exploit her new clout in all matters pertaining to the investigation, but at the same time, she had to appear contrite, downplaying her leadership role in deference to a renewed spirit of cooperation, albeit forced by the heavy hand of the Chief Executive himself. She needed the seasoned cop's unconditional help.

Now!

Their assigned office was in a basement corner of a non-descript low-rise building at the corner of 16th Street and Champa, which housed the regional FBI branch. Catherine was not happy at first with the cramped space, its strong musty order, dirty sink with a leaky faucet and a unisex bathroom situated a few paces down the hall. But she was slowly accepting the less-than-ideal conditions. With a lovely water stained backdrop, one wall in the main office had been covered with a mosaic depicting the life of Thomas Riha and life and death of Galya Tannenbaum. Catherine's analysts and the rookie Fed agent had spent the last three days creating a montage billboard of photographs, newspaper clippings, note cards, maps, and hand drawings of every key element of the case gathered thus far. The postings ranged from a sketch of the cell in which Galya had died, to the costume Riha left in the ladies' room when he snuck past his would-be CIA greeters at Kennedy International Airport.

Xeroxed pages of Galya's diary were also pinned to the wall. The handwriting was exquisite but revealed little.

Agent Benson sipped her coffee; her feet resting on the desktop. She had grown to like Denver. A little. She was surprised that the city was not overrun by cattle roaming in the streets; rather it exhibited genuine traffic jams, some decent restaurants and generally a few cosmopolitan attributes like an acoustically appealing Concert Hall and minor league baseball team. As a result she was no longer angry over the decision to headquarter the investigation here. In fact she had to admit she was glad to be on her own, away from DC and Langley for an extended period, without having to travel abroad.

Catherine swung her feet off the desk, stood and ambled over to the coffee urn to retrieve a second cup. Contemplating the question all morning she had finally decided not to say a word to Detective Bravo about the telephone call she knew he'd received earlier that day.

No reason to rub it in.

We'll be moving in the direction I choose, from this point on. Let's just hope I can steer us on the right course.

Victor arrived only a few minutes past eight. Catherine greeted him at the door. Pleasantries were exchanged among the five and Victor stood by as Catherine ordered her underlings, all except him, to spend the day reviewing the files on Galya's handler prior to and after his departure for Europe. She ordered them to look for any indication that he might have slipped through the tight CIA net thrown over him for his rogue actions to somehow go after Riha in retaliation.

"We still might want to question him even if everything looks clean and we determine he's stayed put in Vienna," Catherine said.

After that was done, Catherine ordered her crew to comb through the list of every student Riha had ever had in class, plus every teacher and administrator with whom he had contact during his teaching career. They were to examine the profiles of anyone who might have shown signs of overt antagonism toward the esteemed professor and shown up in either CIA or FBI archives as extremists apt to harm any Communist that might get in their way.

"That should keep them busy for the rest of the day," Catherine said to Victor in jest and out of earshot of the others. And then she added, "We're going back to Boulder to take another tour of Dr. Riha's love nest."

Victor stifled a recoil at her order but reminded her that, "I've been through the house twice. And it's been months since the last time. I'd be surprised if it hasn't been burglarized. My sense is the Boulder cops had no intention of protecting the scene, if we can call it that... a crime scene."

Further he couldn't resist by saying, "Oh, I forgot. I guess it is a crime scene; your crime, something akin to kidnapping."

"Very funny," Catherine said, taking the gentle ribbing well. She went on. "I understand what you're saying Detective. I just want another look around. Not to say you missed anything; rather just to observe, let's say, from a woman's perspective."

"Whatever you say boss," Victor acknowledged with the smile.

"I still have the key, you know," Victor said as Catherine steered the government-leased Crown Victoria into the Riha driveway. She had insisted on driving. Their trip had taken less than an hour. At one point the speedometer had topped eighty.

"I figured you did, but just in case I had one made," Catherine said.

Victor noticed the For Sale sign in front of neighbor Gustav's house. He was curious about the cause for Gus' move, but didn't say anything.

There were no noticeable signs of mischief around the house as they walked up the steps and Victor inserted his key. When they stepped inside and gazed about, the place was immaculate. The air was stale, but for that, from corner-to-corner the interior appeared scrubbed and polished by maids in the employ of a Park Avenue matron. Hardwood floors sparkled. Furniture shined. Windows glistened. Loving, thoughtful hands and knees had been at work. Either that or a major effort had been put forth to destroy evidence. Catherine and Victor walked around in silence for a time before Victor said, "As I told you before, this joint was an absolute a mess, but a measured or controlled mess."

"Tell me again what you mean by that," Catherine instructed.

"What I noticed before were things overturned, ajar, tossed about, like pillows off the couch but piled nicely on the floor. Lamps tipped over but shades not shattered. Ceramics and figurines resting on their sides in the China cabinet but not broken; all pieces still intact. Wall hangings and pictures askew, but not damaged. Flour and sugar spread over the kitchen floor but almost in an artistic pattern. Beds rumpled but sheets still tucked under the mattress. Now everything here has been put back in its place. It looks like a model home in here. I can even smell the furniture polish."

"Someone's definitely been in here recently. Not a speck of dust anywhere," Catherine calmly observed.

She took her time moving slowly through each room. Her eyes sweeping the surroundings. She climbed the stairs. Her nerves spiking with each step.

"I don't see the necklace," she shouted down to the main floor upon approaching the nightstand in the upstairs master bedroom. Victor was downstairs taking another loop around the kitchen. Her loud voice startled him. He hurriedly bounded up the stairs to join her.

"You did say it was lying right there. Resting on top of a lace doily, or something like that."

"Yes, rather cheap thing it appeared to me, but the lace article was nice, and like I said, the chain was shaped into a heart. The little diamond, if that's what it was, was clipped to the bottom."

"Well someone liked it, whether being a diamond or not." Catherine attempted to control her suddenly faltering speech.

She fought to keep her emotions in check but knew she was failing. Reliving the not-too-distant past. Another time and place, but similar circumstances.

"Let's get out of here," she abruptly ordered; her voice shrill.

"Don't you want to go through the drawers and closets? The bathroom cabinets? I thought you thought I might have missed something. A woman's perspective. Remember?"

Catherine didn't answer. She bolted from the room and dashed down the stairs toward the front door. Out on the dry brown lawn, she squatted and rested her elbows on her knees. She breathed heavily. Dizzy. Her thoughts gripped her gut in a vice.

Victor had stood at the top of the stairs and watched Catherine's rapid descent. He was struck by her abrupt, convulsive change in behavior. From a seasoned professional to an emotional runaway wreck. In an instant. Quite an unexpected turn of events. He would step lightly but would not waste time in delving into the reasons for her altered state.

Leaving the house he found her leaning against the front fender of the Ford gazing into the sky appearing either in search of inspiration or seeking relief from an overwhelming jolt of despair. In either case Bravo's new partner needed his help and he needed answers.

He waited to approach her. Finally she dropped her skyward stare and looked over in his direction. She shook her head in resignation and motioned for him to approach.

Victor stepped toward her cautiously and began to speak when she interrupted him with, "I think I know who did it."

> *City Morgue - Montreal, Canada*
> *December 15, 1971*
> *2:03 pm*

Chapter 41

"The body has been here for nearly thirty days. Unclaimed. There were no documents in the personal effects of the deceased to provide guidance in identifying next of kin or disposing of the remains. It is my understanding that your office did trace his temporary domicile to the Bonaparte Hotel where they found clothing, a significant amount of cash, mostly in American dollars, and some travel papers all of which have proven to be fakeries. We have no idea who this gentleman was, and since no one has stepped forward, we have no choice but to order his burial in a pauper's grave at public cost in the public cemetery. I must clear this cooler immediately. Unfortunately, others await its use."

City Medical Examiner Jacques Lamont paused in presenting his status report to City homicide constable Micah Jordan, soliciting a response. The telephone line, which connected the pair buzzed with unusual static; otherwise momentary silence.

"Are you there constable?"

Finally with resignation in his voice, "It was a brutal slaying. An execution to be more exact. Truly a baffling case Dr. Lamont. There were no witnesses. With the heavy snow and gale-force winds at the probable time of death, the sound of both shots, fired at point blank range, must have been greatly muted, or the gun was silenced. The corpse was not discovered until the next morning when a young man, cross-country skiing on the snowpack, stopped to rest on the park bench. Despite the heavy layer of snow, measuring more than one-half meter in depth, and obscuring the man's form, the skier grew curious and swept it away to discover the well-preserved, frozen remains," Constable Jordan said.

"Truly a stiff indeed. Quite stiff by then," he added in a feeble attempt to bring levity to the conversation.

Ignoring the stab at humor, Dr. Lamont lectured, "Yes, constable, we are well aware of the condition of the body when discovered. The cause of death also was readily apparent. Massive injuries to the head and spine from a through-and-through projectile. Those injuries, of course, were proven instantaneously fatal. We believe that the headshot was the second shot fired, however. The first being the one piercing the man's forearm and abdomen to rest several centimeters inside the liver. That bullet, in and of itself, probably could have ended his life in a slow bleed out, however, the shooter was apparently determined to complete the task quickly, leaving no doubt as to the result and affirming their true intent."

"Execution is an apt description constable."

Again a lull in their exchange.

"I have made one final attempt to solicit an identification by posting on the international wire the physical description and an artist's rendering of the victim both with and without the beard," Jordan offered. "The solicitation will cover law enforcement agencies throughout Canada, the States and Europe. But I must say, I hold out little hope. His facial features were so horribly distorted by the gunshot I find it hard to believe our depiction will match true likings of any missing persons," Jordan added.

"Sadly, I believe you are correct in that assumption constable. Now, for the record, may I re-state my intentions? My office plans to remove the remains day after tomorrow, delivering them to the burial crew at the public cemetery for internment at the earliest possible date. Do you have cause to object to my decision, constable?"

"No sir. I have no objection. You are free to proceed. I will mimeograph the release confirmation at the conclusion of our conversation."

After an additional interlude.

"Have we not concluded constable?"

"I suppose so, but don't you think in looking at this fellow, his refined features, his dress, his apparent impeccable grooming habits, plus the material we found in his hotel room, that he was somebody? I mean in his briefcase there were probably two hundred type- written pages. All neat. Not a misspelling that I could tell. It looked to me like a manuscript; you know, for a book. It was strange. Most of it was written in English, but there were some long passages written in Russian of all things. I had to look up the words to make sure. Russian all right. He was writing about Leon Trotsky. One of those revolutionaries who overthrew the Czar and founded the Soviet Union. I had to look that up too. I was not the best student in world history, sorry to say.

"Anyway, this guy had to have been some sort of author or historian, maybe even an academic, you know, a scholar or a diplomat. Damn, I wish we could turn up something; anything that could put a name to that bloody pulp of a face," Jordan said.

"I understand constable. I'm sympathetic, but I have no choice. Here, he's only taking up space. Much needed space."

"Proceed Dr. Lamont. "I have nothing more to say."

Highway 36
Outside Boulder, Colorado
December 15, 1971
3:05 pm

Chapter 42

Catherine Benson held a death grip on the steering wheel of the Crown Vic. Her glare at the winding road ahead was insanely intense. Much to his relief Victor realized that eastbound traffic toward Denver was light at that time of day, absent evening after-work commuters clogging the roadway. He was very happy about traffic conditions. In her current less-than-stable mental state he would not have liked his new, suddenly distraught partner wielding the big black cruiser through bumper-to-bumper jam-ups.

Catherine had barely spoken since her dramatic declaration some twenty minutes before.

Instead of explaining, she had simply motioned for Victor to resume position in the passenger seat while she re-took the driver's side for the ride back to the Big City. He had tried to elicit an explanation for her case-cracking comment, but she stopped him short with a halting palms-up gesture signifying his questions were unwelcomed and untimely. All she would say at that moment was, "Give me time to think; to sort it out."

So he waited. Nervously; especially now with her driving habits coming into question. From weaving lane to lane at well over seventy she had suddenly slowed down to around forty miles per hour. Horns were blaring at their rear, and middle fingers were commonly displayed by motorists whizzing past. She was in the passing lane, for Christ's sake.

Without warning she abruptly swerved into the right lane, cutting off a speeding delivery truck, and headed toward the off-ramp.

That's enough!

"All right Miss Benson, cut the shit. Pull over right now! I'm driving. You're going to kill us both. What the fuck is the matter with you?"

Victor yelled not so politely.

His outburst seemed to shake her loose from a moored stupor.

As she steered up the ramp to a stoplight, she said calmly, "I'm sorry Victor. Let's find a spot for a cup of coffee. I'm ready to talk now."

Two cups later, plus the best damn apple pie Victor ever tasted, he sat back in the coffee shop booth full from his snack and astonished at what he had just heard. He let it sink in for a short time and then reacted.

"Okay, so you believe since you once tore up a shack pad you shared with your married boyfriend, and then you went back later to straighten it all up, that somehow you think that strange behavior might have been adopted by the former Mrs. Riha? Is that what I'm hearing?" Victor's skepticism could not be missed.

"Look detective," Catherine responded, "I can't be sure. I'm just saying that while walking through that creepy goddamn house it struck me. Like a sledgehammer. There I was, back a few months ago, just like her; like someone intent on ripping the place apart. Destroying everything that meant anything to either one of us. To wipe away the past; the guilt; the memories. And then when I started tossing things around and I dropped a nice expensive vase, I realized something different. A change of heart. Why am I doing this? Why should I deprive myself of these things? But at the same time I wanted to leave my mark. Like a mother lion marking her territory with her urine. I know it sounds crazy. So instead of breaking things I just gently rearranged them out of place. Just like she did, or someone did."

Catherine hurried on. "You described it best. Controlled chaos. Like the intruder was careful not to harm anything yet wanted to express her anger, frustration, disappointment; her betrayal in such a way that he and others might understand, yet she didn't want to destroy anything or get caught for that matter."

"Those are your words; not mine. Remember, I thought it was a burglar until I noticed how the objects were positioned about. And I found the necklace, in the heart shape," Victor pointed out.

"Okay. Maybe not your words, but it's what you meant. Right?"

"I concede."

"That was me. I'm telling you," Catherine continued. "When I broke into our little hideaway that night I was nearly hysterical. But I got control of myself, thank God. I could have been arrested. He was paying the rent. The lease was in his brother's name. We had broken up. I had no right being in there. I could have lost my job; my career, but I still needed to make a statement."

"Did you leave a little love token?"

"What do you mean? Like the necklace lying on the nightstand doily? As a matter of fact I did. How stupid of me. Once he gave me a beautiful little solid-gold toe ring."

"A toe ring?" Victor smiled.

"Yes. A toe ring." Catherine did not smile.

"Is there something unusual about your toes?" Victor probed as any good detective would.

"That's enough. Yes, he liked my toes so he gave me a toe ring and I gave it back that night. I put it in his sock drawer. In one of his socks to be exact."

"Toe fetish to toe fetish, you might say," Victor's smile morphed into a snicker.

"All right. You've had your fun. So, I leave the place like I wanted it. Tossed about but not too bad. Things out of place. Like my life at that time. I'm hoping he'll find it and think he's been burglarized. Then he'll have been violated like he violated me. Indirect revenge. Controlled rage. I don't know what I was thinking."

"Not much and not very clearly, I'd say," Victor offered.

"Yes; acknowledged."

"Then a few days later I was feeling better. No more anger. I'd purged myself of him. The rage was gone. All of a sudden I didn't want him or anyone to know how he had affected me. So I had to put things back in order. I took a chance and hit the place a second time. Luckily no one had been there. Everything was just like it was when I finished the first time. Christ, it was two-thirty in the morning. I'd worked all day, but since the apartment was right there in DC, it was easy to get to. I was exhausted but I went to work. I haven't cleaned a house in ten years but I cleaned that one. At sun rise the place was spotless and I had my toe ring right back on my middle toe where it belongs."

"Let me see," Victor ordered in jest.

"Not on your life."

Neither spoke for a while. Catherine sensed it was Victor's time to think.

"So," he began, "Let's just say you're right. The jilted ex-wife returns. She doesn't play house very nice this time. Riha is a neat freak, so messing up his pad and Galya's sleeping quarters is a good way to get back at both of them. She does a pretty good job but can't let herself go overboard by smashing things up, so, like you, she just pushes things around. Later she's remorseful; goes back and tidies up.

"Not remorseful; no, I don't think so," Catherine interjected.

"What then? Purged herself like you did?"

"Maybe."

"Come on, Catherine. With that and nothing more you think she killed Galya and may have killed Riha? You have to be kidding." Victor's grin was long gone. "She's nothing more than a vandal with a little vanity."

"Victor, one thing I've learned from you in our short time together is that instinct counts. Your gut can be golden if you run with it. That's what I'm doing right now. Humor me. Please."

"You pay the tab. I'm going to the ladies' room. You can drive. And on our way back to the office I'm going to pose a few questions I want you to think about overnight. It's an open book test. I can't wait for your answers."

"Gee, thanks. They better be good because I'm not buying any of this so far."

Chapter 43

Yesterday's events had been exhausting. By the time he and his now somewhat rational partner returned to their makeshift quarters Victor was too damn tired to drive home. He checked into a nearby hotel, notified Dispatcher Smothers of his whereabouts, called and talked with his kids for a while, ordered room service and went to bed around eight o'clock. Yet sleep was fleeting. Catherine's questions served to crowd out the rest he desperately needed. Plus, he was rudely awakened at dawn by an unexpected call from his boss, the Chief.

Victor seldom communicated with Pueblo Police Chief Rutherford B. Haynesworth, the much-heralded head of the city's finest. Victor considered Haynesworth a political hack unworthy of his position, serving only to please the mayor's office and majority on city council. Haynesworth, in turn, left his Captain of Detectives alone most of the time knowing it was best not to challenge his work since Bravo's record reflected well on the Chief and his entire department. Victor was startled when he picked up the hotel telephone on the fifth ring.

"I hope I didn't disturb you Captain," the Chief began gently; a tone and demeanor Victor had never heard from the man he normally considered only a nuisance.

"No sir, just preparing to check out. Planning one more day here before returning home. I'm sure other cases are piling up," Victor said in an effort to head off what he expected to be a critical reproach for the attention he was paying to the Tannenbaum matter.

To his astonishment Haynesworth cheerily came back with, "No, listen; don't worry about a thing here Captain. You take your time up there with those folks; on that case. I've relieved you of all of your other duties. Until further notice, you are assigned exclusively to that task force, working solely on solving the Tannenbaum murder."

"What are you saying, Chief? What happened?"

"Well Captain. It seems you've become somebody pretty special. A celebrity of sorts. Got a phone call yesterday from a guy by the name of Richard Helms. Ever heard of him?"

"No sir. Don't believe I have."

"Well Captain. This Mr. Helms is the head of the Central Intelligence Agency. Know about that organization, Captain?

"Yes, sir. I know about the CIA."

"Well Captain. This Mr. Helms tells me that the Tannenbaum case is an important one, and that I should allow you a free hand to work it since there might be some connection to someone of interest to his Agency. Do you think that might be true Captain?"

"Yes sir; that might be true."

"Kind of thought so. Well, Captain, this morning the mayor called me to say that the City has just received a special federal grant to the tune of five-hundred-thousand dollars. The money, according to the mayor, is to be used generally to fight crime in our city, but the word coming from the mayor, apparently directed by the guy who called him to say the money was on its way; well Captain, the money's first to go to you. What do you think of that Captain?"

"Really don't know what to say Chief."

"Well Captain. Here's the way it's gonna happen. You've been dealt a free hand. Actually you hit the jackpot. All of your expenses related to this case are to be covered by this money. You go wherever you need to go, use it however you see fit; just send the bills to City Hall. No one else has use of the funds unless you say so. When you're done, whatever is left over, can be applied to our budget for the whole Department. Like that Captain? Isn't that appealing Captain?"

"Yes, I suppose it is sir."

"Not the way I've done it, but that's the way it is," the Chief said, then added, "Well Captain, spend it wisely. Hope you leave some for us peons. See you when I see you Captain. And by the way; give my best to the President. I didn't vote for him you know. I think he's a pompous ass. Good day Captain."

The line went dead. Victor returned the receiver to its cradle and lay back down, covering his naked body with the sheets and blanket. He had a chill. It penetrated to his bones.

Two hours later Victor's mood was sour when he arrived to find Catherine pacing the floor in anticipation of his company.

"You're late. You ready to get to work?" Catherine asked rather harshly.

"And good morning to you," Victor offered without sincerity.

She followed him into his assigned office. His was a great deal smaller than the one she occupied.

"Let's do this privately. I don't want the others overhearing until we're sure there's some validity to my leads," Catherine said.

"You mean your intuition. I wouldn't call them leads just yet," Victor said challenging, but then admitted, "I do find some of the questions you're raising; let's say, intriguing."

"Thought you might," she responded in a self-congratulatory tone.

"All right, your point about the extra time card the night of Galya's death. Someone may have been on that ward who didn't belong there. However, that place is notorious for poor record keeping; employee files included. There are always complaints about misplaced time cards. But let's say we did have an interloper.

"Now you speculate Nurse Henderson was directly involved. You re-read my report on my interview with her. You believe she may have administered the lethal doses, and did so by injection. How on earth do you suppose someone would allow a nurse or anyone to stick a needle in them day after day, maybe more than once a day?"

Catherine smiled. From a folder in her hand she produced a copy of Galya Tannenbaum's medical records compiled during her confinement at the Asylum. Highlighted as an entry, a section in neat hand script read:

Diagnosis, Type I Diabetes; blood samples confirmed; immediate commencement of insulin by injection recommended. Applications twice daily; morning and night. Constant blood sugar test monitoring to adjust for proper dosage.

Victor read the passage, shaking his head and sighing in disbelief.

"How did you get this?"

"A little extra persuasion you local cops aren't inclined to use. Putting it mildly."

With that she produced another document. Victor recognized it immediately. Dr. Korman's toxicology report. Catherine had also highlighted a passage. It read:

At special request attaching this addendum: Second examination of blood samples with special emphasis fails to demonstrate signs of Diabetic condition. No abnormal blood sugar levels. No indication of extraneous quantities of insulin to counteract. The notes were scrawled in Harper Korman's mostly illegible handwriting.

"Your special request, I assume. You had him go back a second time and check for diabetes," Victor asked.

"He didn't want to at first, but eventually he came around," Catherine responded a little too haughtily.

And then she produced a third piece of paper. The nurse's log. Signed by one Mary Louise Henderson. Her duty report for a night some months before the murder. Handwriting, a perfect match to the phony entry into Galya's medical records. At the bottom it read:

Patient is terrified of needles. Refuses to self-administer required insulin. Will personally oversee injections.

"God in heaven," was all Victor could say.

He was stunned at the revelations but still remained skeptical.

"So, we agree that Nurse Henderson may have played a role; perhaps a direct role in her death. But I still have two questions. Why and why? Why did she do it and why the extra time card? Did she have an accomplice?"

"You knew her better than all of us. Your interrogation lasted hours on end. Let's think back together," Catherine advised.

After a pause for Victor to reassemble the critical give-and-take with Mary Louise, he said, "Sure I came away suspicious. That's why I had her followed. My plan was to bring her back in, in a day or two, for another round of questioning. I intended to search her home, subpoena her bank records, delve into her personal life and generally make her life miserable until I either cleared her or unearthed a true suspect. Not unlike my approach with Samuel Richards. But I never got the chance. After her death, despite finding the money at the crash site, I admit I moved on to other options, and then this potential link to Thomas Riha cropped up. That sent me on an unexpected detour. Besides, I really didn't have sufficient evidence to garner subpoenas in the first place."

When he paused, Catherine then brought forth document number four. A copy of Mary Louise Henderson's bank statements. Eight entries dating from six months after Galya Tannenbaum's sentence to the Asylum began, to the day of her death. Amounts of direct deposits ranged from a low of ten-thousand dollars to a high of twenty-five. All total, one-hundred-fifty-five thousand dollars.

"Another one of your persuasive maneuvers, bypassing local jurisdictions and possibly violating the law? Don't see no court order here," Victor said half jokingly.

'Let's just say Federally chartered banks have a tough time resisting a friendly request from a sister agency which leaves the impression that an audit is likely in the event of unnecessary resistance."

"Uncle Sam hard at work. You have me at a distinct disadvantage," Victor smiled.

"So, she's a hired killer. She obtains the poison, probably supplied to her since we're now buying into a conspiracy theory. She administers it under the cruel pretense of controlling a phony disease. And much to her relief and amusement, I'm thrown off track immediately by an incompetent medical examiner and a school boy shrink with a perpetual hard-on who any rookie cop without batting an eye would have scooped up as suspect number-one."

"You said it, Captain, I didn't," Catherine said, absent a critical tone.

"In any case when confronted, she tries to run but dies leaving behind most of the cash. Poetic justice, I would say. No one will ever get to spend a dime of it," he allowed, then offered.

"That about sum it up?"

"Sure does. Nice and neat," Catherine agreed.

"What about our mysterious guest wandering the halls that night?"

"You tell me. What do you think?" Catherine responded.

"There was no indication on previous nights that anyone on Nurse Henderson's ward was guilty of screwing up time cards. Except that night. I checked myself. So someone came there to watch. She probably let them in to make sure things went along as planned. There was too much money at stake to bungle the job. Let's call it an act of vile voyeurism. Self gratification and all that."

"That's the way I look at it," Catherine affirmed.

"All right. Now we have the triggerman, or woman, and I suppose you're going to tell me you think our intruder that night was Mrs. Riha? You think she came to oversee the final act, or maybe she gave Galya the fatal dose herself to put an exclamation point on her ultimate revenge."

"That's what I think." Catherine said and continued,

"Victor, in your report you said you discovered three shards of splintered glass, and you believed they were from a broken syringe, accidentally swept under her bed by someone cleaning up."

"That's right. Confirmed by the lab, by the way. They were from a syringe."

His turn to continue. "You don't have to go any further. You're saying Nurse Henderson, skilled at administering drugs, even to unruly, often combative patients, wouldn't have likely dropped a syringe; rather someone less adept and probably anxious and jumpy, hand shaking in the process, did so, forcing the hurried clean up."

"That's my conclusion."

"Okay, but the presence of the former Mrs. Riha certainly would have sparked an outcry by the victim, sounding an alarm that even the accomplished head nurse couldn't control."

"True, but remember what had just happened."

"How could I forget? She had just been laid mightily by the horny apprentice."

"And was probably asleep when they paid her a visit," Catherine interjected.

"But he said he was screwing her when she died," Victor reminded his partner.

"Do you really think so? I think he came back for more tail that night and that's when he found her."

"Possibly."

Catherine then produced document number five.

Transcript from subsequent interview with one Samuel Richards, student of Chiropractics, Chamberlain Community College, Vermont.

"You have to be kidding," Victor said.

Paragraph 17 highlighted read: Yes, sir, I admit that earlier in the evening I made love to Miss Tannenbaum in her chambers at the hospital and it was much later that night that I returned to her quarters with the intent of further lovemaking when I found her dead and notified authorities.

"Let me guess. You got him for molesting a patient on his chiropractor's couch while practicing a back rub."

"No," Catherine laughed, "INS; Immigration and Naturalization Service. He had some passport problems that might have landed him in jail. Seems he didn't get back into the country properly after his ill-fated medical studies in Central America. Carrying a bunch of drugs the FDA frowned upon. Issues went away for him after agreeing to talk openly without his lawyer. Everything he said to you was repeated exactly except his second attempt at coitus with the victim later that fateful night. And the fact he had given her a mild sedative after their first go-round just to calm her nerves."

"So, convenient for them she was out like a light when the nurse and her accomplice paid Galya a final visit," Victor said.

"That's the way I see it."

Victor stood and walked to the door of his office looking through the glass window at their staff working busily in the outer room.

"They get all of this we just talked about?" He asked, motioning toward the group of analysts stationed beyond the door.

"Sure did," Catherine acknowledged proudly.

"Under estimated them; that's for sure."

Victor suddenly gave Catherine a hard look. Dead serious.

"What?" she cringed, taken aback by his change in demeanor.

"Don't be coy with me Agent Benson," Victor snarled. "I'm tired of all this crap you're throwing at me. Who's to say your goddamn Agency, full of its spooks and crooks living high off the hog at taxpayer expense, didn't kill that poor woman? Know what I think? Someone high up, or maybe it was you, decided she got in the way of your little spy game with her boyfriend. Maybe it was you who snuck in there that night, played grab ass with Nurse Henderson, and gave Galya that fatal shot in her pretty behind."

"Now listen here. You stop right there detective!" Catherine shrieked.

He ignored her outrage. "And to cover your tracks, or so you thought, you took in after Mary Louise and likely ran her off the road into that ravine, killing her instantly. At least you didn't make her suffer."

Victor knew he'd struck a raw nerve. Her face was ashen. She was stunned by his virulent accusations. He had to do it, just to make sure. He waited for her to react, but at first she didn't. He pounced into the void again.

"And this bit about your sordid love life entangled like hers with pretty boys who went astray. What bullshit that is! You expect me to believe you tore into your married consort's house just like Mrs. Riha, somehow to vent your frustrations over losing him"

"Please!"

"I think you or your minions ransacked Riha's house and then had second thoughts, went back and cleaned up the mess after I was there the first time."

He took a breath, again permitting a lull. Catherine didn't hesitate this time. Her voice was calm and forceful.

"Detective. I take great offense at what you just said. If you truly believe that, bring charges. Otherwise as of this moment we have dissolved this task force and I will proceed on my own to find Dr. Riha and I'm sure in the process find Galya Tannenbaum's killer. I will not tolerate those scurrilous remarks from you or anyone else."

"Good," Victor responded with a grin.

"Good! What the fuck do you mean good. You bastard!" Her outburst this time was loud enough for their support staff to hear. She stood and signaled all was right in the inner office when in fact she remained furious and on the verge of physical assault.

"That's the way I hoped you would react Catherine. Violent righteous indignation was good. I'm glad we got that out of the way. Now let's get back to work."

"You....."

"Don't say it. Sure, I was testing you. You passed. It's over. I think your organization pulls some pretty sleazy stunts under the cover of national security, but I don't think you deliberately kill your own citizens. What I do believe is somebody out there with excellent connections; someone who could skirt traditional law enforcement boundaries and ride both sides of the fence...one foot inside the law, the other clearly outside...had something to do with these crimes. Someone like that renegade agent of yours. Galya's handler. I want to hear much more about him.

Catherine finally relaxed but she was still highly annoyed. "Don't ever do that again."

"I promise. Now tell me about this guy who's been exiled to....where is it?

"Vienna," Catherine said.

"Yes, Vienna. Must be nice."

Chapter 44

The three men sat at the round iron-mesh table in unpadded straight-back cast metal chairs, all in silence, eyeing each other suspiciously. None had spoken for minutes. It had seemed like hours. Their friendly greeting and tri-party embrace of twenty minutes before was a darkened memory. Their heavy overcoats hung over the backs of the chairs. Their wool suits, two grey in color, the other deep navy blue, were worn uncomfortably by each in the stifling hot café. An overhead fan rattled noisily, forcing blistering air to circulate about the room. Yet their mood was cold to match the espresso in front of all three, left that way for lack of interest. The tile floor was stained with layers of spilled coffee blends. The temperature outside was minus two Centigrade. One man loosened his red, white and blue striped tie worn for the occasion. Since the meeting was arranged he had been anxious about this time with his American friends. Now he was sure he wanted to leave, wishing he'd never come.

Their meeting place had been chosen by the one with the patriotic lash. He was attached to the embassy at Boltzmanngasse 16, some six kilometers and a twenty-minute taxi ride away. He liked the location because the distance from his post reduced the chances of being seen with his companions by a State Department colleague out for a winter stroll.

Since his banishment his duties had been relatively menial. Not much more difficult than processing lost or stolen replacement passports for frantic tourists, petrified at the prospects of prolonged exile at their chosen vacation spot for nothing more than carelessness or being victimized by petty thieves. Occasionally he would interface with local police when drugs were found in student backpacks, believing they deserved what jail time was warranted until the Ambassador would call to intervene on behalf of the incarcerated whose families were major donors in the last Senatorial campaign cycle.

Only then would he apply his now dormant skills in persuading local authorities to accept a hefty fine in lieu of a long-term stay in the dungeon, which currently housed the whimpering amateur narcotics peddler. Senator so-and-so would be most pleased with their release.

His six-month assignment had been extended indefinitely but he never bothered to tell anyone, including his American friends, preferring the comfortable government-paid rent-free apartment and the company of his former protégé. These advantageous conditions prevailed despite her recent refusal to don the worn out nurse's aid uniform. Most of all he coveted the cushy job, which paid as much but lacked the risks he incurred while coaching counterfeiters and killing their killers. In fact he hoped he would never be forced to reenter that shadowy world again. He had all the money he would ever need. But now, after warm greetings and friendly reminiscing, he finds himself staring into the blank, callous faces of Hoover's agents; men he once trusted, men he risked his career, even his life for, who are angry and threatening unless he gives them more. More of what?

He won't kill any more. He's through with that. He has a better life and will never return stateside. He's protected here, ironically by the country he betrayed while its top law enforcers remain oblivious to his deeds. Yet his tableside companions are insistent. They think he will betray them; betray her, and all they worked together to accomplish. They claim unfriendly people are nosing around. Dangerous people getting too close to all of us. He is vulnerable. They all are.

They claim local authorities have linked his ward's death to the Professor's disappearance. They think someone killed the nurse because she was involved in Galya's death. It's all coming unraveled.

And they want me to go back and kill the cop.

He's the one they're most afraid of.

But why can't the FBI stop it all? Cover it up like they usually do when things become unpleasant. You guys were put in charge of the operation; taking over from the CIA. You guys were running the show, turning Riha, recruiting the nurse and eliminating his girlfriend for the sake of national security. Why can't you take care of the cop if he's the big troublemaker? The FBI can do anything. Or maybe not.

To hell with you.

"No, I won't do it. I'm finished. Pack your bags and get out of town or I'll send the goddamn embassy Marines after you," he sneered having grown tired of their nasty obstinacy.

Neither man flinched at the threat. Their anger grew. They hid it well. They knew their mission was futile. She said it would be, but they insisted the trip was necessary to try to lure him back. He had been the perfect cover. Gullible in believing they, his old chiefs from the Chicago bureau, had taken over the assignment from the CIA. He was the steady hand who never wavered, supplying Mary Louise the lethal injections to finish the job on Galya. And then when the nurse became a liability he never questioned the orders that came next, creatively finding a way to sabotage the car to make sure she never came out of it alive.

He said he would go after the cop if needed, but now he's grown soft. She was right. They should have never come. Now they have to make things right.

Without another word both men rose from their seats, gathered their coats, presented crooked smiles and strolled away leaving him alone with resentment and the bill. He watched them exit the café and hurry across the snow-slick street to hail a taxi. He sipped his icy espresso but that was not what caused the chill to run up his spine. He had always been the one with hardened nerves. They were the weak ones; the ones afraid to take the risks. Sure, more money had come his way from her but he earned it because he was exposed while they lurked in the background, protected by his ingenuity and steel will. Now the tables had turned. He was weak, or at least it felt that way. He would not return to the embassy that day. He needed time to walk and think. It had not been a pleasant afternoon. He would meander until he found his way home to the gratis apartment near St. Stephens Cathedral on Spiegelgass and the life and woman he now cherished.

To hell with them. They can't touch me.

Engaged in hot debate, his antagonists rode back to their hotel conveniently located within walking distance of their opponent's up-scale flat. They spoke in Spanish, comfortable that their Austrian driver could not understand. Yet their words remained guarded. Should they act on their own without her consent? Or should they return with excuses, defeated, and admitting her prediction was correct? If they did that, without eliminating the threat, and he ever talked, all would come crashing down around them. They had to act boldly, to shed their fears and take matters into their own hands. She would approve and they would be rewarded once again. She probably knew all along they would face such a decision. Neither had ever done it before. Who would be the one?

An hour passed. Then they moved in his direction, determined yet with caution.

Luckily their target's fourth-floor dwelling was located at the end of a long corridor with entryway offset from the straight-line structure of the building. In quiet isolation. They liked that. They knocked and waited. Footsteps approaching; then stopping.

Tentatively, a shallow voice asked. "Who is it?"

The single hollow point pierced the beveled glass peephole sending razor sharp spires to lodge in his forehead, centimeters above the orbital cavity that once housed his dark blue eye. His head lurched backward as a four-inch diameter portion of his posterior cranial cap disintegrated. He was dead in midair splay before his body struck the floor. A fatal hit on the first attempt. Lucky shot.

The sound of his lifeless remains descending to the floor with a thud was louder than that emitted by the silenced-Berretta 92, one of a matching pair supplied by their employer. With it the killer lowered, took aim and needlessly fired three more times through the door, each shot missing its intended mark. Galya's handler was already sprawled far below the line of fire. In silence they hesitated. Then proceeded. The next round shattered the door handle. They stepped over the threshold, undeterred by the splintered obstruction, which swung wide on its loosened hinges. Although having watched his muse leave the apartment only minutes before, shopping bag in hand, and enter a taxi for an unknown destination they scampered quickly through the six-room flat, pistols at the ready, intent on distilling more death if needed.

For the occasion they were grateful for their training, although for several years neither had taken opportunity to implement the proper technique for sweeping unknown interior spaces for suspects. They secured the area in less than thirty seconds. The only other breathing inhabitant was a hairless Siamese cat perched on an overstuffed chair back, watching the proceedings with saucer-like steely green eyes. Soon the animal grew disinterested and continued with its afternoon self-grooming, licking its claw-extended paws with certain vigor.

It was not necessary for a close inspection of the body to confirm its violent demise. The extent of destruction was evident. One of them heaved and tasted bitter bile at the sight. His partner had speculated their victim would peer through the peephole, wondering who might be calling right before the dinner hour and so soon after the departure of the handler's beloved. He was right and took the auspicious shot. They noticed place settings at the dining table were for two, and water still boiling in pots on the stove. The smell of cooking food made the queasy one nearly vomit this time, but he held back, swallowing hard to resist.

She must have dashed off to the market for something to round out their meal. Her decision saved her life, the shooter thought.

Task completed, they exited to descend by a nearby stairwell leaving the shattered door standing open for easy access and viewing.

She had planned to wear the nurse's outfit for him that night, slipping into it right after dinner. He enjoyed watching her prance around in costume before the zipper slowly slid down to reveal her pleasures. She wanted to please him since he had seemed horribly upset that afternoon, coming home early from a meeting, he said, with people he didn't enjoy, in fact, didn't trust any longer. Was it that incident in Colorado? No, he said, don't worry about that, he said. That's far in the past. But yes, they were Americans, he said, friends he once had, people he once respected.

It was unusual for him to be that way since things had gone so well following their arrival in Vienna those many months before. Actually he didn't want her to leave the apartment at all that afternoon. He had said he had an uneasy feeling. It was silly, he said, for her to be concerned over the absence of bay leaves for the sauce. But she insisted. Not to worry, she said. She wanted everything to be right that night, for him, since he had been so concerned.

The scrawny feline was standing in and licking at a sticky red pool as she stood horrorstruck in the gaping doorway. When her mind finally fully registered the grizzly scene the glass jar housing the seasoning fell to the floor shattering it and her life in a thousand pieces. Her scream sent the cat scampering for cover.

Chapter 44

They were insistent this time, more so than ever in the two years past. Mission accomplished in Vienna so she would allow their game to continue. Their pastime was humiliating and degrading, but she would comply. There was no pleasure for her, yet she sounded and acted as if there was. Her staged enthusiasm was a big part of their amusement. Unless she played along they would not be satisfied and would want more.

Of everything.

At first, actually the first time, she was in control. She was the one who led them to her lair with a sensual smile and promises of unending gratification ahead. Their meeting had been by chance. Pure happenstance.

Tired, broken, ashamed and wracked with self-doubt Helen Riha, unwilling to change her adopted surname for reasons she failed to reconcile, took to drink and other things. After leaving Thomas and his whore, she hid from herself. Ensnared in their trap she had bent to stronger wills and passions she could not match. Her emotions saw no boundaries like an old fashion whirligig spinning, pitching and rolling about in panoply of misguided directions. Thoughts of suicide crowded her brain only inexplicably replaced by fits of robust gaiety lasting days and spanning nights with lovers she found sickening and in two cases physically harmful. Bruises heal but she could not.

Until she overheard their drunken exchange.

At a dive bar off West Monroe Street, a place where Helen knew no one and increasingly cared less if she did, she had heard the name Riha. Not a common name. Not a name most would think was a name at all. At first she had thought she heard one of them say "Hee-Haw" and surmised their blathering was about the popular hillbilly comedy show recently ending its run on network television. But then, the one appearing less inebriated spoke more clearly. "Riha," he had said, "That son-of-a-bitch."

With that Helen had inconspicuously swung her bar stool toward them for better line-of-sight reception. The joint they were in was crowded and noisy for a Friday night. She had to hear more.

It couldn't be. No, impossible, she thought.

"Yea," the man's bleary-eyed buddy responded, "He was that; a SOB but a smart one. How could he have slipped right past us?"

"Easy you fool," the other one scolded with a slur. "We slept through the night until dawn. He was probably a hundred miles away by the time we woke up. Didn't take much intelligence for him to do that. He probably walked right out the front door, and maybe even waved to us as he drove off."

They both howled with laughter and clinked their glasses as if in celebration.

She did not move. Stunned by the banter. One of them glanced up to catch her eye. She caught it and held his view. He looked away and then came back. She was there again. He stared; this time seeking confirmation of her interest. Her turn to look away. His attention waned. He ordered another round of drinks.

She had waited. It was not enough. She needed more to be sure.

Minutes passed. Neither man spoke. She stirred her scotch and soda nervously thinking it was pure coincidence; silently hoping differently.

Then she heard one of them babble, "But he cost us our jobs. He ruined my fucking career. Yours too."

"Right," the other one confirmed, "That little nap of ours. It sure changed everything. But goddamn it, Hoover didn't need to sack us over it. With two weeks severance. No pension. Just like that. Cut our balls off, he did. Denied us our right to appeal. We had no one defending us. Every friend we had in the Bureau ran like rabbits. Just because Hoover wanted to snatch up that Commie bastard and try him for treason so he could go out with a bang was, well, too much. He took it out on us and now we got nothin'.

And then she heard.

"Thomas Riha and that bitch he was shacking up with brought us down for sure. I hope someone finds them in a ditch somewhere. And I hope Hoover dies with his pants down around his ankles."

"Yeah, sitting on the shitter and someone takes his picture to publish in the Chicago Sun Times."

"I'll drink to that," Rico exclaimed.

That's all she needed. She slid off her stool and sashayed over to where they sat.

Agony was suddenly eclipsed by visions of precious vengeance.

Despite the constant schoolboy attention she was forced to pay to the despicable drunks, Helen often found time to reflect on the months succeeding that fateful night at the seedy Monroe Street tavern.

Their plan had been hatched in a short span of three weeks. Early on without much prodding she discovered that Gordon and Rico were former special agents with the Federal Bureau of Investigation. She also quickly learned they were once former, not so cleverly disguised utility linesmen, who J. Edgar Hoover had made certain, would never again find employment in law enforcement. It did not take long for them to become her pawns. Within days she was plying them with sex and money frequently bestowing both in equal quantity. She recalled that their first night together had been tolerable. She made them take turns. It was probably the booze or maybe the dark, twisted euphoria she had felt when the anchor of rejection tore loose from its moorings to launch her journey toward redemption. She allowed herself to become their instrument, their vessel, but in the end she steered them on her designated course. A course tilting all things back into balance.

Money was of no concern. She had plenty. She supported them well with currency from the divorce settlement and a trust fund from her father's medical practice. Not to mention the egg. The egg, which Thomas stupidly thought was a forged Faberge, had turned out to be real. She sold it anonymously through Sotheby's to the Chicago Museum of Art and History for four- hundred-seventy-five thousand dollars less auction concession. The Museum board was ecstatic with a rare find of Russian porcelain and jewels made by the master himself. The object had been Romanov's gift to Czarina Alexandria in February, 1917, a little more than a year before their slaughter at the hands of Thomas' beloved Bolsheviks.

When she staged the contrived melee during her first visit to their divided home, Helen had replaced it with a fake. On the second visit to tidy things up, she dusted it off to brighten its sheen.

Helen justified her sexual favors as a cost of doing business and she insisted that if either one ever declared their affection or strived to gain an advantage she would immediately sever all ties and charge them both with rape. They believed her. She grew callous and cold in the process. Methodical and uncaring. Purposeful in her quest.

In spite of Gordon and Rico's un-ceremonious ouster from the Bureau, they still had some friends in the Chicago field office. When the uncanny connection with Helen Riha was made, they were quick to obtain Galya Tannenbaum's file, including the name and activities of her recruiter and eventual handler for the CIA. Vital details about the man who made a career overseeing the famous counterfeiter were prominently noted. He had a past and it wasn't a good one. His file, before being exposed, had been tightly locked away. Its contents alleged gambling debts, bouts with the IRS for unpaid taxes, and a horrendous civil suit in which a big ugly brown rat played a key role. Seems the huge rodent had gnawed feverously on the toes of an elderly tenant in a run-down rental property, which the handler had owned. The chewy bites spawned an infection and loss of the poor man's left foot. A two-hundred-thousand dollar court judgment plus legal expenses for the amputated appendage were levied against the slumlord essentially spelling his financial ruin.

Still, Gordon had noted, despite his monetary woes, Galya's watchman somehow made the big time by crossing the treacherous career-path moat between federal agencies to land a prestigious post with the Central Intelligence Agency. All because he was the one who accidentally discovered the forger's remarkable talents. However, he was not untouchable, so when his former colleagues approached him with a lucrative proposition to help eliminate their benefactor's hated harlot he became a willing participant. It just took time to formulate the plan, collect the cash and recruit the players including the Night Nurse on Woman's Ward 3.

The cyanide had been Rico's idea. In his glory days before his propensity to sleep on the job, he had investigated a case involving the curious death of a Spanish attaché assigned to the consoler's office in Chicago. Juan Diego Hernandez was a suave and debonair diplomat with immunity and a fat government-backed bank account, who got too close to a bi-polar prostitute with an IQ over 160. Once too often, the envoy apparently stiffed his hired squeeze of her pre-arranged fee and wound up on the floor of his hotel suite, frothing at the mouth and convulsing in a spasmodic fit. His heart stopped three hours later before doctors could pinpoint the cause, treating him instead as an epileptic. The autopsy found not just traces of the poison, but rather a bulk quantity sufficient to knock off ten Spaniards of equal size and weight.

However, it was Helen who had insisted on a slow death for her nemesis. Unhurried, deliberate and horrifically painful. Using her father's medical texts, she researched the effects of cyanide poisoning and concocted the precise formula, dosage and timing for each injection to assure that Galya's health would inevitably deteriorate beyond possible recovery. The almonds were a nice touch. They had originally planned to prolong her suffering. It was the irresistible intern who had altered their schedule. While Galya's trysts ensued it became increasingly difficult for Helen to supervise, and Mary Louise to administer, the deadly serum. In the end Helen decided to finish the job herself, all at once. The final dosage nearly filled the syringe and could have killed a Clydesdale.

Which, that is the syringe, I dropped and broke like a skittish fool, she would unceasingly chastise herself for doing.

Complications stemming from the Night Nurse's willingness to talk with police and then Mary Louise's killer skipping out for the overseas post, leaving Gordon and Rico to cover his tracks, had made Helen's life temporarily intolerable. But not for long. Ordering her minions to hunt him down in Vienna and bring him back to take care of that miserable cop, was so smart of me, she would muse, knowing full well they would have to eliminate the handler on the spot.

They were so stupid to think he would willingly fly home for the hit. I knew they'd have no choice but to do it right there.

And a broad grin would always cross her face when Helen would reflect on the tip Gordon got on Thomas' return from Moscow to the U.S. When Gordon revealed Riha's arrival date, time, and even Aeroflot flight number, supplied by a fellow ex-Fed who also hated the professor for his politics, Helen rewarded him with extra special favors, sending Rico into a rant that lasted for days. That invaluable information had presented Helen with her opening to extract final retribution. She was adamant that she alone would kill him. Gordon and Rico argued to the contrary but she held all the cards and thus her sole stalking began.

To her amazement Helen found joy in shadowing the one she hated most while he hid out in Toronto. She lived as he did on the streets and in the hovels until his move to Montreal and his belief that his trail was cold and his history forgotten. How utterly naïve he had become. For her, the experience was thrilling and invigorating. It further hardened her to don an urchin's costume, forever keeping Thomas in her sights while panhandling and pandering to the downcast in twisted acts of self-degradation. All worth it, no matter the cold, hard asphalt on which she often slept, or the rancid meals she consumed, or the threats of beatings and rapes dispatched with pistol pointed at exposed genitals. Survival. Survivor. Put her to the test.

Preparing myself while descending to his depths.

Nonetheless she was relieved on the day she watched his return to the storage locker to extract his stash for the next leg of exile. Just steps behind, she followed him to the car rental outlet and laughed as he drove off in the shiny red hot-rod. Returning only an hour later, bathed and sheathed provocatively in skin tight and low cut, it only took moments and a hundred-American to convince the clerk to produce the papers pinpointing his destination. Montreal. She loved the city. Visited there once as a child with her parents. Fond memories destined to grow fonder.

Knowing him as she did and sensing a forthcoming life-style transformation, Helen's search for his whereabouts took just a week. At the finer hotels. In the finest restaurants. Close to culture. Then sighting the marquee announcing Chekov's play. He would not miss it. And remain near to see the performances many times. The Bonaparte. Literally next door to the theatre. It had been easy to lurk nearby, once over a coincidental breakfast even befriending a winsome wife in search of strange love and suggesting the bearded man at yonder table, handsome and alone. She became voyeuristically aroused while gazing upon their stairway ascension toward his room.

And then came the day of reckoning. He's run out of time. His joy will cease. He will feel the pain.

They had predicted bad weather on that day and she took the cue waiting through the morning hours for him to step outside into the gray threatening sky. His habit of a vigorous walk each day would not be broken despite the danger of a ferocious blizzard. She knew that about him. Habitual. Seeing him emerge from the hotel lobby, she was particularly impressed with his fashionable wintertime attire and was tempted for a moment to compliment his choice of color and fabric. Chic in disguise to everyone but her. She watched as he swallowed the frigid air and set off almost in a sprint.

Not only was her mind fit for the task, she had shaped a lithe muscular frame with brutal hours of calisthenics and weight lifting, preparing to whisk away into the darkness following the fatal blow. She held back, allowing two-dozen meters to separate them. Time and space. After a short span she noticed a reduced, nearly labored stride, remembering without sympathy his bad ankle and claim of Army injury while in service to the country he loathed. Wisps of snow turning into a torrent. Whimpering winds becoming gale force. His pace slowing and the diversion off his path to find rest. A convenient park bench. The perfect spot. Ideal conditions. Her strut into his view. Cold steel of the lethal weapon nestled and warmed by gloved hand inside her coat pocket. She would cherish the meeting. The conversation that followed. His shock at first and his attempt to lure. Cavalier to the end but never expecting the violence.

But unexpected revulsion at the muffled explosions. The monster I've become gripped her for an instant. Stopping with finality his last feeble attempt to charm, persuade and deceive failed to alter, leaving lingering doubt in her. At that instant, his bloody mouth agape, his dead eyes fixated and bewildered, Helen was trapped, welcoming capture. But why? A demon inside. Her fate.

Find me, was her refrain. Torture me. Render the death penalty, or life in prison knowing my humiliation had made me worse. Than him.

It was the woman passing by the park bench earlier; her swaddled child in the carriage now lost and terrified in the swirling storm that brought Helen back. She first heard their cries, but saw only sheets of swirling white. The anguished sounds startled her as she sat next to Thomas absorbing the sight of her gore. All common sense now abandoned. Reality fled. She would wait for a witness and be taken away. But the distant pleas, echoing through the howling wind, forced her to move; first to close his mouth and shut his eyes to no longer cast her shame. She moved him from slumping grotesquely to upright, in proper pose, crossing limp legs at the knees and folding clawing hands in his lap.

He would soon discolor and the snow would blanket him rigid. Finishing, once again tidying after the chaos, she rose to search. Soon she found them; mother and daughter child, and soon they were warm and safe. All of them. And with their rescue, Helen diverted her destiny and emerged determined to celebrate her achievement.

Her way home took a circuitous route. She remained in Montreal but found Chekov's masterpiece unworthy, leaving the next day's performance after Act One. She avoided the Bonaparte, instead taking weeklong residence at Hotel Le St-James. She drove through the countryside during the day and returned at night. Her rented vehicle also a Camaro. Super-charged, sleek and fast. Exhilarating. She fought the nightmares. They had come after Galya; were more intense with Thomas, but the terror soon faded into satisfying slumber. She shopped manically, replacing every stitch of her clothing with the latest from Paris. Donating her discarded wares to a needy charity. She nearly took a lover on her last night, but declined when he joked about a street-corner beggar shivering in rags seeking only coins for soup. She gave the vagabond twenty-Canadian and told her escort to fuck off. O'Hare welcomed her the next day, arriving buoyant until spotting her charges waiting at the gate.

The facts were that Gordon and Rico had adequately completed their assigned task in Vienna, but the result was sloppy and messy, possibly leaving a trail back to them and to her. Nonetheless, Helen had no choice but to accommodate their cash and carnal requests but under a new set of rules. No longer would they visit her together. And she would pay them separately, not together in a lump sum. They would remain her suitors but the trio was dissolved. They would go forth but only as individual couples. She divided them to even the odds. In the past there were three with Helen disadvantaged, like before. Now she would regain dominance with her rules, and soon turn them into adversaries.

Chapter 45

The classified dispatch from Vienna circulated worldwide to all Agency outposts spoke in stark, vivid terms. As Victor read the transmittal renewed apprehension overtook him. Catherine Benson could sense the unease by the look on her partner's face and how he peered intently at the page. Detective Bravo had a habit of unconsciously narrowing his eyes when he became anxious or angry. His glare became hard and intimidating when squinting at the subject of his concern. He didn't need glasses except for fine-print reading. Otherwise he saw everything clearly with excellent eyesight and insight for a man of his age. Now, however, he was looking through a fog.

Catherine braced herself for his reaction. She expected his suspicions were aroused once again.

"No, we didn't kill him," she proclaimed preemptively in an effort to blunt his oncoming accusations.

"Didn't say you did."

"Well, that's what you were thinking."

"I suppose that's true, but I think your people would have more class; let's say a more refined procedure for murdering an unwanted human being than risking a lucky head shot through a peephole. And then to top it off, traipsing right through the blood pool leaving a defining footprint and a trail down the stairwell right out onto the street. Not very professional if you ask me."

The tight muscles from the tension in Catherine's neck would not ease. She drew a deep breath. She was ready for another one of Victor's scurrilous indictments against her Agency. She was hoping his prior observations were all he had to offer. But he wasn't quite done yet.

"You still had motive. The Agency couldn't afford to have this guy spouting off about the whole affair. Better him dead all around for everyone. You had him and his girlfriend shipped overseas, set him up pretty in a cushy job with plenty of hush money and then when the timing was right, everyone's relaxed, the party's over, you pay him a final visit. Much easier to kill one of your own on foreign soils."

Catherine glared, her challenging gaze intensifying. Jaw taught. Neck muscles rigid. "What will it take to get you off that kick? You really are beginning to annoy me."

"Show me evidence to the contrary."

Furious but in control Catherine smiled with a smirk and reached into the middle drawer of her desk and retrieved a folder similarly marked classified. She slid it across the desktop to him.

"Here, I knew you would jump to conclusions, and piss me off again, so I held this stuff back for a few days until we could match the footprint to the sole pattern and trace the shoes to the buyer. Read all about it detective."

Victor suppressed a grin, flipped open the file and began to read. His went eyes wide. No longer narrow and dubious.

After a few minutes Victor turned to Catherine and asked, "Work from our staff out there in the next room?" He motioned to the three huddled around a portable television set watching an afternoon soup opera.

"Yep," Catherine acknowledged and added, "Between their favorite shows; I think, Days of our Lives and General Hospital."

As he read on Victor was astounded by the stupidity of it all. Standard dress. Hard rubber soles with distinctive ridges. Issued to FBI agents usually reserved for tactical exercises to avoid slipping on wet surfaces; be they asphalt, wood or concrete. And these, size fourteen. Extra large. Not many in service with feet that big. Certainly not hard to identify. Well worn by then, so given to the bearer some time ago.

They might as well have worn their black windbreakers with the yellow F.B.I. lettering on front and back. It was that obvious, Victor thought. He continued reading.....

Recipient of the shoes and one other summarily dismissed on Hoover's direct orders for dereliction of duty over the disappearance of suspect one, Dr. Thomas Riha, wanted for questioning on suspicion of espionage and treason. Special Agents Gordon Peterson and Rico Ramirez relieved of service shortly thereafter. Bureau firearms confiscated at the time of dismissal, but two Berretta 92 handguns easily adaptable with silencer later discovered missing from storage locker used by former partners. Ballistics match those used in the murder of State Department employee Rafael Jones attached to embassy in Vienna whose body was found in rented apartment near American compound preceding month. Peterson and Ramirez known to be in Austrian capital city at the time through use of individual passports still valid and airline tickets purchased in Chicago. Location of suspects unknown at this time.

Victor closed the file, leaned back in his chair and looked over in Catherine's direction. She was examining her fingernails with the offhand thought that a manicure was long overdue. She waited for his response; no, his apology. It didn't come; rather this: "It's not necessary for me to ask whether a manhunt is underway for these characters, is it?"

"Don't be ridiculous," She responded, still pretending to be curious about the condition of her cuticles.

Ignoring her well-deserved condescending tone Victor offered, "I think it's time we got out of this office and did some real police work for a change. What do you say we take a quick trip to the Windy City?"

Catherine glanced up to acknowledge his suggestion, but to his surprise, said, "Sure, Chicago by way of Montreal."

"What? Montreal? What does Montreal have to do with anything?"

Catherine paused, returning Victor's inquisitive gaze.

"A hunch; that's all," Catherine finally stated.

Showing signs of renewed irritation, Victor said, "Okay, spill it. What are you thinking? These guys bound for Canada, or you looking for a new vacation spot?"

"No, I don't think they're that smart, and the last person I'd want to vacation with is you. It's something else."

Victor chuckled, corrected his grin and demanded, "Damn it, what is it?"

"Look here." Catherine produced a third file from the middle drawer. This one carried no warning label that America's secrets were inside, rather a neatly typed police report from the homicide division of the city's Royal Canadian Mounted Police. It was one of hundreds received following a request Langley had made to friendly and not-so-friendly law enforcement agencies in countries across the globe. Victor glanced at it quickly, and still aggravated, said, "So?"

"After Riha vanished from Kennedy Airport I asked Director Helms to solicit information from international police agencies including Interpol on intriguing, unsolved murders in their jurisdictions, particularly those that appeared to be execution style, up-close and personal, taking place in unusual locations. I wanted all male victims. All middle aged. Probably well dressed, sophisticated looking gentlemen meeting their demise unexpectedly, likely at the hands of someone they knew, someone they allowed to get too close. I was thinking gunshots, not stabbings. Don't know why, just felt that way.

Before he could react to another one of her feelings....

"We got hundreds of reports from Panama City to Johannesburg; from Copenhagen to Guadalajara. I had five agency staffers culling through them day after day, presenting me those, which might be linked, to our missing Professor. But none ever fit. Reading dozens of them myself, I just couldn't feel a connection. And I know it was stupid to think that if Riha was dead there would be a body to look at; that his remains weren't three-fathoms deep, or scattered about a pine forest or rotting on a jungle floor never to be identified. None of us think he's still alive, scurrying back to Russia and living high on the hog at a remote dacha outside Leningrad. We'd have found out. The KGB is not that sly, plus the fact that he's more valuable to them back here in the States spouting their propaganda. We don't think they even know he successfully pulled off that little stunt blocking their attempts to restrict our radio signals filled with our own propaganda."

Again Catherine paused, looking away, hesitating to say what was coming next.

"Victor, you're going to think I'm crazy but I got pretty close to that jerk. He was handsome, suave, clever, and even sexy when he'd keep politics out of the conversation. I admit I was attracted to him at one point. I wouldn't say that to anyone but you. And even though he was abhorrent to me we formed a bizarre sort of bond, it seemed. I can understand how women were drawn to him. He was magnetic. And now that he's gone, dead I mean, there's something in that RCMP report that grabbed me. When I read it I just knew, in my gut." She hurried on.

"Bear with me on this, Victor. Read it and tell me I'm wrong. She did it and cleaned up after herself, just like she did at the house in

Boulder; just like before."

Victor's curious look intensified. "Okay, hold on, let me read it," he said, raising his hands to deflect her intensity. He adjusted his glasses and began.

Male, thirty-five to forty-five years of age. Slender build. Black hair, dyed grey. Neatly trimmed grey beard. Expensive winter clothing and footwear. Body discovered seated on a park bench in remote section of St. Lawrence Park covered by a mound of drifted snow following an early season blizzard. Limited decomposition. Virtually frozen state. Remains well preserved for examination once thawing could occur. Cause of death; bullet wound through the left forearm, entering lower abdomen, penetrating liver, resulting in massive internal bleeding, alone likely fatal. Death instantaneous however from second gunshot at close range (less than a meter estimated) piercing victim's upper pallet and exiting through left posterior lobe of the cranium. Body found in casual seated position with hands folded in lap and legs crossed. Likely perpetrator arranged corpse in that manner.

Body removed to morgue. Routine autopsy performed confirming above-stated causes. Body remained unclaimed through maximum legal time period, then interred in pauper's grave. Personal effects found at Bonaparte Hotel, which is last known address. All items including clothing and cash plus extensive written material, found in room, possibly a manuscript written partially in Russian, and letter addressed to the New York Times and placed in hotel safe by female employee. All items now in police possession. Police report no suspects despite intensive investigation.

Victor slowly laid the paper on the desktop. He removed his glasses and rubbed his eyes, suddenly weary of it all. Catherine sat opposite anxious for his response.

"Pattern's there, I have to admit," he finally observed. "Pieces seem to fit. Description certainly tracks to our missing boy. And his position, how they found him, like you said, arranged. I guess we have no choice in the matter; a detour to see our neighbors up north. Can't wait to get my hands on that letter."

Chapter 46

Victor's only previous visit to Canada was with Johnny and two other friends five years past when their group traveled north from Colorado on a fishing trip to the placid, unspoiled lakes of Saskatchewan and Manitoba. On the trip they caught more northern pike than they cared to eat. They stayed drunk for three days to mask the bitter cold north wind, which constantly blew. They lost hundreds of dollars in poker games to female pipe-smoking members of the Nisichawayasihk Cree Nation tribe, but still considered the excursion an immeasurable success, vowing to return annually which hasn't happened despite several attempts to organize it. In explicit detail Victor recounted his expedition to Agent Benson on their flight through Buffalo that morning, but all she could do in the seat beside him was yawn and stretch with manifest boredom at his telling.

Her only attempt at discourse was a demand for him to spell the name of the poker-playing Indian tribe, which surprisingly he did, and to pose the question whether Victor had ever spotted a Mounties or more properly put, a Royal Gendarmerie of Canada, in full regalia. She stirred briefly but bleary-eyed to explain how taken she was by their bright-red tunics, brown belts strapped across their chests and bellies, with holstered revolvers at the ready. She loved the look. Found it erotic, withholding that detail, but saying instead that the Order of Merit of the Police Forces hat was her favorite part of the uniform, perhaps next to the knee-high black leather boots.

All Victor could do in response to her strange recitation was gawk in puzzlement and close his eyes in a futile attempt to sleep.

As she gazed about the cavernous polished-marble foyer, which served as the entry point to the RCMP central office in the Quebec capital, Catherine's quest for just one, that's all that mattered, in full dress, perfectly symbolizing the best of Canadian law enforcement, continued unfulfilled. To her dismay those surrounding her, bustling about noisily unlike the stayed, serene Bobbies of their Motherland, were Canadian cops dressed just like boring old Victor. Dull suits and blue ties sprinkled among those in standard beat patrol garb looking more like meter maids than proud, dashing Gary Cooper look-alikes. Where was Madeleine Carroll? One of Catherine's favorite movie classics was Northwest Mounted Police. Cecil B. DeMille's 1940 production had made a lasting impression on her. She adored the male attire, and thought Madeleine had deserved an Academy Award.

Detective Victor Bravo didn't notice and cared not at all about Catherine's penchant for a Mounties sighting as he quick-stepped through the crowd toward a sign over a door marked Serious Crimes, thinking that might be the best place to find Chief Inspector Russell Crump. He was right. Prior to their departure they had been told Inspector Crump was the major cold-case division head who had handled the unsolved park bench murder of a mangled man, who before his head was nearly blown off, looked more like he belonged on an exclusive ski outing in the Alps.

Abandoning hope of finding Mr. Cooper's clone in the mix, Catherine trotted after Victor as he was already passing through the doorway to Crump's cramped quarters. There was no receptionist to greet them, only the noxious odor of burnt coffee and cigarette smoke and an in-basket in the center of a desk piled eight inches high. Not unlike cop hangouts in most other parts of the world the scene was in stark contrast to the building's opulent entryway,

"Just like home," Victor said, scanning the room.

"Welcome eh," came a voice from over his shoulder and Catherine's who had moved to Victor's side to unblock the doorframe.

Catherine scanned the man's frame as he moved past them toward the desk.

Russell Crump, twenty-two year RCMP veteran with three years left before his pension, could have been Gary Cooper's stunt double if his crew-cut grey hair had been dyed black. He was beautiful Agent Benson quickly concluded. They shook hands all around; Catherine thinking hers was moist to his touch. The Inspector moved overflowing file debris from two wooden side chairs, which stood on either side of his desk and bid his guests to take their seats. He had to close three file cabinet drawers to gain sufficient passage to his chair on the desk's opposite side.

"Lovely accommodations," Catherine said sarcastically.

Her leading man smiled, pleasantly acknowledging her stab at opening-line humor, but announced he was jammed for time since just that morning two bodies had been found in Montreal alleyways, both believed to be French Quebec separatists likely eliminated by unification proponents tired of all the talk of two Canadian nations.

"This little dispute of ours could become the next great North American civil war," the Inspector said, then added, "Yours of course, being the first and the bloodiest."

Ignoring the jab, Victor said, "We appreciate your time Inspector. You know why we're here. The file on the case you sent to us was most helpful."

"Not often do I get requests like that funneled through the prime minister's office. More than just a routine police matter I take it. International implications?" Crump inquired.

"Perhaps, Inspector," Catherine interjected unconsciously wiping her hand on her pant leg. "We need to have the body exhumed. We have dental records and fingerprints. It is imperative we close the loop here. This man, if he is who we think he is, played a key role in a secret overseas operation on behalf of our government. We believe he completed that mission successfully which, by the way, was also of immense importance to your government as a free democracy, but then he disappeared, either voluntarily or not, making his way to this lovely city where he met his unexpected termination."

"Termination? At the hands of unfriendly governments?" Crump probed further.

"We think not," Victor offered.

"How then, may I ask?"

"Unfriendly ex-spouses we believe." It was Catherine's turn.

Crump chuckled. "Eh, at first glance a case full of spies, intrigue and Cold War combatants now downgraded to nothing more than a deadly domestic dispute. I'm not sure I buy all of that, but I don't have time to go any deeper. I apologize for being short, eh, but you see what I have to deal with here. Your request for exhumation was granted this morning by the chief magistrate. I believe equipment is at the gravesite as we speak, and you should have your remains available for examination as early as tomorrow morning. They will be on proper display at the medical examiner's office, which is a mere ten-minute walk from here. I suggest you find acceptable overnight accommodations. I will do my very best to meet you there in the morning. Say 8 a.m. sharp?"

"Would you wear your uniform?" Asked Catherine with a deflecting glance and impish smile directed toward his stern expressionless, now quizzical face.

The sole of Victor's heavy oxford struck Catherine's ankle with a sharp silent rebuking blow. She jerked at impact and let out a tiny squeak.

Crump's quick response was, "Afraid, I haven't worn one of those in nearly twenty years. On duty, that is. Not about to start now. Ceremonial dress, you know. Why do you ask?

"No reason. Pity, however."

"Yes, Inspector we will be there. We hope you will find time to join us," Victor declared, and added, "Might it be possible for you to direct us to the location in the river park where the deceased was found? And more specifically to the location of the park bench where we understand the victim was seated rather formally when discovered?"

"Also if you don't mind provide us the location of the Bonaparte Hotel where we understand he was residing at the time of his death?" Catherine's turn again.

"And assuming our inspection of the remains confirms his identity, I presume we will be granted access to his belongings cited in the international dispatch?" Victor added.

Crump's expression changed from quickened accommodation to outright annoyance.

Hurriedly he said, "Of course. Certainly. Anything you need. You see, I must be going. I will draw you a recommended route to the locations you wish to visit. But your latter request is impossible. Perhaps the report was unclear. The victim's personal effects have been destroyed."

"Is that so?" Catherine hissed, not hiding her anger.

"Yes, afraid so. Somehow mishandled in our property room. However, the items were of little consequence and were taking up much-needed space. Cramped conditions in there, like you see all around us."

"Interesting, inspector. Disappointing so say the least. We had hoped..." Catherine cut him off.

"A Russian language manuscript and letter to the New York Times, were of little consequence?" Catherine's voice rising to a pitch.

"Please. I have no more time to devote to this. You must understand."

Victor's hand went up signaling a halt in the back and forth.

Crump rapidly traced their course on a street-grid map he magically retrieved from an indecipherable stack of additional debris situated on a crammed library table at his back. He slid his finished work across the desktop and abruptly stood, obviously implying his desire to dismiss his unwelcomed guests. Taking the not-so subtle hint Victor grabbed the offering and joined Catherine who by then was moving toward the door.

"Thank you for your precious time inspector," Catherine called out, her back to their host.

Victor offered his hand to Crump who shook it as he watched Catherine storm away.

"Asshole, eh!" Catherine proclaimed as they walked back through the lavish hall toward the exit, directions in hand, ready for a long trek through the heart of Montreal. "I wouldn't go if he offered to take me around town in full Mounties costume seated on a high-stepping chestnut steed with me clinging on the back, arms around his waist. Condescending prick."

Victor ignored her. "Let's take a cab. We'll get enough exercise from our walk through in the park."

Twenty minutes later as their hard-to-find taxi finally pulled to curbside at the park's main entrance, they soon found Montreal's inner-city playground nearly as crowded as Crump's cubicle.

The scene was pandemonium. Literally thousands of people were traversing the greenbelt preserve, walking, jogging, bicycling, skateboarding or by other transport means including wheelchairs and even a few pogo sticks.

Weaving their way through the crowd Victor was the first to speak.

"How could such a violent act go unnoticed? Even at the height of a major blizzard. Must have been a complete, howling whiteout. Yet someone surely heard or saw something. There's so damn many people around."

"What'd you say?" Catherine nearly shouted over the din of a boom box-toting skateboarder.

"Why no witnesses? This place is worse than Central Park on the Fourth of July."

"How do you know? Ever been in Central Park on the Fourth of July?"

"No," Victor admitted sheepishly, "Just seen the pictures."

"Thought so. Yea, I agree. You're right, so strange nobody saw or heard anything."

Not to their surprise Crump's sketch proved difficult to follow, and after several detours through the throng they finally stood in front of the park bench on which Thomas Riha encountered this killer. The seats were empty and looked inviting. They knew they'd walked more than a mile before finding it. All the time still wondering why no witnesses. Granted right then it was daylight, the sky was blue; the wind still, and the ground void of heaps of wet snow, inches accumulating by the minute. Still all these people and no one saw a thing. They both sat. But not for long. An eerie uneasiness suddenly overtook them both. They leaped to their feet as if bounding away from a coiled snake.

"Wow, couldn't handle that," Catherine exclaimed.

"Yep, spooky. Can't tell you why. Just was," Victor acknowledged.

Standing and staring in silence at the murder scene Catherine finally turned away to see a woman lingering nearby, eyes fixed on them, her hands grasping the handle of a baby stroller. A child appeared slumbering inside.

Catherine moved toward her. "Hi," Catherine said. "Can I help you?"

"No one sits there any more," the woman nearly inaudibly whispered.

"What did you say?"

Louder, yet speaking as if at a gravesite, she said again, "No one sits there. Not since they found him. Not since she killed him."

At her words, Victor and Catherine quickly drew closer.

"Miss, what do you mean by that?" Victor asked in a voice masking the sudden tension.

"Please," the woman pleaded in heavy French accent, "Let me pass."

She pulled away, turning the stroller harshly to avoid their oncoming. The child stirred and squealed in protest.

"Miss, we know a few months ago this is where police said they found a man, sitting there on the bench, dead, having been shot," Victor calmly declared. "Do you know something about that? You said, she killed him. How do you know that? Did you see a woman shoot him?"

"Please, I must go, let me pass."

"We're not police, Miss," Catherine said. "The man was a friend of ours. We came here today to see for ourselves where our friend died. The police can't tell us anything about his murder. They've buried our friend in an unmarked grave we can't find, so this was the next best place for us to come to remember him."

The woman stopped. She stooped and lifted the child from its rolling bed, clutching it tightly in her arms. The child cooed and grew quiet.

"She came out of a snowy cloud. Appearing like a ghost. My baby was crying. I was lost. We were freezing. The storm swirled around us. I couldn't see anything, but I heard a pop. Then two. I started toward the noise and then, there she was. Floating toward me. I was terrified at first but then she spoke, offering to help us."

"Have you told the police about this?" Victor quizzed gently.

As if she didn't hear, "She helped us find our way out of the park, back to the street. She gave me money for taxi and food. She saved us. I will always be grateful to her. But there was the blood. On her face; smeared, and on her hands. She didn't seem to mind that I saw it. I didn't say anything. My baby was all that mattered. She saved us. I won't tell the police. I saw the picture in the newspaper the next day. His body covered with snow. Frozen, like my baby would have been if not for her."

Catherine's turn. "Can you describe the woman to us? What did she look like?"

"No, I won't. I remember her face. I remember the blood, but I won't say. She saved us; that's what I say; all that I say. Maybe she didn't shoot. Maybe someone else."

Her child woke again. Fussing.

"I must go." She laid the child back in its place.

Victor and Catherine stepped to each side. The woman scurried away without another word.

Not looking back, she vanished in the crowd.

Chapter 47

Agent Benson and Detective Bravo stood watching the horde into which mother and child had escaped rush away. Leaving no one near. Uncanny calm sans the squawk of circling crows overhead. They were alone with the haunting specter hovering near. No one came to rest on the bench, just like she had said, least of all the agent and cop. Catherine instinctively grasped Victor's arm for solace. Victor welcomed her touch, comforted as well. They turned in the opposite direction of the vanishing swarm that had swallowed their only witness, and walked unobstructed, undisturbed, taking a clear lonely path toward their next destination.

Blocks away, Catherine finally offered the obvious.

"We had no way of detaining her. She was free to go. We lost the one person we desperately needed to solve this thing and thanks to Crump, valuable evidence to seal it once and for all."

"No doubt about that," Victor affirmed.

Their pace was slow. Unspoken thoughts filled their heads.

Unknowingly Crump's crude route had them essentially re-tracing Thomas' trail to his death on that horrific day. They were next in search of the esteemed hotel at which he had resided. As the sky was suddenly growing an ominous grey, only a few passed by on their way to the park's exit. Soon the famed Centaur Theatre came into view. As they approached, the marquee read Joseph Kesselring's Arsenic and Old Lace. They would miss the classic play, its title ironically symbolic of the occasion, but lost on all but Victor and Catherine.

Passing under the marquee, Victor snickered to break the somber mood, "Cyanide and Arsenic, equally effective."

"You're so bad detective," Catherine smiled.

A few blocks later they entered the ornate interior of the landmark lodge and found the front desk off to their right. Each carried an overnight duffel and briefcase, which had been delivered earlier by the well-paid taxi driver who had dropped them off at the river park. A stiff and dour looking tuxedo-clad clerk politely acknowledged their presence.

"Reservations?"

"No, we are trying to locate an employee of yours," Victor responded.

"No reservations? I see. And may I ask about whom you are inquiring?"

"We don't know her name, but we understand that she came into possession of a letter from a former guest of yours; a guest, unfortunately, who has since died. And the letter was turned over to the authorities once they traced his residence back here to the hotel. We'd like to speak with her if possible," Catherine said.

The clerk's expression went from haughty disregard for their lack of reservations to tight-lipped defense.

"We told the police the hotel had no responsibility in that matter. Our employee at the time simply obeyed the request of a guest and placed the letter in safekeeping. She did not, however, forward the letter upon gaining knowledge of the man's death; rather with good sense she turned it over to investigators. That is all the hotel has to say. We have cooperated fully. The incident is closed. Please step aside. Other guests are waiting."

His remarks appeared well rehearsed.

"We are not with the police, sir; in fact we are Americans. The deceased was a friend of ours. We traveled here to Montreal to find out as much as we can regarding the circumstances of his death, and to, frankly, experience some of the pleasurable surroundings we know he had while taking up residence in this great city of yours," Victor said, resisting a backhand slap to the face of the jerk clerk.

"Tragic event; horrible, in fact," their antagonist responded in a tone closely mirroring sympathy. "You are aware, I presume, that your friend's death was not by accident?"

"Yes, we know how he died," Catherine proclaimed and then persisted. "Is it possible to speak with the person who handled the letter? Quite simply, sir, all we are trying to do is determine our friend's state of mind during his time here; how he conducted himself, what his habits were; that sort of thing." Then to bring home the point, "And to find out if he was happy in the end."

The last part of her plea brought on a smirk, and as he suppressed an outright guffaw, a bobbing bowtie-wrapped Adam's apple.

Regaining his composure, he leaned forward to whisper conspiratorially, "I believe your friend had a marvelous time during his stay with us. He paid all in cash and spread around a lot of money in our luxurious lounges and restaurants.

"Further, it is alleged but we have no confirmation that he may have entertained more than a few lonely wives of conventioneers." The clerk, now warming and embracing the thought of such scandalous behavior, added without prompting.

"That's our Thomas all right," Catherine broke in with a snicker of her own.

Without acknowledging the interruption he continued, "I believe he thoroughly enjoyed himself. He made no disturbance, and other than the ladies he escorted around very discreetly, he kept to himself. We understood he was a writer. Most days he remained cloistered in his room. At night, however, he prowled around like an alley cat, as I've already aptly described." By that time the clerk's broad grin was unmistakable.

"No unexpected visitors? Did he ever appear frightened? Perhaps threatened?" Victor asked.

"Heavens, no. Not that we were aware of."

"And the young lady who took the letter?" Catherine's turn.

"Oh, about her. We understand he paid her to keep the letter, only to forward it upon his death. Unfortunately he wasted his money. Shortly after his murder she left employment here, and the letter remained unopened in our safe. She apparently used the funds to move on. We understand she may be in British Columbia."

"No one read it?" Catherine probed.

"I beg your pardon, madam. This hotel protects the personal property and privacy of our guests without exception," he responded indignantly, a scoff returning to his face.

"Privacy? From what you just said, seems like your guests better watch themselves." Catherine declared.

"Now wait just a minute....." he tried to come back.

"In any event her flying the coop sure as hell won't do us any good," Catherine said cutting him off and keeping her turn. "You sure the letter ended up with the police. What did they do with it?"

"Madam, how should I know?"

For the second time that day Victor's hand went up to halt the exchange.

"We appreciate your help, sir; you have been most gracious. By chance do you have rooms available?" Victor inquired.

"Indeed, we do sir. One room or two?"

"Two rooms; two keys," both responded at the same time, "And reservations for dinner, please, for seven o'clock," Victor added.

"Very well. Forgoing the joys your friend experienced while in residence here?"

"Just the keys, please," Victor demanded rather harshly.

The next morning at 8:05 sharp Agent Benson and Detective Bravo stared into the mostly flesh-devoid, empty eye socket, half-torn-away face of Professor Thomas Riha. Inspector Crump was nowhere in sight.

"You're sure it's him?" Victor asked.

"Yes, I'm sure. That bottom tooth, front incisor. See it's crooked; tilted to the right. And his pinky finger on his left hand. He said he broke it when a child, and it never healed properly. That's crooked as well. And see his ankle here?" She moved down to the end of the stainless steel slab and beckoned Victor to follow. "He said he broke it skiing and it didn't heal properly either, causing him to walk with a slight limp. You can still see the jagged line where the bone was once separated. Pretty nasty break. No mistake about it."

"So, crooked might be a good description of this gentleman, eh?" Inspector Crump, unexpectedly offered as he approached through the lab's main entry door.

Catherine glanced up. Drab business suit. Mountie-less. Who cares?

"In many ways, you may be right," Victor conceded.

"So, what do we do now, if I may ask? He's all yours if you want him. We'll wrap him up nicely in a container of sorts that doesn't leak or emit unpleasant odors, he's still pretty ripe, and ship him off to wherever you'd like, courtesy of a United Canadian government. Or we put him back in the frozen ground, cover him up, case closed, and the American government is satisfied their wayward agent is resting peacefully under friendly soil for all eternity," Crump said, failing to hide his disdain for the whole matter.

"We'll further seek your indulgence, Inspector, by returning Dr. Riha to his grave. We've seen all we need to see. This is the man we suspected was murdered here. Our only regret is your failure to find, or even look very hard for his killer. So, thanks to you the case is not closed," Catherine said, deliberately exposing her indignation.

Crump lost his swagger from her verbal assault. "Now, wait a minute Agent Benson..."

"And what did you do with the letter?" she snarled.

"What letter?"

"Don't be coy with us Inspector. The letter Riha wrote and gave to the hotel clerk to send off upon his death."

"Oh, that letter. Like I said. Destroyed. It did contain some very interesting insights into certain schemes often suspected of your government now fully confirmed. If you need more I suggest formal diplomatic channels.

For the third time, Victor's hand went up like a schoolboy crossing guard.

"Inspector, no need to dwell on the matter any further. We appreciate your cooperation. Our work is done here," Victor interceded.

At that moment a lab-coat helper entered the room to announce, "Inspector, there's a reporter and photographer from the Montreal Gazette in the hallway outside who wants a statement; I'm assuming it's about the body here, why it was exhumed and if we know who he was."

"Good God!" Crump exclaimed.

"Guess this one goes back on top of that messy pile on your desk, eh Inspector?" Catherine proclaimed with unmasked glee.

Back in the Bonaparte lounge sipping afternoon tea Victor and Catherine read the banner headlines. The story beneath was mostly accurate, even citing that two unidentified Americans, suspected of being government officials, had forced local authorities to dig up the corpse. The Park Bench Murder exclusive was enhanced by a page-two color photograph catching RCMP Chief Inspector Russell Crump hurriedly attempting to cover the gruesome stainless steel slab-prone remains with a white sheet. A smiling morgue staffer standing nearby. Identified as Timothy Smoltz. The blurry backs of a man and woman in background silhouettes. Unnamed. Mysterious.

The couple exited before reporters could question them. Their involvement in the case could not be verified, the caption read.

Later that evening Victor carried a copy of the afternoon edition under his arm as he and Catherine boarded their flight to Chicago.

Chapter 48

Rico squealed. Like a pig. Loud and disgusting. Helen walled off the noise and cringed as she felt his final thrust. He rolled off, his breath foul and his limpness wet and sticky. Nauseated, she leaped from the bed to flee from his clutch. He whined at her sudden rejection, pleading for her return. She ignored his protestations and slammed shut the bathroom door, securing separation for shelter and to cleanse. She cranked open the shower faucet handle to full velocity and watched steam rise to fog the mirror. She glanced at her nakedness in the reflection, finding her image obscure, without definition, distinction or purpose. She wept as the cloud thickened. Her tears mixing with sweat from her brow.

Inexplicably astounded at her childish outburst her weeping stopped as quickly as it had begun.

Since her plan had taken form she had found no reason to cry; ever, about anything, no matter the misery. But now a weak, distorted melancholic intruder stood in her midst. In the mist. Unrecognizable. Had she grown frail and vulnerable as before? Could she not continue sacrificing body and fortune? Had she reached the end? Revenge fleeting, lost in its allure?

A gentle tap on the door. Another appeal for her return. She buried her face in her hands, screaming at him to go away.

In the weeks preceding, she had found success in driving a wedge between them, deeper and wider by the day. It was not difficult pitting one against the other. They were selfish, juvenile imbeciles, caring only for her gifts and measuring each of her favors. Who was ahead? Who did she prefer? She lied to each, claiming she fancied the one in her bed at that time. As planned she kept them apart, for their own good and hers, demanding absolute partition. Especially since their debacle in Vienna and leaving a trail even a blind man could follow. That part was easy. They were smart enough to disengage and remain hidden in suburban Chicago hovels many miles apart. They could call on her only on alternating weeks, and only for a day, leaving her alone and inaccessible in the interim. She left their cash at two post office boxes in Elmhurst and Evanston even though she knew they were holed up in Oak Lawn and Lincolnwood. She took pleasure in forcing them to drive some distance to retrieve their bloodied blackmail.

She had insisted on the disguises and had spent lavishly on a makeup artist who outfitted them with toupees, moustaches, heavy brows and altered ears. Their eye color also customized with new contact lenses.

She stepped into the simmering heat and gasped at its intensity, her flesh reddening in an instant. Comfort was not her desire. She rubbed in places until they were raw; clawing at her filth but never satisfied it was removed.

Finally giving up, she cut off the scalding cascade and stood dripping, suddenly cold. She sensed he was gone, forgoing more infantile begging, awaiting his next turn. She switched on the radio, searching for soft music to sooth. None came; instead a baritone newscaster shouting that, "the body of a former University of Chicago history professor, missing long ago and feared dead, has been discovered in an unmarked grave in the glorious Canadian metropolis of Montreal.

"He has been positively identified by authorities there," the announcer reported breathlessly.

A rush of air escaped her lungs and the steamy room began to spin. She caught the edge of the sink to steady knees about to buckle. In the fog she found the vanity stool and sat to hear more.

Quoting from newspaper accounts spreading wildly across Quebec Province the shrieking anchorman recited accounts heaping praise on a RCMP investigator who was said to have doggedly pursued the cold case, amply labeled the Park Bench Murder, until he produced sufficient evidence justifying exhumation of the remains and reexamination of previously undisclosed crime-scene evidence.

"Authorities confirm that the body was that of Professor Thomas Riha, a victim of a grizzly execution-style slaying."

"Credit for cracking the case is going to Chief Inspector Russell Crump, a twenty-year veteran of the elite Canadian corps," the announcer barked and added, "Riha was an acclaimed, well respected past member of the University faculty."

And further down the script he read, "Inspector Crump will be appearing at a news conference this afternoon right here in Chicago. "At which time," the throaty newsman proclaimed, "more enticing details of this horrific murder will be forthcoming for all of Chicagoland to hear."

As a postscript he ordered his audience to, "Stay tuned. Inspector Crump will be appearing at Police Headquarters. He is expected to be joined by University President Bertram Huckelbee and several history department faculty members who are mourning their lost colleague and will be demanding Chicago police join the Canadian Mounties in their dedicated search for Riha's killer."

By the time the breathless broadcast had concluded Helen had shed her initial terror and began to plot her next move.

"What a bunch of fucking hypocrites," she yelled at her likeness now gaining clarity as waves of steam dissolved off the mirror. "They were the first to throw him overboard; now they grieve over his death."

But why am I thinking about him? Time for me to run.

At that moment outside on the street below Detective Victor Bravo and CIA Agent Catherine Benson emerged from a Chicago Police squad car, which had pulled to the curb directly in front of Helen's Riha's luxury high-rise condominium complex.

As they stepped onto the sidewalk leading to the building's main entrance they failed to recognize a passerby holding a take-out coffee cup in hand, and sporting a cleverly coiffed hairpiece parted on the side, a carefully trimmed goatee, a business suit starkly pressed and loafers brightly shined. The unnoticed pedestrian, a most-wanted fugitive accused of murderous deeds in Vienna, hurried by, grim-faced and heartsick having just left his only lover not of his own accord. Victor and Catherine also didn't appreciate how the dapper gentleman suddenly turned away and quickened his step almost to a trot when the police vehicle had come to a stop.

After arriving from Montreal Catherine and Victor had briefed Chicago police on their findings and suspicions. They were convinced that the killers of Rafael Jones, late of Vienna, Austria, had snuck back into the States and were likely hiding in or around the City. They were also sure that Helen Riha resided nearby and they had made it clear that it was imperative they find and speak with her at once.

This time, the local cops cooperated and it took no more than twenty minutes for them to pinpoint her address and determine from the doorman in her building that she was home alone. What Catherine and Victor had also learned was that Inspector Crump was on his way to town to receive self-appointed accolades for cracking the case, probably single handedly, and was planning to deliver a sucker punch at the police department for its lax investigative prowess when one of their most prominent former citizens mysteriously vanishes under extremely suspicious circumstances.

In the ride over Catherine had fumed at the news of Crump's grandstanding, calling him a serious motherfucker, while Victor mulled over a strategy for an impending confrontation with a potentially ferocious female assassin. Their escorts, both veteran homicide dicks on orders from their shift commander, had agreed to allow the out-of-towners to approach the suspect solo, while they remained in the shadows as backup.

Helen was almost dressed when the doorbell chimed. Her luggage, opened but empty, laid across her huge king-sized bed. Not waiting for the housekeeper to arrive she had stripped the soiled, putrid-smelling sheets and tossed them onto the floor. Although anticipating a time when she might be questioned about her ex-husband's disappearance, and potentially about the death of his girlfriend, the shock of hearing the news screaming from those radio speakers had forced her to accelerate plans for her own disappearance.

Her destination was South America, first to Brazil, and then to Argentina, eventually settling in Chile. In a wall safe behind an original silkscreen print of a display of Campbell soup cans she'd acquired from an up-and-coming artist named Andy Warhol, Helen had horded fifteen thousand dollars in fifties and hundreds. Much more than that waited for her in various bank accounts in Miami and Puerto Rico. Like she had easily accomplished in so many other things, murder being one, her command of the Spanish language with only six months practice was almost flawless. She would not pay her two rapists another dime, she'd decided. Their abuse was over. They'd used her for the last time. She would find true love in the Southern Hemisphere, plus she wanted to learn to ski in the Andes.

Hearing the chime made her furious. He was back. If he tried to touch her she would stab him in the throat. He would never see her without clothing again. She hurriedly buttoned her fine silk blouse, zipped her skirt, and anticipating another confrontation, walked to the door and angrily swung it open.

Instead of the revolting face of the man she despised she stared into the handsome features of a tall olive-skin stranger presenting a gentle smile that masked piercing, probing eyes. Over his shoulder she caught a glimpse of a pretty brunette whose look was stern yet exhibited a sign of caution. Immediately in her gut Helen knew they were police. She spoke without hesitation.

"You've come about Thomas. I heard on the radio. Please come in," she said with no suggestion of alarm. She stepped aside and waved her arm for them to enter.

Remaining where he stood, Victor, with Catherine moving to his side, responded with, "Are you Mrs. Helen Riha?"

Looking annoyed Helen said, "The former. We're divorced, but I'm sure you know that."

Catherine's turn. "Mrs. Riha, my name is Catherine Benson. I am a federal agent. This is Captain Victor Bravo, a homicide detective from Colorado. If you don't mind we would like to speak with you about your ex-husband, and further, we have questions pertaining to a woman with whom we believe you were acquainted...."

"Cut the crap," Helen snapped, "Of course I knew her and of course I hated her and I'm glad she's dead. And you probably know that too. Now are you going to accept my invitation to come inside or are you going to stand there at my doorstep all day like a couple of Jehovah Witnesses?"

Neither could help breaking into broad grins at Helen's descriptive command, so they quick-stepped through the doorway.

"Have a seat. I'll put on some coffee, or would you rather have tea? Just curious, where are the Chicago cops? The radio said they were getting involved in the case," Helen asked as she stepped toward the kitchen. Catherine instinctively moved to follow her; her hand reaching for the .38 police special strapped under her arm. Victor grabbed her free hand and brought her to a halt.

He whispered, "Let her go. Let's play this out." Catherine reluctantly stopped, and shrugged, indecisively.

"This is a mind game, not a shoot out," he said.

"You better be right. If she comes out blasting I'm gonna haunt you when I'm dead," Catherine sneered.

"You think she'd mess up a place like this?" Victor said, still in a whisper. His arm sweeping outward as if presenting royalty. "Reminds me of the house in Boulder."

They had found their seats on a lovely L-shaped blue velvet sectional sofa. Taupe silk draperies hung open, blocking little sunlight passing through the massive picture windows. The carpet dominated in pale yellow. A four-foot square beveled-glass coffee table stood at their feet, the top supported by an intricately carved teak wood baby elephant about the size of a real newborn. A three-foot longneck cobalt blue Steuben glass vase adorned the tabletop center from which huge bright yellow orchids bloomed in full splendor.

Helen reappeared, unarmed, carrying instead a silver tray balancing fine china cups, saucers and pitchers. Tea in one; coffee in the other. Sugar and cream in matching dispenser and bowl. Silver spoons to stir. She stooped and expertly rested the tray on the glass surface. She took a seat opposite her guests in an overstuffed low-back chair appearing to be upholstered in delicate brushed twill. She motioned for them to help themselves.

Neither did, right away. Instead, Victor began.

"Mrs. Riha, err, do you still prefer being addressed in that manner?"

"Yes, detective, I still prefer the name. Despite it all, he was still my husband and there remains a certain attachment, I suppose."

"Very well, Mrs. Riha, "When was the last time you saw your ex-husband?"

"On the night he and his bitch tried to poison me."

Her guests tried hard to shield their shock at her reply, but neither garnered much success.

Helen was better at it. She carefully hid her delight at detecting how astonished each had become at her remark.

Victor recovered quickly however. "How did you come to suspect they were trying to poison you?"

"You see, I don't have a heart condition. And I don't have thick blood that has a tendency to clot, so there is no reason for me to be on blood thinners. Well, I found it rather curious, you know, when the pharmacy called one day to confirm my prescription for Coumadin; you know, that's nothing more than controlled levels of rat poison."

Helen paused for effect, eyeing her guests to gauge their reaction. Both remained stoic. Disappointed, she continued.

"That's why you might say I became suspicious that they were out to get me. When I confronted them about it, they laughed it off as a joke. It certainly wasn't funny to me, so I picked up one of Thomas' favorite vases, one frankly I thought was hideous, and threw it at him. He ducked, but it hit that bitch hard on the arm...too bad not in the head... and they both came at me, pinned me to the floor, and so it went. A real cat fight for sure. Later that night I packed a bag, called a taxi and off I went, back here to Chicago. Filed for divorce a few weeks later and the rest is history."

She paused again for a moment then quickly added, "Now that you have the story, and apparently you aren't interested in my hospitality, I'd like both of you to leave. I have a plane to catch. I'm off on vacation to South America."

Catherine reached for the tea pitcher and poured herself a full cup, slowly added cream and a single cube of sugar. "I love your necklace Mrs. Riha. Beautiful little diamond on a delicate gold chain. Petite yet stunning." Before she could respond..."How did you become acquainted with Gordon Peterson and Rico Hernandez?"

Helen wasn't so skillful this time. Not without an audible gasp she caught her breath, took the coffee cup from her lips, swallowed hard, and placed it back on the clear glass surface, missing the saucer. Victor noticed that her hand shook slightly producing a tiny cream-colored puddle beside the delicate porcelain beaker.

But Helen, too, recovered quickly after a dainty dab at her lips with a starched linen napkin.

"Well, Miss Benson, what can I say?"

"Just tell us the truth Mrs. Riha," Victor interjected.

"I plan to detective if you will allow me to proceed."

"Please do."

"As I started to say, I am sorry, frankly, to admit this but during my courtship with Dr. Riha, I strayed. I mean I'm ashamed, or at least I was, to discuss it, but I met Gordon Peterson at a rather despicable place, a bar, not far from where he worked at the time; which was, as you also probably know, the branch office of the FBI here in Chicago. It was truly an inglorious fling, if you will, but I cut it off shortly after my relationship with Thomas began to flourish. During this brief interlude I met his partner, Mr. Hernandez, who was, it soon became apparent, equally obnoxious. Both men were so full of themselves; boisterous, loud, self indulgent, a pair of classic chest beating wanna-be-cops in it more for personal glory than service to their fellow citizens."

"And you didn't hire them to kill Galya Tannenbaum and her former CIA hander Rafael Jones?" Catherine queried casually after a sip of delightful tea.

"Pardon me!" Helen shrieked. "How dare you. Of course not, I have had no contact with either of those men for years now."

She abruptly jumped to her feet. "I must ask you to leave. I have been more than accommodating but you have gone too far. Indeed I despised Galya Tannenbaum. She came between me and my husband. She was wicked and deceitful and lured him away from me. She humiliated; even tortured me with her patronizing, cynical lies; never giving me credit; never complimenting me, always criticizing. I hated her and I'm glad she's dead, but I had nothing to do with her death. I've never heard of Rafael Jones, and what is this about the CIA? You say she was some sort of spy?"

"Sit down Mrs. Riha," Victor ordered calmly.

He waited. She slowly retook her seat.

"Please understand we are bound to ask these questions, uncomfortable as they may be, but we not only have the deaths of your ex-husband and Miss Tannenbaum to consider, but there also is the apparent murder of a nurse from my city who attended Galya while being confined at the Asylum, plus now we have the brutal killing of Mr. Jones, a federal employee stationed at our embassy in Vienna, Austria. And all of this seems to revolve around your husband's disappearance and death, coming some months after the fatal poisoning of Miss Tannenbaum. You are the common thread among those two people, and now you admit to having been acquainted with Gordon Peterson and Rico Hernandez. There is simply too much here for us to ignore."

Helen reeled from Victor's summation yet her composure remained intact. Catherine threw a wild left hook to see if it would land.

"You know Helen, through all of your ranting about Galya and how she did this and that to you, not once did you mention Thomas. Was he not complicit in the whole affair? Didn't he go along with his mistress in mocking you, calling you names, denigrating you to the point where literally your life was sucked out of you? Did he not shame you, mortify

R. K. PRICE

you, and beat you down like a mistreated dog? All the while he was
fucking this hateful woman right before your eyes? How could you not
detest him with equal passion and take true delight in blowing his head
off on that park bench in Montreal?"

Helen's glare at her accuser bore laser intensity. Catherine held the
defiant stare without blinking. Eerie silence; her searing words hanging in
the air.

Victor waited, biding his time, then finally asked, "Mrs. Riha, where
were you on the night of March 9, 1971, and the day of November 17,
1971?"

Helen's eyes shifted from Catherine to Victor and then she smiled.
An insolent look; cold, confrontational; challenging, convincing
Catherine she was certifiably mad.

"Please refill your cups, if you'd like. Detective, I don't believe
you've touched yours. Perhaps it's cold by now. I shall return the pot to
the stove to warm it up." Helen rose to stand.

"Please remain seated, Helen," Victor spoke in a low growl, his first
threatening utterance.

"Very well, detective." Helen returned once again to the comfort of
her chair. "I have no idea where I was on either of those two days. More
than likely I was here in Chicago, or perhaps in Cicero visiting my
parents, both of whom are quite elderly and are confined to nursing care
in a private facility. I will have to check those dates against my calendar."

"That will be required, Helen, because we believe you were in
Pueblo, Colorado on the night of March 9, 1971, and you either oversaw
or possibly administered a fatal dose of cyanide that killed Galya
Tannenbaum. And on November 17, 1971 you stalked your ex-husband
through the streets of Montreal, followed him in a blinding snowstorm to
that park bench where he rested and watched the St. Lawrence River
meander by, and then surprised him with a gunshot to the abdomen
followed quickly by a bullet through his mouth exploding through the
back of his head."

Helen brought her hands to her mouth as if in prayer. She closed
her eyes and began to hum a tune. Surprised and somewhat amused
Catherine glanced over at Victor who watched her intently. It took a
moment to identify the melody. Her pitch was perfect. The rhythm on
cue. Catherine recognized it first....The Bee Gees hit, How Can You
Mend A Broken Heart?

She carried the song through two verses before opening her eyes and bringing her hands from her mouth to smooth her skirt. She reached again for her teacup. Catherine noticed it was empty but Helen retrieved it just the same and brought it back to her lips for another sip. She appeared not to notice and swallowed air. Staring at the ceiling she spoke in a gruff, ragged voice.

"I know where they are. I will tell you where to find them. They are both scoundrels. They are the guilty ones. They committed those crimes."

"Who, Mrs. Riha; who are you talking about?" Victor probed.

"Peterson and Hernandez. Don't you know? What kind of detective are you? Who else would I be talking about? Go arrest them but be careful. I suspect they are armed and I'm certain they are dangerous."

"You're now saying you know where these men are? A moment ago you said you had had no contact with either of them for years. Which is it Helen?" Catherine fought to control her anger.

Helen seemed to focus at that moment, resuming her glare at Catherine once more.

"I lied; so I lied. I'm not under oath here, so screw you. I wanted a little pay back, see. I wanted a little revenge; just a little. I was through with Thomas; she could have him, but I wanted to squeeze him; no, pinch him and her just a little, but nothing serious. So I hired those two goons to give them both a small dose of their own medicine."

"Poison, you mean, Mrs. Riha," Victor interrupted.

"Don't be ridiculous. Of course not. Figure of speech; perhaps a poor choice of words."

"I paid them ten-thousand dollars each to use their clout with the FBI to give Thomas and Galya fits over their taxes, to make sure they got plenty of speeding tickets, even mailed a few anonymous letters calling Thomas a traitor for making his speeches against America. I wrote some of them myself. That sort of thing. Nothing really illegal or harmful. They were bad agents, unworthy of carrying badges. It was easy to recruit them for my little game. Plus they needed the money. Some gambling debts for one, I think, and the other liked women other than his wife. So, that's it. The next thing I know Galya's dead, and then Thomas. I have no idea about the man in Austria or the nurse you mentioned. Rico and Gordon came to me, threatening blackmail, saying if I didn't pay them more money they'd implicate me in those murders, since I'm the one who had a motive."

"You did have a motive, much more than they did, Mrs. Riha," Victor said.

"Maybe so, but something went wrong. I'm telling you they acted on their own. For whatever reason they killed those people. It's my word against theirs."

"You'd better have an air-tight alibi; that's all I can say," Catherine warned.

"Gordon's hiding out in a basement apartment in Oaklawn. Rico is in a unit over a garage in the back of a house in Lincolnwood. They are receiving their mail at Post Office boxes in Elmhurst and Evanston. I have the addresses. I'll give them to you."

"How do you know all of this?" Catherine queried harshly. "Especially the Post Office boxes. Why would you know where those are?"

"Because I just sent them money. My last installment. Sure it's blackmail. I know it. That's why I'm leaving the country. I have to escape their harassment. They're vicious men and I'm terrified of them."

"You're not going any where Helen," Victor said assuredly.

"I beg your pardon. You have no basis whatsoever to hold me. Plus you have no jurisdiction here in Chicago to do anything. I am cooperating fully in your investigation, even volunteering vital information about men who should be your prime suspects in two murders, possibly more. I have further chosen to speak with you candidly, absent advice of counsel, which might be foolish on my part but I am compelled to assist you for selfish reasons, frankly, to put all of this behind me; to start a new life, free of all that Galya Tannenbaum burdened me with, in life and in death."

Victor knew she was right and he suspected Catherine did as well. They could not hold her. All circumstantial evidence. She could get up and leave right then, and they couldn't stop her. They had to keep her talking. To bring back those fleeting fits of hysterical instability which seemed to propel her into another round of revealing candor.

Victor sat back into the comfortable cushion and eyed their suspect. Catherine held her edge-of-her-seat posture and Helen's glare.

She did it all right, he thought. Catherine knew it all along. She killed them both, but a confession seems roundly impossible at the moment. Yet it remains our only hope. A new tactic is in order.

Victor reached into the inside pocket of his suit coat, drab and dingy as Catherine had described the style and color that morning, for his notepad and pen. He placed them on the table next to Helen's empty teacup. "Okay, Mrs. Riha, write down those addresses, and as best you can, describe Peterson and Hernandez. If the information you provide proves helpful, Agent Benson and I are willing to speak on your behalf with Chicago police who, by the way, are waiting downstairs to haul you away to Cook County Jail."

"Don't bullshit me, detective," Helen sneered. I could tell by the look on both your faces that you agree with me. You don't have crap. Nothing. I'm free as a bird and you know it, so call off the cops; I'll write it all down for you and then I'm on my way to South America."

She picked up the pen and began to write.

Catherine massaged her forehead, pondering alternatives. On impulse she said, "Captain Bravo will take the information and gather Chicago police units to launch a manhunt. I need to stay with you a while longer. I have a few more questions. What time does your plane leave, Helen?" Her tone had changed. Now polite and sounding respectful.

Victor looked at her curiously. Anticipating an inquisition from him Catherine hastily added, "Its best that we make sure you are protected. If for some reason Gordon and Rico suspected you were cooperating with us, you might be in danger. We can't allow that to happen. We have no idea where either one of them are. For all we know they could be in the building watching our every move."

Helen suppressed a cold chill scampering up her spine. If they only knew how close one of them still might be. Still, she responded with, "I don't need any company Agent Benson. I'm perfectly capable of taking care of myself. Here are the addresses and descriptions. They are both wearing disguises. Fairly sophisticated ones at that. If you have old photographs of them, you won't get very far. The physical images I detail here will give you much better insight into their appearances."

Victor had quickly grasped Catherine's plan. He didn't like it, but saw its merits. They had no reason to doubt the veracity of Helen's information, and Victor knew he should be the one to lead a swat team in pursuit. Yet his concern remained whether Catherine could handle this cold-blooded murderess by herself. She's armed. She's well trained.

She just might take better care of her than I could.

Catherine broke the stillness.

"Helen, I insist on staying with you. In fact, I think it's best for me to accompany you to the airport. Detective Bravo and I would never forgive ourselves if anything happened to you. I won't take no for an answer." Her tone feigned compassion and concern.

Helen didn't miss Catherine's insincerity. Knowing this was the best she could hope for, said, "Very well, but please detective, be on your way, and be extremely careful. Those men will stop at nothing to preserve their freedom."

Victor took the slips of paper from Helen, and in silence, read them carefully before folding and slipping them back into his suit coat pocket. Finally, he stood and moved toward the door. Helen watched him intently. Catherine remained seated and looked up to catch his backward glance as he hesitated before reaching for the handle. She nodded in an effort to signal reassurance. A disquieted grimace overtook his face as he turned away and swung open the door. Instantly he was gone.

Chapter 49

Victor scanned the heavy perimeter established around the basement living unit. He counted twenty-three specially trained combat-ready officers, armed with automatic weapons, shotguns, tear gas canisters and what looked like grenade launchers.

The scene brought back vivid memories. It starkly reminded him of a staged Marine assault on fortified Japanese emplacements he'd witnessed years ago on the infamous island of Okinawa. During that bloody World War II conquest the Navy had allowed him and a few other ship-bound sailors to accompany the troops to land-based battle stations. He regretted receiving that special pass the one and only time he went. He had never witnessed such carnage, and only escaped a counterattack when American airpower was called in from an aircraft carrier fortunately anchored at sea close by.

Victor and the special Chicago squad awaited orders to move in from the police major in command. A neighbor had confirmed that a man with the altered likeness of Gordon Peterson was seen entering the unit two hours before. Enough daylight remained to properly station the force for maximum penetration power and protection, while sealing off all means of possible escape.

Rico was already in custody. He hadn't even put up a fight. A detachment of the combat team had spotted him at his Helen-assigned Post Office box retrieving junk mail and three illicit pornographic magazines wrapped in brown paper and stamped with the Popular Mechanics logo on the covers.

At the time of Rico's arrest Victor was impressed with his dress; impeccably, as Catherine would have put it, and his demeanor. Resigned to his fate and acting like the perfect gentleman, Rico had calmly and with a shrug of acceptance, raised his hands in surrender when approached from all sides by the overwhelming force. Soon it was discovered he carried no firearm. When searched, besides a superb set of phony identification, including driver's license and passport, and five hundred dollars in cash, all he possessed was a color Polaroid of him, in black tie, and an elegantly attired, seductively posed Helen Riha. Both wore beaming smiles for the photographer. Rico's arm was tightly wrapped around Helen's waist. Her head lovingly resting against his shoulder. The perfect, charming, charitable couple. The backdrop of the photo was a sign welcoming attendees to the Annual Fireman's Ball. His only comment before entering the rear of an armored paddy wagon was, "She gave me up. Damn her. God, I loved her so."

Helen had cleared the table service. At first, wary not to let her out of her sight, uninvited, Catherine had followed her into the kitchen to observe. Gradually, the tension between them eased. Catherine surprisingly felt unthreatened. Unconsciously, she relaxed and watched Helen fill the sink with soapy water and gingerly wash the fine flatware and pristine porcelain. Handing her a dishtowel, Catherine accepted Helen's request to dry. They chatted about the weather, of all things, and how the seasons are reversed in South America. There, winter will be fast approaching. Chile is her final destination, Helen advised, for its icy mountains, brilliant skies and unparalleled skiing. She would rent a chalet and look for true love.

My God, I'm sympathetic. That's pathetic, Catherine silently chastised.

Nonetheless, she asked, "Can I help you pack?"

"Of course, perhaps you can help me pick out a few special outfits," Helen responded.

Dishes done and put away, Catherine followed her into the master suite. Another elegant room but this one decorated with Asian flair. Deep red walls, brocade-trimmed silk Oriental draperies at the window, and jade-looking lamps maybe they were real, placed in the center of heavily carved matching rosewood nightstands. A shadow box displaying a collection of intricate cinnabar snuffboxes hung from a wall. A high four-poster bed, adorned with geisha-appearing figures sweetly peering from enclosures imbedded well within the massive poles supporting the bed frame. A fierce dragon, embroidered also in silk, spread across the mattress flaring flames from its nostrils. Catherine took a seat on the edge of a chaise, covered in Chinese print fabric, and watched as Helen carefully laid out her things. Neither spoke for some time, Helen failing to ask her advice on the selections being made. Catherine's position was next to the window, and close to the door to block escape. But she was unconcerned. Why?

Casually, she looked down at the fabric on which she sat and spied a smiling samurai poised between her legs; his spear penetrating obscenely inside her splayed crouch. Her thighs came together quickly and she moved to smother the hysterically animated face.

A light laugh came from her throat.

"What's funny?" Helen asked as she pulled a navy woolen blazer from a hanger.

"Oh, nothing," Catherine replied, and then looking about she noticed a pile of bed sheets stacked in the corner by the chaise on which she now sat ladylike. Curious. They looked out of place. Unkempt housekeeping. Unlike her suspect.

And then a thought, even stranger, came to mind.

Like sisters, they were, Catherine and Helen, with one off to college; the other at home, only a junior, jealous of the adventure the other had in store.

So much like when Catherine lingered while Karen packed for her freshman year at Colgate. Then it was Lionel who had broken Karen's heart and it was then when Catherine discovered the awful truth. How the gentle giant, the baseball slugger who won the regionals with a home run in the ninth, wasn't so gentle. How her sister's bruises weren't from falls from the parallel bars, or from trips while tumbling. How he scoffed when she lost the first-place gold to a freshman, and that night, it was Teri, a second-stringer on the girl's gymnastics squad, who had pleased him in front of the shortstop and left fielder. And how she had to hide behind the Papier-Mâché's of homecoming king and queen for appearances; a storybook high school romance with all the trappings of a teenage fairytale. Fantasy yes; reality, brutal. The bruises covered with makeup for the dance. Karen never told. She let him get away. Escaping to Brown on a full-ride scholarship. Catherine swore revenge. Karen made her promise never to tell. Just leave it be, she had pleaded.

Told once more to forget; to go on, abandon vengeance even when it smells so sweet, Karen had advised those many years later. The helicopter pilot and a whirlwind, globetrotting love affair befitting

Catherine's very own novella if she chose to write it. She was so tempted. Yes, she could ruin his career. Like Lionel. But what was there to gain? Karen was Karen; always right, always sensible, spreading big sister gospel. Yet it left a deep hole in Catherine unfilled. She still burned. She couldn't help it.

You gain a lot dear sister. Vengeance eases the pain.

She spoke with those memories searing her brain.

"Helen, I know you killed them both, and you're not going to believe this, but I don't blame you."

Gordon Peterson was not like Rico Hernandez. His arsenal and his lead-lined firing positions encasing the windows of his apartment were testimonial to that difference. Plus his pledge to die if it came to that. And it was; coming to that. The firefight was raging. Three officers were already down. Paramedics pinned back, unable to render aid. Encircled patrol cars riddled with holes. One set afire. Victor, still in his bad business suit, without proper protective gear was returning fire with a borrowed M-16 on full automatic. Worse than Okinawa, if that was possible. Then the squad commander, bold and brave, for an instant stood up just ten feet away to better take aim. An instant too long. In the open. A single shot to the chest. Victor watched him fall. Instinct to rescue overtook him. He stepped from behind the barricade, and Victor's world went black.

"You don't know shit lady," Helen sneered while folding a lovely silk slip and placing it in the delicates section of her suitcase.

"Listen to me Helen. There's no other explanation. You said it before. You're the only one with a motive. It's pure nonsense to believe that either Peterson or Hernandez would kill on their own unless they were covering their tracks. Which they did when they killed Raphael Jones. He was their only victim."

Helen look amused. Entertained. She waited for Catherine to continue.

"Here's what I think. You left Colorado, justifiably a broken woman. Anyone would be.

"They shamed you. They broke you into a million pieces, a jigsaw puzzle only you could re-assemble. But you couldn't start....healing. The divorce, the money you got, all meant nothing. You probably took lovers, probably more than a few, but found no satisfaction. You drifted. You played happy but you were miserable. You drank, I suspect, heavily at times. And then one lonely night like many before, Rico and Gordon happened along. By pure coincidence. Somehow you overheard them spouting off about Thomas or Galya or something else familiar to you."

Resuming her meticulous task of textbook packing, Helen said, "Continue."

"So you got acquainted and hatched a plan. From deep inside your soul you craved it. Insatiable."

"And what was that, my dear? What was insatiable?"

"Helen, I've been there. I understand. It is a high price. Revenge doesn't come cheap. It cost you dearly I suspect. Your dignity first; your fortune second. But, oh, when it happened, when Nurse Henderson snuck you into Galya's cell that night, and you saw her sleeping soundly, what gratification there was when that needle went into her perfect ass."

"You're crazy you bitch," Helen screamed. She threw a spiked heel in Catherine's direction but her pitch was halfhearted and weak. She fell to her knees and began to cry.

Catherine was tempted to go to her; to comfort her, to embrace her like a good sister should. To release the toxins inside as if piercing an infected boil. But she remained seated, waiting for Helen's sobs to subside. Catherine fought for control of her own emotions. Sure, she wanted the confession but somehow that became secondary.

"Helen, I know this is hard. I am sympathetic. Why do you think I insisted that the detective leave us to ourselves? I want to help."

"You can help by getting the fuck out of my house!" Helen bellowed.

Calmly, in a soothing tone, Catherine said, "Helen, you know I'm not going to leave you. Not like this. You're too fragile." Taking advantage, Catherine pounced again.

"Helen, tell me why, before you killed Thomas, you went back to his house to clean up?"

Helen had managed to sit up and rest her back against the bedroom wall. She faced her accuser, struggling to restore an air of defiance.

After a moment, boldness returning, she smiled as if remembering. "You know Catherine, I loved that house. I loved the things in it. The things we found and bought together. Thomas loved shopping with me around Boulder, looking for interesting items. Not necessarily antiques, although we purchased some, rather, unique pieces with color and character. Art glass. Ceramics. Fine porcelains. I went in there fully intending to demolish everything. To show him I was still alive, still human; that he hadn't destroyed me and that she had no right to enjoy my possessions; the things that mattered to us. They were ours...not hers." Her voice trailed off. She looked away. Insolence fleeting.

But Catherine reeled; choking back a fitful response. Helen caught her reaction. Curious. Appealing. Tables possibly turning. She hastily continued.

"Then, Cathcrine... this is important, I stopped myself. He had to know I was there; that his placid life had been invaded. An uninvited guest, for sure. Remember, those were precious objects to me, so I just turned them over, left them upside down, sideways, in disarray, not in ruin. For some reason I needed to sustain that link between us. If I had smashed everything she would have won, but this way I wedged myself between them."

Catherine could not hide her need to hear more. She understood why. She wanted to say it again, to tell her story, but she held herself in check. Helen was emboldened. She sensed certain vulnerability.

Teeter-totter. Teeter-totter.

Helen leaned toward her for emphasis. "Catherine, look around you. This place is immaculate. I can afford a housekeeper but I choose to clean and polish myself. You won't find a speck of dirt anywhere. I'm a fanatic about it. Soon after my first break-in I went back in to straighten up. I couldn't live with myself. I had nightmares over it. By then Thomas would have realized I was there. They would have cleaned up, but not like I would. Everything had its place in my house, in the space I had for it, not her space, so burglary number two happened. It was then I discovered Thomas and Galya were missing. Everything I had scattered around was undisturbed. Neither one of them had seen my handiwork. My scheme had failed."

"So, from neat-freak cat burglar to vicious killer? That's a giant leap Helen," Catherine pronounced.

Teeter-totter. Teeter-totter.

Helen appeared to ignore Catherine's assertion. "Catherine, what did you mean when you said you had been there? That you understood. Tell me Catherine, have you lost someone? Has your heart been torn from your chest and trampled on by the only man you've ever adored? Tell me Catherine. I'm here for you."

Catherine jumped to her feet, lurching forward to jab her finger toward Helen's face. "Shut up! You shut up. I'm in charge here. You're the suspect. We're not here to talk about me and my past. We're here to investigate two senseless murders, both of which you committed. The evidence is overwhelming," Catherine screeched.

"Now, now Catherine, calm down. You understand me and I understand you." Helen stood to meet her at eye level. "You can tell me. You'll feel so much better, and then you'll let me go."

"You are a lunatic. A psychopath. Stop right there." Catherine stepped back. Retreating, her hand moving to grasp the pistol's handle. "You're under arrest."

Teeter-totter, Teeter-totter.

Helen advanced. "Okay, I'll tell you what you want to hear. Yes, once I found out where she was, I had the bitch tortured. Rico and Gordon compromised Galya's handler. You know that. We recruited the nurse, paid her handsomely and plotted Galya's slow, agonizing death. You know that too. And God, woman, you described it so well, how that needle felt when it punctured her skin. But, dear girl, you'll never prove it. You know that too."

Catherine ignored Helen's last assertion.

"And Thomas, how was it when you blew his head off? Feel good with splattered brains flying in your face?" Catherine's back peddling had stopped. She stood firm.

Teeter-totter, Teeter-totter.

"Thomas was even more satisfying. He had no idea I was in the same hotel. All that time. I'd watch him day after day. Coming and going. Oblivious to it all. Thinking he was safe. Even bedding those old hags he'd pick up in the bar. I've got my own little pistol. It might be right over there in my night stand drawer or it might be in the St. Lawrence River Can't remember which."

Catherine glanced in that direction, sensing Helen might lunge toward it. She freed her holstered weapon but did not draw it.

Helen smiled. "Put your gun away, my dear. Do you really think I'm that stupid? If you thought for a moment you had me, I suspect you would have read me my Miranda rights. And I'd be in handcuffs. But since you have no jurisdiction here or anywhere for that matter, all of this is just a charade."

Catherine's grip loosened. Her gun sliding back down in its place.

Helen smiled and turned to resume packing, placing neatly folded jackets and skirts into a second suitcase, and without prompting, said.

"Before he died he really thought I might come back to him, Catherine. Can you believe that? He tried; he really did, telling me he was wrong to let me go. That's when I shot him. Twice. Once for Galya; once for him. No, the second time was for me. That, darling, you'll never prove either."

"Well, at least his house was clean," Catherine declared sarcastically, and then dug deeper, desperate for anything that might swing back the advantage.

"We found the woman and child you helped after you shot him," Catherine said, offhandedly.

Teeter-Totter, Teeter-Totter.

Helen could not suppress a gasp, but again, quickly recovered. "You don't say. Nice bit of police work. Congratulations."

"Actually, she found us," Catherine admitted, "Came right up to the bloody park bench on which we were sitting, trying to reconstruct the crime, and told us the whole story. Right down to the brain matter plastered in your hair."

"Well, bless her heart. How was that lovely child, by the way? Such a beautiful baby, but horribly fussy, you know. Frankly the kid was a nuisance until its mother calmed down and we found a taxi. Couldn't really tell if it were a boy or a girl."

"We have our eye witness. She'll testify you were there."

"No she won't and you know that as well. I could tell the moment we said goodbye. Thankfulness is an understatement. She'll carry our secret to her grave. I was god-like to her. Saved her and her child from certain death. They would have frozen stiff if I hadn't come along. She knew it. I knew it. She will never utter a word to the authorities. So everything you have is circumstantial, and if you try to bring charges, you know they will be suppressed. All hearsay, and with the lawyers I could hire, you and your case will become a laughingstock. Give up Catherine and tell me if these shoes go well with this belt and necklace."

Teeter-Totter, Teeter-Totter.

The explosion came from inside the apartment unit. Micro-seconds apart. Two percussion grenades pilfered from a FBI storage locker. A fireball and then quiet. Gordon Peterson tossing them to the floor at his feet. He was out of ammunition. He'd kept his promise, never to be taken alive. When the fireball subsided and the smoke cleared they found Detective Bravo.

Teeter-totter, Teeter-totter.

"I felt like killing him," Catherine said, her voice just above a whisper.

"Tell me about it, sweetheart," Helen implored. She continued to pack. Catherine didn't object.

Teeter-totter. Teeter-totter.

"When I broke into his house I saw her picture. He had two kids. They looked just like him."

"It hurts, doesn't it," Helen said, "More than anything. Just two more pairs of shoes and I'll be done. These okay?"

"He lied to me. He made me believe it was real. I was real. I couldn't just go away that easy."

"So you took something back from him. You made him feel vulnerable. Threatened. That's good Catherine. That helps," Helen advised.

"But I couldn't go through with it. I went back, like you, and cleaned up. Put everything back where it was. Like before. Like when we were together. He never knew. I let him go; he'll be a General some day, and now I still suffer. You're the brave one; I'm a coward." Catherine's turn to cry.

Teeter-totter, Teeter-totter.

Sirens blared.

"Extensive blood loss. Bullets entered his right hip and behind his right ear. Faint heart beat. Eyes dilated. He was running toward the wounded squad commander when hit. ETA three minutes," the paramedic screamed above the wail to the emergency room attendant.

Teeter-totter, Teeter-totter.

"I can't let you go," Catherine moaned.

"Yes you can and you will," Helen smiled knowingly.

Teeter-totter, Teeter-totter.

Chapter 50

"Dick, are you prepared if Senator Church or anyone on his panel brings up the 303 Committee? Or its fallout; meaning of course, all that surrounded Thomas Riha and Galya Tannenbaum?" The dreaded question was posed by Bud Wheelon, CIA Director Richard Helms' trusted friend and advisor after receiving their breakfast in the Director's very special private dining room located adjacent to his massive office suite.

The Idaho Senator, already with his eye on a bid for the Democratic Presidential nomination just two years out, had been insisting on Helms' high profile appearance for weeks, and finally under threat of subpoena, the Director had relented, agreeing to appear that afternoon. In keeping with tradition, Wheelon, retaining his top-secret clearance, was brought in to brief the Director on potential topics and review his prepared statement. That assignment, however, took on less importance than keeping his friend calm and confident leading up to the proceedings.

They sipped dark, strong coffee and eyed the ham and eggs and each other. Wheelon waited patiently for Helms to respond.

Finally, "God damn it Bud, you'd think Church and his minions would be more interested in intelligence from Viet Nam, overtures we're making for peace talks, or the Chinese nuclear test, and for Christ's sake, Nixon's trip to China, but no, he's gonna slap me around about Thomas Riha." Helms, said, forlornly, while picking at his plate.

"It's a juicy story, you have to admit, Dick, so let's talk about what you intend to say, or not say," Wheelon urged.

Helms rose from his chair, and in keeping with his habit, when delicate questions commanded precise responses, began to pace. His breakfast growing cold.

"The bodies stacked up quickly," Helms noted with dripping aversion.

"You can't say that!" Wheelon exclaimed.

"Being facetious Bud; take it easy. But where would I start? Where would you start? A simple, little bit of espionage to trick the Soviets into thinking they were still jamming our radio signals, and all of a sudden the murder rate jumps fifteen percent."

"What do our records show, Dick? How much is in the file that Church's committee could obtain and expose?"

"Well, for certain, kidnapping Riha like we did, would be fodder for days of headlines if not life sentences. Aiding and abetting criminal counterfeiting, forgery, and bribing the judiciary in wrongfully committing Galya, also would be interesting for newspaper readers and Church's campaign organization. And then the three-way, Riha, Galya, and the wife, a notorious love triangle on par with Richard Burton, Elizabeth Taylor and Eddie Fisher. Not to mention the diminutive, jilted spouse turning into Lizzy Borden and poisoning her rival with as much glee as a Nazi death camp commandant. That's just for starters."

"You're being overly dramatic, Dick."

"You think? Well, you tell me how to describe it then. Next we have one of my trusted agents blackmailed into allegedly organizing and executing Galya's torture, but now we think the wife may have administered the fatal dose. Nevertheless, his accomplice; that nurse, what's-her-name, runs her car off a cliff, and dies. Accident? Don't think so. She was getting too close to the cops apparently. God knows what actually happened.

"Meanwhile a fine man, a fabulous local homicide detective; big happy family and all of that, begins a proper investigation, but finds himself mixed up in my reeling, out-of-control spy ring. Then, at my request, Nixon himself brings this poor guy into the fold, appealing to his flag-waving sense of patriotism. Cover up all you know, young man, Nixon says, for the good of your country.

"It can't get any worse," Wheelon said hopefully.

"Oh, but it does," his boss responded. Then continued.

"Next I introduce the good cop to my top agent, the one I've put in charge of Riha, who amazingly fulfills his mission, thanks to her expert training, but, after a couple of incompetent field operatives of mine who are now both part-time security guards in Reno, Nevada, fail to spot him coming off the plane in drag, no less, Riha flees to Canada. We're scouring the world for the fugitive professor, but quickly my agent, along with the detective, are hot on his trail. Doesn't take them long but to our dismay they discover Riha's already dead, his brains having been scattered across a Canadian snowfield. His body's already in a pauper's grave. His paper's gone. His link to us, ashes in a fireplace.

"Convenient, I would say," Wheelon offered sarcastically.

"Canadians remain our friendly allies to the north," Helms responded.

Evidence now clearly points to the spurned spouse who had apparently rather skillfully stalked him until she decided his life span was long enough. No hard evidence though, just circumstantial.

"Can't imagine what Church would do with that," Wheelon said.

"I can," Helms said.

By this time Wheelon estimated that Helms had completed fifteen laps around his workplace. Without breaking stride the Director continued.

"We truly underestimated the lovely Mrs. Thomas Riha. She's the last one any of us dreamed could have hatched such a scheme.

"You sure?" Wheelon probed.

This time his question was ignored, but followed with,

"Lost loves are great motivators, Bud. Yet Agent Benson, with more than a little help from Detective Bravo, somehow, someway, figured it all out, or at least they think they did."

"What do you mean? They didn't figure it out?" Wheelon interrupted.

Pausing momentarily, Helms also dodged the question.

Instead he said, "While they're just about ready to grab poor Helen, we have a little incident in Vienna. Seems those Hoover boys, the ones he fired because we got to Riha first, long before had bumped into Mrs. Riha in a dive bar in Chicago. Pure unadulterated coincidence. Million to one shot. But that's how it all began."

Wheelon's brow furrowed inquisitively. But he remained silent.

Helms maintained his pace.

"Remember my rogue, the one who may have killed the nurse? Well, with my permission he's set up with his girlfriend in a cushy job at the American embassy. I had to get him out of the country. Austria's spectacular this time of year. Hoover's boys, now literally performing, we think, for Helen in another twisted love triangle, decide my rogue's a liability, so they put a bullet through his eye leaving the mess for his girlfriend to tidy up. Being Hoover's boys, they leave a trail a mile wide. We quickly determine they're back in the states, possibly in Chicago. Where else would they go? It's their hometown. Come on. Wouldn't you want to go home? I might if Helen Riha was waiting for me."

Twenty laps. Teeter-totter, Teeter-totter.

"Finally we are in Helen's glamorous apartment overlooking the Navy Pier. She's having tea with Catherine and Victor. Chicago cops don't know the details, only that we need to question the woman about some shady activities in Colorado and Canada, far apart geographically but fatally connected. Was a nice afternoon for tea, I'm told. We're not sure how the conversation went, but soon after it started, Victor Bravo leaves. He organizes a huge posse; equipped like a battalion from the 82nd Airborne, and BAM we have a full-blown assault on a fortified bunker in the heart of a Chicago suburb."

Helms paused again to catch his breath and collect his thoughts. He exhaled a deep halting sigh.

"Three dead police. One Hoover boy in custody, the other a puddle at the bottom of a body bag. And, and our man from Colorado, well....."

"Will he live?"

"We think so Bud. But still very critical."

"So Bravo leaves Agent Benson alone with Helen?"

"Yep, that's what happened." Helms again was quiet for a time; then he said, "It gets real sketchy from there. Agent Benson's report is right there on my desk." He points to the top-secret document as if it's a crawling spider. "I've read it twice and had her in here once to go over it, but I'm still not satisfied."

"What do you mean, Dick? What did she say?"

"Not what I wanted her to say."

Teeter-totter, Teeter-totter.

Near the top of the lift she could see across the breathtaking winter landscape below. At an elevation of 3,300 meters she felt momentarily queasy, somewhat lightheaded. She grasped the arm of her handsome instructor snuggling close beside; his arm ready to steady her swooshing glide off the dangling ski lift chair to begin their slow slalom descent down the mountain. They would take Juncalillo, an easy run to the south. "It's for beginners," he cooed to Helen in Spanish. Their elegant fully stocked and expertly bugged ski-in chalet, fireplace crackling and monitors observing their every movement, stood welcoming at bottom.

Teeter-totter, Teeter-totter.

"Dick, one thing among many strange occurrences here that bothers me," Wheelon declared when Helms again paused his phrasing and his pacing to pour a glass of water from a crystal pitcher.

"What's that, Bud?"

"The chance meeting."

"What chance meeting?"

"Peterson and Hernandez and the jilted wife. Pure coincidence? You sure about that?"

Helms turned, and smiled.

"Let's go over my testimony one more time," was the only answer Bud Wheelon got.

Teeter-totter; Teeter-totter.

PART VII

Chapter 51

He is without form, only a perplexing distortion. He aimlessly strides down a winding narrow path. At his feet he ambles along on asphalt and concrete, then with a step further he is onto dirt and into mud. There he slips and stumbles. Falling but coming up clean. A kaleidoscope of colors bursts upon him one moment; deep foggy grays overwhelm him the next. Confusion and bewilderment define his compass. A maze with no exit, turning one corner advances him at right angles to ten more with no signposts to guide. Suddenly he is lost in blackness lasting for days, perhaps seconds, with a return to the unfeeling, drifting to nowhere.

He waits but for what? When there is awareness and his attempt to reenter he melts into another shape, with another face. Handsome then hideous. Whole, then in fragments. There is noise but no sound. He sees flashes but no light, only fierce bolts inflicting pain. Is he dreaming or is he dying? Is he already dead? If not, his plea is it will come soon to end the torture. Make it quick and permanent, he begs. Give me peace, is his supplication. Obliterate that puppet suspended from dancing strings before his eyes. Smiling without joy. It cannot be what God intended unless I deserve His wrath, he ponders. But no, he was good. He tried. I did my job whatever it was. He cannot remember. There is only satisfaction in knowing and feeling. Something. Whatever feelings are; sometimes. Yet they are undefined. Perhaps death has not yet come for him. Just hurt remains, only to depart with the void. Which he welcomes. He closes the curtain once more.

Next, there is sound, sharp and piercing, screeching like an errant bow across a broken violin. Yet it is unlike utterances in the past. It fades and rises from afar and then comes closer to penetrate the tunnel in which he resides. Its walls ragged with deep crevices oozing rancid liquid meant not to refresh, only to repulse and punish. But it is the place in which provides his shelter for now. His home, cold, damp and foreboding. He concentrates, seeking clarity of the noise like twisting the dial of a crackling antique radio. Are those words or only shrill shrieks of haunting banshees invading his tunnel refuge? They are not the echoes from within, but of others. Beyond. God does not beckon to His Kingdom with words. He commands silently, by impression. Then it must not be Him.

Now, that which he hears is more distinct as the reverberations weaken. Light baritone in nature and higher in pitch. Alto. Yes, that's it. I can tell the difference, he reflects, having loved music once and envied those who made it by their voices or with their hands and hearts. He tests the noise to make sure it is not him. He is quiet. They are not. Someone speaks. Are they words yet not complete, incomprehensible. Thoughts only abstract.

"Coma, re...mains, no ign of cog....nition, veg...is...ta...tive tate; ittle ope of cov...er..y.

Slow and halting. He broods and tries to focus but to no avail. He is spent.

Fatigue blankets and blackness returns to consume him once more. In his slumber, overriding the pall, comes light, powerful but this time less damaging. He realizes waning discomfort from the flashes, replaced by vivid images, which commence to take form. An outline at first, pencil thin, but no less a figure, a drawing like those of Picasso. I also loved art, he informs no one, having been fond of impressionists while holding an abiding abhorrence of the surrealists.

Surreal in this instance is apropos. Misshapen, these sketches, the nose to one side, nostrils flaring, an eye set above the other protruding from the forehead. Absent ears, and hair in spiked obelisks. But it is human; still ugly and repulsive. The portrait in his daze does not dissolve like those before. Rather it stands its ground defying the pit, which took all the others. Never to return. Then. Not now. This one remains and moves like a mime. A caricature in motion, stepping over the pit to safety. Declaring a small victory for the others who gather before him, for now there is more than one. Blue fills in the lines of the defiant one. A face. Green is painted inside the outline of another at its side. Pale yellow are the eyes now parallel under the brow. Brown shades fill the inside of another, and the eyes are black but kind not threatening. Their mouths are curled in wavy lines. Lips thin and pursed, thick and wide; teeth gigantic. Then tongues begin to waggle. And sounds begin to spew and words begin to form.

"Damaging effect. Severe hemorrhaging. Typical by a bleeding bullet?"

No, that's not it. Makes no sense. Try again.

"Damaging effect. Severe hemorrhaging is typical; profuse bleeding inherent from cranial bullet wounds."

Those are the words delivered in order. Clear utterances. Sequential. He does hear them. And he understands. They are not his words or thoughts. Not his imagination. Someone is there, speaking, and it's not him. Picasso is replaced by Rockwell. Sure, distinct and bold.

But again he fades. And they, those before him, dissolve as he seeks more time away. From exhaustion, but why? There is nothing to him to tire. Just a fantasy. And the colors and sounds and life forms abound? Unreal. Another dream.

Suddenly months, maybe hours or minutes later, new pain catapults. But does it really hurt? Irritating is more like it. Discomfort, not excruciating, and it is foreign, outside not from within where he dwells in the tunnel avoiding the pit where his Picassos once fell.

Somewhere hiding, this feeling won't go away. He can't touch it but he senses...it... A tickle. What is that? He knows it is there waiting to be dealt with. It grows stronger. Beyond his control.

Explosion, a sound so loud there is ringing. Then another and he is relieved and comforted.

"He sneezed! I'll be a son-of-a-bitch, he sneezed."

"And I think he blinked his eyes."

Back to where he belongs. The tunnel coaxes him to return to where he is safe. That thing that happened. That sound; that blast and those words. They can't be real. Only tricks, more tricks, those in the tunnel with him say. He peers outside searching for the light, for the figures; green and blue and brown; their lips and brows and tongues flapping, but they are gone. Then Norman, not Pablo, turns in his chair, away from his easel and waves to him with his brush.

Waterfall. He is tumbling, rolling over the edge. Miles below it seems, the water churns and boils, yet this time he is not afraid. He does not recoil; rather he welcomes the...what is that? Pressure. Poking. He sees bread dough piled in a heap. Indentations remain after kneaded and rolled elongated by strong hands and fingers. He is over to one side. Norman's clarity has left him but he does not mind. Then the cool wetness. Comforting. Yes, he has drifted to the bottom and he is floating, rolling again.

"Turn him and I will bathe his other side."

More words which he tries to comprehend. Where are they coming from? And then without warning, suddenly he expels, casting out a force, and the pool in which he is suspended suddenly empties and he falls on barren rocks, sharp and biting. Deep and low it is; hurting, truly. He weeps, and the voices are angry.

"Damn, not a second after removing the catheter, he pees all over me."

"Yea, you deserved it. You touched the wound. Be more careful."

Seconds later, maybe decades have passed and he is running along the path, not walking like before, and this time when he falls he does not rise clean. Instead he is covered in soft batter, pure, moist and dripping but absent the slime. He falls again, failing to rise this time, disquiet.

His breath is shallow and he hears those sounds, those words, shouting, like he hears them now, but he becomes whole then, not in the tunnel. He sees it in the distance but resists black hole's calling. He has feet and hands and arms and legs and he knows that he has been violated. Parts of him pierced. Holes created, fluids soaking the ground. He does not acknowledge it as blood, because blood leaving him means it is misplaced

forever. He is lost and angry at the reason for his fall. Yes, he is afraid. Yet he must continue on. Someone is waiting, pleading for his help, but he cannot.........move.

"Virtually in a catatonic state, caused by massive hypovolemic shock, a condition characterized by prolonged restricted delivery of oxygen to the vital organs. Permanently paralyzed, we believe. In his case, shock so severe, coma has been persistent. Infrequently we detect signs of cognitive recognition, but ever so rarely."

Paralyzed. They can't be talking about him. It must be someone else. He has no being. He is just a notion. An observer dangling in space. Brain waves only, occasionally in sync.

Yet he heard the words. And he processed their meaning. He is aware but inside himself still. With great effort he has departed the tunnel and escaped the hideous, circumscriptive maze. Somehow he has found his way out. At least for now. He can not see them but he knows they are not his words, nor his dreams or whatever it was that has kept him dark, inside, dealing with the jagged walls behind which the demons hide. Is this happy, he asks? Because he cannot react to what he hears, only ponder. But that might be good enough for now.

In his brief awakening he does not quite understand what was just said. It doesn't matter who spoke only he must have been the topic of a callous dialogue about insufficient oxygen, a severe, irreversible condition, and no sign of cognition. He understands what those words mean and they are disturbing, if they were talking about me. But who else could be involved? He is the center of their attention because he is down here and they are up there, hovering over him like swarms of wasps ready to strike. Realizing that he must again seek shelter but resist the tunnel, he hides and sees a face. Is it me? He remembers when finding the mirror and looks. There he is as before, no longer with pieces missing, rather whole. I never thought I was handsome, but who cares?

"He was damn lucky that paramedic was close by when he went down. She took the crucial first quick steps that saved his life. Plugging the holes, controlling the bleeding and seepage of vital fluids from the brain, keeping his airways open. CPR; all of it helped, but the trajectory of the bullet made all the difference. Millimeter spans distinguishing the path of the projectile through soft tissue of the brain was the deciding factor sparing his life, regardless of the first aid measures taken at the scene."

"That slug, likely a .30 caliber, entered above the right eyebrow, cleared the skull, students, meaning it was a through and through...in through the forehead and out the back. And the fact that it passed cleanly through the cranium was a fortunate circumstance, believe it or not. A bullet of that size completely clearing the skull helps to limit the opportunity for infection, and it also means the brain bore less of the brunt of the bullet's full energetic load."

"If the victim had been hit in the head with a fastball that contained the same amount of force but not pierced the skull, the brain would have sustained much more damage. In the victim's case the energy dispersed along the bullet's full track was focused like a beam with little chance of diffusion to injure surrounding tissue."

"Further, very fortunate for him, an ambulance was on the scene for transport in a matter of minutes."

"Why was that doctor? Why was an ambulance in close proximity?"

"As I understand it, the patient, a police officer, was involved in a horrific shootout, literally a massive gunfight with a well-armed criminal, holed up in a garage or some such thing. Police had surrounded the building and expected violence, so luckily they had paramedics and emergency vehicles on the scene for evacuation. Only seconds after the patient was hit, three times, trained professionals came to his aid.

"I think I remember that, doctor. Was this the guy who ran out into the open toward two wounded cops who had been shot by some trained sniper who they said might have been a former FBI agent gone mad?"

"Yes, doctor, this is the man. Some call him a hero, others say he was careless since those other officers were already dead, and he exposed himself unnecessarily."

"Wow, and he took one through the frontal lobe, one under the rib cage, lodging in his lung and another through his hip. It's a miracle he didn't die instantly."

"Enough of that. We're clinicians here, not clergy. Shall we now pay attention to our review of the precise neurological surgical procedures that saved this poor man's life, as it is, and engage in some meaningful dialogue regarding the prospects for recovery, miniscule as they are?"

Wait a minute! He shouts without sound. I want to hear more. I want to remember. Hey, tell me what happened before. A bullet through my head! Why was he there in the first place? Doing what? Fighting a gun battle. With whom? Can't be. Who am I, such as I am. Out of his tunnel but still lying on the edge, teetering toward the pit. Without substance, only pitiful. Damn it! Come back!

Chapter 52

"What is this? Who gave these orders?"

"They were received this morning doctor. He is to be moved to Walter Reed Army Medical Center in Washington, DC. They are sending a specially equipped military air transport hospital to pick him up this afternoon. We are to stabilize him as best we can and have him ready for discharge."

"But I am his attending physician. I'm the one who saved his life. Well, among others. I have the final authority over the treatment of my patients. Again, I ask you, who gave these orders?"

"Doctor, the matter is out of my hands. The call came in from the chairman of our board who said he was contacted personally by a very high-ranking government official who solicited our cooperation and, frankly, our discretion in the matter. They say it is best for all of us, including those who will enjoy the uninterrupted continuation of our future research grants, to step aside. Our chairman was told your patient would be given the best care medicine has to offer."

"Well, certainly I am aware of the reputation of Walter Reed, but doesn't the facility cater exclusively to military personnel? I thought my patient was a civilian; rather a police detective, not even from Chicago. Why would they want him at Walter Reed?"

"I have no idea why they are taking this highly unusual step. No one denies that the surgery you performed gave the patient a last ditch fighting chance at survival. Three bullet wounds, all of which singularly could have been fatal, were dealt with the utmost surgical skill. All I can figure is the man is someone special to our government. Someone cares a great deal about his long-term treatment and potential recovery. We all know Walter Reed is renowned for its rehabilitative capabilities particularly applied to wounded combat soldiers suffering head traumas. You know the strides they are making with those returning from Vietnam."

"True, perhaps he will be better off there, but I find it quite odd all the secrecy surrounding the whole affair. I don't even know the poor bastard's name. Do you?"

"No, he's a John Doe, but an important one. I've already given the orders to his attending nurses to begin his preparation, but I thought you would like to supervise."

"Indeed, thank you doctor, I would. Tell me how do you like the dual role of chief-of- staff and administrator? Love the politics of it all?"

"This kind of crap I can do without, I'll tell you that. But there is one more thing. At one point in your post operative report, which by the way, the feds received some days ago, you hypothesized on the potential of hydrostatic shock as a theoretical cause of Mr. Doe's extensive brain injury. I did not know you were among those who prescribed to that line of thinking. With the massive direct cranial damage inflicted by the path of the bullet, please enlighten me as to how gunshot wounds to his chest and upper thigh may have resulted in greater injury to his brain."

"You say they, whoever they are, I presume someone directing my patient's transfer saw my report?"

"Yes, like I said, they've had it for several days now."

"Now I get it. Yes, doctor, I did allude in my report to the premise that his other wounds which, by the way, resulted in more extensive, but certainly pinpointed destruction of the surrounding tissue than the clean shot through his head, may be the tangential cause of his lingering coma and paralysis. And I have read that the military has embarked on an exhaustive study of hydrostatic shock suffered by gunshot victims returning from the Viet Nam Tet Offensive battlefront. Now I see why they want him at Walter Reed. Not only is he a key figure in something none of us may ever know about, apparently they intend to examine my assertions much further."

"Again doctor I implore you, I am not one who thoroughly understands how this could be. I mean what the hell are you talking about?"

"Doctor, there is a growing body of evidence that hydrostatic shock can induce remote neural damage and stimulate incapacitation more quickly than the direct effect of blood loss. Our patient was a victim of "light and fast" projectiles. The bullets that entered his body were high velocity .30 millimeter cartridges fired from a conventional Army-issue M1 carbine. If the assailant had shot him using, say, a .45-caliber weapon, which is "slow and heavy", that man would have been cold and buried in the ground long ago. He was extremely lucky in that sense, however, when those two bullets almost simultaneously hit his chest and upper thigh, the shock waves or hydraulic effects destroying nearby tissues in a wide swath sent liquid-filled particles extending in all directions far beyond the wound axis.

"The pressure waves associated with the explosions hitting his body from these supersonic pieces of metal almost instantaneously caused the remote neural effects to his brain."

"Fascinating, doctor, however, I frankly find it hard to believe that a bullet in his butt is going to send a shock wave to his brain knocking out his full range of sensory modems rendering him a potential invalid for life."

"Believe it doctor, that's what happened in my view. You have to remember his brain suffered incredible trauma, make no mistake, yet entering the frontal lobe, skimming just above the temporal lobe, leaving him the remote prospect of restoration of smell and sound, and only nicking the occipital lobe which may still cause permanent blindness, could not have been on a more fortuitous path. I couldn't have drawn it up any better in a laboratory or in an operating suite."

"And he has been in deep coma for six months now and appears to be permanently paralyzed because he took two to the body, missing vital organs?"

"Yes, indeed, doctor, no one will know for sure until the autopsy, heaven forbid, but I surmise that the hydrostatic pressure congregated most intently in the carotid artery from the wound to his chest. It traveled from that impact location through the pulmonary artery seeking the least route of resistance eventually into the circle of Willis resulting in hemorrhage and sustainable stroke. Again the paramedic saved his life by plugging the holes in his head, preventing massive blood and brain fluid loss.

"God in heaven. That, sir, is incredible."

"I have taken you away from your patient and for that I apologize."

"Thank you doctor I will see to him now."

"If I may? Would you be willing to articulate your conclusions in a more formal paper to me which, in turn, I will present to the medical staff and board as a means of enlightening them on this truly spectacular case?'

"I would be delighted, doctor, however my surgical schedule is very compressed over the next two weeks. May I have it to you, say, by the thirtieth?

"That would be perfectly fine. Thank you."

"Thank you doctor, have a wonderful day....But a final question of you, sir. Something you might also ask members of the hospital board. Are you a hunter?

"No sir, I am not. Why do you ask?"

"Well if you were, you would be joining millions of American sportsmen who have adapted the "light and fast" cartridges. They are cleaner, quicker, leaving smaller entry holes in the game but cause colossal internal devastation from hydrostatic shock. All for surer kills, and the added bonus of prime meat which is much better preserved."

"Was our cop killer a hunter?"

"I suspect he was. Good day, doctor."

Chapter 53

I had this feeling just then. Which is interesting since there isn't anything else in here that occupies his time. Perhaps it was nothing more than a fleeting impression. Like before. Poof and it is gone. The feeling he had, and they come more frequently now, is that time had passed. Time, meaning there was a before and now there is a now. Maybe this before thing lasted no longer than a blink of an eye, maybe it lasted for days, but whatever it was he desperately wants to believe inside here he has begun to sense things that happened in the past and now he's speculating the before is before the now. If that's the case does that mean he has a memory? And if he has a memory then he existed before as some sort of whole being and if his memory is beginning to work then he might be able to recall what happened, presuming he's not dead and all of this isn't just God's cruel hoax, permitting him a quick glimpse back at the life he once had.

Well, if it is a peek into his past on his way to whatever lies ahead, including death, I guess that's okay, because he is visualizing some things that were rather pleasant.

Like when he visited a little boy recently. See, there is a before. This little boy seemed to be happy. He was playing on a lawn, throwing a baseball. He was a strong kid, it appeared, black hair, vigorous, ornery; his father strict and his mother doting. His parents, or at least he's assuming they were, faded in and out of the picture but had a strong influence on the boy. He grew up fast, could run like the wind, and then he was on a big boat in the ocean, wearing a white uniform, but all at once, there was a big bang and flash of light, heat and fire and it reminded him of the light that hurt and the sound that hurt and he decided not to remember. There I go again thinking about a memory. If he is not dead and if God isn't throwing him a bone on his way to somewhere else. Heaven or hell, he doesn't much care. Actually I do. He doesn't want to go somewhere else. He doesn't want to be dead so he won't pay attention to God anymore; that is, if He'll let me.

Not too long after considering there is a before he finds this person again, still a man, still in his white uniform. He salutes another man with metals pinned to his chest and the other man pins some metals on his man's chest and they both salute each other and it's real nice.

His man admires his metals and smiles and then this very pretty girl kisses him. That was the nicest part of all. So, after the kiss, because now he's realizing there's an order of sequence to all of this; occurrences happening one after the other, the pretty girl stays with the man. They remain together. I don't see him alone anymore.

Later, since time may have passed, in the next series of images, he's wearing a blue uniform, and he's walking down a path, but this time he doesn't step off the path into mud and sink or slide or fall. He's solid and steady and he walks straight and goes into a house and there is the pretty girl and they are naked and when they are naked he feels this wonderful sensation, like a surge from inside going outside somewhere, and that was the best thing that ever happened and he hopes he remembers it a long time, if there is time and if he has a memory because memories like that are worth the darkness when it comes and he feels it coming on again so he will have to wait.

"I apologize for the delay and inconvenience it has caused gentlemen, but like I said, last week I was not comfortable in executing the discharge papers. His last episode was simply too strenuous on his precarious condition. Following what appeared to be a seizure and spasms primarily isolated in the pelvic region, in itself quite odd, we detected an extremely disconcerting cardiac arrhythmia, which necessitated immediate defibrillation to bring the heart back into normal rhythmic cycles.

"I hasten to add he did not go into arrest as far as we can tell but the strain sent him back into a deep catatonic state. Further examination has determined there was no permanent damage to the heart muscle, pericardium, or values, and it appears normal uninterrupted blood flow from a heart returning to vigorous productivity. Therefore I'm sure you understand why I was forced to decline your request for his dismissal and send you back to wherever you came from."

"We understand doctor. However, our superiors are growing rather impatient and have urged us to urge you to relinquish your authority over his care and remand him to us for transfer as quickly as possible. Are you prepared to do so, sir?"

"At this point gentlemen, I have no medical basis on which to further postpone his release. However, as an aside, this event, the one we are most recently focused on, has stirred considerable debate among those of us on hospital staff."

"How so, doctor?"

"Well, here we have a patient who for six, almost seven months, is on and off life support, in deep unrelenting coma for most of the time. His blood pressure in peaks and valleys. His brain swelling and constricting like a sponge soaked one minute, wrung dry the next. His vital organs laboring to regain normal function and his immune system in a pitched battle with invading infection, when all of a sudden he sneezes one day, and a few days later has a god damn wet dream!"

What is that? Laughter. What's so funny?

"Indeed, gentlemen, thank God there are signs of life in this remarkable man. Will he ever regain consciousness or any semblance of normal bodily functions, we have no idea. At this point his heart could stop suddenly without explanation despite its dynamic output. His survival depends on one thing...his desire to live, that innate inexplicable human trait that guides us all."

"I am only speculating here, but I suspect when he lands in that bed at Walter Reed the experiments on him will begin in earnest. I realize you and your superiors have a mission in mind with my patient. I am not sure what it is but I have an idea. Whatever you find, if there is discernable evidence that hydrostatic shock blew out those blood vessels in his brain causing his stroke, I warn you, and damn it, hear this well....If this guinea pig you have kidnapped from me is harmed in any way; if you destroy, alter, or inhibit even the slightest chance of his recovery I will bring you all down. I promise you. Give this incredible human phenomenon a chance to live. I implore you!"

"Doctor, thank you for your cooperation. May I ask you to order your staff to place the patient on the gurney for transport?"

"So be it."

Hey, where are you going? Come back here. You had a kind voice and I think you were talking about me. Something about his treatment. It sounded like you were concerned. So, don't leave if you're the one taking care of him.

But does it matter? To anyone. He has nothing for you to care about since he exists only in imagination; his not someone else's. There is no body here, only a mist, shadowy and obscure. Weightless. A shell if even that. Certainly nothing of substance.

Hold on a minute. Why am I floating? Up in the air. Now slammed back down. he doesn't like this. Ouch! Take your hands off him. That hurts. Pain again. He's moving at a high rate of speed, around corners, down straight-aways, reeling, weaving in and out. Bright lights flashing above. There's more noise. A clamor really. Clanking, squealing wheels. Many voices. It's cold. Not like it was before. Warm and comfortable. Faster he goes. Out of control. Like when he was skiing down a mountain. Is that what I'm doing? If so that was fun and he was pretty good at it. He sees the mountains. The trees. The snow. Is that why it's cold?

I've finally stopped. Rising again but supported, lying flat. A noise. Doors shutting. It's dark. The lights are gone. We've moving but at a slower and easier pace. Not frantic like before. He hears a rumbling. Like a motor. He's in a car or on a truck. He feels a touch coming from the outside. A sting. A bee? Those wasps? Warmth flowing inside, meandering like a gentle stream. He feels it.

None of this makes sense. If there is no body and he is just a formless cloud like the faces he saw in fluffy skies on bright summer days, then why all of these sensations?

There must be some connection to movement, the sound, the pain, and warmth and fear. Those things, which come and go must be tied to a body, a real life, living, and breathing being.

Well, that's interesting. God's trickery or God's gift?

I've decided. I'll be an optimist. He's spared him from whatever fate, whomever, or whatever he is, for the time being. He's made him make the connection between fantasy and reality. Okay, I can do that. His thoughts are not just from inside, they are forced from the outside. By someone. Or something. He is reacting to and actually thinking about what's going on to him and around him. So, what do I do about it? He can't just go on reacting. He has to make something happen. He has to let those on the outside know he's in here on the inside no longer lying on the edge of the bottomless pit, or lost in the tunnel, and he feels and thinks and wants to make connections with his body; I guess it's mine, and with them. He wants them to know that he's alive and wants this person working again.

The rumbling motor and swaying box which carries him are more gentle now. Slowing down. Blackness is coming. The warm spring water flowing through him has found its lake and there are no waves. He is calm. The fear is gone replaced by determination. I will make them aware after I...go...to sleep.

Russell Senate Office Building
Closed Door Hearing Convened by
Idaho Senator Frank Church Member
Senate Foreign Relations Committee
Washington, DC
January 29, 1973

Chapter 54

"Senator please let me finish," Richard Helms, Director of the U.S. Central Intelligence Agency, pleaded in elevated pitch, the first time in their four hour closed-door hearing when restraint lost out to irritation.

Ignoring every word, the senior senator from Idaho lectured: "And furthermore, Director Helms, this committee will not tolerate further stonewalling by you or your Agency over the matter of Committee 33, our President's pet project to legitimize flagrant eavesdropping on the Soviet Union. Least I remind you your actions and his have seriously heightened tensions with our sworn enemy during this particularly dangerous period."

"Respectfully Senator, if you will let me speak I will provide you those details as well as any additional intelligence data gathered during the Committee's tenure."

"That certainly would be most welcomed Director Helms because I and the majority members of this Senate panel will find it very difficult to bring your nomination as Ambassador to Iran to the floor for debate, despite your alleged ties to the Shah which may or may not serve you or the nation well in that volatile part of the world."

"Thank you for your astute observations, Senator, and now if I may proceed..."

"By all means."

"As I began to say, Committee 33 was formed and funded on a shoestring budget during the President's first term. It was not, as you allege, an eavesdropping mission. On the contrary. Its purpose was very simple. Find a means to counteract the Soviet's concerted effort to disrupt our broadcast signals, which were carrying messages of democracy and freedom to the oppressed masses inside the Communist bloc.

"KGB and its counterpart organizations in the Soviet Union had manufactured a device which effectively either distorted or completely obliterated U.S. originated radio communications emanating from Western Europe. Radio Free Europe, our Armed Forces Networks, Radio Freedom and all means of U.S. Information Agency broadcasts were being compromised. Their actions were systematically depriving their citizens of our doctrine of hope. President Nixon was adamant that we do everything we could to block them from blocking our signals. And thanks to a team led by the esteemed Dr. Albert "Bud" Wheelon we not only created an ingenious gadget, about the size of a package of gum, to neutralize their appliance and we found a way to install it right under the Kremlin's nose."

"I presume, Director Helms, you are obliquely referring to the escapades of one Dr. Thomas Riha."

"Yes, Senator, Dr. Riha became our vehicle for delivery of Dr. Wheelon's wonderful implement."

"And this gentleman, your mule if you will, is the same individual who some argue was a Soviet spy, while others maintain he was an American counterspy, but in any case is now dead and buried in a pauper's grave in Canada."

"Senator, whatever Thomas Riha was, he carried out his mission for the United States with bravery and aplomb. After entering the country as a special guest, one coveted by the Soviets for his overt anti-American pronouncements, he adroitly found a way to slip the grasp of KGB escorts assigned to control his movements about the Capitol. He discovered the location of the broadcast center in the heart of Red Square, and during their most sacred Bolshevik May Day celebrations, simply entered the communications center, found the main terminal and plugged Dr. Wheelon's pack of Juicy Fruit into the central outlet. Once in place the instrument switched off the computer's instructions to broadcast towers across the country which were aimed at jamming our signals. At the same time the computer told its technicians, hence the Kremlin hierarchy, that all was well; in effect that their dirty blanket still hung over their country denying their citizens the truth."

"A real gumshoe caper, hey Mr. Helms," Church laughed at himself.

"That was a joke fellow committee members," he explained.

A few Democrats on the committee offered polite chuckles.

"Yes, sir, I suppose you could describe it that way," Helms acknowledged with a forced smile.

"Dangerous, to be sure. Is that why you believe he was killed?"

"No sir, we believe it was a domestic dispute that resulted in his death."

"Domestic dispute? I would say that is an understatement when your own report leaked to this committee describes his demise as horrific; shot point blank in the face and belly by none other than his ex-wife."

"Senator, the investigation is on-going. There was no solid evidence that his former spouse was the shooter."

"Well, that's interesting Mr. Helms, since again your own report points to evidence of her involvement in not only Dr. Riha's killing but in the deaths of his ex-lover in a mental institution in Colorado, an attending nurse who worked at that psychiatric center, and two other individuals, one a former FBI agent, and the other a worker at the Austrian embassy who may at one time have been on your payroll."

"Again, Senator, the investigation is ongoing. There are many elements to this case. Several of your questions must be addressed by the FBI which is pursuing its own line of inquiry while others in law enforcement are also heavily engaged to bring forth the facts."

"So I am to assume that fanciful summation presented by your staff for your eyes only but somehow found its way into the hands of my staff, was full of unsubstantiated conjecture? Name the author of this notorious report once again Director?"

"Catherine Benson, Senator."

"Oh yes, a woman. Yes, now I recall. Top agent, trusted, diligent in her pursuit of Riha's killer; somehow roping in a homicide detective who was investigating Riha's lover's death to help her. Then he, this detective, winds up full of holes in a shootout with the now deceased former FBI agent who mows down three other Chicago cops before he blows himself up in a bunker converted from an abandoned garage. Does that about sum it up, Mr. Helms?"

"Once more, Senator, yes, tragic events have surrounded this incident. My agency has been forthcoming with all the facts as we have them at hand today. Agent Benson remains integral to unraveling certain unfortunate occurrences."

"I think I recall in reading her report she used the term teeter-totter; like being on a teeter-totter, a child rising up one moment, descending the next, never striking a balance."

"Yes, I believe she used that term sir."

"Certainly apropos, I would say Mr. Helms. Childish indeed, the way you have handled all elements of his incident."

"I beg your pardon, sir."

"Now let's see what was the last, no, perhaps the second to last entry in Agent Benson's report? Oh, yes, the ex-wife, perhaps a fiendish murderer is now living in Chile. Is that correct Mr. Helms?"

"Yes, we believe she is residing in that country at the moment, Senator."

"And is refusing extradition?"

"Yes, the Chilean government has granted her permanent asylum."

"The same woman allowed to leave the United States on the same day as three Chicago police offers are killed and a Colorado detective is severely wounded and not expected to recover from a bullet through his skull?"

"Yes sir, the same woman, however, again Senator, we have no direct evidence of her culpability in these killings or the regretful circumstances surrounding the wounding of the detective. We pray for his recovery and look forward to the day when he is able to communicate with our investigators. His insight into the series of events leading up to the shootings would be extremely helpful."

"I'm sure of that Mr. Helms; helpful in further covering your tracks."

"I take offense at that remark Senator."

"I'll bet you do, but be very careful in what you say further, Director Helms. Our President strongly believes that you are the man to preserve our fruitful relationship with the powerful oil rich nation of Iran, but I would not hesitate to indefinitely table your nomination for actions contemptuous to this committee and the American people."

"That would be regrettable, Senator. Is that all?"

For now, Mr. Helms, unless the committee members have anything further, you are dismissed."

"Thank you sir."

"Oh by the way, Mr. Helms. Does Committee 33 still exist?"

"No sir, it does not. Mission accomplished."

Chapter 55

I am in another place. And it's different from when he escaped the tunnel and dodged the pit. Where he is now feels real, concrete and substantial. His surroundings are not dark and menacing, abstract or conceptual; rather being here bears truth. For one thing there is the smell. Yes, he detects a certain odor about this place. It's like when that lady, he is reminded, the one who watched over that little boy playing in the yard, would put on rubber gloves and stoop over and pour powder in a toilet and use a brush to scrub it clean, and that little boy would watch her and smell that smell, like something chemical. It was not sweet or sour and certainly not pleasant but that smell took away the other smell coming from the toilet, so it was better after the lady scrubbed and polished with the powder sprinkled in the water.

There are times when that bad smell comes and stays around his new place for a time before someone, not the lady, comes in close. When that happens he's lifted up, and then he's put back down and rolled over and soon the stink goes away and is replaced by that familiar scent of chemicals.

I hope that foul stink isn't coming from me. But wait. If he can produce a bad odor then there must be a body and a mind and maybe the two are connected, and maybe they are him. I hope I don't always stink, but he's fairly sure he has a body and he is this person who offends and can't help it because he is fucking injured and sick and paralyzed and he can't doing anything about it except lie there and shit in this bed and wait for someone to come clean it up.

Who am I kidding? Once he got here, wherever here is because it's different than the first place he was in, he figured it out. It came to him quite suddenly like stepping out of a heavy fog. Problem was he didn't want to face it. Coward as I am. He wanted to scamper back into the darkness, into his land of make believe where he existed only in his head and lived in the tunnel on the edge of the pit. That was sure as hell better than this. He'd peek out of the tunnel and smile even when it thundered black and ripe with storms, thinking he was on a cloud floating billowy white high above, looking down and thinking how lucky he was without a body to torture him with healing.

But no! I had to start feeling. He had to release his senses, see light all around; realize heat, experience pain and shit the bed. Now that's depressing.

To hide he'd visualize that lady hovering over him in the yard and he would go inside to hear her singing when she scrubbed and cleaned, knowing she was his mother because he saw her face when he dreamed and he dreams now because he knows the difference between being awake and being asleep. I loathe being awake. He much prefers being asleep where he's with that beautiful creature, cradling him and soothing his pain. I am there with her once again, a toilet-trained child, innocent, shedding discomfort.

Being awake has no rewards, he believes. He senses there are many people around him all the time now when he is awake. He pretends to sleep but he can't help but hear what they're saying and worst of all he feels what they're doing to him. Often his eyes are open but the cloud is thick and blurry and he can make no connection. He stares into space, and they know there's only void.

He has no way of protesting their invasion. I can't resist at all, because he is a vegetable. Yes, admit it. They could squash him and eat him with their carrots and potatoes and he'd have to let them do it. Make a stew out of him. He has no power other than when he soils the bed sheets, and that gets their attention. Maybe I should do that more often. In the meantime, they can do what they want whenever they want; whatever suits their fancy at the moment. What irritates him the most is when they lift him up and move him around which happens more often these days. They like to pull on his crippled, invalid arms and legs. Yes, he knows he owns decaying extremities and he knows they're just lying there like the rest of him, rotting away. I hate to admit it. But it's true. So what can I say? All of a sudden someone is bending and rotating them, one at a time, and he hears some remark like, "Oh he's getting stronger. Feel that resistance. Muscle tone is coming back. I feel it."

Bullshit lady, you don't feel a thing because he doesn't feel a thing except when you pull too hard and stretch too far and if he could jump up I would knock you flat on the floor.

And then there are those times when he feels a pinch and he knows what's coming next. Needles, dozens of them. Into his withering arms, through his groin, barely missing his shriveling balls. Through his chest, under his ribs, even into his neck. When they are poking him like a pincushion he hears them saying over and over how miraculous it is that I'm alive and how the bullets that struck him, three of them, somehow didn't kill him and it was the ones hitting him in the chest and butt that caused his paralysis and not the one that went through his skull.

Now, I have to say, he may be lying there incapacitated and absent of most human faculties, but he does know one thing. A bullet through someone's brain sure as hell causes greater damage putting them in a state like mine, than a bullet in the ass. Yet he hears all this nonsense about how the body suffers internal trauma from projectiles piercing flesh creating pressure traveling through your arteries exploding in your head to flood the brain and cause a stroke. All he can think is these guys are a bunch of quacks and it scares me to death.

How about that? He's suddenly frightened about the prospect of dying, thinking all these people around him are incapable of providing him proper care and now he's all of a sudden concerned about that when, what....two days ago or maybe six months ago, because he still can't tell time, he was longing for death, actually praying for it to end the suffering. Who knows? Could that mean he might be getting better?

Chapter 56

"Agent Benson, how very nice to see you. I'm glad you could come. Please have a seat," Richard Helms, Ambassador to Iran, and former Director of U.S. Central Intelligence, warmly greeted one of his top spies as she approached the remote corner table at which he stood and held out his hand.

"Nice to see you too sir," Catherine said while tightly grasping the Ambassador's hand.

I won't be intimidated, she thought to herself.

Helms motioned for her to sit. She slid in the booth opposite him and folded her hands on the starched white cloth covering the tabletop. The lamp at her elbow, designed to resemble a single colonial style candle holder, shined brightly in her eyes. She blinked at the irritation and moved her head away from the glare to capture Helm's stare, his eyes fixed and his lips perfectly straight-lined at a veiled attempt at a smile. His look gave her a start. She knew why she had been summoned by her former boss to this unofficial meeting and she had first resisted, but later was persuaded by a trusted friend within the Agency who made it clear that her career was still in jeopardy over the Riha case. "If you don't go, he will most certainly do you in," her friend had warned, adding, "He has as much to lose as you do. He may be your only ally. Remember, you let her go and now she's untouchable somewhere in South America under the protection of a not-so-friendly government."

"But that's where she belongs," Catherine had argued meekly.

A short fire-plug shaped waiter, bald, and sweating and panting as if he'd run a marathon scurried up to the table.

Before he could ask, Helms said, "Martini, dirty, three olives, chilled." And turning to Catherine, "You?"

"Just sparkling water." She had to keep her wits about her.

The waiter scampered off. Helms' Cheshire cat smile returned momentarily; then his lips turned down.

"Have you seen him?" Helms asked.

Knowing full well who him was, she replied, "Yes, sir. I was there the other day, Tuesday. It's awful. He's in such bad shape. Still. So emaciated. He probably weighs less than a hundred pounds. Unable to speak; no control over bodily functions; nothing but an invalid. Makes me so sad. He was such a vibrant man even at his age. And what he did that day. Exposing himself to heavy gunfire to run to aid those officers he didn't even know. I am so ashamed. I should have been there with him. Maybe I could have done something. Instead I stayed behind with her. I, I..."

Interrupting her, "Enough Catherine, please," Helms said soothingly, and adding sympathetically said, "You can't second guess your actions while under stressful conditions in the field. You did what was right and prudent at the time. Staying with the suspect; gathering further information. You had no way of knowing how the situation would evolve. A pitched gun-battle to rival any gangland Chicago, Al Capone-type shootout from the '30's? Come on Catherine, stop blaming yourself."

Her gaze was hard. Hearing his attempt at consolation made her selfish fury rise even further. She had sworn not to become emotional regardless at what he said or did, and just then, at the first mention of Victor's name, she came apart, an inexcusable schoolgirl outpouring over just another partner, just another field operation; this one gone bad, unlike so many others that went so well. By why? Why with Victor, an old worn out Podunk cop with four kids and a backwater wife who has been there to see him only once. And without their kids no less. This guy, such a pain-in-the-ass, consistently condescending, acting superior, always criticizing, never accepting her superior role as commander of the task force. Why did she feel this way? Who cares? She shouldn't, but she does and it makes me sick.

"Okay, Mr. Ambassador, you're right. I need to put this behind me. Funny somehow, calling you Ambassador."

"Yes, taking some getting use to, I suppose, but I'd better get ready since I'm off day after tomorrow. Should be an interesting place, Tehran, and the Shah, a fascinating guy. Just wonder how long he will last."

"As long as we continue to prop him up, I suspect. Don't you think so, sir?"

"Yes, he is a trusted ally, but there is growing discontent among his people as the radical Muslim population stirs animosity, even hatred of the monarchy, especially as their oil reserves are in greater demand, and his wealth, as a result, continues to escalate.

"Again, thanks to the good ole U.S of A. and its love of the sacred automobile."

"Indeed, Catherine, indeed."

"Now why did you want to see me Mr. Ambassador?"

Helms' reply was interrupted as the harried waiter arrived with their drinks. While lifting them from the tray he carried, he tipped one sending a stream of expensive liquor rushing down the sides of the martini glass to puddle around the stem base of the shimmering goblet. Not stopping there he also managed to splash sparkling water and soak the table cloth in front of Catherine as a result of an errant attempt to pour the beverage in a single gush from a bottle too big into a glass too small.

"Can I take your orders?" he panted.

"Give us a minute," Helms grumbled.

"All right then. I'll be back."

"Take your time."

Helms sipped at his drink but did not speak. Catherine sponged up the small lake before her with her only napkin. She waited anxiously, trying desperately to mask her anxiety. She knew what was coming. Had anticipated it for months. But had refused to acknowledge the inevitability. Ever since her final report on the Riha case, re-written not once, but twice at Helms' direction, was sealed in his safe, only to find its way into the hands of a pimply-faced Senate staff intern who happened to be the nephew of a disgruntled CIA clerk who had copied the last version and gave it to him on his 21st birthday along with a large bottle of Aqua Velva.

She was to take the fall. She had become dispensable, excess baggage, a liability. Career over. His continuing uninterrupted. She could not run. Only walk to the exit. Stage right, down the hall, out the door. Taxi waiting at curbside. Limousine waiting for him.

"The specials today are...." He had returned. Lumbering up to the table. Carrying nothing this time to spill. Only sweat dripping and heavy breathing to mark his presence.

"Two cob salads," Helms said.

"You okay with that?" he asked Catherine.

"Sure, Thousand Island, please," she said.

"Make mine ranch," Helms said.

"That it?"

"That's it."

"Back with them in a jiffy," he huffed.

"Take your time," Catherine said.

After further moments of unpleasant silence, finally," Sir, let me save you the trouble," was her offering.

"What do you mean Catherine?"

"The trouble or perhaps the inconvenience of telling me that my time at the Agency is over. The fact that your confirmation as Ambassador was predicated on my falling, or better put, being shoved on to the point of that razor sharp sword." She paused. He held her gaze. Saying nothing. No emotion.

"And I will be the one who quietly steps aside to make room for your advancement; all for the good of the country; especially at this critical diplomatic crossroads in the Middle East.

Right so far?"

He didn't respond.

"Yes, I put her on that plane, even walked her to the gate. She is without a doubt a cold blooded killer, but don't we love them, embrace them, guide and shield them when they have acted unselfishly to protect our most closely guarded secrets? My, how our patriotic fervor rises in time of crisis. You, dear Sir, are equally as culpable in those murders, perhaps more so since you not only recruited her, you found the means to steer the entire course of events.

Another pause. "Still on course, correct?"

Still no response.

"Two cob salads, made to order."

"But that looks like oil and vinegar," Helms said, clearly disgusted with the turn of events.

"I'll bring you another one."

"Don't bother. Just another martini."

Catherine was suddenly famished. She dug into her meal. The dressing was superb. Neither spoke for several minutes. Helms poked at the lettuce, stabbed at the hard boiled eggs and swallowed his second drink in two gulps.

Finally, "Catherine, I'm sorry."

"Don't be Mr. Ambassador. It's only my life."

"I know, but..."

"Let me finish," she growled. "So, in the end nothing was left to chance. Nice and neat. Tidy up. Galya was a dangerous by-product. You had her locked up indefinitely, and with the utmost precision cruelty, planned to slowly cripple her so she became useless to any overly ambitious Capitol Hill sleuth. But when Riha went missing, she had to go. And what better way than priming the spurned spouse, already in your clutches, by handing her a syringe full of lethal medication. The nurse who had been paid off became a real nuisance after a bad interview with Detective Bravo so she ends up in a deep ravine with body parts decorating the countryside. The carnage didn't stop there. You had to get rid of our boy in Vienna. Those two Hoover rejects were the perfect alternates for that little adventure.

"And I'm certain you knew where Riha was all along. Lovely city, that Montreal. So sending her after him was brilliant."

"Stop Catherine."

"No Sir. I'm just beginning. The only one you couldn't control or better put, strangle, was Bravo and that's only because Nixon liked him. Your only mistake was having the President make that telephone call to him. What you didn't count on was the firefight. You thought Gordon and Rico would give up. Too bad one of them nearly blew up an entire neighborhood. And Bravo goes down. A true hero. Nixon likes him even more, so he's given the best possible care the U.S. Government can buy, but let's make sure it's under our watchful eye right here at Walter Reed. He's a vegetable; don't forget, so your lucky streak continues."

"Catherine, you have no idea."

"Come on boss, now is not the time to patronize me. In the end Church and his committee are given just enough of this sordid tale for cover and create the compromise votes for his bill to reform the Agency and its practices. In return, your confirmation is assured. You ride off into the desert sunset with the Shah leaving your successors with many hard choices; either try to run a politically tethered spy apparatus, answerable to a suspicious oversight Congress, or shut it down all together and let the Defense Department and those military geniuses take over."

"Way to go Mr. Ambassador."

She was finally quiet. He sighed heavily but she knew by his banal expression; dull, controlled, acknowledging nothing, yet his eyes could not conceal how many truths he had just heard. At least she thought so. Truth and Consequences? Or Fiction and Fantasy? Teeter-Totter. Teeter-Totter.

"Check please," Helms said when their waiter sauntered by.

"My only question, Mr. Ambassador; am I entitled to severance and a partial pension for my years of service?"

"Maximum severance and full pension," he replied, a slight smile crossing his lips.

"Keep it you bastard."

She slid out of the booth and walked to the door. A taxi waited at curbside. His limo driver leaning against the long black Cadillac parked across the street.

Chapter 57

Catherine Benson, former master spy, once held in high esteem by peers and superiors alike, now assistant manager at Thompson's Books and Historic Documents at the corner of 17th and K Streets, held his hand gently in hers. A little clammy today, she thought. Hope his circulation gets better.

Her visits to Detective Bravo's beside had become a daily ritual since her un-ceremonial dismissal from the Agency those many months before. She had found the new job rather easily. Well qualified, she was, especially with analyzing the authenticity and placing value, real or fake, on the myriad documents crossing her desk. The work was pleasant and often stimulating, especially when she found a forgery and would happily inform the would-be scam artist that their genuine Ben Franklin letter to one of his many French concubines was a genuine counterfeit. She's glad so far having never run into anyone with Galya's skills. Her hours were flexible giving her plenty of time to be there with him.

After a short while she felt a squeeze. Harder this time than before. He knew she was there. He opened his eyes, cloudy at first, blinking away the darkness, searching for her in the clear light. He turned his head toward her. He could not speak. It did not matter. She bent and kissed his cheek. Tomorrow he'll rise from his bed. The first time in too many months to count. Strong enough to begin his painful regimen to become whole again. The wounds have healed. The scars remain but they are fading. Soon she knows he will walk and talk and love again.

Epilogue

...Love, Spies and Cyanide -- Galya's Story is again a tightly-woven tapestry of hard facts and pure fiction.

The mystery of Thomas Riha and Galya Tannenbaum will never die. That's pure fact. I broke the story detailing Galya's death on March 9, 1971, with an exclusive front-page banner headline account in the Pueblo, Colorado, Chieftain daily newspaper.

Since then hundreds of articles have been written, Congressional hearings held with CIA and FBI officials questioned in fervent attempts to explain, or perhaps cover-up, what really went on during the months leading up to Galya's death, and the inexplicable disappearance of her eccentric lover.

Despite it all, the case remains buried deep in Colorado's soul or maybe its soil. But not in Colorado's consciousness. To this day, more than four decades later, walk on the idyllic University of Colorado Boulder campus and ask about long-gone Russian history professor Dr. Thomas Riha, and theories, spanning as wide as the plains stretching east to Kansas, will spring forth with pronounced vigor. Everyone with a keen sense of recent twentieth-century Colorado history will offer an opinion about what happened to Riha, and why his beautiful auburn-haired muse died such a horrible death by poison, trapped in the state's mental institution some one-hundred and thirty miles away.

Still haunting even the most ardent skeptic. Still tantalizing to conspiratorial adherents who gladly latch on to a tale of shadowy spies, gifted forgers, love triangles, greed and graft, all of which makes John LeClaire novels read like grade-school primers.

And that's my story of Galya and Thomas. Involving every one of those sinister characters and the events, which spun around them. Fiction, yes. Facts, many; theories abundant and so much fun to speculate.

I bring back fictional Captain of Detectives Victor Bravo, friend of restaurateur Johnny, and super-cop from I've Already Met the Devil to lead the investigation into Galya's murder. Like Captain Bravo, since breaking the story, not for a moment have I ever believed Galya

Tannenbaum committed suicide in her bleak Colorado prison cell for the criminally insane. It never made sense to me and it certainly doesn't to Detective Bravo that anyone could slowly and methodically kill themselves from months of small but deadly doses of self-inflicted cyanide. But at the time, the coroner did. Why? He wasn't totally incompetent, just perhaps purposefully blind to the facts. Other cops think she killed herself as well. Higher-ups apparently agreed. Based on what? Evidence surely should have pointed them in a different direction.

Were these officials ordered to protect certain secrets Galya took to her cold, hard Colorado grave and were they successful in convincing an inept medical examiner and many others to follow their lead? Why? Meanwhile, as Galya's glamorous remains are dissected to support the pre-determined cause of her demise, the search for Galya's Svengali lover, Dr. Thomas Riha, radical socialist, Soviet-loving Russian history scholar goes on. Is Galya's death tied to Riha's disappearance? I think so; did then, do now. Victor Bravo thinks so. Did someone kill them both? Maybe, Victor believes that's likely. Even today, and this is a fact, no one knows, or probably closer to the truth, no one still alive is saying.

But Victor's not alone in pursuing the truth in Galya's Story. An unexpected ally with a motive and a string of friends and resources stretching all the way to Washington, DC finds him and seeks his help. Her agenda is quite different, however. He's out to solve a baffling murder. CIA special agent Catherine Benson is searching the world for the vanished, perhaps vanquished professor, with whom she has unique ties, not by choice, rather by directives from the inner sanctums at Langley and even the Oval Office. Riha must be found alive or confirmed dead, Catherine tells Detective Bravo, and that's priority over finding Galya's killer. National security is at stake. Bravo disagrees until a very persuasive telephone call convinces him otherwise.

Our story springs from my imagination, but as in all my works, facts imbue between each line. We examine Riha's writings and wonder why he chose to malign his country, turning instead to Marx, Lenin, Khrushchev and Brezhnev as the vehicles by which, in his twisted mind, Socialist doctrine will rise to pluck mankind off its self-destructive path. We are intrigued by and hypothesize about the real-life parts played by then CIA Director Richard Helms, his boss, Richard Nixon, and their nemesis, at the time, Idaho Senator Frank Church. There were unrelenting probes by Church and his committee into Helms' activities, leading to legislation which some charge hamstrung our clandestine operations for decades, spawning the terrorists, which attack us today. All of these famous figures are dead now, but remain much alive in our memories and our suspicions.

We explore the bizarre love triangle within which Thomas and Galya wallowed; scheming and destroying an innocent victim. There is revenge, deceit, and callous redemption. And then who became the victim? Did they deserve to die for casting out an unwanted third-wheel, or did their deaths come, not by the hand of a vengeful vixen, but rather through a simple plot to promote American truth gone awry? Too many tangles to sort through, a teeter-totter for sure. Lifted high one minute, sinking to earth the next, by the sheer weight of guilt or ambition or both. All staged on a playground of danger and death.

Should she have gotten away, free to enjoy, undeterred, the fruits of her hideous labor, or was she the innocent, only to have observed the killings manipulated by those who pawned her sorrow, leveraging it to cover their wanton deeds?

We will never know.

45679040R00224

Made in the USA
San Bernardino, CA
14 February 2017